the
Story
prize

the Story prize

15 Years of Great Short Fiction

Edited by Larry Dark

Catapult  New York

Copyright © 2019 by Strong Words, LLC
First published in the United States in 2019 by
Catapult (catapult.co)

Grateful acknowledgment for reprinting materials
is made to the original publishers of these stories.
Please see Permissions on pages 381–83 for
individual credits.

ISBN: 978-1-936787-63-0

Cover design by Strick&Williams
Book design by Wah-Ming Chang

Catapult titles are distributed to the trade by
Publishers Group West
Phone: 866-400-5351

Library of Congress Control Number: 2018950156

Printed in the United States of America

10 9 8 7 6 5 4 3 2 1

CONTENTS

INTRODUCTION

The founder of The Story Prize, Julie Lindsey, and I began this award in 2004 to address what we perceived to be an existing need: Short story collections were rarely chosen as finalists for major book awards and seldom honored as winners. Yet few would dispute that some of the best English-language fiction written in the last quarter of the twentieth century and the beginning of the twenty-first century has been in the short form. While awards for individual stories and for authors of short fiction already existed, no award specifically for book-length works did. In creating The Story Prize, we aimed to fill that vacuum.

We knew that some of the best writing was and probably always would be in the short form, that it wasn't merely a way for beginners to cut their teeth before moving on to novels, and that it was a challenge that great writers would continue to take on and return to, time and again. It's a long-standing publishing truism that short story collections have limited commercial appeal. As a result, those who endeavor to create them often meet with discouragement. Fortunately, serious writers don't necessarily write to a market. They produce work fueled by their creative drives, and for many authors, one of the strongest creative drives is to write short fiction.

Fifteen years of The Story Prize have more than confirmed our belief in the short form, and though story collections have garnered several more major book awards in that time, the need for a prize focused on such works hasn't diminished. The proof of the vitality and significance of the form is not only in the fourteen books that have become winners (with a fifteenth imminent) but also in the forty-two volumes we've chosen as finalists, the two hundred or so we've included on our long lists, the six we've honored as Spotlight Award winners, and the roughly fifteen hundred that we've received as entries. The list of finalists, excluding winners of the prize, is full of literary luminaries, such as Andrea Barrett, Charles Baxter, Don DeLillo, Tessa Hadley, Jim Harrison, Jhumpa Lahiri, Yiyun Li, Colum McCann, Lorrie Moore, Edith Pearlman, and Joan Silber. Although we would have loved to have been able to include work by all of the finalists, that would have necessitated a multivolume set. For this reason, we're offering stories by the fourteen winners of the prize.

How do we arrive at the winner each year? We read the books we receive as entries, usually more than a hundred of them, not through a critical filter but as knowledgeable readers with open minds. Over the course of the year, we narrow our choices down to a small group of books, usually six or seven, and on New Year's Day, Julie and I have a conversation during which we choose the three finalists. We send these books to a group of three judges: an author, a bookseller or librarian (alternating years), and a third reader who might be an editor or a critic—all of them sophisticated readers. The judges read the books and, independently of one another, communicate their top choice and second choice. We use the second choices to break three-way ties. And from that process, a Story Prize winner emerges.

Reading over these stories again, some after more than a dozen years, has confirmed for me that our choices, and the choices of the judges, have been solid ones. The order of stories in this book is chronological, from the first winner of The Story Prize, for books published in 2004, Edwidge Danticat, to the fourteenth winner, for books published in 2017, Elizabeth Strout. We've chosen to include here the stories that the authors read from at the event each year at which we honor the finalists and announce the winner. This allows many of the stories in this book to match up with the videos of the readings and interviews that we share on

our website, thestoryprize.org, going back to the fourth year of
the prize.

Because our format is to have the authors read from their
work then discuss it with me onstage, I've had the good fortune
of conversing with many writers I admire. All have shared interesting and insightful observations about their own work, the
writing process, and the craft of fiction. So we're introducing
each story with excerpts from the author interviews and, in some
cases, from judges' citations and guest posts on The Story Prize
blog.

If you're looking for themes to mine from the fourteen stories
collected here, good luck. Each is distinctive, sometimes jarringly
different in tone, scope, and language from the story that precedes
or follows it. For instance, Patrick O'Keeffe's elegiac novella set in
rural Ireland hands the baton to Mary Gordon's short humorous
story that takes place in a New York City podiatrist's office. After
Tobias Wolff's brief classic story about a literary critic who experiences a succession of memories in the nanoseconds before he dies
from a gunshot wound, comes Daniyal Mueenuddin's detailed ex-
ploration of the life of a Pakistani servant that unfolds over many
years.

The pronounced juxtapositions and stark differences that oc-
cur from story to story illustrate just a small sample of the scope
and range of contemporary short fiction. They also underscore the
essential truth that the best writers have distinctive voices, inter-
ests, and obsessions. In fact, the most consistent characteristic of
the authors who have won The Story Prize is work so unique to
each of them that, even at the sentence level, the prose identifies the
author as surely as fingerprints or DNA might. At the story level,
the differences are often even more apparent. That's exactly what
is most instructive about what this collection of a mere fourteen
stories says about the current state of short fiction. The story is an
endlessly elastic form that succeeds best when an author finds her

or his own true voice. It's safe to say that five, ten, or fifteen years from now, an anthology of work by Story Prize winners would demonstrate even greater diversity. For now, it's fair to say that you hold in your hands a series of distinctive, beautifully crafted, and transformative reading experiences.

LARRY DARK,
Director, The Story Prize

the Story prize

EDWIDGE DANTICAT

She is able to give us a complicated and engaged socio-political portrait, while at the same time the stories are quite varied in tone and approach as well as in the type of characters she uses and the way she presents their conflicts. She uses the individual stories to create a complex web of connections, and even small asides serve to deepen our appreciation of other stories. And the book comes together very powerfully. . . . There is a real cumulative effect to these stories, which subtly accumulate detail and nuance and bounce off one another in surprising ways.

Each story is strong, powerfully executed, complete. At the same time, each story contributes to the development of the character at the center, the rippling legacy of his actions, or the larger themes of the collection. Much of the time, the stories do all three. The structure of the collection and the choices Danticat made about narrative voice are brilliant.

Citations for The Dew Breaker *from the judges,*
Dan Chaon, Ann Christophersen, and Brigid Hughes

The Book of Miracles

from *The Dew Breaker*

Anne was talking about miracles right before they reached the cemetery. She was telling her husband and daughter about a case she'd recently heard reported on a religious cable access program, about a twelve-year-old Lebanese girl who cried crystal tears.

From the front passenger seat, the daughter had just blurted out "Ouch!"—one of those non sequiturs that Anne would rather not hear come out of her grown child's mouth but that her daughter sometimes used as a shortcut for more precise reactions to anything that wasn't easily comprehensible. It was either "Ouch!" "Cool," "Okay," or "Whatever," a meaningless litany her daughter had been drawing from since she was fourteen years old.

Anne was thinking of scolding her daughter, of telling her she should talk to them like a woman now, weigh her words carefully so that, even though she was an "artiste," they might take her seriously, but she held back, imagining what her daughter's reaction to her suggestions might be: "Okay, whatever, Manman, please go on with your story."

Her husband, who was always useful in helping her elaborate on her miraculous tales and who also disapproved of their daughter's language, said in Creole, "If crystal was coming out of her eyes, I would think she'd be crying blood."

"That's what's extraordinary," Anne replied. "The crystal pieces were as sharp as knives, but they didn't hurt her."

"How big were these pieces?" the husband asked, slowing the car a bit as they entered the ramp leading to the Jackie Robinson Parkway.

Anne got one last look at the surrounding buildings, which were lit more brightly than usual, with Christmas trees, Chanukah and Kwanzaa candles in most of the windows. She tried to keep these visions in her mind, of illuminated pines, electric candles, and giant cardboard Santas, as the car merged into the curvy, narrow lane. She hated the drive and would have never put herself through it were it not so important to her that her daughter attend Christmas Eve Mass with her and her husband. While in college, her daughter had declared herself an atheist. Between her daughter, who chose not to believe in God, and her husband, who went to the Brooklyn Museum every week, to worship, it seemed to her, at the foot of Ancient Egyptian statues, she felt outnumbered by pagans.

Anne was just about to tell her husband and daughter that the crystal pieces, which had fallen out of the Lebanese girl's eyes, were as big as ten-carat diamonds—she imagined her daughter retorting, "I bet her family *wished* she cried ten-carat diamonds"—when they reached the cemetery.

Every time she passed a cemetery, Anne held her breath. When she was a girl, Anne had gone swimming with her three-year-old brother on a beach in Grand Goave, and he had disappeared beneath the waves. Ever since then, she'd convinced herself that her brother was walking the earth looking for his grave. Whenever she went by a cemetery, any cemetery, she imagined him there, his tiny wet body bent over the tombstones, his ash-colored eyes surveying the letters, trying to find his name.

The cemetery was on both sides of them now, the headstones glistening in the evening light. She held her breath the way she imagined her brother did before the weight of the sea collapsed his small lungs and he was forced to surrender to the water, sinking into a world of starfishes, sea turtles, weeds, and sharks. She had gone nowhere near the sea since her brother had disappeared; her heart raced even when she happened upon images of waves on television.

Who would put a busy thoroughfare in the middle of a cemetery, she wondered, forcing the living and their noisy cars to always be trespassing on the dead? It didn't make sense, but maybe the parkway's architects had been thinking beyond the daily needs of the living. Did they wonder if the dead might enjoy hearing sounds of life going on at high speed around them? If this were so, then why should the living be spared the dead's own signs of existence: of shadows swaying in the breeze, of the laughter and cries of lost children, of the whispers of lovers, muffled as though in dreams.

"We've passed the cemetery," she heard her daughter say.

Anne had closed her eyes without realizing it. Her daughter knew she reacted strongly to cemeteries, but Anne had never told her why, since her daughter had already concluded early in life that this, like many unexplained aspects of her parents' life, was connected to "some event that happened in Haiti."

"I'm glad Papa doesn't have your issues with cemeteries," the daughter was saying, "otherwise we'd be in the cemetery ourselves by now."

The daughter pulled out a cigarette, which the father objected to with the wave of a hand. A former chain-smoker, he could no longer stand the smell of cigarettes.

"When you out the car," he said.

"Yes, sir," the daughter replied, putting the loose cigarette back in its pack. She turned her face to the bare trees lining her side of the parkway and said, "Okay, Manman, please, tell us about another miracle."

A long time ago, more than thirty years ago, in Haiti, your father worked in a prison, where he hurt many people. Now look at him. Look how calm he is. Look how patient he is. Look how he just drove forty miles, to your apartment in Westchester, to pick you up for Christmas Eve Mass. That was the miracle Anne wanted to share with her daughter on this Christmas Eve night, the simple miracle of her husband's transformation, but of course she couldn't, at least not yet, so instead she told of another kind of miracle.

This one concerned a twenty-one-year-old Filipino man who'd seen an image of the Madonna in a white rose petal.

She thought her daughter would dismiss this and just say, "Cool," but instead she actually asked a question. "How come these people are all foreigners?"

"Because Americans don't have much faith," her husband quickly replied, turning his face for a moment to glance at his daughter.

"People here are more practical, maybe," the daughter said, "but there, in Haiti or the Philippines, that's where people see everything, even things they're not supposed to see. So if I see a woman's face in a rose, I'd think somebody drew it there, but if you see it, Manman, you think it's a miracle."

They were coming off the Jackie Robinson Parkway and turning onto Jamaica Avenue, where traffic came to an abrupt stop at the busy intersection. Anne tried to take her mind off the past and bring her thoughts back to the Mass. She loved going to Mass on Christmas Eve, the only time she and her husband and daughter ever attended church together.

When her daughter was a girl, before going to the Christmas Eve Mass, they would drive around their Brooklyn neighborhood to look at the holiday lights. Their community associations were engaged in fierce competition, awarding a prize to the block with the best Nativity scenes, lawn sculptures, wreaths, and banners. Still, Anne and her husband had put up no decorations, fearing, irrationally perhaps, that lit ornaments and trimmings would bring too much attention to them. Instead it was their lack of participation that made them stand out, but by then they had already settled into their routine and couldn't bring themselves to change it.

When her daughter was still living at home, the only way Anne honored the season with her daughter—aside from attending the

Christmas Eve Mass—was to put a handful of shredded brown paper under her daughter's bed without her knowledge. The frayed paper was a substitute for the hay that had been part of the baby Jesus' first bed. Over her bedroom doorway, she also hung a sprig of mistletoe. She'd once heard a mistletoe vendor say that mistletoe had all sorts of reconciliatory qualities, so that if two enemies ever found themselves beneath it, they would have to lay down their weapons and embrace each other.

By offering neither each other nor their daughter any presents at Christmas, Anne and her husband had tried to encourage her to be thankful for what she already had—family, a roof over her head—rather than count on what she would, or could, receive on Christmas morning. Their daughter had learned this lesson so well that Christmas no longer interested her. She didn't care about shopping; she didn't watch the endless specials on TV. The only part of the holiday the daughter seemed to enjoy was the drive from block to block to criticize the brightest houses.

"Look at that one," her husband would shout, pointing to the arches of icicle lights draped over one house from top to bottom. "Can you imagine how high their electricity bill is going to be?"

"I wouldn't be able to sleep in a place like that," the daughter would say, singling out a neon holiday greeting in a living room window. "It must be as bright as daylight in there, all the time."

THE TRAFFIC WAS FLOWING AGAIN. As they approached St. Therese's, her husband and daughter were engaged in their own Christmas ritual, her husband talking about the astronomical cost of Christmas decorations and her daughter saying that one lavishly decorated house after another looked like "an inferno." Meanwhile, Anne tried to think of the Christmas carols they would sing during the Mass. "Silent Night" was her favorite. She hummed the peaceful melody and mouthed the words in anticipation.

Sleep in heavenly peace.
Sleep in heavenly peace.

The church was packed even though the Mass would not begin for another fifteen minutes. Their daughter was outside in the cold, smoking. Anne and her husband found three seats in the next-to-last row, near a young couple who were holding hands and staring ahead at the altar. Anne sat next to the woman, who acknowledged her with a nod as Anne squeezed into the pew.

The daughter soon joined them, plopping herself down on the aisle, next to her father. Anne had tried to convince her to wear a dress, or at least a skirt and a blouse, but she had insisted on wearing her paint-stained blue jeans and a lint-covered sweater.

Anne thought the church most beautiful at Christmas. The Nativity scene in front of the altar had a black Mary, Joseph, and Baby Jesus, the altar candles casting a golden light on their mahogany faces. The sight of people greeting one another around her made her wish that she and her husband had more friends, beyond acquaintances from their respective businesses: the beauty salon and the barbershop. She was beginning to rethink the decision she and her husband had made not to get close to anyone who might ask too many questions about his past. They had set up shop on Nostrand Avenue, at the center of the Haitian community, only because that was where they had the best chance of finding clients. And the only reason they rented the rooms in their basement to three younger Haitian men was because they were the only people who would live there. Besides, soon after her husband had opened his barbershop, he'd discovered that since he'd lost eighty pounds, changed his name, and given as his place of birth a village deep in the mountains of Leogane, no one asked about him anymore, thinking he was just a peasant who'd made good in New York. He hadn't been a famous "dew breaker," or torturer, anyway, just one of hundreds

who had done their jobs so well that their victims were never able
to speak of them again.

THE CHURCH GREW SILENT AS the priest walked in and bowed
before the altar. It was exactly midnight. Midnight on Christmas
Eve was Anne's favorite sixty seconds of the year. It was a charmed
minute, not just for her but, she imagined, for the entire world.
It was the time when birds were supposed to begin chirping their
all-night songs to greet the holy birth, when other animals were to
genuflect and trees bow in reverence. She could picture all this as
though it were being projected on a giant screen in a movie theater:
water in secret wells and far-off rivers and streams was turning into
wine; bells were chiming with help only from the breeze; candles,
lanterns, and lamps were blinking like the Star of Bethlehem. The
gates of Paradise were opened, so anyone who died this minute
could enter without passing through Purgatory. The Virgin Mary
was choosing among the sleeping children of the world for some to
invite to Heaven to serenade her son.

Once again, Anne hoped that the Virgin would choose her
young brother to go up to Heaven and sing with the choir of angels. Technically he was not sleeping, but he'd never been buried,
so his spirit was somewhere out there, wandering, searching, and if
he were chosen to go up to Heaven, maybe the Holy Mother would
keep him there.

The priest was incensing the altar, the smoke rising in a perfumed cloud toward the thorn-crowned head on the golden cruci-
fix. Her daughter chose that exact moment to mumble something
to her father, while pointing to someone sitting on the aisle, three
rows down, diagonally ahead of them.

Anne wanted to tell her daughter to be quiet, but her scolding
would mean more conversation, even as her daughter's murmurs
were drawing stares from those sitting nearby. When her daugh-

ter's garbled whispers grew louder, however, Anne moved her mouth close to her husband's ear to ask, "What?"

"She thinks she sees Emmanuel Constant over there," her husband calmly replied.

It was his turn to point out the man her daughter had been aiming her finger at for a while now. From her limited view of the man's profile, Anne could tell he was relatively tall—even in his seated position his head was visible above those around him—had dark brown skin, a short Afro, a beard. All this was consistent with the picture a community group had printed on the WANTED FOR CRIMES AGAINST THE HAITIAN PEOPLE flyers, which had been stapled to lampposts all along Nostrand Avenue a month before. Beneath the photograph of Constant had been a shorthand list of the crimes of which he had been accused—"torture, rape, murder of 5,000 people"—all apparently committed when he ran a militia ironically called Front for the Advancement and Progress of Haiti.

For a month now, both Anne and her husband had been casting purposefully casual glances at the flyer on the lamppost in front of their stores each morning while opening up and again at night while lowering their shutters. They'd never spoken about the flyer, even when, bleached by the sun and wrinkled by the cold, it slowly began to fade. After a while, the letters and numbers started disappearing so that the word *rape* became *ape* and the *5* vanished from *5,000*, leaving a trio of zeros as the number of Constant's casualties. The demonic-looking horns that passersby had added to Constant's head and the Creole curses they'd scribbled on the flyer were nearly gone too, turning it into a fragmented collage with as many additions as erasures.

Even before the flyer had found its way to her, Anne had closely followed the story of Emmanuel Constant, through Haitian newspapers, Creole radio and cable access programs. Constant had created his death squad after a military coup had sent

Haiti's president into exile. Constant's thousands of disciples had sought to silence the president's followers by circling entire neighborhoods with gasoline, setting houses on fire, and shooting fleeing residents. Anne had read about their campaigns of facial scalping, where skin was removed from dead victims' faces to render them unidentifiable. After the president returned from exile, Constant fled to New York on Christmas Eve. He was tried in absentia in a Haitian court and sentenced to life in prison, a sentence he would probably never serve.

Still, every morning and evening as her eyes wandered to the flyer on the lamppost in front of her beauty salon and her husband's barbershop, Anne had to fight a strong desire to pull it down, not out of sympathy for Constant but out of a fear that even though her husband's prison "work" and Constant's offenses were separated by thirty-plus years, she might arrive at her store one morning to find her husband's likeness on the lamppost rather than Constant's.

"Do you think it's really him?" she whispered to her husband.

He shrugged as someone behind them leaned over and hissed "Shush" into her ear.

The man her daughter believed to be Constant was looking straight ahead. He appeared to be paying close attention as the church choir started a Christmas medley.

What child is this, who, laid to rest
On Mary's lap, is sleeping?

Her daughter was fuming, shifting in her seat and mumbling under her breath, all the while keeping her eyes fixed on the man's profile.

Anne was proud of her daughter, proud of her righteous displeasure. But what if she ever found out about her own father? About the things he had done?

After the sermon, the congregation got up in rows to walk to the front of the church to take Holy Communion.

"How lucky we are," said the priest, "that Jesus was born to give of his flesh for us to take into ourselves."

How lucky *we* are, Anne thought, that we're here at all, that we still have flesh.

When her turn came, Anne got up with a handful of people from her pew, including the young couple sitting next to her, and proceeded to the altar. Uninterested and unconfessed, her husband and daughter remained behind.

Standing before the priest, mouthing the Act of Contrition, she parted her lips to receive the wafer. Then she crossed herself and followed a line of people walking back in the other direction, to their seats.

As she neared the pew where her daughter believed Constant was sitting, she stopped to have a good look at the man on the aisle.

What if it were Constant? What would she do? Would she spit in his face or embrace him, acknowledging a kinship of shame and guilt that she'd inherited by marrying her husband? How would she even know whether Constant felt any guilt or shame? What if he'd come to this Mass to flaunt his freedom? To taunt those who'd been affected by his crimes? What if he didn't even see it that way? What if he considered himself innocent? Innocent enough to go anywhere he pleased? What right did she have to judge him? As a devout Catholic and the wife of a man like her husband, she didn't have the same freedom to condemn as her daughter did.

To get a closer look at the man, she simply lowered her body and moved her face closer to his. She did not even pretend to drop something on the ground, as she'd planned.

Up close, it was instantly obvious that though the man bore a faint resemblance to Constant, it wasn't him. In his most recent pictures, the ones in the newspapers, not the one on the WANTED flyer, Constant appeared much older, fatter, almost twice the size of this man. Constant also had a wider forehead, bushier eyebrows, larger, more bulging eyes, and fuller lips.

Anne straightened her body but still lingered in the aisle, glaring down at the man until he looked up at her and smiled. He seemed to think she was a person he knew too, a face he couldn't immediately place. He looked up expectantly as though waiting for her to say something that would remind him of their connection, but she said nothing. Someone tapped Anne's shoulder from behind and she continued walking, her knees shaking until she got back to her seat.

"Not him," she whispered to her husband.

He turned to his daughter and repeated, "Not him."

While slipping into her seat, Anne whispered these words again to herself. "Not him." It was not him. She felt strangely comforted, as though she, her husband, and her daughter had just been spared bodily harm. Her daughter, however, was still staring at the man doubtfully.

Once everyone who wanted to had received communion, the choir began singing "Silent Night." The tranquility of the melody and the solace of the words were now lost on Anne, for she was thinking that she would never attend this Mass, or any other, with her husband again. What if someone had been sitting there, staring at him, the same way her daughter had been staring at that man? And what if they recognized him, came up to him, and looked into his face?

When the choir finished the song, the priest motioned for them to start again so the congregation could join in.

Anne was surprised to see her husband's lips move as though he were trying to follow along. He missed a few of the verses, lowering his head when he did, but he mostly managed to keep up. She was moved by this gesture, knowing he was singing only because he knew it was her favorite. He was trying to please her, take her mind off the agitation the man's presence had caused her.

During the final blessing, her daughter kept her eyes on the man, craning her neck for a better view of his face. As soon as the Mass ended, the priest headed down the aisle to greet the congregants on their way out. The people in the front pews followed him. She and her husband and daughter would have to wait until all the rows ahead of them had been emptied before they could exit.

When his turn came, the man they'd believed was Constant strolled past them, chatting with a woman at his side. As he passed her, their daughter raised her hand as if to grab his arm, but her father reached over, lowered it, and held it to her side until the man was beyond her reach.

"I wasn't going to hit him," the daughter said. "I was just going to ask his name."

The daughter turned to her mother, as if to plead for her understanding and said, "Would it be so wrong, Manman, to ask his name?"

WHEN IT WAS THEIR TURN to greet the priest, her daughter and husband quickly slipped by him, leaving Anne to face him alone.

"It's nice to see you, Anne," the priest said. "I thought you were going to bring your family."

"I did, Father," she said.

From the church entrance, she looked out into the street, where most of the congregation had spilled onto the sidewalk. She pushed her head through the doorway until she spotted her husband and daughter crossing the street and moving toward a house with a plastic reindeer on the front lawn.

"There they are, Father," she said, pointing as they reached the white metal fence bordering the house.

The priest turned to look, but couldn't distinguish them from the others spread out now on both sidewalks.

Anne tried to imagine what her husband and daughter could

be talking about out there, standing next to that light-drenched fence, their heads nearly touching, as if to shield each other from the cold. Were they discussing the Mass, the man, that house?

"Merry Christmas, Anne," the priest said, trying to move her along. His gaze was already on the person behind her.

"Merry Christmas, Father," Anne said. "It was a lovely Mass."

STEPPING OUTSIDE, ANNE JOINED THE crowd on the sidewalk in front of the church, the faces still glowing from the enchantment of the Mass. She didn't rush to cross the street to her husband and daughter, winding her way instead through clusters of families making plans for Christmas dinner, offering and accepting rides, and bundling up their children against the cold.

As she walked the length of the sidewalk, stopping to wish "Merry Christmas" to everyone in her path, she purposely chose families with little boys, stroking their hat-covered heads as she attempted to make small talk with the parents.

"Wasn't it a lovely Mass?"

"Didn't the choir sing well?"

"Papa's ready to go." Her daughter was suddenly at her side, looping her arm through hers. It was a lovely gesture on her daughter's part, her fragile little girl, who'd grown so gruff and distant over the years.

Her husband was still standing across the street. His back was turned to the Christmas house; his hands were buried in his coat pockets, his shoulders hunched against the cold.

"Wasn't it a lovely Mass?" Anne asked her daughter to see whether she was still thinking about the man. If she was, she'd probably say something like, "Yeah, okay, Manman, it was a fine Mass, until that killer came."

Instead, while waving to her father across the street to show that she'd found Anne, the daughter said, "Listen, Manman.

About that guy. I'm sorry I overreacted. Papa thought I was going
to hit him or trip him or something. But I wouldn't do anything
like that. I don't really know what happened. I wasn't there."

But I was, Anne wanted to say, or almost.

It was always like this, her life a pendulum between forgiveness
and regret, but when the anger dissipated she considered it a small
miracle, the same way she thought of her emergence from her occasional epileptic seizures as a kind of resurrection.

Her daughter's breath, mixed in with the cold, was forming an
icy vapor in the air in front of them. Then, moving her lips close,
her daughter pressed them against Anne's cheek until Anne's face
felt warm, almost hot.

"I'm sorry to have to say this too, Manman," the daughter
added, moving away, smiling. "We come every year, but it's always the same thing. Same choir. Same songs. Same Mass. It was
only a Mass. Nothing more. It's never as fabulous as one of your
miracles."

PATRICK O'KEEFFE

The four long stories comprising *The Hill Road* are beautiful and shapely individually, gaining even more power as a group. O'Keeffe's vision never falters, and with each story we gain a greater sense of the secrets, which filter through generations, of the inhabitants of Kilroan. Each story is a world in itself, each character fully rounded—and in the end, the place leaps fully alive before us. O'Keeffe's voice is a marvel and his stories linger in the mind.

Citation for The Hill Road *from the judges,*
Andrea Barrett, Nancy Pearl, and James Wood

The Postman's Cottage

from *The Hill Road*

Every third or fourth Friday, up till thirty or forty years ago, which is long before milking machines were even heard of, and places not even too far in from the road still didn't have electricity, there used to be autumn Fairs in the village of Pallas. After morning milking, the farmers who were selling would gather their heifers and bullocks and hunt them down the fields, along the byroads and the main road to the square in Pallas. For miles around you could hear the cattle lowing along the roads, although louder than them were the shouts of the farmers themselves swinging at and hitting the often restless beasts with their ash sticks.

It was to one of these Fairs that Mrs. O'Rourke sent five fat bullocks one Friday morning on the verge of autumn. The O'Rourkes lived back up in the hills. There were ten children. Eoin was twenty-four, the eldest, who had recently taken charge of the fifteen-acre farm, their father not having survived the flu that spring.

The morning of the Fair his mother boiled him two eggs over the fire, and before her son had eaten the eggs, she had heated a few kettles of water so he could wash and shave himself. His brother Michael, who was less than a year younger, was to say later that his brother was in a fierce hurry finishing up the milking that morning, and was whistling like mad, as he was known to do when he became excited, which was natural enough, for it wasn't every day you got the chance to go to the Fair, not to mention have fine bullocks to sell. Michael also said that his brother took those long strides of his, hunting the cows before him while he combed his black hair out, telling Michael between whistles that the earlier you were at the Fair the better chance you had of getting a good price.

When Eoin sat at the hearth less than an hour later there was no hurry in him as he slipped on his freshly ironed drawers, while his mother, who was frantically ironing his Sunday trousers and shirt on the kitchen table, appealed to him to get a move on and to make sure he left instructions for his brothers and sisters with regards to what jobs they should be doing around the farm and what livestock they needed to keep an eye on while he was in Pallas. Eoin stood up from the hearth whistling, saying to his mother that she should not worry about a thing, reminding her the bullocks were going to make a great price, and that he would have to go for a few jars with the lads after the Fair—you couldn't ever say no to the lads—but he also told her he would not waste too much time in the public house, as this had never been his way.

His brothers and sisters had hunted the bullocks down from the hill and cornered them against the middle gate in the boreen. Mrs. O'Rourke followed her son into the yard, sprinkling holy water on his cap, his back and neck and shoulders. Eoin blessed himself quickly. He began to whistle, then he grabbed the family pram and began pushing it carelessly around the yard, with the youngest child, Timmy, in it, who cried with delight. His mother warned him to stop his foolish carry-on, that he should not take too much for granted and to not forget on his journey back the road to say a prayer for the soul of his father. She was both needing and expecting her eldest to return home that evening with a good sum of money. It had been an exceptionally wet summer and much of the hay had rotted in pikes in the meadows.

That day the square in Pallas was crowded with people from all over selling not only cattle and horses and pigs but also chickens, ducks, turkeys, and eggs from all three. Makeshift stalls had been built around the square, directly across from Ryan's public house and grocery. Winter cabbage was for sale in a few stalls and a line had formed there from early on in the day. A few butchers from Tipperary town were selling bacon. The cattle Jobbers had arrived from all over Munster; they were known to be tough, particularly when they had drink taken, and it was said that without a moment's thought they'd break people's heads with their blackthorn sticks if you were to vex them, but most farmers knew that when it was getting closer to evening you didn't have any dealings or words with a Jobber, no matter what price you got.

Eoin O'Rourke sold the bullocks around one o'clock, he did get an outstanding price, and after the Fair he sauntered laughing through the door of Ryan's with his best friend, Tom Dillon, who at this time was making a living milking cows for the few bigger farmers around Kilroan. (On Saturday and Sunday afternoon he also put in a few hours at the grocer's in the village of Kilroan.) In Ryan's, they joined in a round with two other friends from Kilroan: Francie Houlton and Jim Dwyer were their names. The four young men stood, crushed behind the door of the public house. Eoin's friends clapped him on the back; they called him a boyo and told him he was blessed, his mother would be awfully proud of him, he was a true son of his father's; he was the luckiest man alive in Pallas and Kilroan, or any other place in the world for that matter, and then like every other man in the bar and street they began to discuss the day's cattle prices and last Sunday's hurling match.

Rounds went by; the farmers from Kilroan came and went, chatting and laughing with the young men, on their way in and out the door. Evening drew on. The Pallas Square was washed and swept clean, the stalls had been taken down, and most of the Jobbers had left, when the four friends stopped drinking pints of porter and began to drink John Power's whiskey with water. It was pitch dark outside, around eight o'clock, when Houlton and Dwyer started to make fun of their two friends about Kate Welsh—a grand-looking girl, she was, one of the very best, they all agreed. She lived on a small farm in the townsland of Ballinlough, and over the past few weeks both Tom Dillon and Eoin O'Rourke had walked out with her, although it was presently well known that she was fonder of Tom Dillon, as she had said this openly, and he was cracked about her, which he had also said openly; and behind the door of Ryan's this night Eoin O'Rourke smiled broadly and stuck his face into Tom Dillon's face and told him he could have Kate Welsh for all he cared, and the very best of luck to him. Then the two friends raised their glasses, shook hands, laughed loudly, and Eoin O'Rourke turned to his other two friends and told them in a serious tone that he never had a bit of interest in Kate Welsh in the first place, that girl was not his type at all.

The talk going around at this time in Kilroan and Ballinlough was that Kate Welsh would be doing very well for herself to secure the likes of Dillon, for Dillon, being an only child, would inherit his father's noble cottage, which back then was named Dillon's Cottage. (Years before this it was known as The Butler's Mansion.) The whitewashed cottage was not really a cottage at all but a small house, because it had the two floors. It was located on the left side of the road, right outside of Kilroan village, no more than a ten-minute walk to the church and the grocer's. At the back of the cottage was a semicircle of sycamores; at the front was a stone wall, with a hedge of laurels growing along the top. The cottage had been built by an English landlord—a rake, no doubt, who, it was said, amongst other things, won another man's wife in a card game, and she went off with him, too—anyway, at one time this landlord owned nearly all the land in Kilroan, but on both sides of the Irish Sea he drank and gambled his land and money away, and he'd ordered the cottage built for his coachman or butler, although no one around was fully sure what his job really was up at the landlord's big house. The so-called butler or coachman was a slight, immaculately groomed, polite Englishman, who planted the laurel hedge, grew a lovely flower and vegetable garden in the back, and attended first Mass in Kilroan every Sunday, even though it was plain that he dug with the other foot—but after the landlord had to abscond from Kilroan because of his losses, the Englishman left soon after, and the cottage lay abandoned for many years until Tom Dillon's father, John Joe, was fortunate enough to inherit a sizable amount of money from an old aunt, herself a sheep farmer in New South Wales, and he bought the cottage with the money. He was the gravedigger in Kilroan for thirty years, but apart from digging graves he was otherwise gifted with his hands, and knew well the foundation and the walls and rafters in The Butler's Mansion to be sound, so he went about fixing up the cottage.

When John Joe Dillon died, Tom gave up milking cows and working at the grocer's to take over his father's job as gravedigger, which he did until he landed the luckiest job of all, one he kept till the day he died, as anyone in their right mind would: He became the postman for Kilroan and the surrounding area, and never again did he have to dig a hole to make a living, and the younger lads coming up began referring to Dillon's Cottage as The Postman's Cottage. Tom was a good few years married to Kate Welsh when he became the postman, although their one son was not yet born; they were married five or six years before he appeared.

Around the time of the Pallas Fairs no one would say Tom Dillon was not a great catch, but they did openly admit that Eoin O'Rourke was by far the better-looking man; he also had a kinder nature than Dillon, so they said, but Eoin had no prospects, and this was what he really had against him, when you take into account the few acres on the hill, his mother, the brothers and sisters, who since their father's death fully counted on him.

They did maintain that Kate Welsh, who was nineteen or twenty at this time, was one of the finest-looking girls around, and a very smart young lady, too, although more than one or two people in Ballinlough remarked that she couldn't keep her nose out of other people's business, and when she was a pupil at Ballinlough National School, she was too forward for a girl of her age, and she never listened to those who were older than herself, who naturally knew better.

The morning after Eoin O'Rourke sold the five bullocks, Charlie Ryan was hunting in his cows for milking and noticed a newspaper parcel tied together with string, left atop a big rock in the middle of his field, with a smaller rock on top of the parcel to keep it in place, or so it looked to him that that was what that rock was for. This field, where the Ryans grazed their cows after the hay pikes were in, was beyond the crossroads on the Pallas road, going toward Kilroan; it was large and rectangular and stretched all the way down to the bog and the Main Trench, which all summer had flooded its banks due to a deluge of rain, and the surrounding fields and meadows were under God knows how many feet of water.

Charlie Ryan took one look at the parcel and suspected that something was amiss. He left the cows and the parcel, ran home across the fields, hopped on his bike without saying a single word to his wife or the children, and cycled to the police barracks in Pallas to inform Sergeant Culley, who only a few weeks before had become the new sergeant.

Sergeant Culley, surrounded by the other guards in the barracks, opened the parcel and picked out a pair of drawers, a clean shirt, and a pair of Sunday trousers; in the pocket of the shirt he found a rather peculiar note, written in pencil, in large block letters: *Say a prayer for the awful thing I done. For the poor children who will come after me. Eoin O'Rourke.*

A few hours later, Mrs. O'Rourke read the note in the barracks, and raised her head and claimed to Sergeant Culley that, yes, it was indeed Eoin's handwriting, but the words were barely out of her mouth when she began to weep again, then admitting she had no clue if the handwriting was Eoin's or not, and she rightfully questioned the sergeant as to who in the name of God around here ever paid a bit of attention to how their children wrote, if they were even lucky enough to be able to write one word in the first place. She wiped her eyes and asked him if there was any sign of the money or Eoin's shoes and socks. The sergeant said they hadn't found a thing else. Mrs. O'Rourke dropped her head and cried once more.

That evening she took to the bed. She called Michael to her bedside and told him it was now his duty to run the farm. The parish priest in Kilroan then was Father Gill and he sat at Mrs. O'Rourke's bedside, trying to console and coax her to get out of the bed, explaining it would do her or none of the children any good for her to stay in it, but she told the priest she was too troubled to move; was it not enough to have lost her husband not so long ago, and now this encumbrance.

Was there a fight? Did you lads hear any words said to a stranger, a tinker, or a Jobber in that crowd at Ryan's on his way back and forth to relieve himself? Did you see him with a parcel, perhaps with a change of clothes in it?

These were the questions Sergeant Culley asked Francie Houlton, Jim Dwyer, and Tom Dillon in the barracks the day after Eoin's disappearance. No was their answer to all of them. The sergeant, with his notebook open, sat in a chair next to Tom Dillon and asked him whether young O'Rourke had said anything disturbing of late, had he hinted a word about traveling? A tearful and trembling Tom Dillon told the sergeant if Eoin had such plans he did not tell them to him, and the two of them were the best of friends, not the sort to keep things from each other, for they had known each other since they were barely able to get a solid word out. He then told the sergeant the last he saw and heard of Eoin was at the crossroads just outside of Pallas, where the two of them had walked together after they left Ryan's. Tom said that he took the right fork, cycled on to the graveyard in Ballinlough, a good bit late for his meeting with Kate Welsh, and Eoin walked off, whistling, on the road going toward Kilroan, shouting once into the dark, I'll see you after Mass on Sunday, Tom, please God.

The other two lads had stayed on in the public house. An

accordion appeared from behind the bar and everyone gathered around Francie Houlton, urging him to play; they had to keep at him for half an hour, which was routine, but when his fingers finally touched the buttons, and the first few notes leaped out, he shut his eyes and drifted off into another world, and there was no stopping him till the publican, Mike Ryan, told everyone it was time for the whole lot of them to go on home, that the cows still had to be milked in the morning.

The sergeant questioned all three if they had a good few jars on them and they slowly nodded, as if to say, *well after all it was a Fair day God knows.* Francie Houlton broke down, and then wiped his eyes and nose with the sleeve of his shirt, and proclaimed that it was one of the best Fair days ever—he ended up playing all night. Jim Dwyer said this indeed was the bloody truth, and he dragged his cap off and muttered the truth was that God usually had contrary plans to your own and there was not a thing you or anyone else in the world could do about it, and those congregated in the barracks, including Sergeant Culley, bowed their heads and silently blessed themselves.

The following day Sergeant Culley was overheard saying on the street in Pallas that from his few short years of experience in Pallas he had come to believe that those lads who lived back up in the hills were lacking in more than a little bit upstairs.

—God knows what might go haywire in that young fellow after he had a few drinks taken and all that money in his pocket, the sergeant openly professed that same night in Ryan's, although he did have a good few jars on him when he said it.

In the barracks the next morning he announced his decisions regarding Eoin O'Rourke's disappearance: First things first, the sergeant, as everyone else had done already, dismissed the assumption that Eoin had gone for a drunken swim—you see, back then nobody could, because you couldn't do much swimming in narrow dikes and rivers of stolid water, choked with rushes, and, of course, you couldn't do much swimming either in the rushing waters of a flood. So, the sergeant suggested that Eoin, mad and heedless because of drink taken, walked into Ryan's field to relieve himself, and while he was in there he took a sudden fit, flung the clothes off of himself, and the *awful thing* was that he had run down through Ryan's field, with only his shoes and socks on, and threw himself into the trench; or, in a similar manner, O'Rourke stumbled out of the field, with only his shoes and socks on, and raced like a lunatic down the dark Kilroan road and hung himself from a tree somewhere in one of the fields by the roadside; finally, in a solemn voice, the sergeant recited another version of what he was reported to have said in Ryan's less than twelve hours before this: The recently rich young fellow had it all arranged, had the change of clothes hidden behind Ryan's ditch, and he switched clothes, left the queer note to throw people off, and presently young O'Rourke was becoming familiar with life in America, England, or Australia. When he was finished, those who sat around the table in the barracks bowed their heads and coughed, shoved their chairs back, and did not look at one another in the eye.

Sergeant Culley's accounts were related at the creamery in Pallas later the same morning and news traveled swiftly to the parish of Kilroan. The O'Rourke family and everyone else in Kilroan were livid: Hanging! Is that what he said? Hanging, of all the things that miserable bastard could think of; can you fathom it for one second? Worse even, the poor boy running mad without a stitch on a cold night along the road, and becoming familiar with life abroad, ha! And these people would tell you that they were smart men! God have mercy on us, to be stuck with Peelers like them, but there's the law for you, sure enough. What else could we ever expect?

According to them, Culley and his kind knew nothing, never in their life having seen or spoken one word to Eoin, the most good-natured young fellow God ever put breath in: A responsible, respectable young man like Eoin would never conduct himself in such a manner, bring such misery to his own family, his father's body barely cold in the grave.

—The law is the law, and oftentimes human beings don't behave like human beings, particularly those with certain dispositions, in rare situations they have never confronted before, was Sergeant Culley's arrogant reply, and under his instructions the guards walked in twos and threes with the coats of their uniforms fully unbuttoned, carrying billhooks, rakes, saws, canvas bags, and ropes far in from the roads to scrutinize the trees, thinking they'd find a naked Eoin O'Rourke, with his shoes and socks still on, the money thrown at his feet, hanging from an elm or poplar. They were having a field day for themselves, as the saying goes, and were going to draw it out as long as they could. They even had a bet for a few pints going between them at Ryan's as to whose land and what kind of a tree they'd eventually find him on, whether he would be wearing the shoes and socks or not, but they came across no body hanging from a tree, so the sergeant suggested they drag the ponds, where they also uncovered no body; then the sergeant told them to turn their attention to the rivers and dikes, where they only found the foul and sopping remains of aborted calves and drowned dogs and cats and other things rotted by water and muck beyond recognition.

They did the best they could when it came to searching the bog, and they could not get close to the Main Trench, for the water had spread out in a single enormous sheet, blanketing the meadows and fields, and the only way you could gauge its depth was when the tops of the rushes penetrated above the surface of the water, and this didn't tell you much about how soft the ground might be, and those guards were not knowledgeable about maneuvering through a bog, most of them not being from around Kilroan and Pallas, they not being farmers themselves.

They also searched the hay barns along the Kilroan road to

look up at the rafters, but no trace of Eoin O'Rourke was found
beyond the newspaper parcel on the rock and the queer note in the
shirt pocket.

The next Sunday Father Gill said a special Mass for the safe
return of Eoin O'Rourke. Mrs. O'Rourke unwillingly left the bed,
only to weep throughout Mass. She and her sons and daughters
knelt at the top of the church, as they had that spring, when their
father's coffin lay inside the altar rails. The Tuesday after the Mass,
Sergeant Culley widened the search of the local fields and hay
barns, ponds, and dikes. Nothing. He halted all searches at the end
of the week and he announced in the barracks he now definitely
believed young O'Rourke did run mad, screaming, splashing, and
laughing, with the money in hand, into the bog, where the fierce
waters of the Main Trench brought him to the Shannon and his
body was dragged out like a coffin ship itself into the miserable
and unforgiving Atlantic Ocean.

Most of the people in Pallas and Kilroan, apart from the
O'Rourkes, were beginning to believe that this was most likely
the truth. Eoin was certainly too kind a young fellow to turn his
back on his family and make a run for it, and he was way too easygoing, easygoing and lazy, not gallant enough for such a spirited
adventure, although several months later it was whispered amongst
certain men in Kilroan (these were the men who knelt in the porch
of the church and talked quietly during Mass and left after Holy
Communion to head for Power's public house) that of course there
was some truth to the fact that Eoin made off with the money;
since, according to them, you could not blame a young man, with
a fat purse warming his thigh, a few jars on him to give him a bit of
Dutch courage, for no matter what your outlook on life is, honesty
and God and family have very little to do with it, when you think
about that same young man trudging up a cold and dark hill to a
needy houseful, knowing what was before and around him for the
rest of his life would change very little.

In the end the O'Rourkes had to live with it, because what else can be done when misfortune so cruel and devastating happens? None of them were known to ever again mention Eoin's name or his disappearance in public, and as time went on it felt as though Eoin O'Rourke never existed in the world in the first place, and people in Kilroan were considerate enough to not ever refer to him in the company of an O'Rourke. The same people, though, began to cease talking and speculating; like all news, it became old news. The winter was not far off and people had their own and their livestock to worry about and look after, and it had been such a frightful summer with all the rain.

The O'Rourkes pulled through the autumn and winter as best they could, with the help of neighbors and Father Gill, who continued to visit Mrs. O'Rourke; he eventually cajoled her out of the bed, but never again did she frequent the village or attend Mass, but sat rocking in a chair by her bed; but there was also good news, for in a few short years Michael transformed the hill farm into a noble one, and despite the fact that all of his brothers and sisters had to leave the home place, similar to what everyone else had to do back then, they all married and all prospered in life.

The Fair in Pallas ended a year or two after the Eoin O'Rourke episode, which, in itself, had nothing to do with the Fair closing. The main reason the Fair ended was due to the cattle churning the then unpaved roads to mud with their hooves, their manure and urine splattered and pooled along the roads, and they trampled down the walls of the dikes, and the younger, wilder beasts were well able to leap across the dikes and escape over those ditches to run unhampered through the fields and meadows, and the unlucky farmers who owned those fields and meadows were left with mending fences that those contrary heifers and bullocks had traipsed before them, post and all, into his land; needless to say, this was one of the few drawbacks in those days, or any day for that matter, of having land next to the roadside, but these farmers were the happiest of all when the Fairs closed in the small country villages like Pallas and Emly and moved to the bigger places such as Tipperary town and Limerick City.

IT WAS THE WHISTLING MAN pushing the food trolley into the train carriage that took Kate Dillon's attention from the passing countryside and made her raise her face up to look over the seat opposite her, where the slouched, dark-haired young man had been peacefully dozing since the train left Houston station. She pushed her red scarf halfway back her head and watched the few late-afternoon travelers up ahead stir awake. She knew it was the lively smell of the freshly brewed tea and coffee that was waking them, that and the fact that not too many could sleep through the man's frightfully loud whistling.

The young man sat up, hunched his shoulders, and blinked at the window light. She watched his brow wrinkle and it looked to her the way his eyes were blinking he had no idea who and where he was. She herself could neither read nor sleep on a train, not being used to it, for she had not spent four days away from home since her late husband, Tom, had taken her to Killarney on their honeymoon many years ago. More than anything else, she wouldn't mind the chat, but she was also enjoying watching the countryside between the towns and train stations. It was nearly May and outside of her train window, the fields and trees were green again.

The man pushing the cart was still whistling when he placed a paper napkin before her on the table. The exertion from pushing the trolley and the steam from the tall tanks of hot coffee and tea had reddened his face; his silver hair was tossed and damp, his forehead was shining. She took note of the patches of sweat underneath his arms, and his wrinkled white shirt, the tie tucked inside the shirt halfway down, above his heavy stomach. She knew it would be hard to keep a white shirt clean and fresh with the kind of job he had. He nodded politely, said Hello, Missus, and asked her if she would like a fresh cup of tea.

—No, thank you. She smiled up at him, respectfully nodding her head, as if to say the reason she did not want the tea was because she did not want to put him to all the trouble of pouring it.

—Fair enough, Missus, the man whistled once and turned his attention to the young man.

—And yourself, young fellow?

—Coffee, Mister, thanks very much, lovely day it is.

—Yes, indeed, thank God for it, said the whistling man. —I can bet you, too, that the sun will make an appearance later on.

He had a Cork accent, she now detected, and he was older than she had at first thought, when she had watched him pushing the trolley toward her. She now placed him in his early fifties, as she glanced at the fine wide wedding band on one of the thick hairy fingers gripping the handle of the trolley. She fingered her own wedding band, and turned to look at the young man.

He had put a crumpled pound note on the table, was half-lifted out of the seat, rooting around in his pocket for change, and talking away to the Corkman. She recognized this young man's accent as being from down around her way, but there was also something familiar about his face: a broad, handsome face, with a flicker of kindness in his large hazel eyes that had caused her to smile and feel safe the moment she sat into the seat opposite him at Houston station. She put his age at around seventeen or eighteen. She, herself, had been living for over thirty years in The Postman's Cottage and she guessed that the young man was from one of the many farming families who lived out in the country and came into Kilroan for Mass on Sunday.

Her one child, Christy, was twenty-four. He was a graduating engineering student at the university college in Dublin, and she had phoned him two weeks past, requesting that he come down for a visit, but, he had asked her, for once, would she not take the train up to Dublin and visit him: He said it would do her the world of good to get away from there for a few days, and he was very busy studying for his final exams, and there was his new Dublin girlfriend, Tracy, to consider, who was dying to meet her.

Seán Egan had proposed to Kate Dillon, and this was why she needed to confer with her son, but in her four days in the city, she neither found the courage nor the right moment to ask Christy a thing; in fact, at every twist and turn she felt she was a hindrance to him and the new girlfriend—the two of them were not apart from each other for more than a few minutes, and she could barely get a word in otherwise; then, this morning, while she and Christy were alone in the taxi, on their way to Houston station, he told her he had decided that he was going to work for an American engineering firm in Qatar for five years, said he was sorry that he had forgotten to mention it earlier on, but the money out there was very good and he'd send the few bob home to her, of course, so he and Tracy were heading off this summer, but would spend a few weeks at home before they go, because Tracy was dying to see Kilroan—never happier in my life, Ma, our future, Ma.

The Corkman had gone into the next carriage, although she could still hear a faint whistling. She fingered a paper hankie from underneath the sleeve of her cardigan and began to wipe the mist from the window. They were going through Kildare; outside her window were sweeping, flat fields, where handsome racehorses contentedly grazed. *Our future*—those words would not leave her be from the moment she kissed Christy good-bye and got onto the train, although she was more than well aware that it was herself who had drummed it into him, day after day, when he was going to National School and later when he went to the secondary school in Hospital, that there was no life for him in Kilroan. Drove him like a workhorse from day one, she did, and the postman often telling her to leave the child alone, that she'd turn him into a pure stranger who had no idea who or where he was—nothing and everything to complain about, as usual, is what the postman would say to her at this moment, God rest him.

Seán Egan was Kate Dillon's age, and a bachelor all his life. He was not from Kilroan, but from the coast of Clare, and some fifteen years back he arrived in Kilroan to manage the creamery. A few weeks ago, at her kitchen table, was when he asked her to marry him. She sat across from him; they were drinking tea, like they did every evening when he stopped in on his way home, a habit that began a few weeks after the postman passed way. Seán Egan laid his mug down, interrupting her conversation about plans she had for the garden.

—Kate, would you think about marrying me, he said humbly, —you don't have to give me your word now, Kate, but would you think at all about it? I'm very fond of you and there's not a thing I'd like better in life, but it does not matter a bit if you don't.

He at once rose from his seat at the table and went to her back window, his back turned to her, as he leaned against the cooker and stared through the lace curtain at the rank garden and groaned. She watched his thick body, which she had come to cherish, sitting down and standing up at her table every afternoon, the blackened redness of his wrinkled neck above the stiff white collar, and his gray hair cropped so close that she could see his scalp, his thick, short legs a few feet apart, and his hands gripped so tightly in his pockets that they dragged his trousers up, the gray socks furrowed over his work boots, showing two inches of his white, hairy legs, his trousers clenched so tightly that it shaped his broad, round backside, and even from where he stood, that odd, particular smell of red soap and fresh milk drifting to her; she had first smelled it the afternoon she ran out onto the road and frantically stopped him on his bicycle, she weeping and frantically asking him to help her with the postman, who she said lay dead to the world in the garden.

—I'd have to see what Christy wants, Seán, I'd have to. I

would have to go with whatever the son wants. She turned her eyes from him to the open back door that looked out upon the blooming sycamores.

—Don't I understand that very well, Katie, he whispered, and delicately, as though it were a nightgown, he lifted the edge of her curtain with his two fingers, and continued to silently stare out there for five more minutes.

Kate Dillon sighed and gave the window another quick wipe, while looking across at the handsome young man. She knew by his ruddy complexion, his robust chest straining the buttons of his blue shirt, the words he spoke to the Corkman and the way he had spoken them, how he had dragged that crumpled and soiled pound note from his pocket, that this young fellow before her was no student.

—How is the coffee, young fellow? she asked.

—It's grand, Missus, thank you, he nodded, —I usually drink tea, but on the train, I like coffee just for the change.

—I never touch it myself.

She smiled at him. The train had stopped at a station, whose name she had not got the chance to see. She craned her neck along the window. There wasn't a single soul on the platform but the stationmaster, who was laughing and talking through the window to someone in the next carriage. At the entrance to the train station, an elderly farmer had halted his horse and cart; there were two small milk churns on the cart.

—Portlaoise, this is, Missus, where the big prison is, the young man said.

—Is that right, she said. —Didn't I forget that 'twas here that was.

—Oh, I'm dead sure it's here, Missus, he nodded, watching through the window.

—Your man is coming very late from the creamery, at this hour of the day, she said, pointing to the elderly farmer.

—That's a fact, Missus, but you know the way men like your man will keep talking for hours long after the creamery is long closed.

—You're dead right there, young fellow, God knows.

One or two like him went by her cottage every afternoon. From her kitchen she'd hear the hooves of the ponies clopping leisurely on the road, the muffled voices of the men talking to their ponies. She knew those men by name, and if she happened to be out on the road, out trimming the hedge, they'd stop and have a few words with her. They'd reminisce about what a great man the postman was, how the new postman wasn't half as good, even though he had that nice, comfortable van and all. They'd inquire about the young fellow at the university, and tell her that he was a credit to her, and they'd say how much happier and better off everyone was in the olden days, in spite of how little people had then.

The train began to pull away; the elderly man lifted his cap and waved it high in the air. Kate Dillon and the young man smiled and waved back. The time slipped past her on the station clock. Seán would have locked up the creamery and be cycling past her cottage around now. He would lean his bicycle against the whitewashed wall and look over the gate at the flowers and walk up the path and look in the windows back and front to make sure everything was in its rightful place. She imagined his face pressed against the glass, his darkened shadow stretching into her kitchen. She had given him the key and told him to go in and make himself a cup of tea and a sandwich; she had walked up to the grocer's and filled the fridge for this very reason, but he had told her that sitting at her table wouldn't be the same without her sitting across from him—he'd only feel like a stranger in a strange house.

—The forecast is very good, young fellow. There won't be any rain for a long while, she was looking again at the young man, —I heard that on the radio this morning early.

—Sure it's fine weather all right, Missus. He was gazing at a cloudless sky over the hills. —I'm going home to help my father for a few days in the garden.

—God bless the work, she said, her eyes opened wide with admiration. —You're a very good boy. You work yourself in the city.

—I do, Missus, in the buildings, I do.

—A fine job for a young fellow like yourself, she said, now knowing where those fine strong arms on him came from. —Sure it is far healthier working outside than inside. My husband was the postman, you know, worked outdoors every day of his life.

—Well, Missus, I work indoors, too, I'm a tiler by trade, but I can do everything and anything in that line.

—You can't beat a good honest day's work like that, not many are doing it now, she said mindfully, —and it's good to be earning your own few bob, and half the country out of work and on the dole, but I often think if they really needed the work, they'd find it for themselves.

—Aha, the devil knows. He shook his head at the passing fields, then turned to face her, and wiped his eyes, yawned, without covering his mouth.

—You're putting it aside, I hope. She brought her hand to her mouth, coughed, and sat up stiffly.

—I am, Missus, I take every second of overtime going—

—I have a son up there in the university, she cut him off, —the only one I have, a brand-new man those years have made him. You wouldn't even know him if you saw him. He got so tall and everything these last few years. I didn't know him for a moment myself when he came to meet me at Kingsbridge a few days ago. Of course, he had a new girl with him who I never had met before. Tracy is her name. Never met anyone with that name before, only on the TV.

—Fine job, altogether, Missus, he smiled. —Fine job.

Ballybrophy was the next stop she remembered from the journey up. The young fellow placed his elbows on the table, and took a slug from the paper cup. A stream of coffee dribbled onto the front of his shirt. He did not notice this at all, but kept the cup to his mouth, watching out the window on the other side of the aisle. The seats there were empty. She immediately wanted to tell him about that coffee stain. He could go into the toilet and wash it out and with the heat from the sun through the window, it would be dry before he reached home. Young fellow needs a haircut badly, too. It was too long above his forehead and oiled down around his ears, not tidy the way she'd have it, the way Christy wore his. But the light through the train window put a shiny, clean tint on the young man's hair. She admired the way a few wisps stuck out across his forehead.

—I've worked around that side of the city where the university is a few times, the young man said. He was rearranging his feet and accidentally touched her shin. His ears turned bright red.

—Sure, my son, Christy, is very lucky to go there, she said in haste, —and I don't know if he appreciates all we went through for him, although the postman and me had only the one and that made it an awful lot easier. But I understand too well that he would not be running back home to me. It's not that I'm a pure fool, young fellow. He was always a very good boy to me, mind you, did what he was told, he did, but you yourself wouldn't understand what I'm talking about at all, being too close to being a boy yourself, but that's all before you.

A burst of sunshine through the window made her shift in her seat. She opened a button in her gray cardigan, and she reached her hands up and fully pushed the scarf from her head. She had a long, narrow face and a high forehead. Her hair was jet black and tied back tightly in a bun. She had fine cheekbones, and the tip of her nose went up a little. She tilted her head to the side, and brought her joined hands from her lap and placed them on the table.

—Where are you and your people from? If you don't mind my asking, young fellow.

—Toward Oola, Missus, he turned from the aisle to her.

—Well now, she burst out, well, well. She eyed him—her mind drifting in the second as to where she saw a face like his before.

—I could tell from the moment I saw and heard you that you were from down around my way. I'm from Kilroan myself, not too far from you, and for the life of me I can't think of anyone I know in Pallas anymore, but sure years ago I must have known many. You're a bit young to know anything about the way things and people were back then.

—Well, Missus, my father's family is from up around Kilroan way, but that old place was sold long before my time. There was only the few acres. All are gone from there a long while ago.

She leaned closer to him. He pushed the empty coffee cup to the edge of the table and wiped his mouth and fingers and shoved the napkin into the empty cup. She noted the sun had dried the stain on his shirt.

—And where exactly would the home place be?

—Well, it's a good ways from the village, so I heard my father say once. There was a big family of them, all over the place they are now.

—The truth is, young fellow, that I'm not from Kilroan myself, but I've lived there for more years than I can remember, but the postman himself, God rest him, had the family cottage there.

She sighed and cast her eyes down, squeezed them shut, and brought her hands from the table and joined them on her lap.

—God rest him, the young man whispered and sat up straight. His foot touched her shin again, and he reverently bowed his head. She opened her eyes to a troubled look on his face, a look she immediately wanted to take away.

—Aha, for God's sake, don't let a woman like myself be worrying you at all, young fellow, she waved her hand. —Things could be an awful lot worse. We had a good, long life, the two of us did, thanks be to God for it, and I'm still young and in good health, only a touch of the arthritis in places, but what else can you expect from a woman like myself, after all that I've been through and seen.

—Well, I'm very sorry for your troubles, Missus.

—Well, thank you very much, she smiled and nodded. —I don't know now if I should be telling you things like this at all, but sure what harm. You're old enough to hear such things, but didn't I find him in the garden, five year ago it was. I lifted the curtain and looked out the kitchen window to call him in for his tea and didn't I think at first he was lying down in the drills resting, but I knew the way the spade was lying across him that there was something not right, but lucky for me, God was looking down on me, for didn't Seán Egan, who manages the creamery, happen to be cycling by on the road at that time, because in fright, the first thing I did was run out onto the road to look for someone, and how lucky I was that in the darkest hour of my life a neighbor was there to help me, and help me he did. God does not close a door without opening a window, as that saying goes. My husband died in his favorite place in the whole world, that's what everyone was saying to me at the funeral. A huge funeral it was, too, one of the biggest ever in Kilroan, he being the postman but God took him in his favorite place, Kate Welsh, they all kept saying to me after—couldn't ask for more, they were saying what more could he or me wish for. We had a fine, healthy son, who's doing very well for himself. I suppose that's the truth. Never sick a day in his life the postman wasn't, but there you are now; he was, indeed, a great man in the garden. That's for sure, exactly like yourself, I'm sure.

—My uncle Michael says I'm the best of the lot in the garden—

She did not let him finish, but wagged her finger at him the way a schoolteacher might. —But my son didn't like the garden, and that was a big disappointment to the postman. He thought that the young fellow thought that he was too good for working in the garden and working for the farmers in summertime, which he never did, being good at school and all, that was the only way the postman could see it, but that was not it at all I was tired of telling the postman my whole life. You can't have it every way, I used to repeat to him over and over. There's only one talent God will give you and he gave one to my son, and I made sure he found it, young fellow, and only a few of us have a chance in the first place to even find out he gave us one. You do good work yourself in your job; it sounds to me like you're an honest enough young fellow.

—I do the best I can, Missus, he nodded.

—Good enough, then, she said, —my own son was saying a few years ago when the postman passed away that I should go and live with him in Dublin, and I said I was not leaving my fine, safe cottage and neighbors, no matter what, and now he's off to some foreign place with a stranger of a girl, who could not once look me in the eye when I met her a few days ago, like I was a foreigner myself—but I did the right thing not to leave home, and God knows when I'll see him ever again but sure he was top of his class always, and what more could a woman like myself ask for. I'm very proud of him is the truth of it—and I don't say that out loud ever, to be very honest with you.

—They all come home so easy now, all of them, he spoke at the window.

—No one ever spoke a truer word, he will come home to his home and his mother, she said, —sure it's not like it was years ago at all.

She felt happy as Larry, safe and relieved—and how blessed she was to meet such a smart and kind young fellow.

—Your father farms, she said.

—Yes, Missus, said he solemnly, turning from the sunlit fields.

—They're not easy times for farmers now, not according to my own father, that's for sure. There's talk they're going to shut down all the creameries. I don't mind the farming myself at all. But my father thinks there's no life in it for a young person, that that day

is long over, although my uncle Michael has a massive farm back
in Bruff, with the milking parlor and the silage and slurry-pit and
everything. His son is looking after it now.

She had heard about shutting down the creameries from Seán;
he had said, too, that there was no avoiding it, but he had a good
pension coming to him.

—On the small side then, young fellow, she said, knowing
well she was being too nosey.

He looked from her and blinked at the passing fields.

—Well, now, she said hoarsely, bringing her hand to her
mouth, —I'm terribly sorry, but didn't I forget to ask you your
father's name—I don't know if I've already told you myself that I
am not from Kilroan at all. My real home was in the townsland of
Ballinlough, although I was not too sad to leave it. In fact, I was
lucky enough to leave when I did. I'm from a small place myself,
and don't miss milking cows one bit, that's for sure.

—Can't blame anyone for that, he said, —but as I said earlier
they have the machines now. It's all much easier.

—You're right there, everything is easier, she sighed. —I haven't
been thinking of this journey at all. The chat is a great help, and I
had an awful lot on my mind, but I'm feeling an awful lot better,
and am dying to be back home. I'm not used to the trains and
being away from my own place, but there's nothing grander than
meeting a stranger on a strange journey who's not a stranger at all.

The train had stopped and moved on from Ballybrophy, without either of them noticing. It was now at the platform, in Tem-
plemore. A few people stood and left the carriage. No one came
in. She watched the few country people walking past, a boy and a
girl running and laughing around them, a woman shouting, who
she could not see. *Mind them tracks. You'll knock people down or get
killed dead with that kind of carry-on.* The porter wheeling a trolley
full of boxes and parcels, his jacket fully open, his tie loosened,
and it struck her what a lovely day it had turned into. It would still

be daylight when she reached Limerick Junction, maybe even be warm. The young man gazed at the platform, too. His eyes were motionless, and the look on his face shook her for an instant. His mouth had fallen to one side, like he was biting down on his back teeth. She hoped that she had not upset him with her talk, but all the chatting was making her feel light and girlish.

The children ran up to the window and gawked and stuck their tongues out, then laughed and ran off.

—There's children for you, he sat up and laughed; the look vanished.

—God bless them, she smiled, —I only had one myself, as I told you, but that was more than enough for any woman, and as I said it's all in front of you. That's where life always is, as my friend Seán keeps reminding me, and to be honest I would not want to go back to any of it again.

—This is where they train the gardai, Missus.

—Is that right. She sat up attentively. —I thought it was the other place we passed through above.

—No, Missus, I'm fully sure it's here, didn't I think about joining them myself a year or so ago.

—And you didn't.

—No, I didn't, no.

He was waving and smiling at the children, who had run again to the window. He rolled his eyes and made faces at them. She held back telling him she had once thought that her son should join the gardai, but the postman was insistent that Christy Dillon had too good a head on his shoulders for that work, said that the guards were not as good as people cracked them up to be.

—You'd be fed and found with the gardai is the only thing, and you'd never have to leave home, she said, —and there might even be a bit of excitement.

—There could be, I suppose. He had stopped watching the children and was watching her.

—Not much ever happens for the gardai down our way, mind you.

—It's all in the cities, Missus, robbers, guns, and the drugs, the guards are kept busy there.

—Don't I read that every day in the paper, young fellow, and hear it on the news every morning, sure it's a woefully dangerous job, when I think about it. I am so lucky to be living where I'm living. I would not feel safe in any other place in the whole world, only in my own cottage.

—To be honest, Missus, the marks weren't good enough for the guards, I didn't have much interest in school. I couldn't wait to get away from school is the truth.

—Oh, she said compassionately, slowly, —don't I understand only too well myself that it's not for everyone. When we were young, none of us got a chance to go at all. Only a small few. Those who had the land and the money only had the luxury to care about schooling. There was always too many jobs to be done at home around the farm was the problem, too many jobs and too many mouths to feed, and our mothers and fathers not having the time and patience to think about what was going to happen to a single one of us in a few years.

—Missus, he said, sitting up and smiling broadly, —O'Rourke's my name, by the way, Timmy O'Rourke, after my father.

He put his hand out, and she shook his hand. His fingers were almost too thick for her hand to hold.

—O'Rourke.

Her mouth opened wide. She sat up stiffly, pressed her palms upon the table, and leaned forward.

—From Kilroan, did you say! Which one now did you say your father was?

—Timmy, Missus. According to my mother, he's the younger of them.

—He's a brother to Michael—

—The very man, he threw his head back and laughed. —I can't believe you heard of them. That was my uncle Michael I was talking about earlier with the big farm in Bruff. He had a stroke a few years back but is doing all right. And sure my uncle Eoin went to America years and years ago, and we never hear a word from him, not even a Christmas card do we get.

She squinted at him. How could she tell him? It certainly wasn't her place to—but this is what the O'Rourkes are telling their children? In the name of God, the awful shame of it, to have your own fooling you, but she couldn't tell the young fellow: Your uncle Eoin drowned in the Main Trench, God rest him, the summer it would not stop raining and everyone believed, after, that the deluge had come because God was punishing them; this is what Father Gill told them from the altar—nor could she say, your uncle Eoin was on his way home from the Pallas Fair, and he drowned with all the money, his body pulled into the Atlantic, and not one of your uncles and aunts were the same after; they never got over it, and your poor grandmother died in St. Joseph's Mental Hospital, would not leave the chair in the room; no, indeed, could she ever tell this young fellow a single word of it.

—My husband, God rest him, she said calmly, —my husband, he would have known your uncle Eoin, when they were your age, they were friendly the way young people are at that age. I don't know your father at all or any of your uncles and aunts—but tell me now, Timmy, will your uncle Eoin ever come home and visit us?

She could not, for the life of her, help but inquire.

—That'll never happen, unless a miracle, he was barely able to get those words out.

—Who could blame your uncle Eoin, going out there in very hard times, they were, as most people did. Not like it is today, as you said yourself earlier, Timmy.

—What would I know about any of them, Missus. It's not like they'll tell you.

A lonesomeness had crept into his voice. His face was toward the table, his cheeks heavy. Strands of his hair had loosened and were falling over his forehead. His mouth tightened into a straight line.

—My father and mother would kill me dead, Missus, if they found out I even mentioned his name to anyone outside the house, he said sorrowfully. —They'd go stone mad. My father only talks about him at Christmas, telling us we have an uncle in America, although at the same time he says he's too young to remember him going away, but he remembers well them talking about it after, so he says, and my mother like a mad woman tells him to keep his mouth shut about those things and not be fooling us, and my father shuts his mouth when my mother tells him to.

He had not lifted his face, but was making circles on the table with his finger, pressing his finger hard so that the tip was bent back. —You know the way them older people are, can't say a word or ask them anything ever, excuse me now for saying so, Missus.

—Well, you're right there, was all she could say.

He lifted his face. With the palm of his hand, he pushed the stiff strands of hair from his forehead and turned to the passing fields.

—We shouldn't and won't say another word about any of it, Timmy. Let bygones be bygones, as my husband, God rest him, and my friend Seán says. I've only one thing to tell you about your uncle Eoin, Timmy.

He sat up, turned to her, was all ears.

—Well, when I was a girl, around your age, and like yourself, being too young to know a single thing about anything, and let me tell you you shouldn't be bothering yourself with things you can't know or do a thing about, I walked out once or twice with your uncle Eoin.

—You did not, Missus, his eyes opened wide, innocent as a child's looking out of a pram on a summer's day. —You did not, he repeated it more slowly.

—Oh, I tell you now, I did, Timmy, she said cheerfully. —Well now, I only met him twice now, as I said to you, Timmy, I'd cycle down from Ballinlough after the cows were out in the evening and I'd meet him at the gully not too far beyond Kilroan. Of course he had the few cows to milk himself, but he brought me Bulls Eyes, and he'd put one or two in the pocket of my cardigan out of devilment, knowing they'd stick to the pocket, and I'd find them stuck in there a day or two later, but I have to admit that I'd pull the threads off them and suck away on them. He was a funny one, all right, your uncle Eoin was, a great one for the joking and the whistling—so there was only the three or four times. Small enough world, as they say. You know he told me he was planning to cross the water so that put a stop to us very quickly, and we were only foolish young people then, like yourself is now.

Timmy O'Rourke sat back and looked out, a drifting look on his face, his body shaking to the gentle motion of the train—thank God she'd be home soon. At least she had told the young fellow something of the truth, and what did it matter what she told him anyway, because fairy tales was what all the past was now—but God forgive her for telling him the bare-faced lie about his uncle's plans to cross the water, she fooling him herself like everyone else was, but she could not tell Timmy O'Rourke that on a summer's evening years ago his uncle Eoin stood in front of her bicycle and gripped the handlebars, and he was crying, asking her to give him a chance; there was spittle on his lips, tears rolling down his reddened face, and he was wearing his yellow Sunday shirt, with the wide suspenders, that all the boys had back then, and because of all the rain, the water was loud, tumbling underneath the gully, so that they had to shout, he shouting that things were going good on the hill, there was the bullocks to sell, and when she eventually was able to cycle away from him, she was crying so hard that she could not see the road, crying, *What can I do, Eoin, what in the name of God can I do, my mother and father won't let me, they won't, they won't ever let me,* and he ran up the road after her, gripped the carrier of her bike and she crying, *Please, Eoin, let me go, let me go, Eoin, please, I can't go against them, God forgive me,* pedaling as fast as she could, afraid that she might fall into the blurring ditch, and he running after her, beseeching of her for that chance—can't tell Timmy O'Rourke a single word of that either, unless you're fully off your head you can't. She didn't tell a soul about it back then, not the postman—definitely not him!—that same autumn they began to walk out in a serious way.

Christ Jesus, she prayed, Christ Jesus, forgive me, forgive me and take me home to my home. She meekly glanced up at young Timmy. The sun shone radiantly on his face, on his blue shirt and thick hair. Christ Jesus, but he was the image of Eoin, the same eyes, that sad mouth going sideways, the fine set of teeth; she caught her breath now, just as she caught it back then, when she saw his uncle smoking and laughing with all the lads outside of Sunday Mass, when he cycled, whistling, under the trees toward her on late, warm August evenings, the dust from the road smothering the sunlight under the elm trees where the gully is— the dreadful innocence of a young man's whistle.

She kept her hands as they were and crossed her legs and drew them tightly underneath the seat. She spoke in a quivering voice. —You'll find out, Timmy, that sometimes you don't do the right thing, even when you feel and know in your heart and soul that it's the right thing, and you'll find out, too, that many times they won't let you do the right thing. Mark my words now, young Timmy O'Rourke, and that's the best advice I can give to a grand young fellow like yourself.

—But thank you very much for telling me about him, Missus, and I have something now that I was just thinking about to tell you.

—Go on, like a good boy, she managed a quick smile.

—Well, I haven't told this to anyone, not even to my own father and mother.

—Grand, I won't open my mouth to anyone, go ahead now with it, like a good boy, because we're nearly in Thurles, and although I'm enjoying the chat, young Timmy, thank God we're close to home.

He started by telling her about Uncle Michael getting the stroke a few years ago. Uncle Michael's wife found him out by the silage pit one morning in January. There was snow that morning, and when Uncle Michael's wife came upon him, she thought he was dead; his hands were that cold and stiff. Snow covering his face and he lying on his back in the liquid muck that runs off the silage pits, so he was rushed to the Regional in Limerick. Timmy rang in Oola, Alice and Mary rang in England, Joe and Jack, not spoken to in years, were rang in Australia, Jimmy married in Tramore, Lena and Kathleen married in Dublin.

Timmy O'Rourke held his hand up before his face, counting off his fingers to make sure he mentioned all of them.

—They had the tubes stuck into him and the mask on his face, the tank set up, and the curtain pulled around him, Missus. And we all thought we'd seen the last of him. But then a miracle happened. He rallied, you could not believe it how he did but he did. The doctor said he himself had never seen the likes of his recovery. On the fourth day, he ate a bit; on the sixth, he was able to sit up. The family was rang back all over the place, told to not worry. No need anymore to make the journey.

Then Timmy O'Rourke told Kate Dillon that one afternoon, not too long after the stroke, he ventured in to see his uncle in the hospital. Uncle Michael was very fond of Timmy, Timmy being a very hard worker, good in a garden and good with the cows. They talked about the usual: weather and cows and the hay and silage and the football and the hurling and the dishonest and greedy politicians the country was eternally saddled with and jobs so hard to come by and everyone leaving all over again, like they always did, and the dead Hunger Strikers and that heartless and bitter woman

Mrs. Thatcher. Then Michael O'Rourke stopped talking and the right side of his face started jerking; his eyes spun around to white, he foaming at the mouth the way a tired-out horse would.

—He was taking a fit, Missus, and not a nurse in sight, when you need them.

He told her about the uncle snorting through his nose, then barking like a mad dog out the side of his mouth, barking at Timmy that it was him who should have died. He had luck enough for five people in his life. He reached out his hand and gripped Timmy's wrist, his eyes spinning again and his uncle hisses that one of the friends did it, and the bastard guards in Pallas paid off. He growled at his nephew that he knew that much, that it was one of the bastard friends, his head going from side to side, and he drooling all over the blanket and Timmy's hand, that he would not let go of.

—I'm fully sure now, Missus, that he was talking about an episode he saw on the television, he was mad about John Wayne and Zane Grey and the Virginian and Trampas and Mannix and Steve McGarrett, and used to never stop talking to us about them when we were children. Then he went on like a madman again, Missus, that it was the friend and no one else, says then he saw that friend after, saw it in his eyes, the way they had changed, saw the awful badness in them, saw right down into him—that was all you ever needed to see to know, so my uncle Michael said, but then suddenly, Missus, he put his hand up before his face and stammered, *Enough of that now, not a word, not a word to your father, ever*, his voice settling down a bit, becoming more normal.

—And when men like Uncle Michael say enough that is what they mean, and you know yourself what I mean, and he told me to promise him again that I would never say a word to anyone in the family, especially not to my own father and mother, or uncles and aunts, who I never see anyway—and then the nurses rushed in like an army, Missus, pushed me back and said it was a storm in the brain, delirious, they said. Delirious, I'd never seen him or anyone else like that. It was an episode stuck in his head, stuck in there and never turned off. Behaving like he was in the Mental and not the Regional. A man delirious, they kept saying—but he got over it, is in good enough form now, but in the wheelchair, mind you, but still looks at the television all the time, looks at it and smokes away and says only a few words, and I never said a word to him afterward, but didn't he whisper in my ear a few days after: *Say a prayer for your own who came before you and never forget them, son, never forget them.*

—Never forget them, but what exactly are you supposed to remember, I ask you, he spoke boldly, —I can't often help thinking, Missus.

She stared at him, her dry lips parted a little. He wiped his mouth with the back of his hand, settled back, touched the glass with his fingertips, and pressed his face to it.

Thanks be to God he was done with it. Her elbows and knees had become frightfully sore from being in the same place for too long; she had not taken her tablets, for the joints. He had been speaking too fast and she had drifted in and out of his yarn, he putting his uncle's mad words together for the sake of the story itself, since a young fellow hungry for stories from long ago was who Timmy O'Rourke really was. She could see that now; now when it was too late. Never able to keep your trap shut, is what the postman would say, as he had so often said to her—Christy, from the second he first found words, never asked her or the postman one solid thing about what went on years back, like nothing happened or mattered before the day he was born.

Never forget them. The postman told her when they were first married that Michael O'Rourke was a queer one and to keep out of his way, that he couldn't be trusted one bit, so years ago, if he was walking toward her on the street in Kilroan, she pretended not to see him, and bowed her head and crossed the street.

Jim Dwyer was one of those boys, he went off to America not

too long after she married the postman; he became a fireman in New York, lived in Queens and married an American girl, and the postman and he did not keep in touch beyond the Christmas cards they posted to each other for the first two or three years he went over, and when the postman died, there was no word from Jim Dwyer—but who would have told him, how in God's name would he have known?

Francie Houlton married an older woman; she had a big farm and a public house, up Longford or Leitrim way. She and the postman were not even invited to the wedding; that quick it was, and if Francie Houlton were to walk down the aisle of the Dublin train now she wouldn't know him from Adam.

Those two men were at her wedding, though. Francie Houlton played the accordion; he played it even better than his father used to play it, and the young and old got up to dance. Jim Dwyer got up on the stage and sang "Shanagolden"—but what was she thinking, because they weren't men then, no more than the young fellow across from her was now; young fellows was all they were, and full of devilment and feckless like all young fellows are, wanting each other only, though mad to marry, too, start what they thought would be lives of their own.

The young fellow sitting across from her would marry in a few short years. He'd become an altogether different person and forget completely about his uncle Eoin, and no one would ever tell Timmy O'Rourke, since no one knew anyway, why his uncle flung himself into the Main Trench, ended up down in the sandy mud and the rushes, but it did not matter one bit whether they did or didn't, because like the dead themselves, those who went then were never seen or heard from again.

—Is it dreaming you are? Wake up, Missus, we're nearly here, said Timmy O'Rourke. He was shaking her left arm above the elbow. She opened her eyes, trembled and straightened herself up. She felt her face reddening as he withdrew his hand and sat back.

—Here I am now, indeed, on the train, that's where I am and no place else, Timmy, is the truth. I'm only tired, I usually lie down for an hour or two in the afternoon, and I couldn't do that today of course.

She released her arms and legs and pulled her scarf down low over her forehead, managing somehow to tie the knot, though she did not feel her fingers working. —When you're around as long as I am, you get to see and hear too much, some of it is good news and some is sad, she said, reaching her hand along the table, gently squeezing the back of his warm hand. She had the urge to tell him that he was the image of his uncle Eoin, but she did not want to stir all that up again. —I should have had that cup of tea the Corkman was offering earlier, she said, —and I forgot to take a few tablets. Are we in Thurles yet, Timmy?

—Thurles, Missus, we passed through there a while back. We're close to the Junction, I'm telling you. We're at home.

—I'm going to get married, Timmy, that's what I've been thinking. I am and you're the first one to know, and no one can stop me from doing it this time.

But he had not heard a word of what she had said; too occupied, he was, with the passing countryside, the fields and trees and dung heaps he must know like the back of his own hand, though he stared so hard into them, as if they were vanishing forever, and this was his last chance to take them all in. She squinted at the sunlight bursting along his determined face, the warm April sunlight rippling quickly across both of them. His fixed, unblinking eyes. The speeding, rattling train.

—Thank God we're safe home, can you believe it, Timmy O'Rourke. She leaned forward, whispering, tapping the back of his still hand. —You'll help me with my bag to the taxi, Timmy; it's up in the rack up above me. My son, Christy, said to sit across from a country fellow because he'd help with the bag. The reason I sat here in the first place. When I first laid my eyes on you I

knew that was who you were, and there's not much in the bag at
all, mind you.

He turned from the long row of bushes that grew on the ditch
next to the tracks; the white fences of the racecourse gleamed in
the distance. He leaned his elbows on the table. —Not a bother,
Missus, I was just thinking that I still can't believe you knew him
in the flesh. You knew him when he was only my own age, but
you know what else I was just thinking, too, Missus, he spoke
earnestly. —That this is the happiest part of the journey home for
me, nearly being here but not rightly here, and not knowing what
things are going to be like, but being so close that you think you
can see what'll happen and then you turn around and go away
again and home and all you thought it was never happened at all.
Home never is what you thought it was in the first place.

He groaned then, and sat upright, the sulky look she had noticed earlier fixing itself upon him—in God's name, what else
was he going to unearth upon her and where, I ask you, did a
young fellow like himself find such talk? Beneath her the train
screeched; then it lurched, pushing and pulling her, and then it
abruptly slowed and slipped awkwardly into the inner rail. The
platform suddenly rose up to the window like a brick wall; she
squeezed her eyes shut and opened her eyes to people standing
close to the crawling train; other people stood farther back, smoking and leaning against the pillars, suitcases and bags stretched
along the platform like sleeping cats and dogs. The evening light
covered the front part of the platform at a straight angle, the back
part in shadow, cigarette smoke billowing through the light like
steam from the teapot every day at her back window. The big tub
of red geraniums blooming. She had leaned over four days ago
and smelled them. Thank God they were still there, and time
had done nothing to them. They were glorious, washed in April
sunshine.

—We're at home, Timmy, it looks like, we're safe now.

—Indeed we are, Missus, we're stopped.

He stood tall in the aisle, rolling his sleeves down, buttoning his cuffs, while examining his reflection in the train window, then brushing his hair into place with the palms of his hands; he tightened his belt a notch, pulled at the collar of his shirt, and patted his stomach with both hands. —Right you are, Missus, he said, his eyes shifting from the window to her who yet had to stand up. —We must go on out, he smiled, —unless you want to end up with that whistling fella in Cork, ha. I have your bag here safe with me. We had a great chat, all right. I didn't feel all that time going by one bit, Missus, and I'm sure you yourself didn't feel a bit of it either.

THE POUNDING RAIN AND A dream woke her. The shadowy light at the curtain told her it was around half-six or seven. She heard rain on the flagstone path, rain on the road, and in the sycamore trees. She thought she heard Tony Hartigan hunting his cows. If she didn't, she would hear him any minute now. She had heard different generations of the Hartigans hunting cows every morning since she moved into the cottage.

She needed to get up and make a pot of tea. Seán had dropped a note through the letterbox, saying that he'd stop in before the creamery to see how the journey went, and to make sure she was safe. She knew he would be too polite to ask her about Christy's answer; he'd wait for her to say something. She had knelt at her bedside last night and thanked God for bringing her home safe, thanked him for Christy's good fortune, and asked him to guide her, prayed for the soul of the postman. After she rose, she decided to write a letter to Christy over the next few days; she'd tell him that she was going to marry Seán Egan.

She turned the blanket back and brought her legs out slowly to the floor. Timmy O'Rourke's face was in her dreams, the face

frozen against the fields passing the window. She thought at first
that it was Christy's or the postman's face; it felt that familiar, a
face she had kissed and wiped. In the dream also was the aroma
of freshly brewed coffee, and she heard a man whistling, then the
smell of dirty bog water—Seán would knock at the front door, and
she imagined herself opening the door to the rain rippling off his
umbrella, he in his green raincoat and wellingtons, and his clean-
shaven, red jaw, his generous and timid smile.

She went into the toilet and washed her face and lightly powdered it. She brushed her hair back into a bun. She put on her
underclothes and housecoat and went downstairs, turned left under the stairs, and into her son's small bedroom to check on the
two begonias that had begun to bloom in pots on the windowsill.
She pressed her fingertips into the clay in both pots, and it was
moist. There was the famous picture of Einstein, next to the U2
Boy poster, pinned above her son's single, perfectly dressed bed.
Against the opposite wall was a tall dresser John Joe Dillon had
made years back. This room was her favorite in the house because
of the unusual patterns the sycamore leaves cast in spring and
summer along the floor and the bed. She sat on the edge of the
bed and stroked the cold quilt. So many mornings she had gently
shook the curled-up figure, the growing boy, sat there then and
stared, stunned at how swiftly his body grew bigger, as though
each night he took one more step away from her.

She came out of Christy's room and shut the door. She walked
past the stairs, and opened the door to the kitchen. She went to the
sink at the back window and filled a kettle of water. She put it on
the cooker, and returned to the window and lifted the curtain. The
rain had lightened off a bit, thank God. Thrushes and blackbirds
were singing. Raindrops dripped from the sycamores, and from
clothes on the clothesline she had, before she left, forgotten to
bring in: a shabby old housecoat she had washed a million times,
an old towel that she should have thrown away ages ago, and a

few good shirts belonging to the postman that she had decided to give to Seán. While she had been away, Seán had dug a section of the garden next to the clothesline. He had been saying to her for a long time how sinful it was to let such a fertile piece of ground go to waste.

She had never mentioned Eoin O'Rourke's name to Seán, but Seán would have heard his name spoken of at Power's, that is, if none of the O'Rourkes were in there at the time, for Eoin's name would have come up when one of the older men recollected the summer the Main Trench was transformed into a lake; they would say that was the same time young O'Rourke did away with himself, and the conversation would end at that.

The postman never liked to delve into those olden times. *They're done with for a reason*, was what he had to say about them. This was exactly what Kate Dillon's mother liked about Tom Dillon in the first place. She told her daughter he was a man who was looking ahead, which was the only and right place to look. In the same conversation, her mother never neglected to mention John Joe Dillon's fine cottage.

In the evenings, when Christy was still a child, she'd watch through the window in the front room for the postman's return from work. First, she'd see his hand fumbling with the bolt in the gate, then the front wheel of the bicycle as he maneuvered it onto the flagstone path. Then himself, with his uniform open, his cap sticking out of his pocket and his shoulders drooped, his face to the flagstones, walking the path toward her. She'd have the dinner ready. The paper was laid neatly by his place at the kitchen table. She'd run to the kitchen and pick up anything of Christy's that was left lying around the floor. (He was not allowed to play in the front room.) Then she would tell Christy to go into his room and do his sums, and not to come out unless he was asked, or until all of the sums were done, and to look over the next lesson and try his hand at them. She had to discern what kind of mood the postman was in; most often there was no need for this, but Kate Dillon was the kind of woman who took precautions.

Where's the young fellow?

He's in his room with his books.

What's he doing in there at this hour of the evening, can't he come in and say hello to his own father.

I'll get him, then. Christy, don't be so badly mannered, take your face out of them books and come out here and talk to your father! Them old books don't tell you everything, you know.

Moods and tempers were what she called them—when the mood was good, she could not ask for more: He would let Christy sit on his knee, while he himself sat on in the front room and read the paper, and after he finished with the paper, he'd put the boy on the bar of the bike and take him for rides around the silent country roads outside the village of Kilroan, the boy and himself laughing loudly, the wind making music in the bicycle spokes; then they'd cycle back through the village, where he'd buy the boy and his mother an ice cream cone at the grocer's, then back on the bike again, past the church and down the hill to where the graveyard was, as he boasted to his son what a mighty, hardworking man his grandfather John Joe Dillon was, a man who made sure that a whole generation in Kilroan had dry and safe graves that would not cave-in in a million years, ready forever for the Resurrection.

But on more grim occasions he would walk in from work, enter the kitchen without a word, a deadened, distant, and glassy look in his eyes, and his wife and son and the objects around him, such as doors or stairs, that she had spent all day polishing, were invisible, he, impervious to the four sturdy walls that held him, the woman and the boy who loved and wanted only to please him. On those evenings, he'd sit at his place at the table and eat his dinner in silence; she would not say a word, but serve him his dinner and listen to him chewing. After, he'd go to the front room, sit into the armchair and hold the paper over his face for hours. She did not think that he was reading it.

Five years into the marriage he became the postman. But she was not unhappy or ungrateful; she would not have ever considered or imagined a different life, a life without him, not putting up with his way, not carrying out her duty to him; after all, this was the way God had willed it. So she washed her son's clothes and the postman's uniforms; she prepared delicious lunches and dinners for the two of them. She cleaned and scrubbed the house from top to bottom, and swept and washed the flagstone path. She tended her flowers, and cut the sycamore branches out back when they grew low to the ground. (Christy had run out of the house once and ran right into one, while she and the postman watched in horror from the kitchen table.) Every spring she whitewashed the piers and the gate and trimmed the laurel hedge. In the evenings, while he read the paper in the front room, she sat with Christy for hours in his room and made sure he did all of his homework. It's that job your father has that drives him mad. Being on his own all day. It would drive anyone mad. She had many women friends in Kilroan village, who she spoke to daily when she shopped for groceries. She had the men coming from the creamery in the afternoon who stopped in the road to tell her what news they heard that morning.

There was only the one time he pushed her. It was a few days before Christmas and he'd been delivering all day. People were filling him up with whiskey, and not being used to the drink, it made him irritable, made his behavior unpredictable, and on top of that he'd fallen on the path with the bike on the way in, and then she had made the mistake of serving the young fellow his dinner first, for he had brought home the good news that he had, once again, come in top of his class, and the teacher announced that he was the best student ever to attend Kilroan National School. The postman stood up from the kitchen table and threw the paper aside. He walked over to the cooker, pushed her from it, raised the wooden spoon, and shook it fiercely in her face.

Daddy, Christy shrieked at the table, *Daddy*.

But the postman paid no attention to him. His face had changed bright red, as he bit down on his tongue and shouted: If you only had one solid iota what I have done for you, Kate Welsh, you might not be standing where you are in that nice kitchen.

Later that evening, from behind the paper, he cried in the armchair, and said the business of the season was getting to him, that his legs and back were killing him, and he was frightfully sorry for his ungodly behavior to herself and the child, and that he was going to go to confession tomorrow evening. Was it the surfeit of love she gave so easily to the young fellow? she had often wondered then. Would it have been better if God had blessed them with another child? At night, in bed, he had often lamented that he would dearly love another child, a baby girl this time, but he also said that he was more than lucky to get what God had already given him.

In that nice kitchen. She sat at the table, sipping her tea, eager for Seán's knock on the door, and listening to one of the Hartigans hunting the cows in the field she could not see behind the sycamores. She watched through the back door the rain dripping from the still sycamores. It was at this hour of the morning that she thanked God for her life. She was indeed blessed and she was lucky. She knew many had it an awful lot worse. She had come to understand that what she thought of as her whole life was now becoming a part of it, the two empty places beside her at the table, nobody presently needing anything from anyone. If Christy only knew, indeed, understood it from beginning to end, if he had seen or asked about the thatched cottage she came out of in Ballinlough, most of her brothers and sisters living in England and America. Nobody ever said and did enough good, she knew that; nobody ever had simply goodness in them—that, too.

If Christy had only asked, indeed; all he had not asked and all that she had not told him, like the time years ago, when he was still in the pram, and she discovered the money under the floorboards in their bedroom upstairs. She was cleaning, the postman was at work, and Christy was sleeping in his own room. She had taken the curtains down to wash them. The room was fully lit, and she had dragged the bed out across the floor to sweep under it. When she was dragging the bed, a board underneath the bed came loose. She bent down and lifted up a small square board. And directly beneath the board was an old Halpin's tea canister, the kind people used years ago. She plucked the canister out, and dragged the lid open with her nails. Inside was a large roll of the old money, which went out years ago, wound tightly in two wide elastic bands. She knew the postman was good at saving, was cautious about rainy days in the future, but what surprised her was that he had not put the money in the post office or the bank for safety, for he was usually wise in this way.

When he came home that evening, she tried to coax him out. It was after dinner, and she brought the tea into the front room to him. She put the tea on the hearth beside the armchair and mentioned that when she was sweeping the bedroom upstairs one of the boards came loose on the floor. She watched the legs crossed, the one slipper dangling from the right foot, and the paper covering the upper half of him like he had pulled a curtain. Then she said the board was right under the bed, not a big board at all, just a small square one. An odd one out in the whole lot, it looked like, but it was well hidden, for she had never noticed it before in all her cleaning.

I'll fix it later on when I'm finished with reading this, said he from behind the paper, which did not drop an inch from his face, the top corners of the front pages curled over like pigs' ears. Then she broke down and asked him why he kept such important things concerning herself and Christy's welfare from her, and without shifting the paper, he said he had no idea whatsoever what she was

going on about now, and she could do her complaining later on
when he was finished with reading the paper; didn't he, at least,
deserve these few moments' peace, and what did he ever do but
love the two of them the best way that he could, and what more
could men do for women, and she was not fooling him with that
stupid talk about herself never keeping a thing from him; didn't
he know well about her gossiping on about everyone else's business
with strangers in the road, and then he said that he knew her likes
better than she knew her own self.

But I found all that money, she blurted, and now the paper
slides quickly to the left.

All what money, I have no idea what you're talking about,
woman, is it stone mad you are?

And it took him less than five minutes to sort the whole thing
out; it was his own father, of course: John Joe Dillon himself had
planted the money there years back, and because he had died suddenly, he did not get the chance to tell a soul about it. It was not
until then that the postman told her his father made a prisoner of
every penny he ever came across in his life, and he and his mother
were lucky if they had butter on their bread more than two times
a week, and the postman said he would never have his own live
in that way. She suggested they immediately take that money and
put it in the post office in Kilroan, but he said they didn't want the
Reilly woman, who ran the post office, knowing their business,
and they should take the money to the AIB in Tipperary town,
where no one would know or care who they were.

Which was exactly what they did, and it was not touched until
Christy turned eighteen, when every penny of it went toward his
education. She had thought about it often in the years. A blessing,
it was. Thank God that old John Joe Dillon was such a miser.

She would tell Seán all this by-and-by; she would tell and it
would be a relief to do so—he was running a bit late, because of
the rain? She finished her tea and went into the front room and

began to dust the photographs beneath the picture of the Sacred Heart on the crowded mantelpiece, right above the postman's armchair. She did this every other week. There was a photograph of them on their wedding day outside the new church in Kilroan. Photographs of Christy on his Communion and Confirmation days, the two of them, chins way up, standing next to him, her hat with the feathers, cocked to the left, his good cap to the right, her wearing a fox fur. A black-and-white photograph of the two of them with their backs to her newly whitewashed piers, and the laurel hedge she had trimmed the day before, Christy standing before the whitewashed gate, with his school satchel at his feet. There was a photograph of her own father and mother taken outside their thatched cottage in Ballinlough some thirty-five years ago, and a photo that would have been taken around the same time of the postman—he was not a postman then—with the Kilroan hurling team. Mrs. Hartigan had given her this photograph last Christmas as a gift. (Every Christmas the Dillons gave the Hartigans a box of Jacob's biscuits.) The photograph was in black and white, naturally enough. It was cracked, faded, and out of focus. She had never paid much attention to it because she knew so few of those boys on the team; she was still living in Ballinlough at this time.

The postman was kneeling on one knee in the first row, the hurling stick between his legs, resting against his thigh. She wiped the glass and thought that a youth standing in the back row might very well be Jim Dwyer. She now recalled that, like the youth in the photograph, he did have front teeth like a rabbit—buckteeth, as they'd say. She scanned the line of men, searching for Francis Houlton, but if he were amongst them, she did not recognize him, but there at the very end of the back row was Michael O'Rourke. It was certainly him. The hair and eyes, the way when they smiled their mouths dropped to the right, and she would never have recognized him if she had not met Timmy on the train yesterday. In the photograph, Michael O'Rourke had his arms tightly folded.

He clutched his hurling stick across his chest—the exaggerated, high, thick fringe, the wide, thick shoulders Eoin never had that Timmy had inherited. A mysterious smirk on Michael O'Rourke's face?

She would not yet have met the postman at the time the photograph was taken, but not too long after. Every one of the lads in the photograph would have gone to the Fairs in Pallas, whether they were selling or buying, farmers or not. They would have gone for a day out, the opportunity to laugh in a world with so few of them. They would go cracked with drink and fight, often with their best friends; fight over nothing, things said that they could not even remember, had no significance whatsoever the following day, when all was completely forgotten and forgiven, and yesterday's words, no matter how harmful, were changed into a pure laugh. There was always talk in the villages the day after the Fair about how badly the young men had behaved, though everyone understood that it was natural for young men to conduct themselves in such a way—that the young men had earned and deserved their boyish diversions.

The night Timmy O'Rourke's uncle disappeared forever, the postman was barely able to cycle his bike. He wouldn't, mind you, have been a bit different from any other young fellow who had spent the day in Pallas. She had sat waiting for him for an hour on the low wall of the graveyard in Ballinlough. She knew right well what was happening, what those boys were up to. And when he appeared, he was bent sideways, leading the wobbling bike, his left elbow resting on the saddle. His pants, the shirt and boots, were drenched and covered in muck. There were bits of grass and rushes stuck to his clothes and tossed hair. He let the bike fall onto the road, and stumbled over to the wall to her, telling her they had a great day at the Fair, and Eoin got a great price for the bullocks, and never had he seen a man more satisfied. When she asked him why his clothes were in such a mess, he laughed and told her that he had fallen, bike and all, into the dike on the road beyond the crossroads, that it was so dark he could not even see his own hand in front of him. The battery in his lamp was damp and would not work. He then began to cry. He tottered before her, pulled her to him, and kissed her fervently on the face and mouth, his two mucky hands clutching her head and soiling her scarf. She finally got his hands off her head and persuaded him to sit on the graveyard wall. She told him he'd get sick from being so wet and she took off her scarf and began to wipe the muck from his face and hair and hands, picking the grass and rushes from his jumper. She rubbed his hands in hers, in an attempt to warm him, but he squeezed her hands tightly, and cried loudly, I love you, Katie. You're mine, Katie, and no one else's, now and forever, you'll never again need no one else.

The loud knock on her front door frightened her. She felt her body shrinking, the house vanishing—she had gently taken him by the shoulders and sat him on that graveyard wall and pulled the rushes from his jumper, plucked them from him like quills from naked and dead chickens and turkeys. But wasn't it very dark? Wasn't it frightfully dark? But weren't they only young and wasn't it a very long time ago and wasn't it only grass? Didn't rushes grow in the dikes, too? The cursed rushes, the cold and miserable bog, the shouting and the splashing, the crying and the fighting, his warm and naked young body swallowed under. God having his revenge. A young man, a good-natured boy, who must have cried and cried not to die like that in the dark, without his mother, calling against that beaten, cruel, and bloody land, and not a soul there to help him. Christ Jesus. Christ Jesus.

She was standing behind the front door of The Postman's Cottage. Turning the key was always difficult; it got stuck halfway, and she had to grip the doorknob, pull the door hard toward her, but she lost her will and began to bang as hard as she could on the inside of her own door, with her two fragile fists, as if she were trying to escape. Banging on the cottage door and leaning her forehead against the postman's threadbare uniform coat she might have thrown away a long time ago, she cried, Seán, will you please, please go around to the back, Seán, for God's sake, yes, for God's sake, yes, go around the back, that door's open.

MARY GORDON

"I think I know where I'm going, and I try to allow myself to be open enough to be surprised. All of us have to work this bizarre territory of control and porosity that is what makes the profession so difficult."

"Things almost come to one as if they were music, and that steers something that you never would have thought of on your own."

"One of the things that is exciting about writing stories that one doesn't quite have the luxury of when one is committed to a novel is playing with voice, because the commitment is less long-lived and less intense."

Mary Gordon, from a radio interview with
the three finalists for The Story Prize
(Gordon, Rick Bass, and George Saunders),
The Leonard Lopate Show, *WNYC*
February 27, 2007

My Podiatrist Tells Me a Story About a Boy and a Dog

from *The Stories of Mary Gordon*

He says things to me like "There's no reason why you should feel any pain," and "I'll take care of everything." Why wouldn't I like seeing him?

I first went when I had something called a plantar wart beneath my left big toe. I thought it was called a planter's wart. "A lot of people think that and they're wrong," he said. "But you're a writer, you're interested in words, so you should know the truth." He draws me a diagram of the part of the foot called the planta. "I don't want you to imagine people walking around with shovels in their hands, putting plants into the soil," he said. "Because it's not the truth." I was glad to learn what he had to tell me; now I correct other people, for his sake and in his name.

His daughter plays the French horn in a symphony orchestra. But she's decided she wants to be a vet. To get into veterinary school, "which is already, you understand, very difficult in itself," she has to take more science courses. She lives in Boston. She told him she would take the courses in the local community college.

"'Darling,' I said to her, 'veterinary school is very hard to get into, true or not true?'

"She said what she had to say: 'True.'

"'So what's the best, and I mean the very best place in Boston to take courses?'"

"She said what she had to say: 'Harvard.'

"So I said to her, 'You're my daughter and I want the very best for you. And I can give you the best. So: Harvard.' She thanked me profusely. I can't tell you how profusely she thanked me. She's enjoying her courses very much. Though, of course, they're a challenge."

ON THE BUS HOME, I try to imagine what it would have been like to have a father who said, "I want the very best for you and I can give you the best." My life would have been wholly different.

IT'S NOT WELL KNOWN THAT the subspecialist most consulted by women over forty is the podiatrist. Over the years, many of us have been doing terrible things to our feet. High heels. Pointy toes. Damaging ourselves for vanity. For sex? From fear or from desire? A desire to please whom?

When I went to see him because of the plantar wart, he shaved my calluses, which, he said, were painful in places because of my gait. "Now everybody has a gait," he said. "Everybody's gait means something. In your case, problems. I can take care of them."

He shaved the bad calluses with a very sharp knife, a knife that looked as if it would have to hurt. I stiffened, thinking of my feet, those tender loaves. I've always liked my feet. Sometimes I think of them as my best feature. My second toe is longer than my first; for the Greeks, this is a sign of beauty. Also my toes make, on the top, a fanlike shape that I never look at without pleasure. So I didn't want anything happening to my nice feet. But he said, "You can trust me, I won't hurt you." I didn't believe him: I was looking at that knife. I waited for the shock of pain, which did not come. More than that: over the next days, I noticed that I was free from, if not pain, then a discomfort that had been so habitual I had assumed it was a part of life.

So of course I agreed to come back every three months, to keep myself in the state to which he'd brought me. Besides, he told me stories.

It began when I asked him how he became a podiatrist.

"Long story," he said. "Interesting story, or at least I think it's interesting. Since you're a writer, maybe you'll think it's interesting too."

As he began to speak, his eyebrows, which always had a tendency toward verticality, stood upright like two fuzzy letter *l*s. His small mouth, which I had seen in two positions—cheerfully amused in conversation, or concerned while holding an afflicted foot—became neutral: a vessel of information only.

"IT GOES BACK TO WHEN I was a child. You'll be surprised to hear it. But it goes back to an accident.

"So I can give you a background, so you can understand, you have to know something about my family.

"My father was a successful doctor. We were what you might call wealthy. Definitely wealthy. We lived in New York. It's not like it is now. One day, I was in my father's office with him, playing. By accident, a beaker of acid tipped over and burned my leg, right through to the bone. I became a cripple. And I'd been quite an athletic boy.

"As you can imagine, I grew downhearted. And my father was very guilty because he'd failed to cover the beaker of acid. So he devoted himself to me. He did everything. Built a gym in the basement—we had a brownstone, as I told you we were wealthy—and hired all kinds of teachers for me. Physical education. It was a struggle, but I persevered. And he was with me, urging me on. The thing about him, he was firm but kind. He took me to a podiatrist, who took excellent care of me. So I became interested in the subject, starting, of course, with my own case. The rest of my family became doctors, but studies were hard for me. If I were young now, I'd be called dyslexic.

"But I found the work I love. So you see how everything works out."

I THINK OF HIS QUIZZICAL, cheerful face, but a boy's version. The shock of burning acid. And his poor father. Of all fates, one of the worst: to be implicated in the pain of your own child. I think of the phys ed teachers, with slicked-back hair, mustaches, sleeveless T-shirts, tights, lace-up shoes. I think of the tutors. And the cheerful, quizzical boy, struggling to keep up.

I think of the brownstone, its shining floors, the hanging chandeliers, the smell of coal and laundry in the basement, turned into a gym.

ON ONE OF MY VISITS, the patient before me has come with a standard poodle. I try to understand what's behind the decision to bring your dog with you to the podiatrist. The dog, unleashed, walks around the waiting room, nosing the magazine rack. I hear his master's voice: the voice of Yankee privilege, but suggesting the Maine woods: summers with no running water, bilberries for breakfast, a view from the porch of Daddy's "camp" of half the state. The owner of the dog is a foot taller than the doctor. He tells her he hopes she'll be comfortable, and she says she will be, of course thanks to "your very good work, my friend."

I'm sure they aren't friends. Not like he and I are. I'm sure he doesn't tell her stories.

"NICE ANIMAL," HE SAYS WHEN I sit in the chair. "Very nice animal. I don't do surgery anymore, so I'm glad to have dogs around, as long as they're well behaved. And that one is a real prize. I didn't even know he was there."

He says that everything I'm doing for my feet is exactly right and that the orthotics he made to be inserted into my shoes are working perfectly.

"Funny story about a dog. You want to hear a funny story about a dog?"

I say yes I would, very much.

"Every summer my family went and stayed in a hotel in the Catskills. My father was in New York, except for the weekends, and the rest of the family stayed there all the time. It was an excellent arrangement, suited everyone very well. Of course all meals included and the kitchen was top drawer. Every day, the chef would pack a lunch for me. Always the same thing, a chicken sandwich. He had a way of preparing chicken that I happened to like very much. I would take my lunch and my fishing pole and go down to the dock and fish for hours. Well, one day, I'm sitting on the dock and suddenly at the other end of the dock there's this very big dog. I mean she was big. I saw her looking at me and I looked at her and she didn't look dangerous, although she was so big. I wasn't afraid. I broke off a piece of my sandwich and left it on the dock a certain ways away from where I was sitting. After a while she took it, then she went back into the woods. Next day, same thing, she appears, I leave the piece of sandwich, she takes it and goes away. After a week of this, one day after she takes the piece of sandwich, she lies down next to me on the dock. Then she starts walking me back to the hotel every day. One day, we run into the owner's dog, a German shepherd, not a nice animal, a vicious animal. She takes one look at Brownie, puts her tail between her legs, and runs into the kitchen. I called the dog Brownie because she was brown. Even at that time I had a terrific imagination.

"Well, the end of the summer came and I begged my father

to take Brownie home. But he said no, she was a country dog, a woods dog, she'd be miserable in the city, she'd pine away. Well, I was miserable, but what can I do? I get in the car and put my head against the seat and cry my heart out.

"Now, in those days, they didn't have the superhighways of today, so the fastest my father could go was forty-five miles an hour. After we'd been traveling about an hour and a half, my father yells out, 'Oh, my God.' We didn't know what happened. 'Look out the back,' he says. And there's Brownie, running along the side of the road keeping up with the car.

"So of course my father opened the door. The dog got in. She was so big she had to lie full length on the floor and still there wasn't room for her. She threw up, then she slept all the way home.

"Fortunately, we had a townhouse with a backyard, so she could sleep outside. We just left the back window open and she came and went as she pleased. It wasn't like now, with the crime, which is why I live in Westchester.

"My mother used to worry about me with my lame leg, but she knew she had to give me independence. You have to do that with a boy, and she knew it. So she let me walk to school if Brownie was with me. It was only two blocks away, and she watched me out the window. One day, she's looking out the window and she sees me walking into the street, not paying attention, and the next thing she sees a truck careening around the corner and she sees Brownie grab me by the waist and pull me to safety. I still have scars from the teeth marks, but I wouldn't be here to tell you about those scars if it weren't for that dog.

"She saved my life another time. I was back at the hotel, fishing, but not on the dock, by a creek this time. I was wearing waders and again not paying attention, because, let's face it, that was the kind of kid I was. I walk into the water to get the fish. I walk in too deep and the mud is very soft on the bottom and I don't have the strength in my lame leg to lift myself up because the boots are full of water. I start to be pulled under. The dog comes in and pulls me out. So that was two times my life was saved by that dog.

"Now I'm going to tell you something you didn't know. Until the 1930s, dogs were not licensed in the city of New York. So one day, the notice comes, and my father, who always did things very properly, makes an appointment with our vet, who's a patient of his, to have the dog examined for a license. Well, we go into the office and the vet takes one look at Brownie and gets a strange look on his face. He calls my father into a private office. He says, 'Who does the dog respond to most?' My father says it's me. The vet says, 'We have to put a muzzle on the dog. I have to take some blood.'"

I DON'T WANT TO HEAR any more of this story. I can tell what's coming next: rabies, and this miraculous dog will have to be put down. I think of the little boy with his lame leg in his too-big room in the townhouse where everyone's heels clatter too loudly on the wooden floors.

"SO I PUT THE MUZZLE on the dog, she doesn't give any trouble, she'd do anything for me, but she gives me this terrible look when the doctor sticks the needle into her. My father and I sit in the waiting room, we don't know what's happening, our hearts are in our mouths. Then the doctor comes in and calls my father into his private room.

"'Doctor,' he says to my father, 'I don't know how to tell you this, but this animal you have isn't a dog, it's a wolf. A gray wolf.'"

IMMEDIATELY, I HEAR HOWLS, SEE wild eyes, enormous teeth, huge paws prowling in the moonlight on hard-packed snow that glistens blue and silver. Wolf: danger and magic, poverty and chaos too: the wolf at the door, wolf in sheep's clothing, crying wolf. Life lived at night, remotely, inexplicably.

"MY FATHER ASKS IF HE'S sure. The vet says yes. My father says it's the best dog he's ever had, he tells him how she's saved my life twice.

"The vet says, 'The problem is, Doctor, it's illegal to have a wolf in the city of New York. You'll have to take her back to where she came from or give her to a zoo.'

"My father says, 'Doctor, you have been my patient for twenty years. If you want to go on being my patient, listen to me. This dog is a member of the family. I will not get rid of her. I will not separate her from the people she loves or put her in a cage.'

"The vet says, 'Let me make one call.'

"He finds out that he can get a wildlife license for us. Which he does. And this is how we got to keep Brownie.

"Well, we kept her for another three years. We'd take her up to the Catskills in the summer. She'd sleep in the woods at night and be waiting for us at the hotel in the mornings. One morning she wasn't there. We never saw her again. But I knew it was all right. I knew she'd returned to her pack.'"

"You don't think she just went into the woods to die?" I ask.

"She was too young for that," he says.

"Perhaps she was killed by another animal."

"I believe she went back to join her pack. I'll tell you why. I've made a study of wolves, for reasons I'm sure you find obvious. You see, in a pack, only one female, the alpha female, the dominant one, is allowed to mate. If a beta female wants to mate, she has to leave the pack."

"You think that's what Brownie did?"

"Most definitely, yes, I think so."

"So she left when she was young because she wanted to mate, and then when she got older she wanted to go back to the family."

"I would say so."

"It's sort of a story about female desire, then," I say. "And what happens when that ends, and it's replaced by an urge for conformity."

His eyebrows are almost up to his hairline now. "Maybe it's a story about that for you. For me, it's a wonderful story about a wonderful dog. And I have many more stories about this dog that I could tell you. But I won't be seeing you for quite a while because everything you're doing, from my perspective, is perfect. Just keep doing everything you're doing. One hundred percent."

JIM SHEPARD

"My long-suffering wife has said that I'm the only person she knows who would take a history of the guillotine to the beach. So I'm reading that for pleasure, and then I start to feel an emotional resonance with some of the dilemmas, and I think: 'This could be a story.' Then I start to research as though I'm writing a story."

"The very first story I wrote as an adult featured a triceratops as a protagonist, and it was unsuccessful. And my readers said: 'This is unsuccessful.' So I've always had this weird desire to do stuff like that."

Onstage interview at The Story Prize event
February 27, 2008

Perhaps the biggest impact early on, though, came from a boxed set of J. D. Salinger that a family friend had given me for Christmas. At first I'd been disappointed by the gift—there weren't even illustrations on the covers—but one day when I was kicking around my room, bored, I cracked one open, and was immediately submerged in those voices. I'd always imagined that people who wrote literature needed to sound like writers like Henry James, though I had only the dimmest notion of what writers like Henry James sounded like. Here was a voice that was urgently and comically colloquial and yet somehow never seemed trivial. That was almost certainly where I conceived of the radical notion that there might be hope for somebody like me.

From a post on TSP: The Story Prize blog
January 5, 2012

The Zero Meter Diving Team

from *Like You'd Understand, Anyway*

Guilt, Guilt, Guilt

Here's what it's like to bear up under the burden of so much guilt: everywhere you drag yourself you leave a trail. Late at night, you gaze back and view an upsetting record of where you've been. At the medical center where they brought my brothers, I stood banging my head against a corner of a crash cart. When one of the nurses saw me, I said, "There, that's better. That kills the thoughts before they grow."

Hullabaloo

I am Boris Yakovlevich Prushinsky, chief engineer of the Department of Nuclear Energy, and my younger brother, Mikhail Vasilyevich, was a senior turbine engineer serving reactor Unit No. 4 at the Chernobyl power station, on duty the night of 26 April 1986. Our half brother Petya and his friend were that same night outside the reactor's cooling tower on the Pripyat River, fishing, downwind. So you can see that our family was right in the thick of what followed. We were not—how shall we put it?—very *lucky* that way. But then, like their country, the Prushinskys have always been first to protest that no one should waste any pity on *them*. Because the Prushinskys have always made their *own* luck.

The All-Prushinsky Zero Meter Diving Team

My father owns one photo of Mikhail, Petya, and myself together. It was taken by our mother. She was no photographer. The three of us are arranged by height on our dock over the river. We seem to be smelling something unpleasant. It's from the summer our father was determined to teach us proper diving form. He'd followed the

Olympics from Mexico City on our radio, and the exploits of the East German platform divers had filled him with ambition for his boys. But our dock had been too low, and so he'd called it the Zero Meter Diving Platform. The bottom where we dove was marshy and shallow and frightened us. "What are you frightened of?" he said to us. "*I'm* not frightened. Boris, are *you* frightened?" "*I'm* not frightened," I told him, though my brothers knew I was. I was ten and imagined myself his ally. Petya was five. Mikhail was seven. Both are weeping in the photo, their hands on their thighs.

Sometimes at night when our mother was still alive our father would walk the ridge above us, to see the moon on the river, he said. He would shout into the darkness: he was *Victor Grigoryevich Prushinsky, director of the Physico-Energy Institute.* While she was alive, that was the way our mother—Mikhail's and my mother—introduced him. Petya's mother didn't introduce him to anyone. Officially, Petya was our full brother, but at home our father called him Half-life. He said it was a physicist's joke.

"Give your brother your potatoes," he would order Petya. And poor little Petya would shovel his remaining potatoes onto Mikhail's plate. During their fights, Mikhail would say to him things like "Your hair seems *different* than ours. Don't you think?"

So there was a murderousness to our play. We went on rampages around the dacha, chopping at each other with sticks and clearing swaths in the lilacs and wildflowers in mock battles. And our father would thrash us. He used an ash switch. Four strokes for me, then three for Mikhail and I was expected to apply the fourth. Then three for Petya, and Mikhail was expected to apply the fourth. Our faces were terrible to behold. We always applied the final stroke as though we wanted to outdo the first three.

When calm, he quoted to us Strugatsky's dictum that *reason* was the ability to use the powers of the surrounding world without ruining that world. Striped with welts and lying on our bellies on our beds, we tinted his formulation with our own colorations of fury and misery. Twenty-five years later, that same formulation would appear in my report to the nuclear power secretary of the Central Committee concerning the catastrophic events at the power station at Chernobyl.

Loss

Our mother died of the flu when I was eleven. Petya lost his only protector and grew more disheveled and strange and full of difference. Mikhail for a full year carried himself as though he'd been petrified by a loud noise. Later we joked that she'd concocted the flu to get away, and that she was off on a beach in the Black Sea. But every night we peeped at one another across the dark floor between our beds, vacant and alone.

In the mornings I took to cupping Mikhail's fist with my palms when he was thumb-sucking, as though I were praying. It brought us nose to nose and made me shudder with an enraged tenderness. Petya sucked his thumb as well, interested.

That Warm Night in April

What is there to say about the power station, or the river on which it sits? The Pripyat just a few kilometers downstream drains into the Dnieper, having snaked through land as level as a soccer pitch with a current the color of tea from the peat bogs nearby. In the deeper parts, it's cold year round. For long stretches it dips and loops around stands of young pines.

Mikhail was pleased with the area when he settled there. He was a young tyro, the coming thing, at twenty-eight a senior turbine engineer. There were three secondary schools, a young people's club, festive covered markets, a two-screen cinema, and a Children's World department store. Plenty of good walking trails and fishing. Petya followed him. Petya usually followed him from assignment to assignment, getting odd jobs, getting drunk, getting thrown in jail, getting bailed out of trouble by his brother. Or half brother.

"Why doesn't he ever follow *you?*" Mikhail asked me the night Petya showed up on his doorstep yet again. Mikhail didn't often call. It was a bad connection that sounded like wasps in the telephone line. Petya was already asleep in the dining room. He'd walked the last twenty versts after having hitched a ride on a cement truck.

They found him a little apartment in town and a job on the construction site for the spent fuel depository. As for a residence permit: for that, Mikhail told me on the phone, they'd rely on their big-shot brother.

I was ready to help out. We both treated Petya as though he had to be taught to swallow. "Let *me* do that," we'd tell him, before he'd even commenced what he was going to attempt. Whatever went wrong in our lives, we'd think they *still* weren't as fucked-up as Petya's.

Mikhail's shift came on duty at midnight, an hour and twenty-five minutes before the explosion. Most of the shift members did not survive until morning.

Petya, I was told later, was fishing that night with another layabout, a friend. They'd chosen a little sandbar near the feeder channel across from the turbine hall, where the water released from the heat exchangers into the cooling-pond was twenty degrees warmer. In spring it filled with hatchlings. There was no moon and it was balmy for April, and starry above the black shapes of the cooling towers.

Earthenware Pots

As chief engineer of the Department of Nuclear Energy, I was a mongrel: half technocrat, half bureaucrat. We knew there were problems in both design and operating procedures, but what industry didn't have problems? Our method was to get rid of them by keeping silent. Nepotism ruled the day. "Fat lot of good it's done *me*," Mikhail often joked. If you tried to bring a claim against someone for incompetence or negligence, his allies hectored you, all indignation on his behalf. Everyone ended up shouting, no one got to the bottom of the problem, and you became a saboteur: someone seeking to undermine the achievement of the quotas.

People said I owed my position to my father, and Mikhail owed his position to me. ("More than they know," he said grimly, when I told him that.) At various congresses, I ran my concerns by my father. In response he gave me that look Mikhail called the Dick Shriveler. "Why's your dick big around him in the first place?" Petya once asked when he'd overheard us.

We all lived under the doctrine of ubiquitous success. Negative information was reserved for the most senior leaders, with censored versions available for those lower down. Nothing instructive about precautions or emergency procedures could be organized, since such initiatives undermined the official position concerning the complete safety of the nuclear industry. For thirty years, accidents went unreported, so the lessons derived from these accidents remained with those who'd experienced them. It was as if no accidents had occurred.

So who gave a shit if the Ministry of Energy was riddled through with incompetents or filled with the finest theorists? Whenever we came across a particular idiocy, in terms of staffing, we quoted to one another the old saying: "It doesn't take gods to bake earthenware pots." The year before, the chief engineer during the start-up procedures at Balakovo had fucked up, and fourteen men had been boiled alive. The bodies had been retrieved and laid before him in a row.

I'd resisted his hiring. That, for me, constituted enough to quiet my conscience. And when Mikhail submitted an official protest about sanctioned shortcuts in one of his unit's training procedures, I forwarded his paperwork on with a separate note of support.

Pastorale

The town slept. The countryside slept. The chief engineer of the Department of Nuclear Energy in his enviable Moscow apartment slept. It was a dear night in April, one of the most beautiful of the year. Meadows rippled like silvery lakes in the starlight. Pripyat was sleeping, Ukraine was sleeping, the country was sleeping. The chief engineer's brother, Mikhail, was awake, hunting sugar for his coffee. His half brother, Petya, was awake, soaking his feet and baiting a hook. In the number 4 reactor the staff, Mikhail included, was running a test to see how long the turbines would keep spinning and producing power in the event of an electrical failure at the plant. It was a dangerous test, but it had been done before. To do it they had to disable some of the critical control systems, including the automatic shutdown mechanisms.

They shut down the emergency core cooling system. Their thinking apparently had been to prevent cold water from entering the hot reactor after the test and causing a heat shock. But who knows what was going through their minds? Only men with no understanding of what goes on inside a reactor could have done such a thing. And once they'd done that, all their standard operating procedures took them even more quickly down the road to disaster.

The test was half standard operating procedure, half seat-of-the-pants initiative. Testimony, perhaps, to the poignancy of their longing to make things safer.

Did Mikhail know better? His main responsibility was the turbines, but even so even he probably knew better. Did he suspect his colleagues' imbecility? One night as a boy after a beating he hauled himself off his bed and pissed into our father's boots, already wet from the river. He'd never suspect, Mikhail told us. Mikhail lived a large portion of his life in that state of mind in which you take a risk and deny the risk at the same time, out of rage. No one in his control room knew nearly enough, and whose fault was that? "Akimov has your sense of humor," he told me once about his boss. It didn't sound like good news for Akimov's crew.

Minutes after they began, the flow of coolant water dropped and the power began to increase. Akimov and his team moved to shut down the reactor. But they'd waited too long and the design of the control rods was such that, for the first part of the lowering, they actually caused an *increase* in reactivity.

South Seas

On the evening of 1 May 1986 in Clinic No. 6 in Moscow I made the acquaintance of two young people: another senior turbine engineer and an electrical engineer. They had beds on either side of Mikhail's. The ward overflowed with customers. A trainee was collecting watches and wedding rings in plastic bags. Everyone was on some kind of drip but there weren't enough bowls and bins, so people were vomiting onto the floor. The smell was stunning. Nurses with trays skidded around corners.

Mikhail was a dark brown: the color of mahogany. Even his gums. When he saw my face he grinned and croaked, "South Seas!" A doctor changing his intravenous line explained without looking up that they called it a nuclear tan.

I was there partially in an official capacity, to investigate what had happened at the last moments.

Mikhail said, "Are you *weeping*? The investigator is *weeping*!" But his comrades in the nearby beds were unsympathetic. He interrupted his story in order to throw up in a bin between the beds.

He'd been in the information processing complex, a room a few levels below the control room. Two shocks had concussed the entire building and the lights had flashed off. The building had seemed to tip into the air and part of the ceiling had collapsed. Steam in billows and jets had erupted from the floor. He'd heard someone shouting, "This is an emergency!" and had pitched himself out into the hall. There was a strobe effect from the short circuits. The air smelled of ozone and caused a tickling sensation in the throat. The walls immediately above him were gone and he could see a bright purple light crackling between the ends of a broken high-voltage cable. He could see fire, black ash falling in flakes, and red-hot blocks and fragments of something burning into the linoleum of the floor.

He worked his way up to the control room, where everyone was in a panic. Akimov was calling the heads of departments and sections, asking for help. You could see the realization of what he'd helped to do hitting him. According to the panels, the control rods were stuck halfway down. Two trainees, kids just out of school, were standing around frightened, and he sent them off to *lower the control rods by hand.*

"The investigator is *weeping!*" my brother said triumphantly, again.

"This is a great tragedy," I told him, as though chiding him. The other engineers gazed over from their beds.

"Oh, yes," he said, as though someone had offered him tea. "Tragedy tragedy tragedy."

When it became clear that he wasn't going to go on, I asked him to tell me more.

"We have no protection systems—nothing!" he remembered Perevozchenko saying. Their lungs felt scalded. Their bronchioles and alveoli were being flooded with radionuclides. Akimov had sent him to ascertain the amount of damage to the central hall. He'd made his way to the ventilation center, where he could see that the top of the building had been blown off. From somewhere behind him he could hear radioactive water pouring down the debris. Steel reinforcing beams corkscrewed in various directions. His eyes stung. It felt as though something was being boiled in his chest. There was an acid taste to the steam and a buzz of static on his skin. He learned later that the radiation field was so powerful it was ionizing the air.

"Take that down, investigator," Mikhail said. He tried to drink a little water.

The Maximum Permissible Dose

At 1:23:58 the concentration of hydrogen in the explosive mixture reached the stage of detonation, and the two explosions Mikhail had felt in the information processing complex destroyed the reactor and the reactor building of Unit 4. A radioactive plume extended to an altitude of thirty-six thousand feet. Fifty tons of nuclear fuel evaporated into it. Another seventy tons spewed out onto the reactor grounds, mixing with the structural debris. The radioactivity of the ejected fuel reached twenty thousand roentgens per hour. The maximum permissible dose, according to our regulations for a nuclear power plant operator, is five roentgens per year.

Some Rich Asshole's Just Lost His Job

Petya said the explosions made the ground shake and the water surface ripple in all directions. Pieces of concrete and steel started landing in the pond around them. They could hear the hissing as the pieces cooled. For a while they watched the cloud billow out and grow above the reactor. By then the fire was above the edge of the building. Through a crack in one of the containment walls they could see a dark blue light. "Some rich asshole's just lost his job," he remembered remarking to his friend. I assume he meant someone other than his eldest brother.

And by then they'd both begun to feel dreadful. Their eyes streamed tears as they reeled about, so sluggish and disoriented it took them an hour to traverse the half kilometer to the medical station. By the time they arrived, it resembled a war zone.

The Individual Citizen in the Vanguard

How much difference could an individual bureaucrat really make in our system? That was a popular topic for our drinking bouts.

For the epic bouts, we seemed to require a Topic. The accepted wisdom, which tempered our cynicism enough to smooth the way for our complacency, was that with clever and persistent and assiduous work and some luck, the great creeping hulk that was our society *could* be nudged in this or that direction. But one had to be patient, and work within the system, and respect the system's sheer *size*.

Because, you see, our schools directed all their efforts to inculcating industriousness (somewhat successfully), obedience (fairly successfully), and toadyism (very successfully). Each graduation produced a new crop of little yes-people. Our children learned criticism from their families, and from the street.

The Individual Citizen Still in the Vanguard

By four in the afternoon the day after the explosion, the members of the government commission began to gather, having flown in from everywhere. I'd been telephoned at five that morning by the head of the Party Congress. He was already exhausted. The station managers were assuring him that the reactor itself was largely undamaged and radioactivity levels within normal limits. There was apparently massive damage, however, and they couldn't control the fires. When I told him, rubbing my face and holding the phone, that that made no sense, his response was, "Yes. Well." I was to be on a military transport by eight-thirty. Mikhail, I knew, would be on duty, but when I phoned up Petya, there was no answer.

On the drive in from the airport, we slowed to traverse roads flooded with a white foam along the shoulders. The decontamination trucks we passed made us quiet. When we found our voices, we argued about whether the reactor had been exposed. The design people were skeptical, insisting that this variant was so well conceived that even if the idiots in charge had wanted to blow it up, they couldn't have.

But all that talk petered out when we assembled on the roof

of the Town Committee office and could see over the apartment buildings to Unit 4. Its wall was open and flames were burning straight up from behind it. The air smelled the way metal tastes. We could hear the children down in the courtyard having their hour of physical training. "Which way is the wind blowing?" someone asked, and we all looked at the flags on the young people's club.

We moved back to the Town Committee office and shut the windows and shouted and squabbled for an hour, with contradictory information arriving every moment. *Where is Mikhail?* a voice in my head inquired repetitively. We had no idea what to do. As my mother used to say, it's only thunder when it bangs over your head. It wasn't possible, we were told, to accurately gauge the radiation levels, because no one had dosimeters with the right scales. The ones here went up to a thousand microroentgens per second, which was 3.6 roentgens per hour. So all of the instruments were off the scale wherever you went. But when Moscow demanded the radiation levels, they were told 3.6 roentgens an hour. Since that's what the machines were reading.

The station had had one dosimeter capable of reading higher levels, the assistant to the nuclear power sector reported. But it had been buried by the blast.

Everyone was hoping that the bad news would announce itself. And that the responsibility and blame would somehow be spread imperceptibly over everyone equally. This is the only way to account for our watchmaker's pace, at a time when each minute's delay caused the criminal exposure of all those citizens—all those children—still going about their ordinary day outside.

The deputy chief operational engineer of the number 4 unit was managing to sustain two mutually exclusive realities in his head: first, the reactor was intact, and we needed to keep feeding water into it to prevent its overheating; and second, there was graphite and fuel all over the ground. Where could it have come from?

No one working at the station, we were told, was wearing protective clothing. The workers were drinking vodka, they said, to decontaminate. Everyone had lost track of everyone. It was the Russian story.

The Game of I Know Nothing Played Long Enough
The teachers in the schools heard about the accident through their relatives, who had heard from friends overseas—routine measurements outside Swedish power stations having already flagged an enormous spike in radioactivity—but when they inquired whether the students should be sent home, or their schedule in any way amended, the second secretary of the Regional Committee told them to carry on as planned. The Party's primary concern at that point seemed to be to establish that an accident on such a scale could not happen at such a plant. We had adequate stores of potassium iodide pills, which would at least have prevented thyroid absorption of iodine-131. We were forbidden as yet to authorize their distribution.

So throughout the afternoon children played in the streets. Mothers hung laundry. It was a beautiful day. Radioactivity collected in the hair and clothes. Groups walked and bicycled to the bridge near the Yanov station to get a close look into the reactor. They watched the beautiful shining cloud over the power plant dissipate in their direction. They were bathed in a flood of deadly X-rays emanating directly from the nuclear core.

The fire brigade that had first responded to the alarm had lasted fifteen minutes on the roof before becoming entirely incapacitated. There followed a round-the-clock rotation of firemen, and by now twelve brigades, pulled from all over the region, had been decimated. The station's roof, where the firefighters stood directing their hoses, was like the door of a blast furnace. We learned later that from there the reactor core was generating thirty thousand roentgens per hour.

What about helicopters? someone suggested. What about them? someone else asked. They could be used to dump sand onto the reactor, the first speaker theorized. This idea was ridiculed and then entertained. Lead was proposed. We ended up back with sand. Rope was needed to tie the sacks. None was available. Someone found red calico gathered for the May Day festival, and all sorts of very important people began tearing it into strips. Young people were requisitioned to fill the sacks with sand.

I left, explaining I was going to look at the site myself. I found Mikhail. He was already dark brown by that point. I was told that he was one of those selected for removal by special flight to the clinic in Moscow. His skin color had been the main criterion, since the doctors had no way at that point of measuring the dose he'd received. He was on morphine and unconscious the entire time I was there. As a boy he'd never slept enough, and all of his face's sadness emerged whenever he finally did doze. There in the hospital bed, he was so still and dark that it looked like someone had carved his life mask from a rich tropical wood. At some point I told an orderly I'd be back and went to find Petya.

While hunting his apartment address I asked whomever I encountered if they had children. If they did I gave them potassium iodide pills and told them to have their children take them now, with a little water, just in case.

I found Petya's apartment but no Petya. A busybody neighbor with one front tooth hadn't seen him since the day before but asked many questions. By then I had to return to the meeting. The group had barely noticed I was gone. No progress had been made, though outside the building teenagers were filling sandbags with sand.

All of Them: Heroes of the Soviet Union

By late afternoon the worst of the prevaricators had acknowledged the need to prepare for evacuation. In the meantime untold numbers of workers had been sent into the heart of the radiation field to direct cooling water onto the nonexistent reactor. The helicopters had begun their dumping, and the rotors, arriving and departing, stirred up sandstorms of radioactive dust. The crews had to hover for three to five minutes directly over the reactor to drop their loads. Most managed only two trips before becoming unfit for service.

Word finally came through that Petya too had been sent to the medical center. By the time I got over there he'd been delivered to the airport for emergency transport to Moscow. When I asked how he'd gotten such a dose, no one had any idea.

At ten a.m. on Sunday the town was finally advised to shut its windows and not let its children outside. Four hours later the evacuation began.

Citizens were told to collect their papers and indispensable items, along with food for three days, and to gather at the sites posted. Some may have known they were never coming back. Most didn't even take warm clothes.

The entire town climbed onto buses and was carried away. Many getting on were already intensely radioactive. The buses were washed with decontaminant once they were far enough out of town. Eleven hundred buses: the column stretched for eighteen kilometers. It was a miserable sight. The convoy kicked up rolling billows of dust. In some places it enveloped families still waiting to be picked up, their children groping for their toys at the roadside.

That night when the commission meeting was over, I went my own way. Even the streetlights were out. I felt my way along with small steps. I was in the middle of town and might as well have been on the dark side of the moon. Naturally, I thought, Petya had somehow been there, on the river. Whenever the shit cart tipped over, there was Petya, underneath.

The Zero Meter Diving Team

It turned out Petya was installed on the floor below Mikhail's in Moscow's Clinic No. 6. When I asked an administrator if some sort of triage was going on, she said, "Are you a relative?" When I said I was, she said, "Then no."

He was hooked up to two different drips. He didn't look so bad. He was his normal color, maybe a little pale. His hair was in more riot than usual.

"Boris Yakovlevich!" he said. He seemed happy to see me.

At long last he'd gotten his chance to lie down, he joked. His laziness had always been a matter of contention between us.

"Has Father been by to see me?" he asked. "I've been out of it for stretches."

I told him I didn't know.

"Has he been to see Mikhail?" he asked.

I told him I didn't know. He asked how his brother was holding up. I told him I was going to visit Mikhail directly afterward and would report back.

"Are you feeling sorry for me?" he asked after a pause. A passing nurse seemed surprised by the question.

"Of course I am," I told him.

"With you sometimes it's hard to tell," he said.

"What can I do for you?" I asked after another pause.

"I have what they call a 'period of intestinal syndrome,'" he said glumly. "Which means I have the shits thirty times a day." And these things in his mouth and throat, he added, which was why he couldn't eat or drink. He asked after the state of the reactor, as though he were one of the engineers. Then he explained how he'd ended up near the reactor in the first place. He described his new Pripyat apartment and said he hoped to save up for a motorcycle. Then he announced he was going to sleep.

"Get me something to read," he said when I got up to leave. "Except I can't read. Never mind."

The next floor up, the surviving patients were sequestered alone in sterile rooms. Mikhail was naked and covered in a yellow cream. Soaked dressings filled low bins in the hall. Huge lamps surrounded the bed to keep him warm.

"Father's been to see me," he said instead of hello.

He said that four samples of bone marrow had been extracted and no one had told him anything since. Most of the pain was in his mouth and stomach. When he asked for a drink, I offered some mango juice I'd brought with me. He said it was just the thing he wanted. He was fed up with mineral water. He shouted at a passing doctor that the noise of her heels was giving him diarrhea.

"When we got outside, graphite was scattered all around," he said, as if we'd been in the middle of discussing the accident. "Someone touched a piece of it and his arm flew up like he'd been burned."

"So you knew what it was?" I asked.

I assumed I wasn't allowed to touch him because of the cream. He was always the boy I'd most resented and the boy I'd most wanted to be. I'd been the cold one, but he'd been the one who'd made himself, when he'd had to be, solitary and unreachable.

An orderly wheeled in a tray of ointments, tinctures, creams, and gauzes. He performed a counterfeit of patience while he waited for me to leave.

"Have you had enough of everything?" I asked Mikhail. "Is there anything I can bring?"

"I've had the maximum permissible dose of my brother Boris," he said. "Now I need to recuperate." But then he went on to tell me that Akimov had died. "As long as he could talk, he kept saying he did everything right and didn't understand how it had happened." He finished the juice. "That's interesting, isn't it?"

Mikhail had always said about me that I was one of those people who took a purely functional interest in whomever I was talking to. Father had overheard him once when we were adults and had laughed approvingly.

"Someone's going to have to look after Petya," he said, his eyes closed, some minutes later. I'd thought he'd fallen asleep. As far as I knew, he wasn't aware that his brother was on the floor below him.

"I have to get on with this," the orderly finally remarked.

When I told him to shut up, he shrugged.

There Is No Return. Farewell. Pripyat, 28 April 1986

Two years later, at four in the morning, my father and I drove into the Zone. The headlamps dissolved picturesquely into the predawn mist, but my father's driver refused to slow down. It was like being in a road rally. The driver sat on a lead sheet he'd cadged from an X-ray technician. For his balls, he explained when he saw me looking at it. Armored troop carriers with special spotlights were parked here and there working as chemical defense detachments. The soldiers wore black suits and special slippers.

Even through the misty darkness we could see that nature was blooming. The sun rose. We passed pear trees gone to riot and chaotic banks of wildflowers. A crush of lilacs overwhelmed a mile marker.

Mikhail had died after two bone marrow transplants. He'd lasted three weeks. The attending nurse reported final complaints involving dry mouth, his salivary glands having been destroyed. But I assumed that that was Mikhail being brave, because the condition of his skin had left him in agony for the final two weeks. On some of my visits he couldn't speak at all, but only kept his eyes and mouth tightly closed, and listened. I was in Georgia at the start-up of a new plant the day he died. He was buried, like the others in his condition, in a lead-lined coffin that was soldered shut.

Petya was by then an invalid on a pension Father and I had arranged for him. He was twenty-five. He found it difficult to get up to his floor, since his building had no elevator, but otherwise, he told me when I occasionally called, he was happy. He had his smokes and his tape player and could lie about all day with no one to nag him, no one to tell him that he had better amount to something.

"It's a shame," my father mused on the ride in. "*What* is?" I asked, wild with rage at the both of us. But he looked at me with disapproval and dropped the subject.

At Pripyat a sawhorse was set up as a checkpoint, manned by an officer and two soldiers. The soldiers had holes poked in their respirators for cigarettes. They'd been expecting my father, and he was whisked off to be shown something even I wasn't to be allowed to see. His driver stuck his feet out the car's open window and began snoring, head thrown back. I wandered away from the central square and looked into a building that had been facing away from the reactor. I walked its peeling and echoing hallways and gaped into empty offices at notepads and pens scattered across floors. In one there was a half-unwrapped child's dress in a gift box, the tulle eaten away by age or insects.

Across the street in front of the school, a tree was growing up from beneath the sidewalk. I climbed through an open window and crossed the classroom without touching anything. I passed through a solarium with an empty swimming pool. A kindergarten with little gas masks in a crate. Much had been looted and tossed about, including a surprising number of toys. At the front of one room over the teacher's desk someone had written on a red chalkboard, *There Is No Return. Farewell. Pripyat, 28 April 1986.*

Self-Improvement

The territory exposed to the radioactivity, we now knew, was larger than one hundred thousand square kilometers. Many of those who'd worked at Chernobyl were dead. Many were still alive and suffering. The children in particular suffered from exotic ailments, like cancer of the mouth. The director of the Institute of Biophysics in Moscow announced that there hadn't been one documented case of radiation sickness among civilians. Citizens who applied to the Ministry of Health for some kind of treatment were accused of radiophobia. Radionuclides in large amounts continued to drain into the reservoirs and aquifers in the contaminated territories. It was estimated that humans could begin repopulating the area in about six hundred years, give or take three hundred years. My father said three hundred years. He was an optimist. Nobody knew, even approximately, how many people had died.

The reactor was encased in a sarcophagus, an immense terraced pyramid of concrete and steel, built under the most lethal possible circumstances and, we'd been informed, already disintegrating. Cracks allowed rain to enter and dust to escape. Small animals and birds passed in and out of the facility.

I left the schoolyard and walked a short way down a lane overhung with young pines. Out in the fields, vehicles had been abandoned as far as the eye could see: fire engines, armored personnel carriers, cranes, backhoes, ambulances, cement mixers, trucks. It was the world's largest junkyard. Most had been scavenged for parts, however radioactive. Each step off the road added a thousand microroentgens to my dosimeter reading.

The week after Mikhail died, I wrote my father a letter. I quoted him other people's moral outrage. I sent him a clipping decrying the abscess of complacency and self-flattery, corruption and protectionism, narrow-mindedness and self-serving privilege that had created the catastrophe. I retyped for him some graffiti I'd seen painted on the side of an abandoned backhoe: that the negligence and incompetence of some should not be concealed by the patriotism of others. I typed it again: *the negligence and incompetence of some should not be concealed by the patriotism of others.* Whoever had written it was more eloquent than I would ever be. I was writing to myself. I received no better answer from him than I'd received from myself.

Science Requires Victims

My father and I served on the panel charged with appointing the commission set up to investigate the causes of the accident. The roster we put forward was top-heavy with those who designed nuclear plants, neglecting entirely the engineers who operated them. So who was blamed, in the commission's final report? The operators. Nearly all of whom were dead. One was removed from hospital and imprisoned.

During his arrest it was said he quoted Petrosyants's infamous remark from the Moscow press conference the week after the disaster: "Science requires victims."

"Still feeling like the crusader?" my father had asked the day we turned in our report. It had been the last time I'd seen him. "Why not?" I'd answered. Afterward I'd gotten drunk for three days. I'd pulled out the original blueprints. I'd sat up nights with the drawings of the control rods, their design flaws like a hidden pattern I could no longer unsee.

But then, such late-night sentimentalities always operate more as consolation than insight.

I could still be someone I could live with, I found myself thinking on the third night. All it would take was change.

A red fox, its little jaws agape, sauntered across the road a few meters away. It was said that the animals had lost their skittishness around man, since man was no longer about. There'd been a problem with the dogs left behind going feral and radioactive, until a special detachment of soldiers was bused in to shoot them all.

Around a curve I came upon the highway that had been used for the evacuation. The asphalt was still a powdery blue from the dried decontaminant solution. The sky was sullen and empty. A rail fence ran along the fields to my left. While I stood there, a rumble gathered and approached, and from a stand of poplars a herd of horses burst forth, sweeping by at full gallop. They were followed a few minutes later by a panicked and brindled colt, kicking its legs this way and that, stirring up blue and brown dust.

"Was I ever the brother you hoped I would be?" I asked Mikhail toward the end of my next-to-last visit. His eyes and mouth were squeezed shut. He seemed more repelled by himself than by me, and he nodded. All the way home from the hospital that night, I saw it in my mind's eye: my brother, nodding.

TOBIAS WOLFF

"Writing, for me, is a continual process of negotiation with what I've written before. I think it is for a lot of writers."

"There are just so many stories that are snowflake perfect. They're perfect. You're always after that with what you're writing. I'm sure it's no less true for novels, but there's something about the size and manageability of the short story. You can walk around it, sculpt it here and there, lean back, see it whole. Perfection is something you're always after. But as you change over time, so does your notion of perfection."

"The matter you have to decide for yourself is: Is this as good as I can make it, as I am now? You don't know all your deficits. You don't know your blind spots. You just have to hold yourself to the best standard that you're capable of. If you can answer that question for yourself—say, 'This is as good as I can make it'—then you're done with it."

Onstage interview at The Story Prize event
March 4, 2009

Bullet in the Brain

from *Our Story Begins*

Anders couldn't get to the bank until just before it closed, so of course the line was endless and he got stuck behind two women whose loud, stupid conversation put him in a murderous temper. He was never in the best of tempers anyway, Anders—a book critic known for the weary, elegant savagery with which he dispatched almost everything he reviewed.

With the line still doubled around the rope, one of the tellers stuck a POSITION CLOSED sign in her window and walked to the back of the bank, where she leaned against a desk and began to pass the time with a man shuffling papers. The women in front of Anders broke off their conversation and watched the teller with hatred. "Oh, that's nice," one of them said. She turned to Anders and added, confident of his accord, "One of those little human touches that keep us coming back for more."

Anders had conceived his own towering hatred of the teller, but he immediately turned it on the presumptuous crybaby in front of him. "Damned unfair," he said. "Tragic, really. If they're not chopping off the wrong leg or bombing your ancestral village, they're closing their positions."

She stood her ground. "I didn't say it was tragic," she said. "I just think it's a pretty lousy way to treat your customers."

"Unforgivable," Anders said. "Heaven will take note."

She sucked in her cheeks but stared past him and said nothing. Anders saw that her friend was looking in the same direction. And then the tellers stopped what they were doing, the other customers slowly turned, and silence came over the bank. Two men wearing black ski masks and blue business suits were standing to the side of the door. One of them had a pistol pressed against the guard's neck. The guard's eyes were closed, and his lips were moving. The other man had a sawed-off shotgun. "Keep your big mouth shut!" the man with the pistol said, though no one had spoken a word. "One of you tellers hits the alarm, you're all dead meat."

"Oh, bravo," Anders said. "*'Dead meat.'*" He turned to the woman in front of him. "Great script, eh? The stern, brass-knuckled poetry of the dangerous classes."

She looked at him with drowning eyes.

The man with the shotgun pushed the guard to his knees. He handed the shotgun to his partner and yanked the guard's wrists up behind his back and locked them together with a pair of handcuffs. He toppled him onto the floor with a kick between the shoulder blades, then took his shotgun back and went over to the security gate at the end of the counter. He was short and heavy and moved with peculiar slowness. "Buzz him in," his partner said. The man with the shotgun opened the gate and sauntered along the line of tellers, handing each of them a plastic bag. When he came to the empty position he looked over at the man with the pistol, who said, "Whose slot is that?"

Anders watched the teller. She put her hand to her throat and turned to the man she'd been talking to. He nodded. "Mine," she said.

"Then get your ugly ass in gear and fill that bag."

"There you go," Anders said to the woman in front of him. "Justice is done."

"Hey! Bright boy! Did I tell you to talk?"

"No," Anders said.

"Then shut your trap."

"Did you hear that?" Anders said. "'Bright boy.' Right out of *The Killers.*"

"Please, be quiet," the woman said.

"Hey, you deaf or what?" The man with the pistol walked over to Anders and poked the weapon into his gut. "You think I'm playing games?"

"No," Anders said, but the barrel tickled like a stiff finger and he had to fight back the titters. He did this by making himself stare into the man's eyes, which were clearly visible behind the holes in the mask: pale blue and rawly red-rimmed. The man's left eyelid kept twitching. He breathed out a piercing, ammoniac smell that shocked Anders more than anything that had happened, and he was beginning to develop a sense of unease when the man prodded him again with the pistol.

"You like me, bright boy?" he said. "You want to suck my dick?"

"No," Anders said.

"Then stop looking at me."

Anders fixed his gaze on the man's shiny wing-tip shoes.

"Not down there. Up there." He stuck the pistol under Anders's chin and pushed it upward until he was looking at the ceiling.

Anders had never paid much attention to that part of the bank, a pompous old building with marble floors and counters and gilt scrollwork over the tellers' cages. The domed ceiling had been decorated with mythological figures whose fleshy, toga-draped ugliness Anders had taken in at a glance many years earlier and afterward declined to notice. Now he had no choice but to scrutinize the painter's work. It was even worse than he remembered, and all of it executed with the utmost gravity. The artist had a few tricks up his sleeve and used them again and again—a certain rosy blush on the underside of the clouds, a coy backward glance on the faces of the cupids and fauns. The ceiling was crowded with various dramas, but the one that caught Anders's eye was Zeus and Europa—portrayed, in this rendition, as a bull ogling a cow from behind a haystack. To make the cow sexy, the painter had canted her hips suggestively and given her long, droopy eyelashes through which she gazed back at the bull with sultry welcome. The bull

wore a smirk and his eyebrows were arched. If there'd been a caption bubbling out of his mouth, it would have said HUBBA HUBBA.

"What's so funny, bright boy?"

"Nothing."

"You think I'm comical? You think I'm some kind of clown?"

"No."

"You think you can fuck with me?"

"No."

"Fuck with me again, you're history. *Capiche?*"

Anders burst out laughing. He covered his mouth with both
hands and said, "I'm sorry, I'm sorry," then snorted helplessly
through his fingers and said, "*Capiche*—oh, God, *capiche*," and at
that the man with the pistol raised the pistol and shot Anders right
in the head.

THE BULLET SMASHED ANDERS'S SKULL and plowed through
his brain and exited behind his right ear, scattering shards of bone
into the cerebral cortex, the corpus callosum, back toward the basal
ganglia, and down into the thalamus. But before all this occurred,
the first appearance of the bullet in the cerebrum set off a crackling
chain of ion transports and neurotransmissions. Because of their
peculiar origin these traced a peculiar pattern, flukishly calling to
life a summer afternoon some forty years past, and long since lost
to memory. After striking the cranium the bullet was moving at
nine hundred feet per second, a pathetically sluggish, glacial pace
compared with the synaptic lightning that flashed around it. Once
in the brain, that is, the bullet came under the mediation of brain
time, which gave Anders plenty of leisure to contemplate the scene
that, in a phrase he would have abhorred, "passed before his eyes."

It is worth noting what Anders did not remember, given what
he did recall. He did not remember his first lover, Sherry, or what
he had most madly loved about her, before it came to irritate

him—her unembarrassed carnality, and especially the cordial way
she had with his unit, which she called Mr. Mole, as in *Uh-oh,
looks like Mr. Mole wants to play*. Anders did not remember his
wife, whom he had also loved before she exhausted him with her
predictability, or his daughter, now a sullen professor of econom-
ics at Dartmouth. He did not remember standing just outside his
daughter's door as she lectured her bear about his naughtiness and
described the appalling punishments Paws would receive unless
he changed his ways. He did not remember a single line of the
hundreds of poems he had committed to memory in his youth so
he could give himself the shivers at will—not "Silent, upon a peak
in Darien," or "My God, I heard this day," or "All my pretty ones?
Did you say all? O hell-kite! All?" None of these did he remember;
not one. Anders did not remember his dying mother saying of his
father, "I should have stabbed him in his sleep."

He did not remember Professor Josephs telling his class how
Athenian prisoners in Sicily had been released if they could recite Aeschylus, and then reciting Aeschylus himself, right there, in
the Greek. Anders did not remember how his eyes had burned at
those sounds. He did not remember the surprise of seeing a college
classmate's name on the dust jacket of a novel not long after they
graduated, or the respect he had felt after reading the book. He did
not remember the pleasure of giving respect.

Nor did Anders remember seeing a woman leap to her death
from the building opposite his own just days after his daughter
was born. He did not remember shouting, "Lord have mercy!" He
did not remember deliberately crashing his father's car into a tree,
or having his ribs kicked in by three policemen at an antiwar rally,
or waking himself up with laughter. He did not remember when
he began to regard the heap of books on his desk with boredom
and dread, or when he grew angry at writers for writing them.
He did not remember when everything began to remind him of
something else.

This is what he remembered. Heat. A baseball field. Yellow grass, the whir of insects, himself leaning against a tree as the boys of the neighborhood gather for a pickup game. He looks on as the others argue the relative genius of Mantle and Mays. They have been worrying this subject all summer, and it has become tedious to Anders: an oppression, like the heat.

Then the last two boys arrive, Coyle and a cousin of his from Mississippi. Anders has never met Coyle's cousin before and will never see him again. He says hi with the rest but takes no further notice of him until they've chosen sides and someone asks the cousin what position he wants to play. "Shortstop," the boy says. "Short's the best position they is." Anders turns and looks at him. He wants to hear Coyle's cousin repeat what he's just said, though he knows better than to ask. The others will think he's being a jerk, ragging the kid for his grammar. But that isn't it, not at all—it's that Anders is strangely roused, elated, by those final two words, their pure unexpectedness and their music. He takes the field in a trance, repeating them to himself.

The bullet is already in the brain; it won't be outrun forever, or charmed to a halt. In the end it will do its work and leave the troubled skull behind, dragging its comet's tail of memory and hope and talent and love into the marble hall of commerce. That can't be helped. But for now Anders can still make time. Time for the shadows to lengthen on the grass, time for the tethered dog to bark at the flying ball, time for the boy in right field to smack his sweat-blackened mitt and softly chant, *They is, they is, they is.*

DANIYAL MUEENUDDIN

"One thing I've observed is that people basically live within the same range of emotion, so even a very poor person in Pakistan will basically have the same experiences of their own wealth and power and food as you will have in America. People are very resilient."

"The world is a kind of place where you can make choices, of being a romantic or a cynic. But I think you end up being happier if you're romantic."

"One of the problems for writers is that they live as writers, and that doesn't provide you with very much material. I've been very lucky that way."

Onstage interview at The Story Prize event
March 3, 2010

Saleema

from In Other Rooms, Other Wonders

Saleema was born in the Jhulan clan, blackmailers and bootleggers, Muslim refugees at Partition from the country northwest of Delhi. They were lucky, the new border lay only thirty or forty miles distant, and from thieving expeditions they knew how to travel unobserved along canals and tracks. Skirting the edge of the Cholistan Desert, crossing into Pakistan, on the fourth night they came to a Hindu village abandoned by all but a few old women. They drove them away and occupied the houses, finding pots and pans, buckets, even guard dogs, which grew accustomed to them.

During Saleema's childhood twenty years later the village was gradually being absorbed into the slums cast off by an adjacent provincial town called Kotla Sardar. Her father became a heroin addict, and died of it, her mother slept around for money and favors, and she herself at fourteen became the plaything of a small landowner's son. Then a suitor appeared, strutting the village on leave from his job in the city, and plucked her off to Lahore. He looked so slim and city-bright, and soon proved to be not only weak but depraved. These experiences had not cracked her hard skin, but made her sensual, unscrupulous—and romantic.

One morning she lay on the bed of the cramped servants' quarters in Lahore where she and her husband lived. He was gone for the day, aimless and sloping around the streets, unwanted at the edge of the crowd in a tea stall. Though he knew right away that she slept with Hassan the cook, in this house where she served as a maid, the first time he opened his mouth she made to slap him and pushed him out of the room; and next day as usual he hungrily took the few rupees she gave—to buy twists of rocket pills, his amphetamine addiction.

She picked at the chipped polish on her long slim toe, feeling sorry for herself. Her oval face, taller than broad, with deep-set eyes, had a grace contrasting with her bright easy temperament. At twenty-four this hard life had not yet marked her, and when she smiled her dimples made her seem even younger, just a girl; she still had some of the girl's gravity. It was true, the cook Hassan had gotten everything from her, as always she'd given it too soon. She had been a maidservant in three houses so far, since her husband lost his job as peon in an office, and in every one she had opened her legs for the cook. She'd been here at Gulfishan, the Lahore mansion of the landlord K. K. Harouni, only a month, and already she'd slept with Hassan. The cooks tempted her, lording it over the kitchen, where she liked to sit, with the smell of broth and green vegetables cooking and sauce. And she had duties in the kitchen, she made the *chapattis*, so thin and light that they almost floated up to the ceiling. She had that in her hands. Mr. Harouni had called her into the dining room at lunch one day and said he'd never in seventy years eaten better ones, while she blushed and looked at her bare feet. And then, the delicacies that Hassan gave her—the best parts, things that should have gone to the table, foreign things, pistachio ice cream and slices of sweet pies, baked tomatoes stuffed with cheese, potato cutlets. Things that she asked for, village food, curry with marrow bones and carrot *halva*. The entire household, from the sahib on down, had been eating to suit her appetite.

"Ask for it, my duckling," said Hassan in the mornings, when she drank her tea sitting beside him, hunched together in the kitchen. "I need to fatten you up, I like them plump."

"Don't talk that way, I come from a respectable family."

"Well, whatever kind of family, what should I stuff that rounded little belly with today?"

And he wobbled off to market on his bicycle with a big woven basket strapped on the back, riding so slowly that he could almost have walked there faster, pedaling with his knees pointed out.

•

BUT THAT HAD ENDED SOON enough. Why are cooks always vicious? She knew that at lunchtime today she would go silently into
the kitchen and begin making the *chapattis*, that Hassan would be
standing at the stove, banging lids, ignoring her. She hadn't done
anything, she had told the slut sweepress who was always hanging
around the kitchen to fuck off somewhere else, and he exploded.
Hassan ruled the hot filthy kitchen. He made food both for the
master's table and for all the servants, more than a dozen of them.
For days on end the servants' food would be inedible—keeping
with Hassan's policy of collective punishment. Once, when the accounts manager had quite mildly commented on Hassan's reckless
padding of the bills, they had eaten nothing but watery lentils for
more than a week, until the manager backed down. "Well, I've got
to cut corners *somewhere*," Hassan kept saying, shaking his grizzled head. Anyway, Saleema knew that he was through with her,
would sweeten up and try to fuck her now and then, out of cruelty
as much as anything else, to show he could but the easy days were
over, now she had no one to protect her. In this household a man
who had served ten years counted as a new servant. Hassan had
been there over fifty, Rafik, the master's valet, the same. Even the
nameless junior gardener had been there four or five. With less
than a month's service Saleema counted for nothing. Nor did she
have patronage. She had been hired on approval, to serve the master's eldest daughter, Begum Kamila, who lived in New York, and
who that spring had come to stay with her father. Haughty and
proud, Kamila allowed no intimacies.

SALEEMA NEXT ANGLED FOR ONE of the drivers—forlorn
hope!—a large man with a drooping mustache who didn't ever
speak to her. The two drivers shared quarters, a room next to the

cool dark garage where two aging Mercedes stood, rarely driven, because the old man rarely went out. Day and night the drivers kept up a revolving card game, with the blades from a nearby slum, the fast set. She would linger past the door of the room where they sprawled on a raft of beds. At night they sometimes drank beer, hiding the bottles on the floor.

As she walked past their room a second time on a breezy spring morning, one of the men in the room whistled.

"Go to hell," she said.

That made it worse.

"Give us some of that black mango. It's a new variety!"

"No, it's smooth like ice cream, I swear to God my tongue is melting."

"You can wipe your dipstick after checking the oil!"

One of them pretended to be defending her. "How dare you say that!"

She went into the latrine, holding back her tears. She didn't even have a place to herself for that, she shared the same toilet as the men. The dark room stank, there were cockroaches in the corners. She closed the wooden door of the stall behind her, pushed her face and arms against the flaking whitewashed wall, and began softly to cry.

"What is it, girl?"

Someone must have been in the shower, next to the toilet. Usually she called before entering.

"Who the hell is that?"

"Stay in there, my clothes are on the wall. I'm just finished."

She recognized the voice of Rafik, the valet.

"You can go to hell too. I'm done with you fuckheads."

"That's all right, quiet down, I'm just leaving." His thin arm reached to take the clothes hanging from a nail pounded into the wall behind the door. She heard him dress and go out, pulling the door shut gently.

•

SHE SQUATTED IN THE DARK, pulling down her *shalvar* and trying to pee. Nothing came. His voice had been gentle. Three bars of light filtered across the air above her head, alive with motes of dust, and this filled her with hope. The summer would be here in a month, the cold winter had passed. She loved the heat, thick night air, and the smell of water and dust, the cool shower spraying her breasts, water splashing on the furry walls in the dank room; and her body, coming out into the evening, drying her hair, head sideways, ear to her shoulder, combing its hanging length.

Rafik sat in the servants' courtyard on one of the dirty white metal chairs, smoking a hookah, not looking at her as she sat down on a low wooden stool, almost at his knees.

He cupped the mouthpiece of the hookah with blunt weathered hands, a heavy agate ring on his index finger. She had never before looked closely at Rafik. He wore clean plain clothes, a woolen mountain vest—spoke with the curling phlegmy accent of the Salt Range, despite having served in Lahore for fifty years. Black shoes cracked where the toes bent, polished. He said the five daily prayers, the only servant who did. A week earlier he had dyed his hair red with henna, to keep him cool as summer came. Hair parted in the middle, looking almost martial but without any swagger; a small brush of mustache, thick ears of an aging man. He must be sixty, came into service as a boy, fifty years ago. He spent more time with the master than anyone else, woke the old man and put him to bed, brought him tea, massaged his feet, dressed him, brought him a single whiskey at night. All of Old Lahore knew Rafik, the barons, the landlords and magnates and politicians, the old dragons, the hostesses of forty years ago.

She let herself cry a few more tears—she could cry whenever she wanted, she thought of herself, alone, her husband on drugs, that dried-up stick who picked her out of the village, when she thought he was saving her. She was still a girl, not just then, but now too. She cried harder, wiping her eyes with the corner of her *dupatta.*

Rafik's mouth worked, distorting his patient resigned face. He took a long pull on the hookah, the tobacco thick in the air.

They were alone, they could hear Hassan in the kitchen making lunch, pounding something. The drivers sat in their quarters playing cards, the gardeners tended their plants, the sweepers were in the house washing the toilets or the floors, or sweeping the leaves from the long tree-shaded drive at the front of the house.

"I know what you all think," she began. "You think I'm a slut, you think I poison my husband. Because of him I'm alone, and you all do with me as you like. I'm trying to live here too, you know. I'm not a fool. I also come from somewhere." Her words poured out clearly, evenly, angrily, entirely unplanned.

He didn't say anything, smoked, his heavy-lidded eyes half shut.

After a moment she got up to leave.

"Stay a minute, girl. I'll bring you tea."

He shifted to get up, putting aside the bamboo stem of the hookah.

"All right, Uncle. But let me bring it." His offering this meant so much to her.

Going boldly into the kitchen, she ladled tea into two chipped cups—the servants' crockery—from a kettle that simmered on a back burner morning till night. Hassan ignored her.

She brought the cups and handed one to Rafik, hoping as she sat down on a bench that someone would come and see them together.

Touching the hot tea to her lips, she peered at him.

He poured tea into the saucer and blew the clotted cream away, then sipped. "It's good, isn't it?" he said.

She wanted to stop it, because it seemed too soon after her

tears, but a smile came over her, rising up. She beamed, her girlish yet knowing face lit and transformed.

"What are you laughing at?"

"Nothing. You look like my uncle, except he was huge and fat and you're thin. He always blew on his tea and then he sipped it and looked sort of gloomy and important, like you do."

"Gloomy?" He said it in the funniest way, startled.

I can get him, she thought, and it sent a shiver of happiness through her.

"I'm just joking with you. You're completely different from my uncle. Is that better?"

He smiled, not as a grown-up does, but like a child, smiling with his eyes and mouth and the wrinkles bitten into his face, cheerfully. She noticed this, and thought, He smiles all over, the same way I do.

"You're making fun of me. Well, go ahead, I'm an old man. It's time for me to be a fool."

She thought of disagreeing with him, saying he would never be a fool—but stopped herself. Instead she said, "Well, whatever time it is, I don't think foolishness wears a watch."

"You're full of riddles, little girl."

"Little girl." Finishing her tea, she took both her cup and his into the kitchen and washed them carefully. Going out again and walking past him, she said, "Thank you, I feel better for talking to you, Uncle."

In her room, she sat on the bed cross-legged, closed her eyes, leaned back against the wall, and thought, *After all, why not? Why shouldn't I?*

SALEEMA AVOIDED RAFIK DURING THE next few days, watching him, but not presuming on the intimacy of their one conversation. She had never been discreet, so that although she did this almost unconsciously, it suggested to her new possibilities of relation, defined not by constraint—which she understood—but by delicacy. Then fate stepped in to reward her. Every year, at the time of the wheat harvest, K. K. Harouni went for a week to his farm at Dunyapur, on the banks of the Indus. His daughter Begum Kamila that year accompanied him, and therefore Saleema went too.

Early on the morning of the departure the two cars stood in the front of the house, one under the portico, for the sahib and Kamila, and the other for the servants. The drivers polished the cars while they waited, leaning over to clean the windshields, experts. Saleema had tied her clothes in a bag. She had bought a new pair of sandals the day before, and now the red plastic straps were cutting into her feet. When the master came out, leaning on Rafik's arm, those who were sitting on their haunches stood up sharply. He got into the car, called Shah Sahib the accounts manager over, spoke to him briefly through the lowered window, and then the car pulled away, passed under the alley of ancient flame-of-the-forest trees, and turned out the gate. Everyone relaxed, Shah Sahib lit a cigarette, looked without interest over the scene, and returned to his office.

"Come on, come on, get it done," Samundar Khan driver said to the gardeners, who were loading provisions into the trunk of the second car.

Hassan sat in the front, wearing a lambskin cap that brushed the roof, Rafik and Saleema in the back, a basket of food on the seat between them. She had never before ridden in a private car. Sitting with her hands on her knees, she looked out the window at the old shops along the Mall, Tollington Market, where Hassan went on his bicycle to buy chickens and meat, then the mausoleum of Datta Sahib.

I suppose people looking in must wonder who I am, she thought.

As they came across the Ravi River bridge she asked if she could open her window, not so much because she wanted to, as to register her presence. Hassan and Samundar Khan were arguing about whether the fish in the river had been getting bigger or smaller in the last few years.

"Oh, for God's sake," said Hassan, "what do you know about it. I'm a cook, and I've been cooking fish longer than you've been breathing. Listen to me, once upon a time the fish used to be half as big as this car."

"For you old guys everything used to be bigger."

With Hassan, this could go on for hours. Saleema asked again, "Can I open the window, please?"

They were stuck in traffic going through the toll.

"Go ahead," Samundar Khan said. "The air's free."

She couldn't find the handle. Rafik leaned over and touched the button, and the window glided down. He pointed out at the river. The rising sun threw a broad stripe of orange on the chocolate brown water. Bicycles and donkey carts and gaudy Bedford trucks streamed in and out of the city over the bridge. He gestured with his eyes at Samundar Khan and Hassan debating nonsense in the front. "Wisdom against youth," he whispered.

SALEEMA DROVE BACK INTO HER childhood, through towns the same as those around her home a hundred miles to the east, rows of ugly concrete buildings, crowded bazaars, slums, ponds of sewage water choked with edible water lilies, then open country, groves of blossoming orange trees, the ripe mustard yellow with flowers; but she rode in an immaculate car instead of a bus crashing along thick with the odor of the crowd. She had painted her nails the night before; her hand rested on the sill of the window, the spring air brushing her fingers. She felt pretty. They drove through mango orchards, fields of harvest wheat. Rafik sat telling a rosary of worn plastic beads, mouthing the ninety-nine names of Allah, his eyes dull, allowing the landscape to pass through him.

They turned onto a single-lane road, which led first through barren salt flats, then irrigated fields, and finally into an orchard of old mango trees.

"All this belongs to Mian Sahib," said Rafik.

They drove up a packed dirt road bordered with jasmine, along the brick wall that enclosed the house, running for several acres, and then into a cul-de-sac planted with rosewood trees. Ten or twelve men sat on benches and stools—the managers and other rising men who wanted to be noticed by the landowner. Rafik stepped out of the car and embraced them one by one. Several of them looked over at Saleema and said, "*Salaam*, Bibi jee."

After they had tea Rafik said to her, "Come on, I'll show you where Begum Kamila's room is."

They went through an ornate wooden door, set in the wall, and into a lush garden that stretched away and became lost among banyans and rosewood trees and open lawns.

She paused, shading her eyes with her hand, taking in the green sward.

"There's more than you can see. If you like, I'll show you later."

Walking through a grassy courtyard, Rafik came to a door, removed his shoes, and knocked.

"Come in," called Begum Kamila. She was sitting in an armchair reading a book. "So you've come, have you?"

She must once have been a very beautiful woman. She wore saris in bright colors and colored her long hair jet black, and on her third finger she wore an immense emerald set in gold, which Saleema once found lying next to the bathtub, and held in her palm for a long time, feeling the heft of the stone, guessing what it must be worth.

"Shall I light the fire, Begum Sahiba?" asked Rafik.

"Go ahead, it'll take away the damp. I suppose Daddy's about to call for lunch."

Rafik kneeled in front of the fire, twisting sheets of newspaper into sticks.

Kamila's bags had been placed on a long desk by the window, which overlooked another garden. Lines had been chalked in the grass for tennis and a net strung. Saleema took the toiletries into the bathroom and laid them out. Unlike the house in Lahore, where the doors were smudged with fingerprints and the paint flaked off the walls in strips, these rooms had been newly painted. The rugs were bright and clean, the brick floors had been washed, vases of flowers, badly arranged, had been placed all around, marigolds and roses.

Going out again into the dark chilly bedroom, Saleema found Rafik still kneeling at the hearth, the flames orange on his orange face.

"Is Bibi gone?"

"They announced lunch."

"May I sit down?"

He moved over.

"It's amazing. My village would fit in a corner of this garden, and we were thirty families. And it's so clean and comfortable, out here in the middle of nowhere."

"Harouni Sahib is a lord, and we're poor people. And then, these are the games that the managers play. The better the house and gardens look, the more comfortable he is, the less Mian Sahib notices the tricks they all get up to on the farms. I don't know what they're storing it up for, stealing fertilizer and the water and cheating in the books. In the old days no one dared. Mian Sahib made these people—the fathers ate his salt, and now the sons have forgotten and are eating everything else."

The fire cracked, the dry mango wood catching hungrily.

She threw a little twig into the fire. "At least their bellies are full."

•

IN THE MORNING SHE WASHED Begum Kamila's clothes, sitting by a faucet outside in the back garden, beside the unused tennis court. Foam on her arms, water splashing onto her bodice from the big orange bucket, she looked up at the trees blowing in the wind, the birds. She was alone. The swaybacked tennis net and the odd chalked lines made the lawn seem expectant, prepared. Last night she had taken a bowl of food quickly into her own room. She heard the men outside around a fire telling stories about the old tough managers and light-fingered servants, now dead, or about happenings on the farm, cattle thefts, dowries. Hassan and Rafik and even the drivers, who had after all been in service fifteen or twenty years, had old friends here.

Churning the clothes in the bucket, squeezing them out, she felt happier perhaps than she ever had been. The April sun had bite, even in the morning, reflecting off the whitewashed walls enclosing this back garden. The earth cooled the soles of her bare feet. Her thoughts ducked in and out of holes, like mice. I'll avoid him, she thought, settling on this as a way forward, knowing that she would be seeing Rafik at lunch if not before. Her love affairs had been so plainly mercantile transactions that she hadn't learned to be coquettish. But the little hopeful girl in her awoke now. Spreading the clothes to dry on a long hedge that bordered the tennis court, bright red and white and yellow patches against the healthy green, she sat there alone in the sun until lunchtime, undisturbed except once, by a gardener, who walked past with a can, stooping to water the potted plants arranged next to the building.

AT LUNCH SHE MADE THE *chapattis*—no one in the village could do that properly. Hassan came into the big hot kitchen, which had a row of coal-burning hearths set at waist level in one wall, and lifted the covers off the saucepans and casseroles prepared by the farm cook enough for several dozen people.

"Hey, boy," he said to the gangly farm cook, "I've never heard of chickens with six legs. I suppose you're one of those guys—if you cooked a fly you'd keep the breast for yourself. At least you could waft it past your lord and master once."

He pinched Saleema under her arm as she stood flattening the *chapattis* between her hands.

"Here's where the real meat is."

He laughed without mirth, a drawn-out wheeze.

The young cook didn't know what to say. He hadn't slipped anything away yet, though he certainly planned to.

Rafik stood beside another servant, who was spooning the food into serving dishes. The room had high ceilings, and a long wooden table in the middle. In the old times food for scores of people had been cooked here, when the master came on weeks-long hunting trips, with large parties and beaters and guides. Fans that had been broken for years hung down on long pipes, like in a railway station hall.

Saleema had become rigid when Hassan pinched her, raising her shoulders but keeping her eyes on the skillet.

Resting a hand on Hassan's shoulder, Rafik said, "Uncle, why do you bother this poor girl? What has she done to you?"

"You should ask, what *hasn't* she done to me." Then, after a moment, "The hell with it, she's a virgin ever since she rowed across the river, how's that? Don't 'Uncle' me, when you're my own uncle."

He threw down his apron, and left the kitchen, saying to the village cook, "Watch out for Kamila Bibi, young man. Mian Sahib doesn't care what he eats."

As he walked past Saleema, carrying a tray of food to the living room, Rafik made a funny stiff face and then winked.

•

THAT EVENING THE WEATHER CHANGED. This wasn't the season for rain, but just before dark the wind from the north had begun to blow across the plain, bending the branches of the rosewood trees like a closed hand running up the trunk to strip off the leaves, throwing in front of it a scattering of crows, which flew sloping and tumbling like scraps of black cotton. The rain spattered and made pocks in the dust, cold as rain is before hail. Then it fell heavily. Rafik had taken the drinks into the living room at seven, as he did every day. The food sat warming over coals, there was nothing further to be done till the bell for dinner rang at eight-thirty. The others were in the verandah of the servants' sitting area. Saleema leaned against the long table, while across from her Rafik sat on a stool. The dim bulbs with tin shades hanging from the ceiling threw a yellow light which left the corners of the room dark. Neither of them could think of anything to say, and Saleema kept wiping her eyes and her face with her *dupatta* as if she were hot.

When the rain became hard she said, "Come on, let's go see it come down."

They walked awkwardly through the empty dining room, which smelled of dust and damp brick, then through an arcade to the back verandah. A single banyan tree stood in the middle of the back lawn, the rain cascading down through its handsbreadth leaves. Saleema leaned against a pillar, Rafik stood next to her, his hands behind his back.

"God forgive us, there's going to be a lot of damage to the straw that hasn't been covered," he said.

"This will even knock down the wheat that hasn't been cut. Look at how hard it's coming down."

She looked over at him, his serious wrinkled face, his stubble. Despite the rain, moths circled around the lamps hanging from the ceiling. She kept bumping her hip against the pillar. *Come on, come on*, she thought.

Finally, he said, "Well, at least they haven't started planting the cotton yet."

She turned, with her back to the pillar. "Rafik, we're both from the village, we know all this."

He looked over at her quickly. His face seemed hard. She had startled him. Then he did come over.

She put her arms around him. "You're thin," she said, as if she were pleading, "you should eat more," exhaling. The water splashed in the gutter spouts. He also pulled her into his body and held her, melted into her, she was almost exactly as tall as him, his thin body and hers muscular and young. He kissed her neck, not like a man kissing a woman, but inexpertly, as if he were kissing a baby. She kept her eyes open, face on his shoulder.

The electricity went, with a sort of crack, night extinguishing the house and the rain-swept garden.

"Let's go, little girl," he whispered in her ear. "They'll be calling for me." In the darkness, with the other servants hurrying to bring lamps and candles, no one noticed when Saleema and Rafik returned to the kitchen.

But the next morning, when the servants were eating their *parathas* and tea, he came over and sat down next to her, saying nothing, sipping the tea and chewing noisily because of his false teeth, his mouth rotating. So everyone knew. After that he ate his meals next to her, and when they had no duties went off into the empty back garden and sat talking. But they didn't make love, or even do more than hold hands.

At the end of the week Harouni and his retinue drove back to Lahore, Rafik, Saleema, and the rest.

THE SERVANTS HAD A GAME that they played, with Rafik surprisingly enough not just acquiescent but the ringleader. Up in Rafik's native mountains marijuana grew everywhere, along the sides of the roads, and thickest along the banks of open sewers running through the rocky pine woods below the villages, the blooming plants at the end of summer competing in sweetness and stench with the odor of sewage. Hash smoke clouded the late-night air in the little village tea stall when he was a young man. Now, every spring Rafik planted a handful of seeds behind some trees in a corner of the Lahore garden, and in the fall he dried the plants and ground up the leaves. He played tricks on the others, making a paste called *bhang* and slipping it into the food of one or another servant. Sometimes they would taste it and stop eating, but often not.

A few weeks after the visit to the Harouni farm at Dunyapur, Rafik began secretly compounding a batch of his potion in his quarters, with the help of Saleema. Kamila Bibi had gone back to New York, but Saleema had been kept on, through Rafik's intervention. The accounts manager Shah Sahib had been planning to tell the master that the girl was "corrupt" and a "bad character"— saying these words in English—and toss her out. But now he held his tongue, not wanting to cross Rafik. And Rafik spoke for her one evening as the old man went to sleep, with Rafik massaging his legs.

"I beg your pardon, sir, about the maid Saleema, who has been serving Begum Kamila. She's a poor girl and her husband is sick and she's useful in the kitchen. She makes the *chapattis*. If you can give her a place it would be a blessing."

The old man did not merely lack interest in the affairs of the servants—he was not conscious that they had lives outside his purview.

"That's fine."

NOW SALEEMA WATCHED IN RAFIK'S quarters as he boiled the dried leaves in water over an electric ring.

"Hey, girl, close the door, don't let anyone see."

She sat down on the edge of the bed, swinging her bare feet, kicking off her sandals, which fell by the door. Rafik squatted, stirring the leaves with a wooden spoon and peering into the cauldron. They still hadn't made love, though now he would lie with her in the afternoon during the servants' naptime, his hand on her breasts. He made no attempt to hide their relations, and all the servants thought they must be sleeping together. She would fold him into her body, and stroke his thinning hennaed hair while he slept.

"This is a strange kind of cooking for an old man."

"You're the strange one, following this old man around like a little sheep. Most shepherds are young boys."

"Please don't say that." She never in her life had spoken in these gentle tones.

He looked up at her, eyes smiling, pointing with the spoon. "Be careful or I'll give you a taste of this!"

"No, thanks."

"No, I'm serious. When Mian Sahib goes to 'Pindi I want everyone to take some. I'll have it too."

"Are you kidding?"

"It'll be fun. And we'll be together. You can trust me."

TWO DAYS LATER K. K. Harouni flew to Rawalpindi, to attend a meeting of the board of governors of the State Bank—one of the few positions he still held, a sinecure—the real policy was decided elsewhere, Harouni and other eminences unknowingly acting to camouflage self-serving deals and manipulations.

Shah Sahib, who had accompanied his master to the airport, stood next to Samundar Khan in the parking lot, leaning against the hood of the car, wearing a gray suit with excessively broad lapels.

A jet taxied out and came hurtling down the runway, then climbed smoothly through haze, toward Rawalpindi to the west, locking its wheels up.

"Let's go," said Shah Sahib.

As they drove out the airport gate, Samundar Khan said, "May I take you home?"

Shah Sahib glanced over at him. "I need to pick up some things for my wife. *Then* you can take me home."

"WELL, SHAH SAHIB'S OUT OF the way," Samundar Khan said, walking into the kitchen.

Hassan stood at the stove over an enormous pot of boiling oil, cooking the *samosas*, which Rafik and Saleema were assembling at a table, filling them with meat and *bhang*. Rafik had told the servants that he would be passing around *samosas* to celebrate good news from home, but everyone saw through this. The drivers and their gang were fully on board, and had sent Samundar Khan to make sure they got a heaping plate. The old gardener had left, but the younger one had sidled into the drivers' quarters and wanted to join in. The oldest of the sweepers, a thin balding man with a meek, servile expression, sat out in the courtyard hoping that he would be included. Whenever he could afford it he would buy himself a stick of hash to smoke at home after the day's work.

All the *bhang* had been used up. A pile of *samosas* steamed in a plate.

"Okay, now it's us," said Rafik.

Hassan turned his back and raised the lid on a saucepan. "Not me."

But he ended up having some.

Saleema and Rafik sat in his room eating *samosas*. At first she had refused, but he pressed her.

"Now what?" she said.

"Sit here and tell me a story. Tell me about when you were a girl."

Neither of them had spoken much of their pasts or their homes. She knew that he had a wife and children, two sons, and shied away from anything bringing it to mind.

"What shall I say? I was brought up with slaps and harsh words. We had nothing, we were poor. My father sold vegetables from a cart, but when he began smoking heroin he sold everything, the cart, his bicycle, the radio, even the dishes in the kitchen. Once a man—a boy—gave me a little watch—he brought it from Multan—and my father pushed me to the ground and took it from my wrist."

"Poor girl, little girl, how could he do it?" He rolled her over onto the bed and kissed her neck, under her chin. Stopping for a moment, he stood and locked the door.

She didn't tell him the worst, much worse things. Her father came into her room at night and felt under her clothes.

For the first time, Rafik touched between her legs. She opened the drawstring of her *shalvar*, then took off her shirt sitting up on the bed. Her small breasts stood out, her ribs.

He turned off the lights, but she said, "No, I want to see you."

"This old body? Leave it, there's nothing to see."

"For me you're not old."

The *bhang* had begun to affect her, she felt the dimensions of the room, the light, the calendar on the wall that showed a picture of the Kaaba, the black cloth covering the stone and crowds circling around it. How strange, she had never before seen the roof, made of bricks and metal rods, the little high window to let in air. She felt aroused, yet wanted to get up, to go somewhere. She took off his clothes, peeling off his tan socks. Their skin touched. Standing up and going to the corner, she bent down on purpose to pick up her shirt, letting him see her. She saw reflected in his eyes the beauty of her young body. They made love, he came almost immediately, then lay on her.

"Stay inside of me," she said.

Her thoughts were racing, from idea to idea. Oh, would he marry her, and she knew he wouldn't. She had been taken by so many men; could have given herself to him so much more pure.

"Now turn off the lights," she said.

"No, let's go out in a minute. Let's go in the garden and look at the flowers."

In the garden he even held her hand. "Don't be afraid," he said. "If you have strange thoughts, remember it's the *bhang*. Be happy."

"Well, it's warm," she said. The sun beat down, the dust on the roses seemed heavy, under a banyan tree the grass didn't grow. She kicked off her shoes, felt the cool earth.

"Lie down here," she said, "next to me, hold me."

And though they might have been seen, he did.

ALL THE AFTERNOON THEY WALKED around together, even in the house, looking at the paintings, the furniture. Rafik wanted to sit with the drivers, but she said no, she wanted to be with him alone. Hassan banged around the kitchen, he had eaten too many of the *samosas*.

That evening she said to Rafik, "I'll be back in half an hour." She went to her own room. Her husband lay on the bed, on his pills, twitching his fingers.

"Look," she said, standing over him. "You're a mess. You've been a mess for two years. Now I'll never sleep in your bed again."

He began to cry, his emaciated face, his long yellow teeth. This she hadn't expected. He sobbed, real tears. She sat down on the broken chair in the corner, looking at the shelf on which she kept her few things, a metal jar of eyeliner, a tin box thrown out by Kamila that once held chocolates.

"Will I still get my money?"

Then she stood up again. "Yes, but if you ever say one funny word, that's it."

She took some clothes, and when she hung them from a nail in Rafik's room he said nothing. She held him all night, his face in her breasts.

Only once, waking, she thought, That was our marriage feast, drugged *samosas*, and she felt sad and worn and frightened.

NOW SHE SLEPT EACH NIGHT in Rafik's bed, leaving her husband to his addiction. Fall and winter came, the leaves fell, at night they slept under a heavy quilt that the managers at the farm sent to Rafik as a present. She slept naked, which still after five months disturbed him. Rafik woke before dawn, to say his prayers, then went into the kitchen and had tea with Hassan. The sahib woke early, and Rafik had duties until mid-morning. When he came to wake her, she would pretend still to be asleep, face hidden in the quilt—she always slept with her head covered. He would bring a cup of tea and some toast.

"Come in with me," she would say, moving over in the bed, leaving a warm spot, and sometimes he would. Her long hair hung down, and she would brush it, while he told her about the guests who had come for bridge, or about some feud in the kitchen. He read the Urdu paper *New Times*, sitting in the morning sun, wearing ancient horn-rimmed glasses with thick lenses. She bought him a warm woolen hat and carefully washed and mended his clothes. She wanted everyone to see how well she cared for him. She said, "You wear me on your back, and I wear you on my face." Her face had softened.

She missed one period, then a second, but said nothing to Rafik.

They had finished making love one afternoon, and were talking, her head on his shoulder.

He was stroking her belly.

"I might as well tell you. See how I'm bigger? I'm pregnant."

He pushed her head away and sat up. "That's bad."

"If that's how you feel, I'll go to my village and get rid of it."

"I'm married. I have a son your age."

She got out of bed, dressed, and went out, turning for a moment at the door. "I'll never forget what you said when I told you."

Where to go? She walked out the gate, in the direction of Lawrence Gardens, a few blocks away. Looking up into the cradle of branches in an enormous flame-of-the-forest tree, she thought, God, I'm nothing, look at how small I am next to this tree. It must be hundreds of years old. But I won't give up the baby. I'd rather have the baby than Rafik.

That night she had nowhere else to sleep, and so went into Rafik's quarters—she couldn't bear to be with her husband, who used more and more of the rocket pills and stayed up all night smoking cigarettes.

"Forgive me," Rafik said.

"I'm going to have it, you can keep me here or throw me out. In any case, I'll have it in my village, there are no women here to help me."

The next day he went to the bazaar in the morning, and when she came to his room for the afternoon nap he gave her a tiny suit, blue knitted trousers, a blue shirt, mittens, and a hat with a pompom, printed with little white rabbits.

So he accepted her condition and would run his hands over her growing belly, speaking to the life within. When it moved, she would put his hand there to show him. None of the other servants said anything openly, though they had expected it; and of course she could claim it was her husband's child. Hassan once jokingly congratulated her, but she responded so gently that he too became silent.

Rafik obtained a month's leave for her.

Before she left for the village he gave her a lot of money, ten thousand rupees, which he had saved up over the years, even after sending maintenance to his family.

"I can't take this."

"For me, for our baby—in case you need a doctor."

SHE ARRIVED AT HER VILLAGE at dusk, taking a rickshaw from the bus station. The open field next to the village had become a collecting pool for the sewage from the city, the water black.

"Look, Saleema's come," the neighbors said, as she walked through the narrow lane to her mother's house, carrying two plastic bags full of food, meat and sugar, tea, carrots, potatoes. The walled compound didn't have a door, just a dirty burlap cloth made of two gunnysacks sewn together. Children ran behind her and peeked in.

Her mother sat on a *charpoy*, peeling potatoes, her long thin hair braided and red with henna.

She didn't even get up, she kept peeling the potatoes.

"I'm back."

"Are you in trouble? You're pregnant."

"No," she lied.

"I bought a goat with the money you sent."

"I can see." The goat, tied to a stake, nibbled at a handful of grass.

The single room was almost completely bare, not even a radio.

Saleema made a curry, sitting by the little hearth, over a fire of twigs.

As they ate, sitting on the bed, Saleema asked, "Where's my brother?"

"Bholu doesn't come here much. I don't give him money."

"Where do you get money besides what I send?"

"It isn't easy anymore, that I can tell you. You'll find out someday what it's like to be old. I sweep the Chaudreys' house, I sell milk from the goat."

The next day she told her mother about Rafik and the baby.

"Did your husband throw you out?"

"I forgot about him long ago."

She wanted to explain that she had become a respectable woman, but knew that her mother would never understand.

Her mother found out about the money and wheedled day and night. Saleema kept the money in a pouch that she wore under her shirt. Late one night, she woke to find her mother stealthily untying the pouch with thin practiced hands.

When Saleema sat up, her mother at first said, "I thought I saw a scorpion." Then, "You owe me, you gravid bitch, coming here puffed up after your whoring. This isn't a hotel."

"It's not my money. And I've been buying all the food."

"It sure seems like your money."

The mother lay in her bed, coughing.

The old midwife from the village, with filthy hands and a greedy heart, brought the baby into the world, a tiny little boy.

RAFIK IMMEDIATELY BONDED WITH HIS son. He had been in Lahore when his other children, conceived during ten-day leaves, were born and grew up. He named the child Allah Baksh, God-gifted one.

Saleema sat leaning against the wall of the quarters while Rafik played with the little baby, which held his finger in its tiny hand. He clapped and made a crooning sound, till the baby laughed, showing its red toothless gums.

"His teeth are like yours. Plus you two think alike." She saw that Rafik really did think like the baby, he would sit all afternoon playing with it, engaged with it and seeing the world through its eyes, till it tired. When she opened her blouse to feed the baby, Rafik would look away, embarrassed, lighting his hookah as a distraction, while it smacked and sucked, its tiny throat moving.

Happy months passed, then a year, Saleema became more rounded, she was at the peak of her strange long-faced beauty. Her breasts were heavy with milk.

Rafik sat cross-legged on the lawn one morning, holding the baby. He heard the screen door leading from Harouni's room open, and the master came out. Rafik quickly stood up.

"*Salaam*, sir."

"Hello, Rafik." He was in a good mood. "Is this Saleema's baby?"

The master touched the baby with the flat of his hand. The baby, which had been sleeping, smacked its lips. Rafik always dressed him too warmly, a knitted suit with feet, a floppy hat.

"I must say, he's the spitting image of you," Harouni said, teasingly.

Rafik's face broke involuntarily into a broad smile. "What can I say, Hazoor, life takes strange turns. These are all Your Honor's blessings."

Harouni shouted with laughter. "There are some blessings that you shouldn't attribute to me!"

The old retainer's gentle face colored.

A LETTER ARRIVED FROM RAFIK'S wife. He kept it in his pocket all day, and that night showed it to Saleema. She literally began trembling, sat down on the bed with her head bowed.

"Will you read it to me?"

"All right." The village *maulvi* had taught Rafik to read as a boy, so that he could recite the Koran.

He took his battered glasses from a case in his front pocket and began.

As-Salaam Uleikum.

I am writing to you because you have not been home in so many months more than eighteen months and your sons and also I miss you and speak of you at night. The old buffalo died but the younger one had two calves both female so we will have plenty of milk though for a short while we have none. Khalid asks to come to Lahore and find a job there you can find a job for him perhaps with God's help. Your brother's shop was robbed but they found no money and now he wants to buy two marlas of land so he will not have cash which is better. The land is on the other side of Afzal's piece. Everything else is well. Please dear husband come home when Mian Sahib can spare you. We all send our respects.

As he read the *salaam*, Rafik had breathed, "*Va leikum as-salaam.*"

She had signed the letter, written by a neighbor, with an X.

"Look," said Rafik, "she wept on the paper."

"Or watered it. What will you do?"

"I'll have to go."

She turned her face to the wall and held herself rigid when he touched her.

"Have I done you some wrong?"

"No," she said, "I've done you wrong."

"My wife is sixty years old, little girl. She and I have been together for almost fifty. She stood by me, she bore me two sons, she kept my house, my honor has always been perfectly safe in her hands."

"Honor." Saleema began to cry. "That's bad. You're tiring of me and this situation. Imagine how it feels for me."

He tried to reassure her, but she could tell that the letter had shaken him, as a man of principle. The baby and her love had made him gentler and more philosophical, taking a long view of life as he began to grow old—but the same gentleness would bend him toward his duty, which always would be to his wife and grown sons. He would punish himself and thus her for not loving his wife and for loving Saleema so much and so carnally.

She made him give her a phone number before he left, of a shop near his house, and every evening she wanted to use it, the paper burned in her pocket; but she never dared, what would she say, who would she say was calling? When he returned to Lahore he had changed. He had told his wife about little Allah Baksh.

A FEW DAYS LATER, RAFIK'S son and his wife came to stay in the Lahore house. Saleema was dusting the living room and happened to see them arrive, through a window looking out onto the drive in front. She heard the harsh puttering of a rickshaw, and then an old woman emerged, led by a young man with glistening hair and a strong manner. She knew immediately who this must be, her destruction come in this feeble guise. Panic overcame her, mixed with jealousy and a strange pride that came of knowing they had traveled with her in their minds, planning against her. She watched as they walked up the drive and through the passage to the servants' area. Suddenly remembering her son, who was with Rafik, she raced through the house to the back. But she arrived too late, the old woman had come to the quarters and found Rafik playing with the baby. Saleema walked past the open door, pretending to be on some errand, expecting to hear shouting and tears. The old woman sitting on the bed looked up at Saleema with rheumy eyes that expressed neither reproach nor disliking but simply a flat dismissal. She knew who this young girl must be.

Rafik brought the child to Saleema's quarters, where she had retreated.

"At least this one belongs to me," she whispered.

The grown son, when he met Saleema later that afternoon in the servants' sitting area, said to her, "*Salaam*, Auntie."

I'm younger than you, you country fool, she thought spitefully. She would much rather have been attacked, for then she could react.

That night she sat in the kitchen till midnight, the sleeping baby in her arms, watching the cockroaches scurry across the dirty floor. Finally going to her own room, she roughly pushed her husband over on the bed. He had become so thin that his face looked like a broken steel lantern, a gash of mouth and skin stretched over wires.

"Don't smoke," she ordered. "And don't touch me, stay against the wall."

"I lost all that long ago." He knew why she had come back to his bed.

Lying and staring at the ceiling, nursing the baby when it woke, she felt her love for Rafik tearing at her breast, making her a stranger to herself, breaking her. Now she slept again next to this man who disgusted her, while her love must be sleeping beside his ancient wife, who had known him in his youth, who knew all about him. How she loved the baby, its tiny feet and hands, its contented smacking noises and warmth beside her.

The next day she hid in her room with the doors closed. When Rafik knocked she said, "Please, I beg you. You'll only hurt me. Tell them I'm sick, and leave me alone."

"*Are* you sick?" he asked, concerned.

"What do you think?"

She heard his measured footsteps walking away.

She thought, If just once he would act rashly or even quickly, suddenly, without thinking. But he wouldn't. She remembered how slowly he had surrendered to her.

•

THREE DAYS PASSED. SHE AND Rafik barely spoke, and when they passed each other she saw from his broken and haunted look that he missed her as she missed him. Yet also she saw how resolutely he had turned from her. Just once, when they were alone in the kitchen, at night, he reached over and touched her hand.

"You know, don't you . . ." he said.

The well inside her stirred, all the sorrows of her life, the sweet thick fluid in that darkness, which always lay at the bottom of her thoughts, from which she pulled up the cool liquid and drank.

"I know." And they knew that she forgave him.

Still she hoped. The wife sat in Rafik's room all day, the door open, cross-legged on the bed, eyes not responding to passersby, heavy and settled—Saleema couldn't help walking past on her way to the latrine.

ONE MORNING VERY EARLY SHE heard the master's bell ring, and then people rushing around. She rose and went to the kitchen.

Hassan told her as soon she walked in, "The old man's sick, they're taking him to the hospital."

The other servants milled around the kitchen, no one spoke. The household rested on Harouni's shoulders, their livelihoods. Late that night he died. The daughters had come, Kamila from New York, her sister Sarwat from Karachi. Even Rehana, the estranged middle daughter, who lived in Paris and hadn't returned to Pakistan in years, flew back. A pall fell over the house. Already the bond among the servants weakened.

Hassan disappeared to his quarters, his face fallen in.

The house was full of mourners, the governor came, ambassadors, retired generals. There was nothing to do, no food would be served.

Rafik sought her out. He came to her room, where she sat on the bed, contemplating the emptiness of her future. Even the

child had become silent. When Rafik came in she stood up, and he
leaned against her and sobbed.

She couldn't understand what he said, except that he repeated
how he had fastened the old man's shirt the last evening in the
hospital; but he kept saying *butters* instead of *buttons*. He couldn't
finish the sentence, he repeated the first words over and over. Finally he became quiet, face streaked.

THAT WAS THE LAST TIME ever that she held him. After a week
Sarwat called all the servants into the living room. She sat wearing
a sari, her face collapsed and eyes ringed, arms hung with gold
bracelets.

"I'm going to explain what happens to you. Rafik and Hassan
I've spoken to, as well as the old drivers. The ones who've been in
service more than ten years will get fifty thousand rupees. The rest
of you will get two thousand for each year of service. If you need
recommendations I'll supply them. You served my father well, I
thank you. This house will be sold, but until it is you'll receive your
salaries and can stay in your quarters." She stood up, on the brink
of tears, dignified. "Thank you, goodbye."

Crushed, they all left. They had expected this, but somehow
hoped the house would be kept. It must be worth a tremendous
amount, with its gardens and location in the heart of Old British
Lahore, where the great houses were gradually being demolished,
to make way for ugly flats and townhouses. That all was passing,
houses where carriages once had been kept, flags lowered at sunset
to the lawns of British commissioners. Gone, and they the servants
would never find another berth like this one, the gravity of the
house, the gentleness of the master, the vast damp rooms, the slow
lugubrious pace, the order within disorder.

•

SHE FOUND HASSAN IN THE kitchen, muted for once.

"What'll become of me?" she asked. After all, something must come of his intimacy with her. She had slept with him, held him. The stark fact of her body shown to him, given to him, must be worth something. She wished for this, and knew that it wasn't so. With Rafik it had been different, he had raised her up, but Hassan had degraded her. She saw her hopes receding. Again she became the stained creature who threw herself at Hassan, for the little things he gave her.

"You came with nothing, you leave with nothing. You've been paid and fed for some time at least. You have decent clothes and a little slug of money."

"What of you and Rafik?"

"We're being put in the Islamabad house."

"And did Rafik say anything to the mistresses about me?"

"Nothing," Hassan said cruelly. "Not a word." He put his hands on the counter and looked directly in her face. "It's over. There never *was* any hope. I spent my life in this kitchen. Look at me, I'm old. Rafik's old."

So Rafik had renounced her. At the end of the month she had found another place, with some friends of Harouni, who took her because she came from this house.

Before leaving she said to Rafik one day, "Meet me tonight in the kitchen. You owe me that."

SHE FOUND HIM WAITING FOR her, under a single bulb. He had aged, his face thin, shoulders bent. Worst of all, his eyes were frightened, as if he didn't understand where he was. K. K. Harouni had been his life, his morning and night, his charge, his wealth.

"What of the child?" she asked. "Will you help him? When he's grown will you find him a job?"

"I'll be gone long before that, dear girl."

"Say that once you loved me."

"Of course I did. I do. I loved you more."

WITHIN TWO YEARS SHE WAS finished, began using rocket pills, which she once had so much despised, lost her job, went on to heroin, leaving her husband behind without a word. She knew all about that life from her husband and father.

The man who controlled the lucrative corner where she ended up begging took most of her earnings. This way she escaped prostitution. She cradled the little boy in her arms, holding him up to the windows of cars. Rafik sent money, a substantial amount, so long as she had an address. And then, soon enough, she died, and the boy begged in the streets, one of the sparrows of Lahore.

ANTHONY DOERR

"One of the many strengths of short story collections is that they can potentially range more widely than a novel, maybe encompass a greater variety of human experience. If you think of a writer's interest as a courtyard, you can make a lot more windows onto that courtyard in a story collection."

"I don't see my own life as necessarily all that interesting. I'm not mining or cannibalizing my own direct experience to write stories. I'm sure those of you who are writers have all heard this advice: Write what you know. Fundamentally that is good advice. You're writing about heartbreak or feeling lost or feeling scared or feeling anxious—these things that you have gone through. But that doesn't mean necessarily that if you are a violinmaker for sixty years, you should only write stories about violinmakers. You should assume that there are enough commonalities in human experience that you can write about a Finnish washerwoman in 1512."

Onstage interview at The Story Prize event
March 2, 2011

The world is so fundamentally interesting and it makes me fall in love with it a dozen times a day. Part of my goal as a writer is to say to a reader: Look at this life we're living, look how enormous the scales of time are, look how incredibly old and marvelous this situation is we've lucked into.

From a post on TSP: The Story Prize blog
July 26, 2010

Memory Wall

from *Memory Wall*

Tall Man in the Yard

Seventy-four-year-old Alma Konachek lives in Vredehoek, a suburb above Cape Town: a place of warm rains, big-windowed
lofts, and silent, predatory automobiles. Behind her garden, Table
Mountain rises huge, green, and corrugated; beyond her kitchen
balcony, a thousand city lights wink and gutter behind sheets of
fog like candleflames.

One night in November, at three in the morning, Alma wakes
to hear the rape gate across her front door rattle open and someone
enter her house. Her arms jerk; she spills a glass of water across
the nightstand. A floorboard in the living room shrieks. She hears
what might be breathing. Water drips onto the floor.

Alma manages a whisper. "Hello?"

A shadow flows across the hall. She hears the scrape of a shoe
on the staircase, then nothing. Night air blows into the room—it
smells of frangipani and charcoal. Alma presses a fist over her heart.

Beyond the balcony windows, moonlit pieces of clouds drift
over the city. Spilled water creeps toward her bedroom door.

"Who's there? Is someone there?"

The grandfather clock in the living room pounds through the
seconds. Alma's pulse booms in her ears. Her bedroom seems to be
rotating very slowly.

"Harold?" Alma remembers that Harold is dead but she cannot help herself. "Harold?"

Another footstep from the second floor, another protest from
a floorboard. What might be a minute passes. Maybe she hears
someone descend the staircase. It takes her another full minute to
summon the courage to shuffle into the living room.

Her front door is wide open. The traffic light at the top of the street flashes yellow, yellow, yellow. The leaves are hushed, the houses dark. She heaves the rape gate shut, slams the door, sets the bolt, and peers out the window lattice. Within twenty seconds she is at the hall table, fumbling with a pen.

A man, she writes. *Tall man in the yard.*

Memory Wall

Alma stands barefoot and wigless in the upstairs bedroom with a flashlight. The clock down in the living room ticks and ticks, winding up the night. A moment ago Alma was, she is certain, doing something very important. Something life-and-death. But now she cannot remember what it was.

The one window is ajar. The guest bed is neatly made, the coverlet smooth. On the nightstand sits a machine the size of a microwave oven, marked *Property of Cape Town Memory Research Center.* Three cables spiraling off it connect to something that looks vaguely like a bicycle helmet.

The wall in front of Alma is smothered with scraps of paper. Diagrams, maps, ragged sheets swarming with scribbles. Shining among the papers are hundreds of plastic cartridges, each the size of a matchbook, engraved with a four-digit number and pinned to the wall through a single hole.

The beam of Alma's flashlight settles on a color photograph of a man walking out of the sea. She fingers its edges. The man's pants are rolled to the knees; his expression is part grimace, part grin. Cold water. Across the photo, in handwriting she knows to be hers, is the name *Harold.* She knows this man. She can close her eyes and recall the pink flesh of his gums, the folds in his throat, his big-knuckled hands. He was her husband.

Around the photo, the scraps of paper and plastic cartridges build outward in crowded, overlapping layers, anchored with pushpins and chewing gum and penny nails. She sees to-do lists, jottings, drawings of what might be prehistoric beasts or monsters. She reads: *You can trust Pheko.* And *Taking Polly's Coca-Cola.* A flyer says: *Porter Properties.* There are stranger phrases: *dinocephalians, late Permian, massive vertebrate graveyard.* Some sheets of paper are blank; others reveal a flurry of cross-outs and erasures. On a half-page ripped from a brochure, one phrase is shakily and repeatedly underlined: *Memories are located not inside the cells but in the extracellular space.*

Some of the cartridges have her handwriting on them, too, printed below the numbers. *Museum. Funeral. Party at Hattie's.*

Alma blinks. She has no memory of writing on little cartridges or tearing out pages of books and tacking things to the wall.

She sits on the floor in her nightgown, legs straight out. A gust rushes through the window and the scraps of paper come alive, dancing, tugging at their pins. Loose pages eddy across the carpet. The cartridges rattle lightly.

Near the center of the wall, her flashlight beam again finds the photograph of a man walking out of the sea. Part grimace, part grin. That's Harold, she thinks. He was my husband. He died. Years ago. Of course.

Out the window, beyond the crowns of the palms, beyond the city lights, the ocean is washed in moonlight, then shadow. Moonlight, then shadow. A helicopter ticks past. The palms flutter.

Alma looks down. There is slip of paper in her hand. *A man*, it says. *Tall man in the yard.*

Dr. Amnesty

Pheko is driving the Mercedes. Apartment towers reflect the morning sun. Sedans purr at stoplights. Six different times Alma squints out at the signs whisking past and asks him where they are going.

"We're driving to see the doctor, Mrs. Alma."

The doctor? Alma rubs her eyes, unsure. She tries to fill her lungs. She fidgets with her wig. The tires squeal as the Mercedes climbs the ramps of a parking garage.

Dr. Amnesty's staircase is stainless steel and bordered with ferns. Here's the bulletproof door, the street address stenciled in the corner. It's familiar to Alma in the way a house from childhood would be familiar. As if she has doubled in size in the meantime.

They are buzzed into a waiting room. Pheko drums his fingertips on his knee. Four chairs down, two well-dressed women sit beside a fish tank, one a few decades younger than the other. Both have fat pearls studded through each earlobe. Alma thinks: Pheko is the only black person in the building. For a moment she cannot remember what she is doing here. But this leather on the chair, the blue gravel in the saltwater aquarium—it is the memory clinic. Of course. Dr. Amnesty. In Green Point.

After a few minutes Alma is escorted to a padded chair overlaid with crinkly paper. It's all familiar now: the cardboard pouch of rubber gloves, the plastic plate for her earrings, two electrodes beneath her blouse. They lift off her wig, rub a cold gel onto her scalp. The television panel shows sand dunes, then dandelions, then bamboo.

Amnesty. A ridiculous surname. What does it mean? A pardon? A reprieve? But more permanent than a reprieve, isn't it? Amnesty is for wrongdoings. For someone who has done something wrong. She will ask Pheko to look it up when they get home. Or maybe she will remember to look it up herself.

The nurse is talking.

"And the remote stimulator is working well? Do you feel any improvements?"

"Improvements?" She thinks so. Things do seem to be improving. "Things are sharper," Alma says. She believes this is the sort of thing she is supposed to say. New pathways are being forged. She is remembering how to remember. This is what they want to hear.

The nurse murmurs. Feet whisper across the floor. Invisible

machinery hums. Alma can feel, numbly, the rubber caps being twisted out of the ports in her skull and four screws being threaded simultaneously into place. There is a note in her hand: *Pheko is in the waiting room. Pheko will drive Mrs. Alma home after her session.* Of course.

A door with a small, circular window in it opens. A pale man in green scrubs sweeps past, smelling of chewing gum. Alma thinks: There are other padded chairs in this place, other rooms like this one, with other machines prying the lids off other addled brains. Ferreting inside them for memories, engraving those memories into little square cartridges. Attempting to fight off oblivion.

Her head is locked into place. Aluminum blinds clack against the window. In the lulls between breaths, she can hear traffic sighing past.

The helmet comes down.

Three Years Before, Briefly

"Memories aren't stored as changes to molecules inside brain cells," Dr. Amnesty told Alma during her first appointment, three years ago. She had been on his waiting list for ten months. Dr. Amnesty had straw-colored hair, nearly translucent skin, and invisible eyebrows. He spoke English as if each word were a tiny egg he had to deliver carefully through his teeth.

"This is what they thought forever but they were wrong. The truth is that the substrate of old memories is located not inside the cells but in the extracellular space. Here at the clinic we target those spaces, stain them, and inscribe them into electronic models. In the hopes of teaching damaged neurons to make proper replacements. Forging new pathways. Re-remembering.

"Do you understand?"

Alma didn't. Not really. For months, ever since Harold's death, she had been forgetting things: forgetting to pay Pheko, forgetting to eat breakfast, forgetting what the numbers in her checkbook meant. She'd go to the garden with the pruners and arrive there a minute later without them. She'd find her hairdryer in a kitchen cupboard, car keys in the tea tin. She'd rummage through her mind for a noun and come up empty-handed: Casserole? Carpet? Cashmere?

Two doctors had already diagnosed the dementia. Alma would have preferred amnesia: a quicker, less cruel erasure. This was a corrosion, a slow leak. Seven decades of stories, five decades of marriage, four decades of working for Porter Properties, too many houses and buyers and sellers to count—spatulas and salad forks, novels and recipes, nightmares and daydreams, hellos and good-byes. Could it all really be wiped away?

"We don't offer a cure," Dr. Amnesty was saying, "but we might be able to slow it down. We might be able to give you some memories back."

He set the tips of his index fingers against his nose and formed a steeple. Alma sensed a pronouncement coming.

"It tends to unravel very quickly, without these treatments," he said. "Every day it will become harder for you to be in the world."

Water in a vase, chewing away at the stems of roses. Rust colonizing the tumblers in a lock. Sugar eating at the dentin of teeth, a river eroding its banks. Alma could think of a thousand metaphors, and all of them were inadequate.

She was a widow. No children, no pets. She had her Mercedes, a million and a half rand in savings, Harold's pension, and the house in Vredehoek. Dr. Amnesty's procedure offered a measure of hope. She signed up.

The operation was a fog. When she woke, she had a headache and her hair was gone. With her fingers she probed the four rubber caps secured into her skull.

A week later Pheko drove her back to the clinic. One of Dr. Amnesty's nurses escorted her to a leather chair that looked something like the ones in dental offices. The helmet was merely a vibration at the top of her scalp. They would be reclaiming memories, they said; they could not predict if the memories would be good ones or bad ones. It was painless. Alma felt as though spiders were stringing webs through her head.

Two hours later Dr. Amnesty sent her home from that first session with a remote memory stimulator and nine little cartridges in a paperboard box. Each cartridge was stamped from the same beige polymer, with a four-digit number engraved into the top. She eyed the remote player for two days before taking it up to the upstairs bedroom one windy noon when Pheko was out buying groceries.

She plugged it in and inserted a cartridge at random. A low shudder rose through the vertebrae of her neck, and then the room fell away in layers. The walls dissolved. Through rifts in the ceiling, the sky rippled like a flag. Then Alma's vision snuffed out, as if the fabric of her house had been yanked downward through a drain, and a prior world rematerialized.

She was in a museum: high ceiling, poor lighting, a smell like old magazines. The South African Museum. Harold was beside her, leaning over a glass-fronted display, excited, his eyes shining— look at him! So young! His khakis were too short, black socks showed above his shoes. How long had she known him? Maybe six months?

She had worn the wrong shoes: tight, too rigid. The weather had been perfect that day and Alma would have preferred to sit in the Company Gardens under the trees with this tall new boyfriend. But the museum was what Harold wanted and she wanted to be with him. Soon they were in a fossil room, a couple dozen skeletons on podiums, some as big as rhinos, some with yardlong fangs, all with massive, eyeless skulls.

"One hundred and eighty million years older than the dinosaurs, hey?" Harold whispered.

Nearby, schoolgirls chewed gum. Alma watched the tallest of

them spit slowly into a porcelain drinking fountain, then suck the spit back into her mouth. A sign labeled the fountain *For Use by White Persons* in careful calligraphy. Alma felt as if her feet were being crushed in vises.

"Just another minute," Harold said.

Seventy-one-year-old Alma watched everything through twenty-four-year-old Alma. She *was* twenty-four-year-old Alma! Her palms were damp and her feet were aching and she was on a date with a living Harold! A young, skinny Harold! He raved about the skeletons; they looked like animals mixed with animals, he said. Reptile heads on dog bodies. Eagle heads on hippo bodies.

"I never get tired of seeing them," young Harold was telling young Alma, a boyish luster in his face. Two hundred and fifty million years ago, he said, these creatures died in the mud, their bones compressed slowly into stone. Now someone had hacked them out; now they were reassembled in the light.

"These were our ancestors, too," Harold whispered. Alma could hardly bear to look at them: They were eyeless, fleshless, murderous; they seemed engineered only to tear one another apart. She wanted to take this tall boy out to the gardens and sit hip-to-hip with him on a bench and take off her shoes. But Harold pulled her along. "Here's the gorgonopsian. A gorgon. Big as a tiger. Two, three hundred kilograms. From the Permian. That's only the second complete skeleton ever found. Not so far from where I grew up, you know." He squeezed Alma's hand.

Alma felt dizzy. The monster had short, powerful legs, fist-size eyeholes, and a mouth full of fangs. "Says they hunted in packs," whispered Harold. "Imagine running into six of those in the bush?" In the memory twenty-four-year-old Alma shuddered.

"We think we're supposed to be here," he continued, "but it's all just dumb luck, isn't it?" He turned to her, about to explain, and as he did shadows rushed in from the edges like ink, flowering over the entire scene, blotting the vaulted ceiling, and the schoolgirl who'd been spitting into the fountain, and finally young Harold himself in his too small khakis. The remote device whined; the cartridge ejected; the memory crumpled in on itself.

Alma blinked and found herself clutching the footboard of her guest bed, out of breath, three miles and five decades away. She unscrewed the headgear. Out the window a thrush sang *chee-chweeeoo*. Pain swung through the roots of Alma's teeth. "My god," she said.

The Accountant

That was three years ago. Now a half dozen doctors in Cape Town are harvesting memories from wealthy people and printing them on cartridges, and occasionally the cartridges are traded on the streets. Old-timers in nursing homes, it's been reported, are using memory machines like drugs, feeding the same ratty cartridges into their remote machines: wedding night, spring afternoon, bike-ride-along-the-cape. The little plastic squares smooth and shiny from the insistence of old fingers.

Pheko drives Alma home from the clinic with fifteen new cartridges in a paperboard box. She does not want to nap. She does not want the triangles of toast Pheko sets on a tray beside her chair. She wants only to sit in the upstairs bedroom, hunched mute and sagging in her armchair with the headgear of the remote device screwed into the ports in her head and occasional strands of drool leaking out of her mouth. Living less in this world than in some synthesized Technicolor past where forgotten moments come trundling up through cables.

Every half hour or so, Pheko wipes her chin and slips one of the new cartridges into the machine. He enters the code and watches her eyes roll back. There are almost a thousand cartridges pinned to the wall in front of her; hundreds more lie in piles across the carpet.

Around four the accountant's BMW pulls up to the house. He

enters without knocking, calls "Pheko" up the stairs. When Pheko comes down the accountant already has his briefcase open on the kitchen table and is writing something in a file folder. He's wearing loafers without socks and a peacock-blue sweater that looks abundantly soft. His pen is silver. He says hello without looking up.

Pheko greets him and puts on the coffeepot and stands away from the countertop, hands behind his back. Trying not to bend his neck in a show of sycophancy. The accountant's pen whispers across the paper. Out the window mauve-colored clouds reef over the Atlantic.

When the coffee is ready Pheko fills a mug and sets it beside the man's briefcase. He continues to stand. The accountant writes for another minute. His breath whistles through his nose. Finally he looks up and says, "Is she upstairs?"

Pheko nods.

"Right. Look. Pheko. I got a call from that . . . physician today!" He gives Pheko a pained look and taps his pen against the table. Tap. Tap. Tap. "Three years. And not a lot of progress. Doc says we merely caught it too late. He says maybe we forestalled some of the decay, but now it's over. The boulder's too big to put brakes on it now, he said."

Upstairs Alma is quiet. Pheko looks at his shoetops. In his mind he sees a boulder crashing through trees. He sees his five-year-old son, Temba, at Miss Amanda's school, ten miles away. What is Temba doing at this instant? Eating, perhaps. Playing soccer. Wearing his eyeglasses.

"Mrs. Konachek requires twenty-four-hour care," the accountant says. "It's long overdue. You had to see this coming, Pheko."

Pheko clears his throat. "I take care of her. I come here seven days a week. Sun tip to sundown. Many times I stay later. I cook, clean, do the shopping. She's no trouble."

The accountant raises his eyebrows. "She's plenty of trouble, Pheko, you know that. And you do a fine job. Fine job. But our time's up. You saw her at the boma last month. Doc says she'll forget how to eat. She'll forget how to smile, how to speak, how to go to the toilet. Eventually she'll probably forget how to swallow. Fucking terrible fate if you ask me. Who deserves that?"

The wind in the palms in the garden makes a sound like rain. There is a creak from upstairs. Pheko fights to keep his hands motionless behind his back. He thinks: If only Mr. Konachek were here. He'd walk in from his study in a dusty canvas shirt, safety goggles pushed up over his forehead, his face looking like it had been boiled. He'd drink straight from the coffeepot and hang his big arm around Pheko's shoulders and say, "You can't fire Pheko! Pheko's been with us for fifteen years! He has a little boy now! Come on now, hey?" Winks all around. Maybe a clap on the accountant's back.

But the study is dark. Harold Konachek has been dead for more than four years. Mrs. Alma is upstairs, hooked into her machine. The accountant slips his pen into a pocket and buckles the latches on his briefcase.

"I could stay in the house, with my son," tries Pheko. "We could sleep here." Even to his own ears, the plea sounds small and hopeless.

The accountant stands and flicks something invisible off the sleeve of his sweater. "The house goes on the market tomorrow," he says. "I'll deliver Mrs. Konachek to Suffolk Home next week. No need to pack things up while she's still here; it'll only frighten her. You can stay on till next Monday."

Then he takes his briefcase and leaves. Pheko listens to his car glide away. Alma starts calling from upstairs. The accountant's coffee mug steams untouched.

Treasure Island

At sunset Pheko poaches a chicken breast and lays a stack of green beans beside it. Out the window flotillas of rainclouds gather over the Atlantic. Alma stares into her plate as if at some incomprehensible puzzle. Pheko says, "Doctor find some good ones this morning, Mrs. Alma?"

"Good ones?" She blinks. The grandfather clock in the living room ticks. The room flickers with a rich, silvery light. Pheko is a pair of eyeballs, a smell like soap.

"Old ones," Alma says.

He helps her into her nightgown and squirts a cylinder of toothpaste onto her toothbrush. Then her pills. Two white. Two gold. Alma clambers into bed muttering questions.

Wind-borne rain starts a gentle patter on the windows. "Okay, Mrs. Alma," Pheko says. He pulls the quilt up to her throat. "I got to go home." His hand is on the lamp. His telephone is vibrating in his pocket.

"Harold," Alma says. "Read to me."

"I'm Pheko, Mrs. Alma."

Alma shakes her head. "Goddammit."

"You've torn your book all apart, Mrs. Alma."

"I have? I have not. Someone else did that."

A breath. A sigh. On the dresser, three lustrous wigs sit atop featureless porcelain heads. "Ten minutes," Pheko says. Alma lies back, bald, glazed, a withered child. Pheko sits in the bedside chair and takes *Treasure Island* off the nightstand. Pages fall out when he opens it.

He reads the first paragraphs from memory. *I remember him as if it were yesterday, as he came plodding to the inn door, his sea chest following behind him in a hand-barrow; a tall, strong, heavy, nut-brown man . . .*

One more page and Alma is asleep.

B478A

Pheko catches the 9:20 Golden Arrow to Khayelitsha. He is a little man in black trousers and a red cable-knit sweater. In the bus seat, his shoes barely touch the floor. Gated compounds and walls of bougainvillea and little bistros lit with colored bulbs slide past. At Hanny Street the bus pauses outside Virgin Active Fitness, where three indoor pools smolder with aquamarine light, a last few swimmers toiling through the lanes, an elephantine waterslide disgorging water in the corner.

The bus fills with township girls: office cleaners, waitresses, laundresses, women who go by one name in Cape Town and another in the townships, housekeepers called Sylvia or Alice about to become mothers called Malili or Momtolo.

Drizzle streaks the windows. Voices murmur in Xhosa, Sotho, Tswana. The gaps between streetlights lengthen; soon Pheko can see only the upflung penumbras of billboard spotlights here and there in the dark. *Drink Opa. Report Cable Thieves. Wear a Condom.*

Khayelitsha is thirty square miles of shanties made of aluminum and cinder blocks and sackcloth and car doors. At the century's turn it was home to half a million people—now it's four times bigger. War refugees, water refugees, HIV refugees. Unemployment might be as high as sixty percent. A thousand haphazard light towers stand over the shacks like limbless trees. Women carry babies or plastic bags or vegetables or ten-gallon water jugs along the roadsides. Men wobble past on bicycles. Dogs wander.

Pheko gets off at Site C and hurries along a line of shanties in the rain. Windchimes tinkle. A goat picks its way through puddles. Torpid men perch on fenders of gutted taxis or upended fruit crates or beneath ragged tarps. Someone a few alleys over lights a firework and it blooms and fades over the rooftops.

B478A is a pale green shed with a sandy floor and a light blue door. Three treadless tires hold the roof in place. Bars seal off the two windows. Temba is inside, still awake, animated, whispering, nearly jumping up and down in place. He wears a T-shirt several sizes too large; his little eyeglasses bounce on his nose.

"Paps," he says, "Paps, you're twenty-one minutes late! Paps, Boginkosi caught three cats today, can you believe it? Paps, can you make paraffin from plastic bags?"

Pheko sits on the bed and waits for his vision to adjust to the dimness. The walls are papered with faded supermarket circulars. Dish soap for R1.99. Juice two for one. Yesterday's laundry hangs from the ceiling. A rust-red stove stands propped on bricks in the corner. Two metal-and-plastic folding chairs complete the furniture.

Outside the rain sifts down through the vapor lights and makes a slow, lulling clatter on the roof. Insects creep in, seeking refuge; gnats and millipedes and big, glistening flies. Twin veins of ants flow across the floor and braid into channels under the stove. Moths flutter at the window screens. Pheko hears the accountant's voice in his ear: *You had to see this coming.* He sees his silver pen flashing in the light of Alma's kitchen.

"Did you eat, Temba?"

"I don't remember."

"You don't remember?"

"No, I ate! I ate! Miss Amanda had samp and beans."

"And did you wear your glasses today?"

"I wore them."

"Temba."

"I *wore* them, Paps. See?" He points with two fingers to his face.

Pheko slips off his shoes. "Okay, little lamb. I believe you. Now choose a hand." He holds out two fists. Temba stands barefoot in his overlarge jersey, blinking his brown eyes behind his glasses.

Eventually he chooses left. Pheko shakes his head and smiles and reveals an empty palm.

"Nothing."

"Next time," says Pheko. Temba coughs, wipes his nose. He seems to swallow back a familiar disappointment.

"Now take off your glasses and give me one of your barnacle attacks," says Pheko, and Temba stows his glasses atop the stove and leaps onto his father, wrapping his legs around Pheko's ribs. They roll across the bed. Temba squeezes his father around the neck and back.

Pheko rears up, makes exaggerated strides around the little shed while the boy clings to him. "Paps," Temba says, talking into his father's chest. "What was in the other hand? What did you have this time?"

"Can't tell you," says Pheko. He pretends to try to shake off the boy's grip. "You got to guess right next time."

Pheko stomps around the house. The boy hangs on. His forehead is a stone against Pheko's sternum. His hair smells like dust, pencil shavings, and smoke. Rain murmurs against the roof.

Tall Man in the Yard
Monday night Roger Tshoni brings the quiet little memory-tapper named Luvo with him up into the posh suburb of Vredehoek and breaks, for the twelfth time, into Alma Konachek's house. Roger has white hair and a white beard and a nose like a large brown gourd. His teeth are orange. He gives off a reek of cheap tobacco. The band of his straw hat has *Ma Horse* printed three times around the circumference.

Each time Roger has picked the lock on the rape gate, Alma has woken up. He thinks it might have to do with an alarm but he has not seen any alarms inside the house. Roger has given up trying to hide anyway. Tonight he hardly bothers to keep quiet. He waits in the doorway, counting to fifteen, then leads the boy inside.

Sometimes she threatens to call the police. Sometimes she calls him Harold. Sometimes something worse: boy. Or kaffir. Or darkie. As in, Get to work, boy. Or: Goddammit, boy. Sometimes she stares right through him with her empty eyes as if he were made of smoke. If he frightens her he simply walks away and smokes a cigarette in the garden and breaks back in through the kitchen door.

Tonight Roger and Luvo stand in the living room a moment, both of them wet with rain, looking out at the city through the glass balcony doors, a few red lights blinking among ten thousand amber ones. They wipe their shoes; they listen as Alma mutters to herself in the bedroom down the hall. The ocean beyond the waterfront is an invisible blackness in the rain.

"Like an owl, this lady," whispers Roger.

The boy named Luvo takes off his wool cap and scratches between the four ports installed in his head and climbs the stairs. Roger crosses into the kitchen, takes three eggs from the refrigerator, and sets them in a pot to boil. Before long Alma comes shambling out from the bedroom, barefoot, bald, no bigger than a girl.

Roger's hands whisper across his shirtfront, find an unlit cigarette tucked into his hatband, and return to his pockets. It's his hands, he has learned, more than anything else, that terrify her. Long hands. Brown hands.

"You're—" hisses Alma.

"Roger. You call me Harold sometimes."

She drags a wrist across her nose. "I have a gun."

"You don't. You couldn't shoot me anyway. Come, sit." Alma looks at him, confounded. But after a moment she sits. The blue ring of flame on her cooktop casts the only light. Down in the city the pinpoints of automobile lights dilate and dissolve as they travel between raindrops on the windowglass.

The house feels close around Roger tonight, with its ratcheting grandfather clock and spotless sofas and the big display cabinet in the study. He wants desperately to light his cigarette.

"You got some new cartridges today from your doctor, didn't you, Alma? I saw that little houseboy of yours drive you down to Green Point."

Alma keeps silent. The eggs rattle in their pot. She looks as if time has stopped inside her: rope-veined, birdlike, expressionless. A single blue artery pulses crosswise above her right ear. The four rubber caps are seated tightly against her scalp.

She frowns slightly. "Who are you?"

Roger doesn't answer. He shuts off the burner and lifts out the three steaming eggs with a slotted spoon.

"I am Alma," Alma says.

"I know it," Roger says.

"I know what you're doing."

"Do you?" He places the eggs on a dishtowel in front of her. A dozen times now over the past month they've done this, sat at her kitchen table in the middle of the night, Roger and Alma, tall black man, elderly white woman, the lights of Trafalgar Park and the railway yards and the waterfront strewn below. A tableau not quite of this world. What does it mean, Roger wonders distantly, that the countless failures of his life have funneled him into this exact circumstance?

"Eat up now," he says.

Alma gives him a dubious look. But moments later she takes an egg and cracks it on the surface of the table and begins to peel it.

The Order of Things

Things don't run in order. There is no A to B to C to D. All the cartridges are the same size, the same redundant beige. Yet some take place decades ago and others take place last year. They vary in intensity, too: Some pull Luvo into them and hold him for fifteen or twenty seconds; others wrench him into Alma's past and keep him there for half an hour. Moments stretch; months vanish during a breath. He comes up gasping, as if he has been submerged underwater; he feels catapulted back into his own mind.

Sometimes, when Luvo comes back into himself, Roger is standing beside him, an unlit cigarette fixed in the vertex of his lips, staring into Alma's cryptic wall of papers and postcards and cartridges as if waiting for some essential explanation to rise up out of it.

Other times the house is noiseless, and there's only the wind sighing through the open window, and the papers fluttering on the wall, and a hundred questions winding through Luvo's head.

Luvo believes he is somewhere around fifteen years old. He has very few memories of his own: none of his parents, no sense of who might have installed four ports in his skull and set him adrift among the ten thousand orphans of Cape Town. No memories of how or why. He knows how to read; he can speak English and Xhosa; he knows Cape Town summers are hot and windy and winters are cool and blue. But he cannot say how he might have learned such things.

His recent history is one of pain: headaches, backaches, bone aches. Twinges fire deep inside his neck; migraines blow in like storms. The holes in his scalp itch and leak a clear fluid; they are not nearly as symmetrical as the ports he has seen on Alma Konachek's head.

Roger says he found Luvo in the Company Gardens, though Luvo has no memory of this. Lately he sleeps in Roger's apartment. A dozen times now, the older man has kicked Luvo awake in the middle of the night; he hustles Luvo into a taxi and they climb from the waterfront into Vredehoek and Roger picks two locks and lets them into the elegant white house on the hill.

Luvo is working from left to right across the upstairs bedroom, from the stairwell toward the window. By now, over a dozen nights, he has eavesdropped on perhaps five hundred of Alma's memories. There are hundreds more cartridges to go, some standing in towers on the carpet, far more pinned to the wall. The numbers engraved into their ends correspond with no chronology Luvo can discover.

But he feels as if he is working gradually, clumsily, toward the center of something. Or, if not toward, then away, as if he is stepping inch by inch away from a painting made of thousands of tiny dots. Any day now the picture will resolve itself; any day now some fundamental truth of Alma's life will come into focus.

Already he knows plenty. He knows that Alma as a girl was obsessed with islands: mutineers, shipwrecks, the last members of tribes, castaways fixing their eyes on empty horizons. He knows that she and Harold worked in the same property office for decades, and that she has owned three silver Mercedes sedans, each one for twelve years. He knows Alma designed this house with an architect from Johannesburg, chose paint colors and doorknobs and faucets from catalogs, hung prints with a level and a tape measure. He knows she and Harold went to concerts, bought clothes at Gardens Centre, traveled to a city called Venice. He knows that the day after Harold retired he bought a used Land Cruiser and a nine-millimeter Crusader handgun and started driving out on fossil-hunting trips into a huge, arid region east of Cape Town called the Great Karoo.

He also knows Alma is not especially kind to her houseman, Pheko. He knows that Pheko has a little son named Temba, and that Alma's husband paid for an eye operation the boy needed when he was born, and that Alma got very angry about this when she found out.

On cartridge 5015 a seven-year-old Alma demands that her nanny hand over a newly opened bottle of Coca-Cola. When the nanny hesitates, grimacing, Alma threatens to have her fired. The nanny hands over the bottle. A moment later Alma's mother appears, furious, dragging Alma into the corner of a bedroom. "Never, ever drink from anything one of the servants has put her lips on first!" Alma's mother shouts. Her face contorts; her little teeth flash. Luvo can feel his stomach twist.

On cartridge 9136 seventy-year-old Alma attends her husband's funeral service. A few dozen white-skinned people stand beneath chandeliers, engulfing roasted apricot halves. Alma's meticulous little houseman, Pheko, picks his way through them wearing a white shirt and black tie. He has a toddler in eyeglasses with him; the child winds himself around the man's left leg like a vine. Pheko presents Alma with a jar of honey, a single blue bow tied around the lid.

"I'm sorry," he says, and he looks it. Alma holds up the honey. The lights of a chandelier are momentarily trapped inside. "You didn't need to come," she says, and sets the jar down on a table.

Luvo can smell the nauseating thickness of perfume in the funeral home, can see the anxiety in Pheko's eyes, can feel Alma's unsteadiness in his own legs. Then he is snatched out of the scene, as if by invisible cords, and he becomes himself again, shivering lightly, a low ache draining through his jaw, sitting on the edge of the bed in Alma's guest room.

Soon it's the hour before dawn. The rain has let up. Roger is standing beside him, exhaling cigarette smoke out the open bedroom window, gazing down into the backyard garden.

"Anything?"

Luvo shakes his head. His brain feels heavy, explosive. The lifespan for a memory-tapper, Luvo has heard, is one or two years. Infections, convulsions, seizures. Some days he can feel blood vessels warping around the columns installed in his brain, can feel the neurons tearing and biting as they try to weave through the obstructions.

Roger looks gray, almost sick. He runs a shaky hand across the front pockets of his shirt.

"Nothing in the desert? Nothing in a Land Cruiser with her husband? You're sure?"

Again Luvo shakes his head. He asks, "Is she sleeping?"

"Finally."

They file downstairs. Memories twist slowly through Luvo's thoughts: Alma as a six-year-old, a dining room, linen tablecloths, the laughter of grown-ups, the soft hush of servants in white shirts bringing in food. Alma sheathing the body of an earthworm over the point of a fishhook. A faintly glowing churchyard, and Alma's mother's bony fingers wrapped around a steering wheel. Bulldozers and rattling buses and gaps in the security fences around the suburbs where she grew up. Buying a backlot brandy called white lightning from Xhosa kids half her age.

By the time he reaches the living room, Luvo is close to fainting. The two armchairs and the lamp and the glass balcony doors and the massive grandfather clock with its scrollwork and brass pendulum and heavy mahogany feet all seem to pulse in the dimness. His headache is advancing, irrepressible; it is an orange flame licking at the edges of everything. Each beat of his heart sends his brain reverberating off the walls of his skull. Any moment his field of vision will ignite. Roger tugs the boy's wool cap over his head for him, loops a long arm under his armpit, and helps Luvo out the door as the first strands of daylight break over Table Mountain.

Tuesday Morning

Pheko arrives just after dawn to the faint odor of tobacco in the house. Three fewer eggs in the refrigerator. He stands a minute, puzzling over it. Nothing else seems disturbed. Alma sleeps a deep sleep.

The estate agent is coming this morning. Pheko vacuums, washes the balcony windows, polishes the countertops until they shine a foot deep. Pure white light, rinsed by last night's rain, pours through the windows. The ocean is a gleaming plate of pewter.

At ten Pheko drinks a cup of coffee in the kitchen. Two tea towels, crisp and white, are folded over the oven handle. The floors are scrubbed, the dishwasher empty, the grandfather clock wound. Everything in its place.

It occurs to Pheko that he could steal things. He could take the kitchen television and some of Harold's books and Alma's music player. Jewelry. Coats. The matching pea-green bicycles in the garage—how many times has Alma ridden hers? Once? Who even

knows those bicycles are here? Pheko could call a taxi right now
and load it with suitcases and take them into Khayelitsha and before nightfall a hundred things Alma didn't know she had could
be turned into cash.

Who would know? Not the accountant. Not Alma. Only
Pheko. Only God.

Alma wakes at ten thirty, groggy, muddled. He dresses her, es-
corts her to the breakfast table. She sits in her chair, tea untouched,
hands quivering, strands of her wig stuck in her eyelashes. "I used
to come here," Alma mutters. "Before."

"You don't want your tea, Mrs. Alma?"

Alma gives him a bewildered look.

Upstairs the memory wall ruffles in the wind. The estate
agent's sedan glides into the driveway at 11:00, precisely on time.

The South African Museum

Luvo wakes in the afternoon in Roger's one-room apartment in the
Cape Flats. Beside him is a table and two chairs. Pans in a cupboard, a paraffin stove, a row of books on a shelf. Not much more
than a prison cell. Roger's one window reveals the bottom corner
of a billboard, perhaps twenty feet away. On the billboard a white
woman in a whiter bikini reclines on a beach holding a bottle of
Crown Beer. From where he lies Luvo can see the lower half of her
legs, her ankles crossed, the pale bottoms of her bare feet flecked
with sand.

Through the walls and ceiling ride the racket of the Cape
Flats, laughter, babies, squabbles, sex, the rumbles of engines and
fans. Six or seven times, in the month or so Luvo can remember
sleeping here, he has heard the drumbeat of gunfire. Women with
glossy nails and chokers around their throats drift through the
open hallways; every evening someone comes past the door whispering, "Mandrax, Mandrax."

Roger is out. Probably following around Alma. Luvo sits at the

table and eats a stack of saltines and reads one of Roger's books. It
is an adventure novel about men in the Arctic. The adventurers are
out of food and hunting seals and the ice is thin and it seems any
moment someone will break through and fall into freezing water.

After an hour or so Roger is still not back. Luvo takes two
coins from a drawer and scrubs his face and hands in the sink and
runs a wet paper towel over the toe of each sneaker. He fixes his
watchcap over the ports in his head and rides a bus to the Company Gardens.

He enters the South African Museum around 4 p.m. and steps
past the distrustful looks of two warders and into the paleontology
gallery. Hundreds of fossils are locked in glass cases, specimens
from all over southern Africa: shells and worms and nautiluses and
seed ferns and trilobites, and minerals, too; yellow-green crystals
and gleaming clusters of quartz; mosquitoes in drops of amber;
scheelite, wulfenite.

In the reflections in the glass it is as if Luvo can see the papers and cartridges pinned to Alma's wall floating in the dimness
above the stones. Bones, teeth, footprints, fishes, the warped ribs
of ancient reptiles—in Alma's memories Luvo has watched Harold
return from the Karoo boiling with ardor, enthusing about dol-
erite and siltstone, bonebeds and trackways. The big man would
chisel away at rocks in the garage, show Alma whole amphibians,
a footlong dragonfly embedded in limestone, little worm tracks in
hardened mud. He'd come into the kitchen, flushed, animated,
smelling of dust and heat and rocks, safety goggles pushed up over
his forehead, waving a walking stick he'd picked up somewhere,
nearly as tall as he was, made of ebony, wrapped with red beads on
the handle and with an elephant carved on the top.

The whole thing infuriated Alma: the safari-tourist's walking
stick, the goggles, Harold's boyish avidity. Forty-five years of marriage, Alma would announce, and now he had decided to become
a lunatic rockhound? What about their friends, what about going

for walks together, what about joining the Mediterranean Cruise Club? Retirees, Alma would yell, were supposed to move *toward* comforts, not away from them.

Here is what Luvo knows: Inside Roger's frayed, beaten wallet is a four-year-old newspaper obituary. The headline reads *Real Estate Ace Turned Dinosaur Hunter.* Below it is a grainy black-and-white of Harold Konachek.

Luvo has asked to see the obituary enough times that he has memorized it. A sixty-eight-year-old Cape Town retiree, driving with his wife on backveld roads in the Karoo, had stopped to look for fossils at a roadcut when he had a fatal heart attack. According to the man's wife, just before he died he had made a significant find, a rare Permian fossil. Extensive searches in the area turned up nothing.

Roger, with his straw hat and white beard and tombstone teeth, has told Luvo he went out to the desert with dozens of other fossil hunters, even with a group from the university. He says several paleontologists went to Alma's house and asked her what she'd seen. "She said she couldn't remember. Said the Karoo was huge and all the hills looked the same."

Interest slackened. People assumed the fossil was unrecoverable. Then, several years later, Roger saw Alma Konachek leaving a memory clinic in Green Point with her houseboy. And he started following them around town.

"*Gorgonops longifrons,*" Roger told Luvo a month ago, on the first night he brought the boy to Alma's house. Luvo has engraved the name into his memory.

"A big, nasty predator from the Permian. If it's a complete skeleton, it's worth forty or fifty million rand. World's gone crazy for this stuff. Movie stars, financiers. Last year a triceratops skull sold to some Chinaman at an auction for thirty-four million American dollars."

Luvo looks up from the display case. Footfalls echo through

the gallery. Knots of tourists mill here and there. The gorgon skeleton the museum has on a granite pedestal is the same one Harold showed Alma fifty years before. Its head is flat-sided; its jaw brims with teeth. Its claws look capable of great violence.

The plaque below the gorgon reads *Great Karoo, Upper Permian, 260 million years ago.* Luvo stands in front of the skeleton a long time. He hears Harold's voice, whispering to Alma through the dark hallways of her memory: *These were our ancestors, too.*

Luvo thinks: We are all intermediaries. He thinks: So this is what Roger is after. This incomprehensibly old thing.

Wednesday Night, Thursday Night

When Luvo wakes, Roger is standing over him. It's after midnight and he is back inside Roger's apartment. The shock of coming into his own, tampered head is searing. Roger squats on his haunches, inhales from a cigarette, and glances at his watch with a displeased expression.

"You went out."

"I went to the museum. I fell asleep."

"Am I going to have to start locking you in?"

"Locking me in?"

Roger sits on the chair above Luvo, sets his hat on table, and looks at his half-smoked cigarette with a displeased expression.

"Someone put a realty sign in front of her house today."

Luvo presses his fingertips into his temples.

"They're selling the old lady's house."

"Why?"

"Why? 'Cause she's lost her mind."

Spotlights shine on the tanned legs of the Crown Beer woman. Below her leaves blot and unblot the cadmium-colored lights of the Cape Flats. Dim figures move now and then through the trees. The neighborhood seethes. The tip of Roger's cigarette flares and fades.

"So we're done? We're done going over there?"

Roger looks at him. "Done? No. Not yet. We've got to hurry up." Again he glances at his wristwatch.

An hour later they're back inside Alma Konachek's house. Luvo sits on the bed in Alma's upstairs bedroom and studies the wall in front of him and tries to concentrate. In the center, a young man walks out of the sea, trousers rolled to his knees. Around the man orbit lines from books, postcards, photos, misspelled names, grocery lists underscored with a dozen hesitant pencil strokes. Trips. Company parties. *Treasure Island*.

Each cartridge on Alma's wall becomes a little brazier, burning in the darkness. Luvo wanders between them, gradually exploring the labyrinth of her history. Maybe, he thinks, at the beginning, before the disease had done its worst, the wall offered Alma a measure of control over what was happening to her. Maybe she could hang a cartridge on a nail and find it a day or two later and feel her brain successfully recall the same memory again—a new pathway forged through the dusklight.

When it worked, it must have been like descending into a pitch-black cellar for a jar of preserves, and finding the jar waiting there, cool and heavy, so she could bring it up the bowed and dusty stairs into the light of the kitchen. For a while it must have worked for Alma, anyway; it must have helped her believe she could fend off her inevitable erasure.

It has not worked as well for Roger and Luvo. Luvo does not know how to turn the wall to his ends; it will only show him Alma's life as it wishes. The cartridges veer toward and away from his goal without ever quite reaching it; he founders inside a past and a mind over which he has no control.

On cartridge 6786 Harold tells Alma he is reclaiming something vital, finally trying to learn about the places he'd grown up, grappling with his own infinitesimal place in time. He was learning to see, he said, what once was: storms, monsters, fifty million years of Permian protomammals. Here he was, sixty-some years old, still limber enough to wander around in the richest fossil beds outside of Antarctica. To walk among the stones, to use his eyes and fingers, to find the impressions of animals that had lived such an incomprehensibly long time ago! It was enough, he told Alma, to make him want to kneel down.

"Kneel down?" Alma rages. "Kneel *down*? To who? To what?"

"Please," Harold asks Alma on cartridge 1204. "I'm still the same man I've always been. Let me have this."

"You're out of your tree," Alma tells him.

On cartridge after cartridge Luvo feels himself drawn to Harold: the man's wide, red face, a soft curiosity glowing in his eyes. Even his silly ebony walking stick and big pieces of rocks in the garage are endearing. On the cartridges in which Harold appears, Luvo can feel himself beneath Alma, around her, and he wants to linger where she wants to leave; he wants to learn from Harold, see what the man is dragging out of the back of his Land Cruiser and scraping at with dental tools in the study. He wants to go out to the Karoo with him to prowl riverbeds and mountain passes and roadcuts—and is disappointed when he cannot.

And all those books in that white man's study! As many books as Luvo can remember seeing in his life. Luvo is even beginning to learn the names of the fossils in Harold's display cabinet downstairs: sea snail, tusk shell, ammonite. He wants to spread them across the desk when he and Roger arrive; he wants to run his fingers over them.

On cartridge 6567, Alma weeps. Harold is off somewhere, hunting fossils probably, and it is a long, gray evening in the house with no concerts, no invitations, nobody ringing on the telephone, and Alma eats roasted potatoes alone at the table with a detective show mumbling on the kitchen television. The faces on the screen blur and stray, and the city lights out the balcony windows look to Luvo like the portholes of a distant cruiseliner, golden and warm and far away. Alma thinks of her girlhood, how she used to stare at photographs of islands. She thinks of Billy Bones, Long John Silver, a castaway on a desert beach.

The device whines; the cartridge ejects. Luvo closes his eyes. The plates of his skull throb; he can feel the threads of the helmet shifting against the tissues of his brain.

From downstairs comes Roger's low voice, talking to Alma.

Friday Morning

An infection creeps through Site C, waylaying children shanty by shanty. One hour radio commentators say it's passed through saliva; the next they say it's commuted through the air. No, township dogs carry it; no, it's the drinking water; no, it's a conspiracy of Western pharmaceutical companies. It could be meningitis, another flu pandemic, some new child-plague. No one seems to know anything. There is talk of public antibiotic dispensaries. There is talk of quarantine.

Friday morning Pheko wakes at four thirty as always and takes the enameled washbasin to the spigot six sheds away. He lays out his razor and soap and washcloth on a towel and squats on his heels, shaving alone and without a mirror in the cool darkness. The sodium lights are off, and a few stars show here and there between clouds. Two house crows watch him in silence from a neighbor's eave.

When he's done he scrubs his arms and face and empties the washbasin into the street. At five Pheko carries Temba down the lane to Miss Amanda's and knocks lightly before entering. Amanda pushes herself up on her elbows from the bed and gives him a groggy smile. He sets still-sleeping Temba on her couch and the boy's eyeglasses on the table beside him.

On the walk to the Site C station Pheko sees a line of schoolgirls in navy-and-white uniforms, queuing to climb onto a white bus. Each wears a paper mask over her nose and mouth. He climbs the ramp and waits. Down in the grassy field below them forgotten concrete culverts lie here and there like fallen pillars from some foregone civilization, spray-painted with signs: *Exacta* and *Fuck* and *Blind 43. Rich Get Richer. Jamakota dies please help.*

Trains shuttle to and fro like rattling beasts. Pheko thinks, Three more days.

Cartridge 4510

Alma seems more tired than ever. Pheko helps her climb out of bed at 11:30. A clear liquid seeps from her left eye. She stares into nothingness.

This morning she lets Pheko dress her but will not eat. Twice an agent comes to show the house and Pheko has to shuttle Alma out to the yard and sit with her in the lounge chairs, holding her hand, while a young couple tools through the rooms and admires the views and leaves tracks across the carpets.

Around two Pheko sighs, gives up. He sits Alma on the upstairs bed and screws her into the remote device and lets her watch cartridge 4510, the one he keeps in the drawer beside the dishwasher so he can find it when he needs it. When she needs it.

Alma's neck sags; her knees drift apart. Pheko goes downstairs to eat a slice of bread. Wind begins thrashing through the palms in the garden. "Southeaster coming," says the kitchen television. Then ads flicker past. A tall white woman runs through an airport. A yardlong sandwich scrolls across the screen. Pheko closes his eyes and imagines the wind reaching Khayelitsha, boxes cartwheeling past spaza shops, plastic bags slithering across roads, slapping into fences. People at the station will be pulling their collars over their mouths against the dust.

After a few more minutes, he can hear Alma calling. He walks upstairs, sits her back down, and pushes in the same cartridge again.

Chefe Carpenter

Friday Roger shepherds Luvo up a sidewalk in front of a different house than Alma Konachek's, on the opposite side of the city. The house is wrapped by a twelve-foot stucco wall with broken bottles embedded in the top. Nine or ten eucalyptus trees stand waving above it.

Roger carries a plastic sack in one hand with something heavy inside. At a gate he looks up at a security camera in a tinted bubble and holds up the sack. After perhaps ten minutes a woman shows them through without a word. Two perfumed collies trot behind her.

The house is small and walled with glass. The woman seats them in an open room with a large fireplace. Above the fireplace is a fossil of what looks like a smashed, winged crocodile spiraling out of a piece of polished slate. All around the room, Luvo realizes, are dozens more fossils, hung from pillars, on pedestals, arrayed in a backlit case. Some of them are massive. He can see a coiled shell as big as a manhole cover, and a cross-section of petrified wood mounted on a door, and what looks like an elephant tusk cradled in golden braces.

A moment later a man comes in and leans over the collies and scratches them behind the ears. Roger and Luvo stand. The man is barefoot and wears slacks rolled up to the ankles and a soft-looking shirt that is unbuttoned. A great upfold of fat is piled up against the back of his skull and a single gold bracelet is looped around his right wrist. His fingernails gleam as if polished. He looks up from the dogs and sits in a leather armchair and yawns hugely.

"Hello," he says, and nods at them both.

"This is Chefe Carpenter," Roger says, though it's not clear if he is saying this to Luvo or not. Nobody shakes hands. Roger and Luvo sit.

"Your son?"

Roger shakes his head. The woman reappears with a black mug

and Chefe takes it and does not offer Luvo or Roger anything. Chefe drinks the contents of the mug in three swallows, then sets the mug down and grimaces and cracks some bones in his back and rolls his neck and finally says, "You have something?"

To Luvo's surprise Roger produces from the plastic sack a fossil Luvo recognizes. Roger has taken it from Harold's cabinet. This one contains the impressions of a seed fern, three fronds pressed almost parallel into it, nearly white against the darker stone. Looking at it in Roger's hands makes Luvo want to run his hands across the leaves.

Chefe Carpenter looks at it for perhaps four or five seconds but does not get up from his armchair or reach out to take it.

"I can give you five hundred rand."

Roger lets out a forced, unctuous laugh.

"Come now," Chefe says. "In the sunroom right now I have a hundred of these. What can I sell these for? What else do you have?"

"Nothing right now."

"But where is this big one you're working on?"

"It's coming."

Chefe reaches down for his mug and peers inside and sets it back on the floor. "You owe money, don't you? Men are coming to collect money from you, aren't they?" He glances over with a soft look at Luvo, then looks back. "You have a long way to go to repay your debt, don't you?"

Roger says, "I'm working on the big one."

"Five hundred rand," Chefe says.

Roger gives a defeated nod. "Now," Chefe says, and stands up, and his big, shiny face brightens, as if a cloud has moved away from the sun. "Shall I show the boy the collection?"

Upstairs

There are blanks on Alma's wall, Luvo is learning, omissions and gaps. Even if he reorganized her whole project, arranged her life

in a chronological line, first memory to last, Alma's history running in a little beige file down the stairs and around the living
room, what would he learn? There'd still be breaks in time, failure
in his understanding, months beyond his reach. Who is to say a
cartridge even exists that contains the moments before Harold's
death?

Friday night he decides to abandon his left-to-right method.
Whatever order once existed in the arrangement of these cartridges has since been shuffled out of it. It's a museum arranged
by a madwoman. He starts watching any cartridge that for some
unnameable reason stands out to him from the disarray pinned
to the wall. On one cartridge nine- or ten-year-old Alma lies back
in a bed full of pillows while her father reads her a chapter from
Treasure Island; on another a doctor tells a much older Alma that
she probably will not be able to have children. On a third Alma has
written *Harold and Pheko*. Luvo runs it through the remote device
twice. In the memory Alma asks Pheko to move several crates of
books into Harold's study and arrange them alphabetically on his
shelves. "By author," she says.

Pheko is very young; he must be newly hired. He looks as if
he is barely older than Luvo is now. He wears an ironed white
shirt and his eyes seem to fill with dread as he concentrates on her
instructions.

"Yes, madam," he says several times. Alma disappears. When
she returns, what might be an hour later, Harold in tow, Pheko
has put practically every book on the shelves in Harold's office
upside-down. Alma walks very close to the shelves. She tilts a couple of titles toward her, then sets them back down. "Well, these
aren't in any kind of order at all," she says.

Confusion ripples through Pheko's face. Harold laughs.

Alma looks back to the bookshelves. "The boy can't read," she
says.

Luvo cannot turn Alma's head to look at Pheko; Pheko is a

ghost, a smudge outside her field of vision. But he can hear Harold behind her, his voice still smiling. He says, "Not to worry, Pheko. Everything can be learned. You'll do fine here."

The memory dims; Luvo unscrews the headgear and hangs the little beige cartridge back on the nail from which he plucked it. Out in the garden the palms clatter in the wind. Soon the house will be sold, Luvo thinks, and the cartridges will be returned to the doctor's office, or sent along with Alma to whatever place they're consigning her to, and this strange assortment of papers will be folded into a trash bag. The books and appliances and furniture will be sold off. Pheko will be sent home to his son.

Luvo shivers. He thinks of Harold's fossils downstairs, waiting in their cabinet. He can hear Chefe Carpenter's voice as he showed Luvo several smooth, heavy teeth that he said belonged to a mosasaur, hacked out of a chalk pit in Holland. "Science," Chefe had said, "is always concerned with context. But what about beauty? What about love? What about feeling a deep humility at our place in time? Where's the room for that?"

"You find what you're looking for," Chefe had said to them before they left, "you know where to bring it."

Hope, belief. Failure or success. As soon as they stepped outside Chefe's gate, Roger had lit a cigarette and started taking shaky, hungry pulls.

Luvo stands in Alma's upstairs bedroom in the middle of the night and hears Harold Konachek whispering as if from the grave: *We all swirl slowly down into the muck. We all go back to the mud. Until we rise again in ribbons of light.*

This wind, Luvo realizes, right now careering around Alma's garden, has come to Cape Town every November that he can remember, and every November Alma can remember, and it will come next November, too, and the next, and on and on, for centuries to come, until everyone they have ever known and everyone they ever will know is gone.

Downstairs

Three eggs steam on a towel in front of Alma. She cracks one
open. Out the window the sky and ocean are very dark. The tall
man with the huge hands is waving his fingers around in her
kitchen. "Running out of time," he says. "You and me together,
old lady."

He begins stalking the kitchen, pacing back and forth. The
balcony rails moan in the wind, or else it's the wind moaning, or
the wind and railing together, her ears unable to unbraid the two.
The tall man raises a hand to the cigarette in his hatband and puts
it between his lips, unlit. "You probably think you're a hero," he
says. "Up there waving your sword against a big old army."

Roger waves an imaginary sword, slashing it through the air.
Alma tries to ignore him, tries to focus on the warm egg in her
fingers. She wishes she had some salt but does not see a shaker
anywhere.

"But you losing. You losing bad. You losing and you going
to end up just like all them other old, rich junkies—you going
to blitz out, zone out, drift away, feed yourself a steady stream of
those memories. Until there's nothing left of you at all. Aren't you?
You're just a tube now, hey, Alma? Just a bleeding tube. Put something in the top and it drops right out the bottom."

In Alma's hand is an egg she has evidently just peeled. She
eats it slowly. In the face of the man in front of her something
suppressed is flickering and showing itself, an anger, a lifelong con-
tempt. Without turning her head she has the sense that out there
in the darkness beyond her kitchen windows something terrible is
advancing toward her.

"And what about the houseboy?" the tall man is saying. She
wishes he would stop talking. "From one angle it probably has the
look of sacrifice. Oh, a good boy, fit, speaks English, disease-free,
got himself a little piccanin, rides ten miles each way on the bus
from the townships to the suburbs to make tea, water the garden,

comb out her wigs. Fill the refrigerator. Clip her fingernails. Fold her old-lady underthings. Apartheid's over and he's doing women's work. A saint. A servant. Am I right?"

Two more eggs sit in front of Alma. Her heart is opening and closing very quickly in her chest. The tall black man is wearing his hat indoors. A sentence from *Treasure Island* comes back to her, as if from nowhere: *Their eyes burned in their heads; their feet grew speedier and lighter; their whole soul was bound up in that fortune, that whole lifetime of extravagance and pleasure, that lay waiting there for each of them.*

Roger is tapping his temple with one finger. His eyes are whirlpools into which she must not look. I am not here, Alma thinks.

"But from another angle what does it look like?" the man is saying. "Houseboy lets himself in the gate, through the door, watches you dodder about, moves beyond the edges of your memory. Lined up for his inheritance, surely. Fingers in the till. He eats the sausages, too, doesn't he? Probably pays the bills. He knows the kind of money you're spending with that doctor."

"Stop talking," says Alma. She thinks, I am not here. I am not anywhere.

"I did it to the boy," he says. "I can tell you, you don't even know what I'm saying. I found him in the Company Gardens and who was he? Just an orphan. I paid for the operation. I fed him, I took care of him. I brought him back. I keep him healthy, don't I? I let him wander around."

The headlights of a passing car swing through the yard, drain through the trees. Alma's fear rises into her throat. The headlights fade. The wind flies over the house.

"Stop talking right now," she says.

"You eat now," says Roger. "You eat and I'll stop talking and the boy upstairs will find what I'm looking for and then you can go die in peace."

She blinks. For a moment the man in her kitchen has transformed into a demon: imperious, towering; he peers down at her from beneath a limestone brow. He is waving his terrible hands.

"We all have a gorgon in here," the demon says. He points to his chest.

"I know who you are." She says this quietly and with great intensity. "I see you for what you are."

"I bet you do," says Roger.

Nightmare

In a nightmare Alma finds herself in the fossil exhibit she went to with Harold fifty years before. All the gallery's overhead lights have been switched off. The only illumination comes from sweeping, powder-blue beams that slice through the room, catching each skeleton in turn and leaving it again in darkness, as if strange beacons are revolving in the lawns outside the high windows.

The gorgon Harold was so excited about is no longer there. The iron brace that supported the skeleton remains, and a silhouette of dust marks where it stood. But the gorgon is gone.

Alma's heart quickens; her breath catches. Her hands are at her sides, but in the dream she can feel herself clawing at her own throat.

A column of blue light, swinging through the arcade of museum windows, shows cobwebs, shows the skeletal monsters in their various postures, shows the empty pedestal, shows Alma. Shadows rear up and are sucked back into darkness. The roof above her makes oceanic groans. The purpose of her errand veers past her, there, then gone.

Then she sees. In the window looms a demon. Nostrils, a jaw, a face chalked white with dry skin, and two yellow canine incisors, each as long as her forearms, extend from a scaly pink gum. It exhales through its wet, reptilian nose; twin ovals of vapor cloud the window. Saliva hangs from its lower jaw in pendulous bobs. The light veers past; the beast ducks lower. Its pleated throat convulses; it peers at her with one eye, spiderwebbed with filigrees of blood vessels, whole tiny river systems trundling blood deeper and deeper into the yellow of its eyeball, unknowable, terrible, wet—it is a demon dredged up from some black corner of memory; even from across the gallery, she can see into the crypt of its eye, huge and unblinking, and she can smell it, too; the creature smells like a swamp, riparian, of mire and ooze, and a thought, a scrap, a line from a book, rises to her from some abscess of memory and she wakes with a sentence on her lips: *They are coming. They are coming and they don't mean well.*

Saturday

The southeaster throws a thick sheet of fog over Table Mountain. In Vredehoek everything looks hazy and tenuous. Cars loom up out of the white and disappear again. Alma sleeps till noon. When she wakes she comes tottering out with her wig in proper alignment, her eyes bright. "Good morning," she says.

Pheko is startled. "Good morning, Mrs. Alma."

He serves her oatmeal, raisins, and tea. "Pheko," she says, enunciating his name as if tasting it. "You're Pheko." She says his name several more times.

"Would you like to sit indoors today, Mrs. Alma? It's awfully damp out there."

"Yes, I'll stay inside. Thank you."

They sit in the kitchen. Alma shovels big spoonfuls of oatmeal into her mouth. The television burbles out news about rising tensions, farm attacks, violence outside a health clinic.

"Now, my husband," Alma says suddenly, not quite speaking to Pheko but to the kitchen at large, "his passion was always rocks. Rocks and the dead things in them. Always off to do, as he put it, some grave-robbing. Mine was less obvious. I did care about houses. I was an estate agent before many women were estate agents."

Pheko sets a hand on top of his head. Except for a mild unsteadiness in her voice, Alma sounds much as she did a decade ago. The television drones. Fog presses against the balcony windows.

"There were times when I was happy and times when I was not," continues Alma. "Like anyone. To say a person is a happy person or an unhappy person is ridiculous. We are a thousand different kinds of people every hour." She looks at Pheko then, though not quite directly at him. As if a guest floats behind him and to his left. Fog seeps through the garden. The trees disappear. The lounge chairs disappear. "Don't you think?"

Pheko closes his eyes, opens them.

"Are you happy?"

"Me, Mrs. Alma?"

"You should have a family."

"I do have a family. Remember? I have a son. He is five years old now."

"Five years old," says Alma.

"His name is Temba."

"I see." She drives her spoon into what's left of the oatmeal and lets go and watches its handle slowly fall down to touch the rim of the bowl. "Come with me."

Pheko follows her up the stairs into the guest bedroom. For a full minute she stands beside him, both of them facing her wall of papers and cartridges. She crouches, moving here and there along the wall. Her lips move silently. On the wall in front of Pheko is a postcard of a little island ringed by a turquoise sea. Two years ago Alma worked every day on this wall, posting things, concentrating. How many meals did Pheko bring her up in this room?

She reaches for the photo of Harold and fingers its corner a moment. "Sometimes," she says, "I have trouble remembering things."

Behind her, out the window, the fog cycles and cycles. The sky is invisible. The neighbor's rooftops are gone. The garden is gone. Everything is white. "I know, Mrs. Alma," Pheko says.

Vapor Lights

It's 9:30 p.m. and the wind is shrieking against the ten thousand haphazard houses in Site C. As soon as he walks in the door, Pheko can tell by the way Miss Amanda has her lips pinched under her teeth that Temba has become ill. A foot away, he can feel the heat radiating off the boy's body. "Little lamb," whispers Pheko.

The queue at the twenty-four-hour clinic is already long, longer than Pheko has ever seen it. Mothers and children sit on upturned onion crates or sleep on blankets. Behind them a bus-length mural depicts Jesus stretching supernaturally long arms across a wall. Dried leaves and plastic bags scuttle down the road.

Two separate times over the next few hours Pheko has to get out of line because Temba has soiled his clothes. He cleans his son, wraps him in a towel, and returns to wait outside the clinic. The vapor lights on their towers above Site C rock back and forth like some aggregation of distant moons. Scraps of paper and skeins of dust fly through the air beneath them.

By 2 a.m. Pheko and Temba are still nowhere near the front of the line. Every hour or so a bleary nurse walks up and down the queue and says, in Xhosa, how grateful she is for everybody's patience. The clinic, she says, is waiting for antibiotics.

Pheko can feel Temba's sweat soaking through the towel around him. The boy's cheeks are the color of dishwater. "Temba," Pheko whispers. Once the boy raises his face weakly and Pheko can see the wobbling pinpoints of the light towers reflected in the sheen of his eyes.

That Same Hour

Roger and Luvo enter Alma Konachek's house in the earliest hours of Sunday morning. Alma doesn't wake. Her breathing sounds steadily from the bedroom. Roger wonders if perhaps the house-boy has given her a sedative.

Luvo tromps upstairs. Roger opens the refrigerator and closes it;

he contemplates stepping out into the garden to smoke a cigarette. He feels, very keenly tonight, that he is almost out of time. Down below the balcony, somewhere past the fog, Cape Town sleeps.

Absently, for no reason, Roger opens the drawer beside the dishwasher. He has stood in this kitchen on seventeen different nights but has never before opened this drawer. Inside Roger can see butane lighters, coins, a box of staples. And a single beige polymer cartridge, identical to the hundreds upstairs.

Roger picks up the cartridge and holds it to the window. Number 4510.

"Kid," Roger calls, raising his voice to the ceiling. "Kid." Luvo does not reply. Roger walks upstairs and waits. The boy is hooked into the machine. His torso seems to vibrate lightly. After another minute the machine sighs, and Luvo's eyes flit open. The boy sits back and grinds his palms into his eyesockets. Roger holds up the new cartridge.

"Look at this." There is a shakiness in Roger's voice that surprises them both.

Luvo reaches and takes it. "Have I seen this before?"

Cartridge 4510

Alma is in a movie theater with Harold. They are perhaps thirty years old. The movie is about scuba divers. Onscreen, white birds with forked tails soar above a beach. Light touches the tops of breaking waves. Alma and Harold sit side by side, Alma in a bright green dress, green shoes, green plastic earrings, Harold in an expensive brown shirt. The side of Harold's knee presses against the side of Alma's. Luvo can feel a dim electricity traveling between them. Now the camera slips underwater. Rainbows of fish flit across the screen. Reefs scroll past. Alma's heart does its steady work.

The memory jerks forward; Alma and Harold are in a cab, Alma's camera bag on the bench seat between them. They travel through a place that looks to Luvo like Camps Bay. Everything out the windows is vague; it is as if, for Alma, there is nothing to look at all. There is only feeling, only anticipation, only her young husband beside her.

In another breath they are climbing the steps of a regal, cream-colored hotel, backed by moonlit cliffs. Gulls soar everywhere. A little gold-lettered sign reads *Twelve Apostles Hotel*. Inside the lobby a willowy woman in a white shirt and white pants with a gold belt buckle gives them a key on a brass chain; they pad down a series of hallways.

In the hotel room Alma lets out a succession of bright, genuine laughs. She gulps wine. Everything is pristine; two spotless windows, a wide white bed, richly ruffled lampshades. Harold switches on a music player and takes off his shoes and dances clumsily in his socks. Out the windows, range after range of spotlit waves fold over onto a beach.

After what might be a few minutes Harold leaps the balcony railing and takes off his shirt and socks. "Come with me," he calls, and Alma takes her camera bag and follows him down onto the beach. Alma laughs as Harold charges into the wave-break. He splashes around a bit, grinning hugely. "Freezing!" he shouts. As he walks out of the water, Alma raises her camera, and takes a photograph.

If they say anything more to one another, it is not remembered, not recorded on the cartridge. In the memory Harold makes love to Alma twice. Luvo feels he should leave, should yank out the cartridge, send himself back into Alma's house in Vredehoek, but the room is so clean, the sheets are so cool beneath Alma's back. Everything is soft; everything seems to vibrate with possibility. Alma tastes the sea on Harold's skin. She feels his big-knuckled hands hold on to her ribs, his fingertips touch the knobs of her spine.

Near the end of the memory Alma closes her eyes and seems to slip underwater, as if back into the film at the moviehouse, watching a huge black urchin wave its spines, noticing how the water is not silent but full of soft clicks, and soon the pastels of coral are scrolling past her vision, and little slashes of needlefish are dodging her fingers, and Harold's body seems not to be on top of hers at all, but drifting instead beside her; they are swimming together, floating slowly away from the reef toward a place where the sea floor falls away and the bottom is too far away to see, and there is only light filtering into deep water, bottomless water, and Alma's blood seems to swell out to the very edges of her skin.

Sunday, 4 a.m.

Alma sits up in bed. From the ceiling comes the unmistakable sounds of footfalls. On her nightstand there is a glass of water, its bottom daubed with miniature bubbles. Beside it is a hardcover book. Though its jacket is missing and half the binding is torn away, the title appears sparkling and whole in her mind. *Treasure Island.* Of course.

From the ceiling comes another creak. Someone is in my house, Alma thinks, and then some still-functional junction in her brain coughs up an image of a man. His teeth are orange. His nose looks like a small brown gourd. His trousers are khaki and stained and a tear in the left shoulder of his shirt shows his darker skin beneath. A faded jaguar winds up the underside of his wrist.

Alma jerks herself onto her feet. A demon, she thinks, a burglar, a tall man in the yard.

She hurries across the kitchen into the study and opens the heavy, two-handled drawer at the bottom of Harold's fossil cabinet. A drawer she has not opened in years. Toward the bottom, beneath a stack of paleontology magazines, is a cigar box upholstered with pale orange linen. Even before she finds it, she is certain it is there. Indeed, her mind feels particularly clear. Oiled. Operable. You are Alma, she thinks. I am Alma. She retrieves the box, sets it on the desk that once was Harold's and opens it. Inside is a nine-millimeter handgun.

She stares at it a moment before picking it up. Blunt and color-less and new-looking. Harold used to carry it in his glove compart-ment. She does not know how to tell if it is loaded.

Alma carries the gun in her left hand through the kitchen to the living room and sits in the silver armchair that offers her a view up the stairwell. She does not turn on any lights. Her heart flutters in her chest like a moth.

From upstairs winds a thin strand of cigarette smoke. The pendulum in the grandfather clock swings back and forth. Out the windows there is only a dim whiteness: fog. Everything seems irradiated with a meaning she is only now recognizing. My house, she thinks. I love my house.

If Alma keeps her eyes straight ahead, and does not look to her right or left, it is possible to believe Harold is about to settle into the matching chair beside her, the lamp and table between them. She can just sense the weight of his body shifting over there, can smell something like rock powder in his clothes, can perceive the scarcely perceptible gravitational tug one body exerts upon an-other. She has so much to say to him.

She sits. She waits. She tries to remember.

Leaving the Queue

At 4:30 a.m. Pheko and Temba are still twenty or so people from the clinic entrance. Temba is sleeping steadily now, his arms and legs limp, his big eyelids sealing him off from the world. The wind has settled down. Clouds of gnats materialize above the shacks. Pheko squats against the wall with his son in his lap. The boy looks emptied out, his cheeks depressed, the tendons in his throat showing.

Above them the painted Jesus stretches his implausibly long arms. The light towers have been switched off and a dull orange glow reflects off the undersides of the clouds.

My last day of work, Pheko thinks. Today the accountant will pay me. A second thought succeeds that one: Mrs. Alma has antibiotics. He is surprised he did not think of this sooner. She has piles of them. How many times has Pheko refreshed the little army of orange pill bottles standing in her bathroom cupboard?

Bats cut silent loops above the shanty rooftops. A little girl beside them unleashes a chain of coughs. Pheko can feel the dust on his face, can taste the earth in his molars. After another minute he lifts his sleeping son and abandons their place in the queue and carries the boy down through the noiseless streets to the bus station.

Harold

"Maybe it's something the houseboy didn't want her to see?" murmurs Roger. "Something that made her upset?"

Luvo waits for the memory to fade. He studies Alma's wall in the dimness. *Treasure Island. Gorgonops longifrons. Porter Properties.* "That's not it," he says. On the wall in front of them float countless iterations of Alma Konachek: a seven-year-old sitting cross-legged on the floor; a brisk, thirty-year-old estate agent; a bald old lady. An entitled woman, a lover, a wife.

And in the center Harold walks perpetually out of the sea. His name printed below it in shaky handwriting. A photograph taken on the very night when Harold and Alma seemed to reach the peak of everything they could be. Alma had placed that picture in the center on purpose, Luvo is sure of it, before her endless rearranging had defaced the original logic of her project. The one thing she wouldn't move.

The photograph is faded, slightly curled at the edges. It must be forty years old, thinks Luvo. He reaches out and takes it from the wall.

Before he feels it, he knows it will be there. The photograph is slightly heavier than it should be. Two strips of tape cross over its back; something has been fixed underneath.

"What's that?" asks Roger.

Luvo carefully lifts away the tape so as not to tear the photograph. Beneath is a cartridge. It looks like the others, except it has a black X drawn across it.

He and Roger stare at it a moment. Then Luvo slides it into the machine. The house peels away in slow, deciduous waves.

Alma is riding beside Harold in a dusty truck: Harold's Land Cruiser. Harold holds the steering wheel with his left hand, his face sunburned red, his right hand trailing out the open window. The road is untarred and rough. On both sides grassy fields sweep upward into crumbled mountainsides.

Harold is talking, his words washing in and out of Alma's attention. "What's the one permanent thing in the world?" he's saying now. "Change! Incessant and relentless change. All these slopes, all this scree—see that huge slide there?—they're all records of calamities. Our lives are like a fingersnap in all this." Harold shakes his head in genuine wonderment. He swoops his hand back and forth in the air out the window.

Inside Alma's memory a thought rises so clearly it's as if Luvo can see the sentence printed in the air in front of the windshield. She thinks: Our marriage is ending and all you can talk about is rocks.

Occasional farm cottages rush past, white walls with red roofs; derelict windpumps; sun-ravaged sheep pens; everything tiny against the backdrop of the peaks growing ever larger beyond the hood ornament. The sky is a swirl of cloud and light.

Time compresses; Luvo feels jolted forward. One moment a rampart of cliffs ahead glows chalk-white, flickering lightly as if composed of flames. A moment later Alma and Harold are in among the rocks, the Land Cruiser ascending long switchbacks. The road is composed of rust-colored gravel, bordered now and then by uneven walls of rock. Sheer drops open off the left, then right sides. A sign reads, *Swartbergpas*.

Inside Alma, Luvo can feel something large coming to a head. It's rising, frothing inside her. Heat prickles her under her blouse; Harold downshifts as the truck climbs through a nearly impossible series of hairpin turns. The valley floor with its quilting of farm fields looks a thousand miles below.

At some point Harold stops at a pullout surrounded by rock-fall. He produces sandwiches from an aluminum cooler. He eats ravenously; Alma's sandwich sits untouched on the dash. "Just going to have a poke around," Harold says, and does not wait for a reply. From the back of the Land Cruiser he takes a jug of water and his ebony walking stick with the elephant on the handle and climbs over the drystone retaining wall and disappears.

Alma sits, bites back anger. Wind plays in the grasses on both sides of the road. Clouds drag across the ridgetops. No cars pass.

She'd tried. Hadn't she? She'd tried to get excited about fossils. She'd just spent three days with Harold in a game lodge outside Beaufort West: a cramped row of rooms encircled by rocks and wind, ticks on her pant legs, a lone ant paddling slow circles atop her tea. Lightning storms scoured the horizon. Scorpions patrolled the kitchenette. Harold would leave at dawn and Alma would sit in a fold-up chair outside their room with a mystery novel in her lap and the desolation of the Karoo shimmering in all directions.

A glitter, a madness. The Big Empty, people in Cape Town called the Karoo, and now she saw why.

She and Harold had not been talking, not sleeping in the same bed. Now they were driving over this pass toward the coast to spend a night in a real hotel, a place with air-conditioning and white wine in silver buckets. She would tell him how she felt. She would tell him she had reached a certain threshold. The prospect of it made her feel simultaneously lethargic and exhilarated.

The sun lapses across the ridgelines. Shadows swing across the road. Time skids and ripples. Luvo begins to feel nauseous, as if he and Alma and the Land Cruiser are teetering on the edge of a cliff, as if the whole road is about to slough off the mountain and plunge into oblivion. Alma whispers to herself about snakes, about lions. She whispers, "Hurry up, goddamn it, Harold."

But he does not come back. Another hour passes. Not a single car comes over the pass in either direction. Alma's sandwich disappears. She urinates beside the Land Cruiser. It's nearly dusk before Harold clambers back over the wall. Something is wrong with his face. His forehead is crimson. His words come fast, quick convoluted strings of them, as if he is hacking them out.

"Alma, Alma, Alma," he's saying. Spittle flies from his lips. He has found, he said, the remains of a *Gorgonops longifrons* on a ledge halfway down the escarpment. It is toothy, bent, big as a lion. Its long, curved claws are still in place; its entire skull is present, its skeleton fully articulated. It is, he believes, the biggest fossilized gorgon ever found. The holotype.

His breathing seems only to pick up pace. "Are you okay?" asks Alma, and Harold says, "No," and a second later, "I just need to sit for a moment."

Then he wraps his arms across his chest, leans against the side of the Land Cruiser, and slides into the dust.

"Harold?" shrieks Alma. A slick of foamy, blood-flecked saliva spills down the side of her husband's throat. Already dust begins to cling to the wet surfaces of his eyeballs.

The light is low, golden, and merciless. On the veld far below, the zinc rooftops of distant farmhouses reflect back the dying sun. Every shadow of every pebble seems impossibly stark. A tiny rockslide starts beneath Alma's ribs. She turns Harold over; she opens the rear door. She screams her husband's name over and over.

When the memory stimulator finally spits out the cartridge, Luvo feels as if he has been gone for days. Patches of rust-colored light float through his vision. He can still feel the monotonous, back-and-forth motion of the Land Cruiser in his body. He can still hear the wind, see the silhouettes of ridgelines in his peripheral vision, feel the gravity of the heights. Roger looks at him; he flicks a cigarette out the open window into the garden. Strands of fog pull through the backyard trees.

"Well?" he says.

Luvo tries to raise his head but it feels as if his skull will shatter.

"That was it," he says. "The one you've been looking for."

Tall Man in the Yard

Alma is thirsty. She would like someone to bring her some orange juice. She runs her tongue across the backs of her teeth. Harold is here. Isn't Harold in the chair beside her? Can't she hear his breathing on the other side of the lamp?

There are footfalls on the stairs. Alma raises her eyes. She is almost giddy with fear. The gun in her left hand smells faintly of oil.

Birds are passing over the house now, a great flock, harrying across the sky like souls. She can hear the beating of their wings.

The pendulum in the grandfather clock swings left, swings right. The traffic light at the top of the street sends its serial glow through the windows.

The fog splits. City lights wink between the garden palms. The ocean beyond is a vast, curved shield. It seems to boom outward toward her like a loudspeaker, a great loudspeaker of reflected starlight.

First there is the man's right shoe: laceless, a narrow maw between the toe and sole. Then the left shoe. Dark socks. Unhemmed trouser legs.

Alma tries to scream but only a faint, animal sound comes out of her mouth. A man who is not Harold is coming down the stairs and his shoes are dirty and his hands are out and he is opening his mouth to speak in one of those languages she never needed to learn.

His hands are huge and terrible. His beard is white. His teeth are the color of autumn leaves.

His hat says Ma Horse, Ma Horse, Ma Horse.

Virgin Active Fitness

The bus grinds to a halt in Claremont and Temba sits up and looks out bleary-eyed and silent at Virgin Active Fitness, not yet open for the day. His gaze tracks the still-lit, unpopulated swimming pools through his eyeglasses. Submerged lights radiating out through green water.

The bus lurches forward again. Looking up through the window, the boy watches the darkness drain out of the sky. The first rays of sun break the horizon and flow across the east-facing valleys of Table Mountain. Fat tufts of fog slide down from the summit.

A woman in the aisle stands with her back very straight and peers down into a paperback book.

"Paps?" Temba says. "My body feels loose."

His father's arm closes around his shoulders. "Loose?"

The boy's eyes shut. "Loose," he murmurs.

"We're going to get you some medicine," Pheko says. "You just rest. You just hang on, little lamb."

Dawn

Luvo is detaching himself from the remote device when he hears Roger say, from the stairwell, "Now, wait one minute." Then something explodes downstairs. Every molecule in the upstairs bedroom feels as if it has been jolted awake. The windows rattle. The cartridges on the wall quiver. In the shuddering concussion afterward Luvo hears Roger fall down the stairs and exhale a single sob, as if expelling all of his remaining breath at once.

Luvo sits paralyzed on the edge of the bed. The grandfather clock resumes its metronomic advance. Someone downstairs says something so quietly that Luvo cannot hear it. His gaze catches on a small, inexplicable watercolor of an airborne boat among the hundreds of papers on the wall in front of him, a sailboat gliding through clouds. He has seen it a hundred times before but has never actually looked at it. Sails straining, clouds floating happily past.

Gradually the molecules in the air around Luvo seem to return to their former states. He hears no more from downstairs except the grandfather clock, banging away in the living room. Roger has been shot, he thinks. Someone has shot Roger. And Roger has the cartridge with the X on it in his shirt pocket.

A low breeze drifts through the open window. The pages on Alma's wall fan out in front of him like a flower, like a mind turned inside out.

Luvo listens to the clock, counts to a hundred. He can still see Harold in the gravel beside the Land Cruiser, his face a mask, dust stuck to his eyes, saliva gleaming on his chin and throat.

Eventually Luvo crawls across the floor and peers down the stairwell. Roger's tall body is at the bottom, slumped over onto itself, folded almost in half. His hat is still on. His arms are crimped underneath him. A portion of his face is gone. A halo of blood has pooled around his head on the tile.

Luvo lies back on the carpet, sees Alma's immaculate room at the Twelve Apostles Hotel, sees a mountain range rush past the dusty windscreen of a truck. Sees Harold's legs twitching beneath him in the gravel.

What is there in Luvo's life that makes sense? Dusk in the Karoo becomes dawn in Cape Town. What happened four years ago is relived twenty minutes ago. An old woman's life becomes a young man's. Memory-watcher meets memory-keeper.

Luvo stands. He plucks cartridges off the wall and sticks them in his pockets. Forty, fifty of them. Once his pockets are full he moves toward the stairwell, but pauses and looks back. The little room, the spotless carpet, the washed window. On the bedspread a thousand identical roses intertwine. He takes the photograph of Harold walking out of the sea and slips it inside his shirt. He sets Cartridge 4510 in the center of the coverlet where someone might find it.

Then he stands at the top of the stairwell, collecting himself. From the living room—from Roger—rises a smell of blood and gunpowder. An odor more grim and nauseating than Luvo expected.

Luvo is about to walk down the stairs when the rape gate rattles and he hears a key slip into the deadbolt of the front door.

Clock

Perhaps the last thing in the world Pheko is prepared to see is a man facedown at the bottom of Alma's stainless-steel staircase lying in a puddle of blood.

Temba is asleep again, a hot weight across his father's back. Pheko is out of breath and sweating from carrying the boy up the hill. He sees the dead man first and then the blood but still it takes him several more seconds to absorb it all. Parallelograms of morning light fall through the balcony doors.

Down the hallway, in the kitchen, Alma is sitting at the kitchen table, steadily turning the pages of a magazine. She is barefoot.

The questions come too quickly to sort out. How did this man get in? Was he killed with a gun? Did Mrs. Alma do the killing? Where is the gun? Pheko feels the heat radiating off his son into his back. He wants suddenly for everything to go away. The whole world to go away.

I should run, he thinks. I should not be here. Instead he carries his son over the body, stepping over the blood, past Alma in the kitchen. He continues out the back door of the kitchen and into the garden and sets the boy in a lounge chair and returns inside to retrieve the white chenille blanket off the foot of Alma's bed and wraps the boy in it. Then inside again for Alma's pill bottles. His hands shake as he tries to read the labels. He ends up choosing two types of antibiotic of which there are full bottles and crushing them together into a spoonful of honey. Alma does not look up from the pages as she turns them, one, then the next, then the next, her stare lost and unknowable and reptilian.

"Thirsty," she says.

"Just a moment, Mrs. Alma," says Pheko. In the garden he sticks the spoon in Temba's mouth and makes sure the boy swallows it down and then he goes back into the kitchen and pockets the antibiotics and listens to Alma snap the pages forward awhile, and puts on the coffeepot, and when he is sure he will be able to speak clearly he pulls his telephone from his pocket and calls the police.

Boy Falling from the Sky

Temba is looking into the shifting, inarticulate shapes of Alma's backyard leaves when a boy falls from the sky. He crashes into some hedges and clambers out onto the grass and places his head in the center of the morning sun and peers down at Temba with a corona of light spilling out around his head.

"Temba?" the silhouette says. His voice is hoarse and unsteady. His ears glow pink where the sunlight passes through them. He speaks in English. "Are you Temba?"

"My glasses," says Temba. The garden is a sea of black and white. The face in front of him shifts and a sudden avalanche of light pierces Temba's eyes. Something bubbles inside his gut. His tongue tastes of the sweet, sticky medicine his father spooned into his mouth.

Now hands are putting on Temba's glasses for him. Temba squints up, blinking.

"My paps works here."

"I know." The boy is whispering. Fear travels through his voice. Temba tries whispering, too. "I'm not supposed to be here."

"Me either."

Temba's eyesight comes back to him. Big palms and rosebushes and a cabbage tree loom against the garden wall. He tries to make out the boy standing over him against the backdrop of the sun. He has smooth brown skin and a wool cap over his lightly felted head. He reaches down and tugs the blanket up around Temba's shoulders.

"My body is sick," says Temba.

"Shhh," whispers the boy. He takes off his hat and presses three fingers against his temple as if reining in a headache. Temba glimpses strange outlines on the boy's scalp, but then the boy puts his cap back on and sniffs and glances nervously toward the house.

"I'm Temba. I live at B478A, Site C, Khayelitsha."

"Okay, Temba. You should rest now."

Temba looks toward the house. Its sleek profile looms up above the hedges, cut with silver windowframes and chrome balcony railings.

"I'll rest now," he says.

"Good," whispers the boy with the smooth skin and the glowing ears. Then he takes five quick steps across the backyard and leaps up between the trunks of two palms and scales the garden wall and is gone.

The Days Following

Harold's dying face, Roger's crumpled frame, and the filmy eyes of Temba all rotate through Luvo's thoughts like some appalling picture show. Death succeeding death in relentless concatenation.

He spends the rest of Sunday hiding inside the labyrinthine paths of the Company Gardens, crouched among the leaves. Squirrels run here and there; city workers string Christmas lights through a lane of oaks. Are people looking for him? Are the police?

Monday Luvo crouches in the alley outside a chophouse watching the news on a bar television through an open window. It takes several hours before he sees it: An elderly woman has shot an intruder in Vredehoek. A reporter stands on Alma's street, a few houses away, and talks into a microphone. In the background a stripe of red-and-yellow police tape stretches across the road. The reporter says nothing about Alma's dementia, nothing about

Pheko or Temba, nothing about accomplices. The whole report lasts perhaps twenty-five seconds.

He does not return to Roger's apartment. No one comes for him. No Roger shaking him awake in the night, hustling him into a taxi. No Pheko come to demand answers. No ghosts of Harold or Alma. Tuesday morning Luvo rides a bus up to Derry Street and walks up onto the slopes of Table Mountain, through the sleek, hushed houses of Vredehoek. There is a blue van in front of Alma's house and the garage door is open. The garage is absolutely empty. No Mercedes, no realty sign. No lights. The police tape is still there. As he stands beside the gutter a moment a dark-skinned woman passes behind a window pushing a vacuum cleaner.

That afternoon he sells Alma's memory cartridges to a trader named Cabbage. Cabbage calls a red-eyed teenager out from the trees to run them through a ramshackle memory machine. The transaction takes more than two hours. "They real," affirms the teenager finally, and Cabbage looks Luvo up and down before offering him 3,300 rand for the whole batch.

Luvo studies the cartridges in the bottom of his backpack. Sixty-one of them. Pinpoints of a life. He asks the trader if he can buy the remote device, with its dirty-looking, warped headgear, but Cabbage only grins and shakes his head. "Costs more than you'll ever have," he says, and snaps his bag shut.

Afterward Luvo walks back up through the Company Gardens to the South African Museum and stands in the fossil room with his money in his pocket. He gazes into every display case. Brachiopod, paper mussel, marsh clam. Horsetail, liverwort, seed fern.

Outside a light rain starts to fall. A warder ambles through, announces to no one in particular that it's closing time. Two tourists come through the door, glance about, and leave. Soon the room is empty. Luvo stands in front of the gorgon a long time. It's a slender-headed skeleton, stalking something on its long legs, its huge canine incisors showing.

At the street market in Greenmarket Square Luvo buys the following things: a kelly-green duffel bag, nine loaves of white bread, a paint scraper, a hammer, a sack of oranges, four two-liter bottles of water, a polyester sleeping bag, and a puffy red parka that says *Kansas City Chiefs* across the back. When he's done, he has 900 rand in his pocket, all the money left him in the world.

B478A

Pheko gazes up into the darkness of his little house and listens to the rain rattle on the roof. Beside him Temba blinks his big eyes, waiting for sleep to fall away. The boy's fever has broken; he is slowly coming back into himself.

Pheko is thinking about his cousin who says he might be able to find him work loading powdered cement into bags for shipping. He's thinking about the fur of dead insects on the window screens, the tracks of ants marching along the floor. And he's thinking about Alma.

For six hours the police asked Pheko questions. He did not know where Temba had been taken; he hardly knew where he was. Then they released him. They let him keep the antibiotics, they even paid his train fare. After leaving her kitchen that morning with the police, Alma still turning the pages of that thick, five-year-old fashion magazine, he has not seen Alma again.

All around the little house are things he has been given by Harold and Alma over the years, castoffs and hand-me-downs: a dented soup pot, a plastic comb, an enameled mug that says *Porter Properties Summer Picnic*. A dish towel, a plastic colander, a thermometer. How many hours had Pheko spent with Alma over the past twenty years? She is engraved into him; she is part of him.

"I saw a boy," Temba says. "He looked like an angel from church."

"In your dream?"

"Maybe," says Temba. "Maybe it was a dream."

Swartberg Pass

On the morning bus heading east from Cape Town there's the impossible straightness of the N1 cutting across the desert all the way to the horizon. The road is swallowed by the bus's big tinted windscreen like an infinite black ribbon. On either side of the N1, dry grasslands run away from the highway's edges into sheaves of brown mountains. Everywhere there is light and stone and unimaginable distance.

Luvo feels simultaneously frightened and awed. As far as he can remember, he has never been outside of Cape Town, though he has Alma's memories riding along inside him, the bright blue coves of Mozambique, rain in Venice, a line of travelers in suits standing in a first-class queue in a Johannesburg train station.

He pulls the photograph of Harold from his backpack. Harold, half-grinning, half-grimacing, walking out of the sea. He thinks of Roger, lying dead on the floor of Alma's living room. He hears Chefe Carpenter say, "You owe money, don't you?"

It's afternoon when Luvo clambers off at the intersection for Prince Albert Road. A gas station and a few aluminum trailers huddle under a brass-colored sun. Black eagles trace slow ovals a half-mile above the road. Three friendly-looking women sit beneath a vinyl umbrella and sell cheese and marmalade and sticky rolls. "It's warm," they tease. "Take off your hat." Luvo shakes his head. He chews a roll and waits with his duffel bag. It's nearly dusk before a Bantu sales representative in a rented Honda slows for him.

"Where you going?"

"The Swartberg."

"You mean over the Swartberg?"

"Yes, sir."

The driver reaches across and pushes the door open. Luvo climbs in. They turn southeast. The sun goes down in a wash of orange and moonlight spills onto the Karoo.

The pavement ends. The man drives the last hour through the

badlands in silence, with the startled eyes of bat-eared foxes reflecting now and then in the high beams and a vast spread of stars
keeping pace above and curtains of dust floating up behind the
rear tires.

The car vibrates beneath them. Soon there is no traffic in either
direction. Great walls of stone rear up, darker than the sky. They
come around a turn and a rectangular brown sign, its top half
pocked from a shotgun blast, reads *Swartbergpas*. Luvo thinks:
Harold and Alma saw this same sign. Before Harold died they
drove right past this spot.

Fifteen minutes later the Honda is climbing past one of the
road's countless switchbacks when Luvo says, "Please stop the car
here."

The man slows. "Stop?"

"Yes, sir."

"You sick?"

"No, sir."

The little car shudders as it idles. Luvo unclips his seat belt.
The man blinks at him in the darkness. "You're getting out here?"

"Yes, sir. Just below the top."

"You're joking."

"No, sir."

"Ag, it gets cold up here. It *snows* up here. You ever seen snow?"

"No, sir."

"Snow is terrible cold." The man tugs at his collar. He seems
about to asphyxiate with the strangeness of Luvo's request.

"Yes, sir."

"I can't let you out here."

Luvo stays silent.

"Any chance I can talk you out of this?"

"No, sir."

Luvo takes his big duffel and four bottles of water from the
backseat and steps out into the darkness. The man looks at him a

full half-minute before pulling off. It's warm in the moonlight but Luvo stands shivering for a moment, holding his things, and then walks to the edge of the road and peers over the retaining wall into the shadows below. He finds a thin path, cut into the slope, and hikes maybe two hundred meters north of the road, pausing every now and then to watch the twin red taillights of the salesman's Honda as it eases up the switchbacks high above him toward the top of the pass.

Luvo finds a lumpy, level area of dry grass and rocks roughly the size of Alma Konachek's upstairs bedroom. He unrolls his sleeping bag and urinates and looks out over the starlit talus below, running mile after mile down onto the plains of the Karoo far beneath him.

He takes a drink of water and climbs into his sleeping bag and tries to swallow back his fear. The rocks on the ground are still warm from the sun. The stars are bright and impossibly numerous. The longer he looks into a patch of sky, the more stars emerge within it. Range upon range of suns burning out beyond the power of his vision.

No cars show themselves on the road. No airplanes cross the sky. The wind makes the only sound. What's out here? Millipedes. Buzzards. Snakes. Warthogs, ostriches, bushbuck. Farther off, on the northern tablelands: jackals, wild dogs, leopards. A last few rhinos.

First Day

Dawn finds Luvo warm and bareheaded inside his sleeping bag with a breeze washing over the ports in his scalp. A truck grinds up the switchbacks of the road in the distance, *Happy Chips* painted across its side.

He sits up. Around his sleeping bag are rocks, and beyond his little level spot of grasses are more rocks. The slopes below him and above him are littered with rocks in every size, pressed half

into the earth like grave markers. Beyond them cliffs have calved
off slabs the size of houses. Indeed, there seem to be sandstone and
limestone blocks everywhere, an infinity of rocks.

The *Happy Chips* truck disappears around another hairpin. No
souls, only a few spindly trees—only boulders and distances. On its
pedestal at the museum, the gorgon had seemed huge, big as a dinosaur, but out here the scale of things feels new. What was a dinosaur compared to cliffs like these? Without turning his head Luvo
can see ten thousand rocks in which a gorgon might be hidden.

Why did he think he could find a fossil out here? A fifteen-
year-old boy who knows only adventure novels and an old woman's
memories? Who has never found a fossil in his life?

Luvo eats two pieces of bread and walks slow circles around his
sleeping bag, turning over stones with his toes. Splotches of lichen
grow on some, pale oranges and grays, and the rocks include grains
of color, too, striations of black, flecks of silver. They are lovely but
they contain nothing that looks like the fossils in the museum, in
Harold's cabinet, in Alma's memories.

All that first day Luvo makes wider and wider circles around
his little camp, carrying a bottle of water, watching his shadow
slip across the hillsides. Clouds drift above the mountain range
at the horizon and their shadows drag across the farms far below.
Luvo remembers Harold talking to Alma about time. Younger was
"higher in the rocks." Things that were old were deep. But what
is higher and lower here? This is a wilderness of rocks. And every
single stone Luvo turns over is plain and carries no trace of bone.

Maybe one car comes over the pass every two hours. Three
eagles soar over him in the evening, calling to one another, never
once flapping their wings as they float over the ridge.

The Great Karoo

In dreams Luvo is Alma: a white-skinned estate agent, pain-free,
well-fed. He strides through the Gardens Centre; clerks rush to

help him. Everywhere circular racks gleam with clothes. Air-conditioning, perfumes, escalators. Clerks open their bright, clean faces to him.

His headaches seem to be intensifying. He has a sense that his skull is slowly being crushed, and that the metallic taste seeping into his mouth is whatever is being squeezed out.

On his second day up on Swartberg Pass, ants chew a hole through one of his bread bags. The sun roasts his arms and neck. Lying there at night Luvo feels as if the gorgon is at the hub of a wheel out of which innumerable spokes rotate. Here comes Luvo on one spoke, and Roger on another, and Temba on the next, and Pheko and Harold and Alma after that. Everything coursing past in the night, revolving hugely, almost unfathomably, like the wheel of the Milky Way above. Only the center remains in darkness, only the gorgon.

From his memory Luvo tries to summon images of the gorgon at the museum, tries to imagine what one might look like out here, in the rocks. But his mind continually returns to Alma Konachek's house.

Roger is dead. Harold is dead. Alma is either in jail or tucked into a home for the rich and white-skinned. If there's anything left of who she was, it's a scrap, a shred, some scribbled note that a cleaner or Pheko has guiltily unpinned from her wall and thrown into the trash. And how much longer can Luvo be any better off, with these ports throbbing in his skull? A few more months?

Here is the surprise: Luvo likes the strange, soothing work of looking into the rocks. He feels a certain peace, clinging to the side of Swartberg Pass: The clouds are like huge silver battle-ships, the dusks like golden liquids—the Karoo is a place of raw light and monumental skies and relentless silence. But beneath the silence, he's learning, beneath the grinding wind, there is al-ways noise: the sound of grass hissing on the cliffsides and the clattering of witgat trees tucked here and there into clefts. As he lies in his sleeping bag on his third night he can hear an almost imperceptible rustling: night flowers unveiling their petals to the moon. When he is very quiet, and his mind has stilled the chewing and whirling and sucking of his fears, he imagines he can hear the coursing of water deep beneath the mountains, and the movements of the roots of the plants as they dive toward it—it sounds like the voices of men, singing softly to one another. And beyond that—if only he could listen even more closely!—there was so much more to hear: the supersonic screams of bats, and, on the most distant tablelands, the subsonic conversations of elephants in the game reserves, grunts and moans so deep they carry between animals miles apart, forced into a few isolated reserves, like castaways on distant islands, their calls passing through the mountains and then shuttling back.

That night he wakes to the quivering steps of six big antelope, shy and jittery, the keratin of their hooves clacking against the rocks, the vapor of their breath showing in the moonlight as they file past his sleeping bag, not fifty feet away.

On Luvo's fourth morning, wandering below the pass, perhaps a half mile from the road, he turns over a rock the size of his hand and finds pressed into its underside the clear white outline of what looks like a clam shell. The shell is lighter than the stone around it and scalloped at the edges. The name of the fossil rises from some corner of his brain: brachiopod. He sits in the sun and runs the tips of his fingers over the dozens of grooves in the stone. An animal that lived and died eons ago, when this mountainside was a seabed, and galaxies of clams flapped their shells at the sun.

Luvo hears Harold Konachek's big, enthusiastic voice: *Two hundred fifty million years ago this place was lush, filled with ferns and rivers and mud.* Flesh washing away, minerals penetrating bones, the weight of millennia piling up, bodies becoming rock.

And now this one little creature had risen to the surface, as the earth was weathered away by wind and rain, in the way a long-frozen corpse sometimes bobs to the surface of a glacier, after being mulled over in the lightless depths for centuries.

What Endures?

His dreams stray farther and farther from his reality, dreams that feel as if they emerge not from his own forgotten childhood but from lives that have been passed to him through his blood. Dreams of ancestors, dreams of long-ago men who dragged their own aching heads through this arid place, centuries of nations pursuing herds across the sands, whole bands passing in the haze with ocher on their faces and spears in their fists and great ragged tents folded and strapped to their backs, the long poles nodding as they marched, dogs trotting at their feet, tongues lolling. Thick-bodied herds, rain-animals and handprints, lines of dots descending from a sky and plugging into a rhinoceros horn. Men with antelope heads. Fish with the faces of men. Women dissolving into mists of red.

The fifth morning on Swartberg Pass finds Luvo exhausted and hollow and in too much pain to rise from his sleeping bag. He pulls the curled photograph of Harold from his duffel and studies it, running his fingers over the man's features. Pinpoints of sky show through the little holes in each corner.

Luvo tries to cut through his headache, tries to coax his memory back toward the moments before Harold's death. Harold was talking about geology, about death. "What's the permanent thing in the world? Change!" Windpumps, sheep pens, a sign that reads *Swartbergpas.*

Luvo remembers Alma's sandwich on the dashboard, the wind in the grass beside the road, Harold finally returning over the apron of the road, staggering as he muttered Alma's name. Pink foam coming out of his mouth. Alma punching telephone buttons in vain. Gravel pushed into Harold's cheek and dust on his eyeballs.

Luvo stares at the photograph of Harold. He has begun to feel as if Alma's wall of papers and cartridges has been reiterated out here a hundredfold on the mountainside, these legions of stones like identical beige cartridges, each pressed out of the same material. And here he is doomed to repeat the same project over and over, hunting among a thousand things for a pattern, searching a convoluted landscape for the remains of one thing that has come before.

Dr. Amnesty's cartridges, the South African Museum, Harold's fossils, Chefe Carpenter's collection, Alma's memory wall—weren't they all ways of trying to defy erasure? What is memory anyway? How can it be such a frail, perishable thing?

The shadows turn, shorten; the sun swings up over a ridge. Luvo remembers for the first time something Dr. Amnesty told Alma on one of the cartridges. "Memory builds itself without any clean or objective logic: a dot here, another dot here, and plenty of dark spaces in between. What we know is always evolving, always subdividing. Remember a memory often enough and you can create a new memory, the memory of remembering."

Remember a memory often enough, Luvo thinks. Maybe it takes over. Maybe the memory becomes new again.

In Luvo's own memory a gun explodes. Roger slumps down the stairs and lets out a last breath. A five-year-old boy sits in a lounge chair wrapped in a blanket blinking up at the sky. Alma tears out a page of *Treasure Island* and nails it to a wall. Everything happens over and over and over.

A body, Harold told Alma once, vanishes quickly enough to take your breath away. As a boy, he said, his father would put a dead ewe on the side of the road and in three days the jackals would have reduced it to bones and wool. After a week, even the bones would be gone.

"Nothing lasts," Harold would say. "For a fossil to happen is a miracle. One in fifty million. The rest of us? We disappear into the grass, into beetles, into worms. Into ribbons of light."

It's the rarest thing, Luvo thinks, that gets preserved, that does not get erased, broken down, transformed.

Luvo turns the photograph in his hands and a new thought rises: When Harold was leaning against the Land Cruiser, clutching his chest, his breath coming faster and faster, his heart stopping in his chest, he was not holding his walking stick. The tacky ebony walking stick with the elephant on top. The stick that used to drive Alma mad. When Harold left the Land Cruiser, he took his walking stick from the back of the truck. And when he returned, a couple of hours later, he no longer had it.

Maybe he'd dropped it on the way back to the Land Cruiser. Or maybe he'd left it in the rocks to mark the gorgon's location. Four years had passed and the walking stick could have been picked up, or washed over a cliff in a storm, or Luvo could be remembering things wrong, but he realizes it had been here once, on the north side of Swartberg Pass, somewhere below the road. Near where Luvo is camped. And it might be here still.

Luvo wants to find the gorgon, needs to find it, for himself, for Alma, for Pheko, for Roger, for Harold. If the walking stick is still here, he thinks, it will not be too hard to find. There are no trees up here so big, no branches nearly as long as that walking stick. No wood as dark as ebony.

It's a small thing, perhaps, but it's enough to get Luvo on his feet, and start him searching again.

The Gorgon

For that whole day and the next, Luvo walks the sea of stones. He has only one two-liter bottle of water left and he rations it carefully. He works in circles, in rectangles, in triangles. Belts and swaths and carpets of stones. He looks now for something dark, bleached by sun perhaps, a few red beads strung around its handle, the wooden elephant carved on top. Such staffs he has seen sold by children along the airport road and at tourist shops and in Greenmarket Square.

The sixth evening it starts to rain and Luvo drapes his sleeping bag over a bush and crawls beneath it and sleeps a dreamless sleep and around him spiders draw their webs between the branches. When he wakes, the sky is pale.

He stands, shakes the water drops off his sleeping bag. His head feels surprisingly light, almost painless. It's morning, Luvo thinks. I slept through an entire rainstorm. He climbs perhaps fifty feet onto a flat, smooth rock and sits chewing a slice of bread and then sees it.

Harold's walking stick is sticking up from between two boulders two hundred meters away. Even from where he sits Luvo can see the hole almost near the top, a tiny space carved between the elephant's legs and its torso.

Every second, walking those two hundred meters, is like leaping into very cold water, in that first instant when the body goes into shock, and everything you are, everything you call your life, disintegrates for an instant, and all you have around you is the water and the cold, your heart trying to send splinters through a block of ice.

The walking stick is sun-bleached and the beads are no longer on the handle but it's still standing upright. As if Harold has left it there for Luvo to find. He stares at it awhile, afraid to touch it. The morning light is sweet and clear. The hillside trickles quietly around him with last night's rain.

There is a carefully stacked pile of stones right beside it and even after Luvo has clawed most of them away, it takes him a few minutes to realize he is looking down at a fossil. The gorgon is white against the grayer limestone and the outline of the animal inside seems interrupted in places. But eventually he can make out its form from one foreleg to the tip of its tail: It is the size of a crocodile, tilted onto its side, and sunk as if into an enormous bathtub of cement. Its big, curved claws are still in place. And its skull sits separate from the rest of the stone entirely, as if it has been set there by the recession of a flood. It is big. Bigger, he thinks, than the one at the museum.

Luvo lifts away more rocks, sweeps away gravel and dust with his hands. The skeleton is fully articulated, looped into the stone. It is perhaps ten feet long. His heart skids.

With the hammer it takes Luvo only about two hours to break the skull free. Little chips of darker rock fly off as he strikes it and he hopes he is not damaging the thing he has come to find. As big as an old box-television, made entirely of stone, even once it's free of the matrix surrounding it, the skull seems impossible for him to lift. Even the eyeholes and nostrils are filled with rock, a lighter color than the surrounding skull. Luvo thinks: I won't be able to move it by myself.

But he does. He unzips the sleeping bag and folds it over the skull, padding it over on all sides, and using the walking stick as a lever, begins to roll the skull, inches at a time, toward the road. It's dark and Luvo is out of water before he gets the skull to the bottom of the retaining wall. Then he goes back to the rest of the skeleton, covers it again with rocks and gravel, marks it with the walking stick, and brings his camp up to the road.

His legs ache; his fingers are cut. Rings of starlight expand out over the ridgeline. The insects in the grass around him exult in their nighttime chorus. Luvo sits down on his duffel bag with the last of his oranges in his lap and the skull waiting six feet below, wrapped in a sleeping bag. He puts on his bright red parka. He waits.

The moon swings gently up over the mountains, huge, green, aswarm with craters.

Return

Three English-speaking Finnish women stop for Luvo after midnight. Two are named Paula. They seem mildly drunk. They ask shockingly few questions about how ragged Luvo looks or how long he has been sitting on the side of one of the most remote roads in Africa. He keeps his hat on, tells them he has been fossil hunting, asks them to help him with the skull. "Okay," they say, and work together, pausing now and then to pass around a bottle of Cabernet, and in fifteen minutes have heaved the skull over the wall and made room for it in the back of their van.

They are traveling across South Africa. One of them has recently turned forty and the others are here to celebrate with her. The floor of their camper van is knee-deep with food wrappers and maps and plastic bottles. They pass around a thick, half-hacked-apart shank of cheese; one of the Paulas cuts wedges of it and stacks them on crackers. Luvo eats slowly, looking at his torn fingernails and wondering how he must smell. And yet, there is reggae music washing out of the dashboard, there is the largeness of these women's laughter. "What an adventure!" they say, and he thinks of his paperbacks sitting in the bottom of his duffel. When they stop at the top of the pass and pile out and ask Luvo to take their photograph beside the beaten brown sign that reads *Die Top*, Luvo feels as if perhaps they have been sent to him as angels.

Dawn finds them eating scrambled eggs and chopped tomatoes in the rickety and deserted dining room of the Queens Hotel in a highway town called Matjiesfontein. Luvo drinks an ice-cold Fanta and watches the women eat. Their trip is ending and they show each other photos on the camera's screen. Ostriches, wineries, nightclubs.

When he's done with the first Fanta Luvo drinks another one, the slow fans turning above, and the kind, sweaty smiles of the three women turn on him now and then, as if in their worlds black and white are one and the same, as if the differences between people didn't matter so much anymore, and then they get up and pile into the van for the drive back to Cape Town.

One of the Paulas drives; the other two women sleep. Out the windows communication wires sling past in shallow parabolas from pole to pole. The road is relentlessly straight. Paula-the-driver looks back now and then at Luvo in the backseat.

"Headache?"

Luvo nods.

"What kind of fossil is it?"

"Maybe something called a gorgon."

"Gorgon? Like the Medusa? Snakes for hair, all that?"

"I'm not sure."

"Well, those are the gorgons all right. Medusa and her sisters. Turn you to stone if you look them in the eyes."

"Really?"

"Really," says forty-year-old Finnish Paula.

"This gorgon is very old," says Luvo. "From when this whole desert was a swamp, and big rivers ran all through it."

"I see," says Paula. She drives awhile, tapping her thumb on the wheel in time with the music. "You like that, Luvo? Going out and digging up old things?"

Luvo looks out the window. Out there, beyond the fence-lines, beneath the starlit, flat-topped hills, beneath the veld, beneath the dwarf scrub, beneath the endless running wind of the Karoo, what else remains locked away?

"Yes," he says. "I like it."

The Twelve Apostles Hotel

Paula parks the van outside Chefe Carpenter's stucco wall and the four of them get out and Luvo waves at the security camera but nothing seems to happen so they sit on the curb waiting. Not ten minutes later Chefe in his robe comes up the street walking his two collies. He regards Luvo and then the women with their matted hair and wrinkled shirts and when they open the back of the van and lift away the shredded remains of Luvo's sleeping bag, he looks at the fossil for a full minute without saying anything. His eyes seem both incredulous and dreamy, as if he is not entirely sure

that what is happening is real. With his trembling lip and soft eyes
he looks to Luvo as if he is about to cry.

Twenty minutes later they stand in Chefe's spotless garage
drinking coffee with the skull sitting naked on the painted floor.
This one huge head retrieved from the past and stripped from its
context. Chefe makes a call and an Indian man comes over and
looks at the skull with his hand on his chin and then makes several
more telephone calls. His excitement is obvious. Within an hour
three more men come in to look at the skull and the three yawning
Finnish women and the strange boy in the wool cap.

Eventually Chefe disappears into the house and reemerges
dressed in a trim blue suit. He says he can offer 1.4 million rand.
The jaws of the Finnish women drop simultaneously. They thump
Luvo on the back. They shriek and jump around the garage. Luvo
asks what he can give him now and Chefe says, "Now? As in today?"

"That's what he said," says one of the Paulas. After another
half hour of waiting Chefe gives Luvo 30,000 rand in cash. There
is enough money that he has to give it to Luvo in a paper shopping
bag. Luvo asks that the remainder be sent in a complete sum to
Pheko Garrett, B478A, Site C, Khayelitsha.

"All of it?" Chefe asks, and Luvo says, "All of it."

"How do we know you'll do that?" asks Paula, and Chefe Carpenter looks up at all three of them, taking his eyes off the skull
for the first time in several minutes, as if he is not sure who has
spoken. He blinks his eyes once. "You can go now," he says.

Three blocks away Luvo says goodbye to the Finnish women,
who hug him each in turn and give him their email addresses on
little white cards, and one of the Paulas is crying softly to herself as
they watch Luvo climb out of their rented camper van.

Near the entrance to the Company Gardens is a little English
bookshop. Luvo walks inside with his paper shopping bag full of
money. He finds a paperback of *Treasure Island* and pays for it with
a 1,000-rand note.

Then he flags down a waterfront cab and tells the driver to take him to the Twelve Apostles Hotel. The driver gives him a look, and the woman at the desk at the hotel gives him the same look, but Luvo has cash and once he has paid she leads him down a hundred-meter-long cream-colored runner of carpet to a black door with the number 7 on it.

The room is as clean and white as it was in Alma's memory. Off the balcony jade-colored waves break onto a golden beach. In the bathroom tiny white tiles line the floor in diamond shapes. Crisp white towels hang on nickel-plated rods. There's a big, spotless, white toilet. White fluffy bathmats sit on the floor. A single white orchid blooms in a rectangular vase on the toilet tank.

Luvo takes a forty-five-minute shower. He is somewhere around fifteen years old and he has perhaps six months left to live. After his shower he lies on the perfect white sheets of the bed and watches the huge afternoon sky flow like liquid out the window. Rafts of gulls sail above the beach. He thinks of Alma's memories, both those carried inside his head and the ones somewhere out in the city—Cabbage will have traded them away by now. He thinks of Alma's memory of this place, of the movie about the fish, gliding out into the great blue. He sleeps.

When he wakes, hours later, he stares awhile into cobalt squares of night out the windows and then he turns on his lamp and opens *Treasure Island*.

I remember him as if it were yesterday, he reads, *as he came plodding to the inn door, his sea chest following behind him in a handbarrow; a tall, strong, heavy, nut-brown man . . .*

The Gorgon

It takes six weeks for a crew of six men to excavate the skeleton. They work in daylight only and park their cars two bends away from the easiest route and when they have to bring in the crane they do it at night. They bring it back to Cape Town in an unmarked truck. The dealer who buys it from Chefe Carpenter brings it to a black-market auction house in London. In London it is cleaned and prepared and varnished and mounted on a titanium brace. It sells at an anonymous cloak-and-dagger auction for 4.5 million dollars, the fourth-highest sum anyone has ever paid for a fossil. The skeleton travels from London on a container ship through the Mediterranean and the Suez Canal and across the Indian Ocean to Shanghai. A week later it is installed by trained preparators on a pedestal in the lobby of a fifty-eight-story hotel.

No fake vegetation, no color, just a polyvinyl acetate sprayed along the joints and a Plexiglas cube lowered down over it. Someone sets two big potted palms on either side but two days later the hotel's owner asks for them to be taken away.

Pheko

In late February Pheko goes to the post office behind the spaza shop and in his mailbox is a single envelope with his name on it. Inside is a check for almost 1.4 million rand. Pheko looks up. He can hear, all of a sudden, the blood trundling through his head. The ground swivels out from underneath him. Madame Gecelo, behind the counter, looks over at him and looks back at whatever form she is filling out. A bus with no windows passes. Dust rides up over the little post office.

No one is looking. The floor steadies. Pheko peeks again into the envelope and reads the amount. He looks up. He looks back down.

On the subject line the check says, *Fossil Sale*. Pheko locks his post office box and hangs his key around his neck and stands with his eyes closed awhile. When he gets home he shows Temba his two fists. Temba looks at him through his little eyeglasses, then looks back at the fists. He waits, thinking hard, then taps the right fist. Pheko smiles.

"Try the other one."

"The other one?"

Pheko nods.

"You never say to try the other one."

"This time I say try the other one."

"This isn't a trick?"

"Not a trick." Temba taps the left hand. Pheko opens it. "Your bus card?" says Temba. Pheko nods.

"Your bus card?" repeats Temba.

They stop in the market on the way to the station and buy swimming shorts, red for Pheko and light blue for Temba. Then they ride the Golden Arrow toward the city. Pheko carries the plastic shopping bag containing the swimming trunks in his right hand but will not let Temba see inside. It is a warm March day and the edges of Table Mountain are impossibly vivid against the sky.

Pheko and Temba disembark at the Claremont stop and walk two blocks holding hands and enter a branch of the Standard Bank of South Africa two storefronts down from Virgin Active Fitness. Pheko opens an account and shows his identification and the clerk spends ten minutes typing various things into his computer and then he asks for an initial deposit. Pheko slides the check across.

A manager shows up thirty seconds later and looks at the check and takes it back behind a glass-walled office. He speaks into a phone for maybe ten minutes.

"What are we doing?" whispers Temba.

"We're hoping," whispers Pheko.

After what seems like an hour the manager comes back and smiles at Pheko and the bank deposits the check.

Ten minutes later Temba and Pheko stand in the glaring, cloudless sunlight in front of the glass walls of Virgin Active Fitness. Above them they can see people on treadmills, toiling away, and straight ahead, down through the walls, through their own reflections, they can see the three indoor pools, swimmers toiling through lanes, lifeguards in chairs, and children shooting through the channels of the twisting green waterslide.

At the entry Pheko gives the attendant a 1,000-rand note and she grumbles for a minute about change but passes some over and Pheko fills out a form on a clipboard and then they walk into a big locker room, lined with mahogany-fronted lockers, a few men here and there shaving or lacing tennis shoes or knotting ties and here comes Pheko with Temba trotting behind, adjusting his little eyeglasses with a happy incredulousness, and Temba chooses locker number 55 and they pull on their brand-new swim trunks, red for Pheko and light blue for Temba. Then they pass through a tile hallway lined with dripping showers and descend twelve steps and step through a glass door and into the roiling, chlorinated air of the indoor pools.

Temba whispers something to himself that Pheko cannot hear. Lifeguards in red polo shirts sit in chairs. The slide gushes; the shouts of children echo off the ceiling.

Pheko leads Temba up the long waterslide staircase, holding his little hand, the pools below growing smaller, the pink backs of the children in front of them wet with drops of water. Toward the top there is a short wait, each person in front of them climbing into place, then releasing, shooting down the slide, sweeping through the turns, and within a minute Pheko and Temba have climbed the last few steps and they stand together at the top of the waterslide.

Pheko sits in the slide and lifts his son and sets him between his legs. Warm water rushes through their trunks and races down the slide and disappears beyond the first turn. Pheko takes off his son's glasses and holds them in his fist.

Temba looks back at him, his eyes naked. "It looks very fast, Paps."

"It sure does."

Pheko looks down the steep channel into the first turn and then over the wall to where the pool looks very, very far below, the swimmers like little drowsy bees, the pure sunlight pouring through the windows, the traffic gliding noiselessly past.

He says, "Ready?"

"Ready," says Temba.

Alma

Alma sits in the community dining room in a yellow armchair. Her hair is short and silver and stiff. The clothes she is wearing are not hers; clothing seems to get mixed up in this place. Out the window to her left she can see a concrete wall, the top half of a flagpole, and a polygon of sky.

The air smells of cooked cabbage. Fluorescent lights buzz softly in the ceiling. Nearby two women are trying to play rummy but they keep dropping the cards. Somewhere else in the building, perhaps the basement, someone might be howling. It's hard to say. Maybe it's only the air, whistling out of heating ducts.

A ghost of a memory flits past Alma: there, then gone. A television at the front of the room shows a man with a microphone, shows a spinning wheel, shows an audience clapping.

Through the door walks a big woman in a white tank top and white jeans. In the light of the entryway her dark skin is almost invisible to Alma, so that it looks as if a white outfit has become animated and is walking toward her, white pants and a white top and white eyeballs floating. She walks straight toward Alma and begins emptying boxes onto the long table beside her.

A nurse in a flowered smock behind Alma claps her hands together. "Time for fine arts class, everyone," she says. "Anyone who would like to work with Miss Stigers can come over."

Several people start toward the table, one pushing a walker on wheels. The woman in white clothes is setting out buckets, plates, paints. She opens a big Tupperware bin. She looks over at Alma.

"Hi, sweetheart," she says.

Alma turns her head away. She keeps quiet. A few minutes

later some others are laughing, holding up plaster-coated hands. The woman in white clothing sings quietly to herself as she tends to the residents' various projects. Her voice rides beneath the din.

Alma sits in her chair very stiffly. She is wearing a red sweater with a reindeer on it. She does not recognize it. Her hands, motionless on her lap, are cold and look to her like claws. As if they, too, might have once belonged to someone else.

The woman sings in Xhosa. The song is sweet and slow. In a back room across town, inside a memory clinic in Green Point, a thousand cartridges containing Alma's memories sit gathering dust. In her bedside drawer, among earplugs and vitamins and crumpled tissues, is the cartridge Pheko gave her when he came to see her, Cartridge 4510. Alma no longer remembers what it is or what it contains or even that it belongs to her.

When the song is done a man at the table in a blue sweater breaks into applause with his plaster-coated hands. The piece of sky out Alma's window is warm and purple. A jetliner tracks across it, winking a golden light.

When Alma looks back, the woman in white is standing closer to her. "C'mon, sweetheart," she says with that voice. A voice like warm oil. "Give this a try. You'll like it."

The woman places a foil pie plate in front of Alma. There is newspaper over the tablecloth, Alma sees, and paint and silk flowers and little wooden hearts and snowmen scattered here and there in plastic bowls. The singing woman pours smooth, white plaster of Paris out of her Tupperware and into Alma's pie plate, wiping it clean with a Popsicle stick.

The plaster of Paris possesses a beautiful, creamy texture. One of the residents has spread it all over the tablecloth. Another has some in her hair. The woman in white has started a second song. Or perhaps she is singing the first song again,

Alma cannot be sure. *Kuzo inzingo zalomhlaba,* she sings. *Amanda noxolo, uxolo kuwe.*

Alma raises her left hand. The plaster is wet and waiting. "Okay," she whispers. "Okay."

She thinks: I had somebody. But he left me here all by myself.

Kuzo inzingo zalomhlaba. Amanda noxolo, uxolo kuwe, sings the woman.

Alma sinks her hand into the plaster.

STEVEN MILLHAUSER

"I deliberately avoid being too self-conscious about what drives me as a writer, but I'm perfectly aware that a good number of my stories have a somewhat similar pattern of beginning with something more or less simple and normal, and then a more extreme version of it, and a more extreme version of that. I think it's how my imagination works."

"I don't disdain modern technological things, but they don't have the kind of wonder for me that the technologies of age eleven had. They have their own kind of wonder, but it's mixed with intellect rather than magic."

Onstage interview at The Story Prize event
March 21, 2012

"Most American writers begin with the story and then become novelists. For them, the short story is a kind of apprenticeship. My own history is backward. I began as a novelist and later turned to the short story. Why this is so remains mysterious even to me, but the crucial thing is that I didn't turn to the story as a form of preparation for something larger or more important. It's as if the novel were a kind of preparation for the rigorous pleasures of the shorter form. For me, the shortness of a great story is part of its greatness. In any case, I love and revere this form of writing and hold it second to no other form."

Acceptance speech on winning The Story Prize
March 21, 2012

Snowmen

from *In the Penny Arcade*

One sunny morning I woke and pushed aside a corner of the blinds. Above the frosted, sun-dazzled bottom of the glass I saw a brilliant blue sky, divided into luminous rectangles by the orderly white strips of wood in my window. Down below, the backyard had vanished. In its place was a dazzling white sea, whose lifted and immobile waves would surely have toppled if I had not looked at them just then. It had happened secretly, in the night. It had snowed with such abandon, such fervor, such furious delight, that I could not understand how that wildness of snowing had failed to wake me with its white roar. The topmost twigs of the tall backyard hedge poked through the whiteness, but here and there a great drift covered them. The silver chains of the bright yellow swing-frame plunged into snow. Snow rose high above the floor of the old chicken coop at the back of the garage, and snow on the chicken-coop roof swept up to the top of the garage gable. In the corner of the white yard the tilted clothespole rose out of the snow like the mast of a sinking ship. A reckless snow-wave, having dashed against the side of the pole, flung up a line of frozen spray, as if straining to pull it all under. From the flat roof of the chicken coop hung a row of thick icicles, some in sun and some in shade. They reminded me of glossy and matte prints in my father's albums. Under the sunny icicles were dark holes in the snow where the water dripped. Suddenly I remembered a rusty rake-head lying teeth down in the dirt of the vegetable garden. It seemed more completely buried than ships under the sea, or the quartz and flint arrowheads that were said to lie under the dark loam of the garden, too far down for me to ever find them, forever out of reach.

I hurried downstairs, shocked to discover that I was expected

to eat breakfast on such a morning. In the sunny yellow kitchen
I dreamed of dark tunnels in the snow. There was no exit from
the house that day except by way of the front door. A thin, dark,
wetly gleaming trail led between high snowbanks to the two cement steps before the buried sidewalk, where it stopped abruptly,
as if in sudden discouragement. Jagged hills of snow thrown up by
the snowplow rose higher than my head. I climbed over the broken
slabs and reached the freedom of the street. Joey Czukowski and
Mario Salvio were already there. They seemed struck with wonder.
Earmuffs up and cap peaks pulled low, they both held snowballs
in their hands, as if they did not know what to do with them.
Together we roamed the neighborhood in search of Jimmy Shaw.
Here and there great gaps appeared in the snow ranges, revealing a
plowed driveway and a vista of snowy yard. At the side of Mario's
house a sparkling drift swept up to the windowsill. A patch of
bright green grass, in a valley between drifts, startled us as if waves
had parted and we were looking at the bottom of the sea. High
above, white and black against the summer-blue sky, the telephone
wires were heaped with snow. Heavy snow-lumps fell thudding.
We found Jimmy Shaw banging a stick against a snow-covered
stop sign on Collins Street. Pagliaro's lot disturbed us: in summer
we fought there with trash-can covers, sticks, and rusty cans, and
now its dips and rises, its ripples and contours, which we knew
as intimately as we knew our cellar floors, had been transformed
into a mysterious new pattern of humps and hollows, an unknown
realm reminding us of the vanished lot only by the distorted swell-
ing of its central hill.

Dizzy with discovery, we spent that morning wandering the
newly invented streets of more alien neighborhoods. From a roof
gutter hung a glistening four-foot icicle, thick as a leg. Now and
then we made snowballs, and feebly threw ourselves into the con-
ventional postures of a snowball fight, but our hearts were not really in it—they had surrendered utterly to the inventions of the

snow. There was about our snow a lavishness, an ardor, that made us restless, exhilarated, and a little uneasy, as if we had somehow failed to measure up to that white extravagance.

It was not until the afternoon that the first snowmen appeared. There may have been some in the morning, but I did not see them, or perhaps they were only the usual kind and remained lost among the enchantments of the snow. But that afternoon we began to notice them, in the shallower places of front and back yards. And we accepted them at once, indeed were soothed by them, as if only they could have been the offspring of such snow. They were not commonplace snowmen composed of three big snowballs piled one on top of the other, with carrots for noses and big black buttons or smooth round stones for eyes. No, they were passionately detailed men and women and children of snow, with noses and mouths and chins of snow. They wore hats of snow and coats of snow. Their shoes of snow were tied with snow laces. One snowgirl in a summer dress of snow and a straw hat of snow stood holding a delicate snow parasol over one shoulder.

I imagined that some child in the neighborhood, unsettled by our snow, had fashioned the first of these snow statues, perhaps little more than an ordinary snowman with roughly sculpted features. Once seen, the snowman had been swiftly imitated in one yard after another, always with some improvement—and in that rivalry that passes from yard to yard, new intensities of effort had led to finer and finer figures. But perhaps I was mistaken. Perhaps the truth was that a child of genius, maddened and inspired by our fervent snow, had in a burst of rapture created a new kind of snowman, perfect in every detail, which others later copied with varied success.

Fevered and summoned by those snowmen, we returned to our separate yards. I made my snowman in a hollow between the swing and the crab-apple tree. My first efforts were clumsy and oppressive, but I restrained my impatience and soon felt a passionate discipline come over me. My hands were inspired, it was as if I were coaxing into shape a form that longed to spring forth from the fecund snow. I shaped the eyelids, gave a tenseness to the narrow nostrils, completed the tight yet faintly smiling lips, and stepped back to admire my work. Beyond the chicken coop, in Joey's yard, I saw him admiring his own. He had made an old woman in a babushka, carrying a basket of eggs.

Together we went to Mario's yard, where we found him furiously completing the eyes of a caped and mustached magician who held in one hand a hollow top hat of snow from which he was removing a long-eared rabbit. We applauded him enviously and all three went off to find Jimmy Shaw, who had fashioned two small girls holding hands. I secretly judged his effort sentimental, yet was impressed by his leap into doubleness.

Restless and unappeased, we set out again through the neighborhood, where already a change was evident. The stiffly standing snowmen we had seen earlier in the afternoon were giving way to snowmen that assumed a variety of poses. One, with head bent and a hand pressed to his hat, appeared to be walking into a wind, which blew back the skirt of his long coat. Another, in full stride, had turned with a frown to look over his shoulder, and you could see the creases in his jacket of snow. A third bowed low from the waist, his hat swept out behind him. We returned dissatisfied to our yards. My snowman looked dull, stiff, and vague. I threw myself into the fashioning of a more lively snowman, and as the sun sank below a rooftop I stood back to admire my snowy father, sitting in an armchair of snow with one leg hooked over the arm, holding a book in one hand as, with the other, he turned a single curling page of snow.

Yet even then I realized that it was not enough, that already it had been surpassed, that new forms yearned to be born from our restless, impetuous snow.

That night I could scarcely sleep. With throbbing temples and burning eyes I hurried through breakfast and rushed outside. It was just as I had suspected: a change had been wrought. I could feel it everywhere. Perhaps bands of children, tormented by white dreams, had worked secretly through the night.

The snowmen had grown more marvelous. Groups of snowy figures were everywhere. In one backyard I saw three ice-skaters of snow, their heels lifted and their scarves of snow streaming out behind them. In another yard I saw, gripping their instruments deftly, the fiercely playing members of a string quartet. Individual figures had grown more audacious. On a backyard clothesline I saw a snowy tightrope walker with a long balancing stick of snow, and in another yard I saw a juggler holding two snowballs in one hand while, suspended in the air, directly above his upward-gazing face. . . . But it was precisely a feature of that second day, when the art of the snowman appeared to reach a fullness, that one could no longer be certain to what extent the act of seeing had itself become infected by these fiery snow-dreams. And just when it seemed that nothing further could be dreamed, the snow animals began to appear. I saw a snow lion, a snow elephant with uplifted trunk, a snow horse rearing, a snow gazelle. But once the idea of "snowman," already fertile with instances, had blossomed to include animals, new and dizzying possibilities presented themselves, for there was suddenly nothing to prevent further sproutings and germinations; and it was then that I began to notice, among the graceful white figures and the daring, exquisite animals, the first maples and willows of snow.

It was on the afternoon of that second day that the passion for replication reached heights none of us could have foreseen. Sick with ecstasy, pained with wonder, I walked the white streets with Joey Czukowski and Mario Salvio and Jimmy Shaw. "Look at that!" one of us would cry, and "Cripes, look at that!" Our own efforts had already been left far behind, but it no longer mattered, for the town itself had been struck with genius. Trees of snow had been composed leaf by leaf, with visible veins, and upon the intricate twigs and branches of snow, among the white foliage, one could see white sparrows, white cardinals, white jays. In one yard we saw a garden of snow tulips, row on row. In another yard we saw a snow fountain with arching water jets of finespun snow. And in one backyard we saw an entire parlor all of snow, with snow lamps and snow tables and, in a snow fireplace, logs and flames of snow. Perhaps it was this display that inspired one of the more remarkable creations of that afternoon—in the field down by the stream, dozens of furiously intense children were completing a great house of snow, with turrets and gables and chimneys of snow, and splendid rooms of snow, with floors of snow and furniture of snow, and stairways of snow and mirrors of snow, and cups and rafters and sugar bowls of snow, and, on a mantelpiece of marble snow, a clock of snow with a moving ice pendulum.

I think it was the very thoroughness of these successes that produced in me the first stirrings of uneasiness, for I sensed in our extravagant triumphs an inner impatience. Already, it seemed to me, our snowmen were showing evidence of a skill so excessive, an elaboration so painfully and exquisitely minute, that it could scarcely conceal a desperate restlessness. Someone had fashioned a leafy hedge of snow in which he had devised an intricate snow spiderweb, whose frail threads shimmered in the late afternoon light. Someone else had fashioned a kaleidoscope of snow, which turned to reveal, in delicate ice mirrors, changing arabesques of snow. And on the far side of town we discovered an entire park of snow, already abandoned by its makers: the pine trees had pinecones of snow and individual snow needles, on the snow picnic tables lay fallen acorns of snow, snow burrs caught on our trouser legs, and under an abandoned swing of snow I found, beside an empty Coke bottle made of snow, a snow nickel with a perfectly rendered buffalo.

Exhausted by these prodigies, I sought to pierce the outward shapes and seize the unquiet essence of the snow, but I saw only whiteness there. That night I spent in anxious dreams, and I woke feverish and unrefreshed to a sunny morning.

The world was still white, but snow was dripping everywhere. Icicles, longer and more lovely, shone forth in a last, desperate brilliance, rainspouts trickled, rills of bright black snow-water rushed along the sides of streets and poured through the sewer grates. I did not notice them at first, the harbingers of the new order. It was Mario who pointed the first one out to me. From the corner of a roof it thrust out over the rainspout. I did not understand it, but I was filled with happiness. I began to see others. They projected from roof corners, high above the yards, their smiles twisted in mockery. These gargoyles of snow had perhaps been shaped as a whim, a joke, a piece of childish exuberance, but as they spread through the town I began to sense their true meaning. They were nothing less than a protest against the solemnity, the rigidity, of our snowmen. What had seemed a blossoming forth of hidden powers, that second afternoon, suddenly seemed a form of intricate constriction. It was as if those bird-filled maples, those lions, those leaping ballerinas and prancing clowns, had been nothing but a failure of imagination.

On that third and last day, when our snowmen, weary with consummation, swerved restlessly away, I sensed a fever in the wintry air, as if everyone knew that such strains and ecstasies were bound to end quickly. Scarcely had the gargoyles sprouted from the roofs when, among the trees and tigers, one began to see trolls and ogres and elves. They squatted in the branches of real elms and snow elms, they peeked out through the crossed slats of porch aprons, they hid behind the skirts of snow women. Fantastical snowbirds appeared, nobly lifting their white, impossible wings. Griffins, unicorns, and sea serpents enjoyed a brief reign before being surpassed by splendid new creatures that disturbed us like half-forgotten dreams. Here and there rose fanciful dwellings, like unearthly castles, like fairy palaces glimpsed at the bottoms of lakes on vanished summer afternoons, with soaring pinnacles, twisting passageways, stairways leading nowhere, snow chambers seen in fever dreams.

Yet even these visions of the morning partook of the very world they longed to supplant, and it was not until the afternoon that our snowmen began to achieve freedoms so dangerous that they threatened to burn out the eyes of beholders. It was then that distorted, elongated, disturbingly supple figures began to replace our punctilious imitations. And yet I sensed that they were not distortions, those ungraspable figures, but direct expressions of shadowy inner realms. To behold them was to be filled with a sharp, troubled joy. As the afternoon advanced, and the too-soon-darkening sky warned us of transitory pleasures, I felt a last, intense straining. My nerves trembled, my ears rang with white music. A new mystery was visible everywhere. It was as if snow were throwing off the accident of accumulated heaviness and returning to its original airiness. Indeed these spiritual forms, disdaining the earth, seemed scarcely to be composed of white substance, as if they were striving to escape from the limits of snow itself. Walking the ringing streets in the last light, my nerves stretched taut, I felt in that last rapture of snow a lofty and criminal striving, and all my senses seemed to dissolve in the dark pleasures of transgression.

Drained by these difficult joys, I was not unhappy when the rain came.

It rained all that night, and far into the morning. In the afternoon the sun came out. Bright green grass shone among thin patches of snow. Joey Czukowski, Mario Salvio, Jimmy Shaw, and I roamed the neighborhood before returning to my cellar for a game of ping-pong. Brilliant black puddles shone in the sunny streets. Here and there on snow-patched lawns we saw remains of snowmen, but so melted and disfigured that they were only great lumps of snow. We did not discuss the events of the last few days, which already seemed as fantastic as vanished icicles, as unseizable as fading dreams. "Look at that!" cried Mario, and pointed up. On a telephone wire black as licorice, stretched against the bright blue sky, a blue jay sat and squawked. Suddenly it flew away. A dark yellow willow burned in the sun. On a wooden porch step I saw a brilliant red bowl. "Let's do something," said Joey, and we tramped back to my house, our boots scraping against the asphalt, our boot buckles jangling.

CLAIRE VAYE WATKINS

My thinking is there's no such thing as a bad idea for a story. Or perhaps what I mean is every idea for a story is bad until you make it good. Any time I've written anything good I've spent the vast majority of the composition process convinced it was an utter stinker. And they were stinkers, until they weren't, at which point they were done. The only way to get from one to the other is work. . . . Debunking the myth of the good idea is essential for the short story writer. It is, I think, essential for any writer working in any genre other than film or television. There's a reason fiction writers don't pitch their books (imagine Toni Morrison saying, "Picture this! Ghost baby has sex with her mom's boyfriend! It'll win a Nobel!"). The idea is a formality, mere permission. The triumph is what you do with it.

From a post on TSP: The Story Prize blog
January 7, 2013

"So many people that I admire take the fact that we are, as readers, really curious about the writer and use that as part of the reading experience—acknowledge it, fold it in, and see what they can do with it."

"Whatever I was curious about, I went towards it. Whatever I didn't know, I went towards it. Whatever freaked me out, I just went onward marching towards it."

Onstage interview at The Story Prize event
March 13, 2013

Ghosts, Cowboys

from *Battleborn*

The day my mom checked out, Razor Blade Baby moved in. At the end, I can't stop thinking about beginnings.

The city of Reno, Nevada, was founded in 1859 when Charles Fuller built a log toll bridge across the Truckee River and charged prospectors to haul their Comstock silver across the narrow but swift-moving current. Two years later, Fuller sold the bridge to the ambitious Myron Lake. Lake, swift himself, added a gristmill, kiln, and livery stable to his Silver Queen Hotel and Eating House. Not a bashful man, he named the community Lake's Crossing, had the name painted on Fuller's bridge, bright blue as the sky.

The 1860s were boom times in the western Utah Territory: Americans still had the brackish taste of Sutter's soil on their tongues, ten-year-old gold still glinting in their eyes. The curse of the Comstock Lode had not yet leaked from the silver vein, not seeped into the water table. The silver itself had not yet been stripped from the mountains, and steaming water had not yet flooded the mine shafts. Henry T. P. Comstock—most opportune of the opportunists, snatcher of land, greatest claim jumper of all time—had not yet lost his love Adelaide, his first cousin, who drowned in Lake Tahoe. He had not yet traded his share of the lode for a bottle of whiskey and an old, blind mare, not yet blown his brains out with a borrowed revolver near Bozeman, Montana.

Boom times.

Lake's Crossing grew. At statehood in 1864, the district of Lake's Crossing, Washoe County, was consolidated with Roop County. By then, Lake's Crossing was the largest city in either. The curse, excavated from the silver vein and weighted by the heavy ore, settled on the nation's newest free state.

•

OR BEGIN THE STORY HERE:

In 1881 Himmel Green, an architect, came to Reno from San Francisco to quietly divorce Mary Ann Cohen Magnin of the upscale women's clothing store I. Magnin and Company. Himmel took a liking to Reno and decided to stay. He started designing buildings for his friends, newly rich silver families.

Reno's Newlands Heights neighborhood is choked with Green's work. In 1909, 315 Lake Street was erected. A stout building made of brick, it was one of Himmel's first residential buildings, a modest design, a small porch off the back, simple awnings, thoroughly mediocre in every way. Some say construction at 315 Lake stirred up the cursed dust of the Comstock Lode. Though it contaminated everyone (and though we Nevadans still breathe it into ourselves today), they say it got to Himmel particularly, stuck to his blueprints, his clothing, formed a microscopic layer of silver dust on his skin. Glinting silver film or no, after his divorce was finalized Himmel moved in with Leopold Karpeles, editor of the *B'nai B'rith Messenger.* Their relationship was rumored a tumultuous one, mottled with abuse and infidelity. Still, they lived together until 1932, when the two were burned to death in a fire at Karpeles's home, smoke rising from the house smelling like those miners boiled alive up in Virginia City mine shafts.

OR HERE. HERE IS AS good a place as any:

In March 1941, George Spahn, a dairyman and amateur beekeeper from Pennsylvania, signed over the deed to his sixty-acre farm to his son, Henry, packed four suitcases, his wife, Helen, and their old, foul-tempered calico cat, Bottles, into the car, and drove west to California, to the ocean.

He was to retire, bow out of the ranching business, bury his tired feet in the warm Western sand. But retirement didn't suit George. After two months he came home to their ticky-tacky rental on the beach and presented Helen with plans to buy a 511-acre ranch at 1200 Santa Susana Pass Road in the Santa Susana Mountains. The ranch was up for sale by its owner, the aging silent-film star William S. Hart.

The Santa Susana Mountains are drier than the more picturesque Santa Monica Mountains that line the California coast. Because they are not privy to the moist winds rolling in off the sea, they are susceptible to fires. Twelve hundred Santa Susana Pass Road is tucked up in the Santa Susanas north of Los Angeles, off what is now called the Ronald Reagan Freeway. Back in 1941, when George was persuading Helen to move again, taking her knobby hand in his, begging her to uproot the tendrils she'd so far managed to anchor into the loose beige sand of Manhattan Beach—*Just a bit east this time, sweet pea*—the city of Chatsworth was little more than a Baptist church, a dirt-clogged filling station, and the Palomino Horse Association's main stables, birthplace of Mr. Ed. Years later, in 1961, my father, still a boy, would start a wildfire in the hills above the PHA stables. He would be eleven, crouched in the dry brush, sneaking a cigarette. But let's not get ahead of ourselves.

At the heart of the ranch was a movie set, a thoroughfare of a Western boomtown: bank, saloon, blacksmith, wood-planked boardwalk, side streets and alleys, a jail. Perhaps the set dazzled Helen. Perhaps she—a prematurely arthritic woman—recalled the aching cold of Pennsylvania winters. Perhaps she spoiled her husband, as her children claim. Whatever the reason, Helen laid her hand on her husband's brow and said, "All right, George." And though by all accounts Helen came to like the ranch, on the day George took her out to view the property for the first time her journal reads:

> *The property is quite expansive, surrounded by mountains. G. giddy as a boy. Not such a view as the beach,*

though. The road out is windy and narrow, sheer can-
yon walls on either side. Seems I am to be once again
separated from the sea. And what a brief affair it was!
Looking west I felt a twinge like something had been
taken from me, something a part of me but never truly
mine.

Within a week of the Spahns' move up to 1200 Santa Susana
Pass Road, Bottles the cat ran away.

But George was more adaptable than Bottles, and luck-
ier. In 1941, Westerns were still Hollywood's bread and butter.
George ran his movie set like he'd run his dairy ranch, building strong relationships with decision makers, underpricing the
competition. It certainly didn't hurt business when Malibu Bluff
State Recreation Area annexed Trancas Canyon and sold off its
many sets, making Spahn's Ranch the only privately owned—
and therefore zero-permit—outdoor set for seventy-five miles.
The Spahns enjoyed a steady stream of business from the major
studios, charging them a pretty penny to rent horses and shoot
films at the ranch, among them *High Noon*, *The Comstock Boys*,
and David O. Selznick's 1946 classic *Duel in the Sun*, starring
Gregory Peck. TV shows were also shot at the ranch, including
most episodes of *The Lone Ranger* and—before Warner Brothers,
coaxed by Nevada's tax incentives and the habits of its big-name
directors, moved production to the Ponderosa Ranch at Lake
Tahoe—*Bonanza*.

WE MIGHT START AT MY mother's first memory:

It's 1962. She is three. She sits on her stepfather's lap on a plastic lawn chair on the roof of their trailer. Her older brother and
sister sit cross-legged on a bath towel they've laid atop the chintzy
two-tab roof, the terry cloth dimpling their skin. They each wear

a pair of their mother's—my grandmother's—oversize Jackie O. sunglasses. It is dusk; in the eastern sky stars are coming into view—yes, back then you could still see stars over Las Vegas—but the family faces northwest, as do their neighbors and the teenage boys hired to cut and water the grass at the new golf courses and the city bus drivers who have pulled over to the side of the roads and the tourists up in their hotel rooms with their faces pressed to the windows. As does the whole city.

Their stepfather points to the desert. "There," he says. A flash of light across the basin. An orange mushroom cloud erupts, rolling and boiling. Seconds later, she hears the boom of it, like a firework, and the trailer begins to sway. Impossibly, the heat warms my mother's face. "Makes you think," her stepfather says softly in her ear. "Maybe there's something godly out there after all."

The blast is a 104-kiloton nuclear explosion. It blows a hole into the desert rock, creating the deepest crater of all the Nevada Test Site's 1,021 detonations: 320 feet deep. The crater displaces seven hundred tons of dirt and rock, including two tons of sediment from a vein of H. T. P. Comstock's cursed soil, a finger reaching all the way down the state, now blown sky-high in the blast. The July breeze is gentle, indecisive. It blows the radiation northeast, as it always does, to future cancer clusters in Fallon and Cedar City, Utah, to the mitosing cells of small-town downwinders. But today it also blows the curse southeast, toward Las Vegas, to my mother's small chest, her lungs and her heart. And it blows southwest, across the state line, all the way to the dry yellow mountains above Los Angeles. These particles settle, finally, at 1200 Santa Susana Pass Road.

WE MIGHT START WITH GEORGE'S longest year:

For nearly twenty years, George's letters to his son, Henry, back home in Pennsylvania were characteristically dry, questions about herd count, tips for working the swarm at honey harvest; he hardly mentioned his own ranch, which to his son would not have seemed a ranch at all.

But by the early 1960s the demand for Westerns began to wane and George Spahn blamed, among others, Alfred Hitchcock. He increasingly ended his notes about farm business with aggravated rants about "cut-'em-ups," and "sex-crazed" moviegoers' fixation on horror films, probably meaning Hitchcock's *Psycho*, the second-highest-grossing film of 1960, after *Swiss Family Robinson*. On the first day of February 1966, George Spahn filed for bankruptcy. By then, unbeknownst to George, his wife's kidneys were marbled with tumors. Six weeks later, at UCLA Medical Center, Helen died from renal failure on the same floor where my father would die thirty-four years later. The coroner's report noted that her tumors were visible, and in the glaring light of the microscope seemed "like hundreds of hairlike silver ribbons."

After Helen's death, George neglected the few already tenuous ties he had at the big studios. He wrote Henry often, spoke of the ranch deteriorating, of weeds pushing up through the soil in the corrals.

"I'm tired," he wrote to his son on July 23, 1966. "Let most everyone [three part-time ranch hands] go. It is hot here. So hot I have to wait for dusk to feed the horses. They get impatient down in the stalls and kick the empty troughs over. Boy, you wouldn't believe the noise of their hoofs against the metal . . ."

In the end it was the horses, thirsty or not, that kept Spahn's Ranch afloat. Spahn rented the horses to tourists for self-guided rides through the hills. Occasionally, a few of George's old studio friends would throw business his way, sending for six or eight paints when a scene couldn't have needed more than two. And so the horses became George's main source of income, meager as it was. The Los Angeles County tax records show Spahn's annual income in 1967 to be $13,120, less than a quarter of what it was in 1956.

In previous letters, George rarely wrote of Helen. When he did his lines were terse, referring to her only along with other ranch business: "Storm coming in. Your mother's knuckles would have swelled. Lord knows we need the rain."

That year, George continued to write even as his eyesight failed, his lines sometimes piling atop one another. He began to write of Helen more frequently, sometimes devoting an entire page to her blackberry cobbler or the fragrance of her bath talcum. These are the only letters in which George, otherwise a deliberate and correct writer, slips into the present tense.

In September, George reported discovering a tiny bleached skull in the hills above his cabin. "Bottles," he wrote, "picked clean by coyotes."

OR HERE. BEGIN HERE:

When a group of about ten young people—most of them teen-agers, one of them my father—arrived at the ranch in January of 1968, having hitchhiked from San Francisco, George was nearly blind. Surely he smelled them, though, as they approached his porch—sweat, gasoline, the thick semi-sweet guff of marijuana. The group offered to help George with chores and maintenance in exchange for permission to camp out in the empty façaded set build-ings. Though he'd broken down and hired a hand a couple weeks earlier—a nice kid, a bit macho, went by "Shorty," wanted to be, what else?, an actor—George agreed, perhaps because he wouldn't have to pay them. Or perhaps because the group's leader—a man named Charlie—offered to leave a young girl or two with George twenty-four-seven, to cook his meals, tidy the house, keep up with the laundry, and bed him whenever he wanted.

My father didn't kill anyone. And he's not a hero. It isn't that kind of story.

Nearly everyone who spent time at Spahn's that summer

wrote a book after it was over, Bugliosi's only the most lucrative. We know, from the books of those who noticed, that a baby was born at Spahn's Ranch, likely April ninth, though accounts vary. In her version, Olivia Hall, who'd been a senior at Pacific Palisades High School and an occasional participant in group sex at the ranch, wrote of the birth: "The mother, splayed out on the wood floor of the jail, struggled in labor for nearly fourteen hours, through the night and into the early morning, then gave up." In *The Manson Murders: One Woman's Escape*, Carla Shapiro, now a mother of four boys, says the struggling girl "let her head roll back onto a sleeping bag and would not push. Then Manson took over." My father's book reads, "Charlie held a cigarette lighter under a razor blade until the blade was hot and sliced the girl from vagina to anus." The baby girl slipped out, wailing, into Charlie's arms. My father: "The place was a mess. Blood and clothes everywhere. I don't know where he found the razor blade."

Charlie had a rule against couples. The group had nightly orgies at the ranch and before it in Topanga, Santa Barbara, Big Sur, Santa Cruz, Monterey, Oakland, San Francisco, the list goes on. You know this part, I'm sure. The drugs, the sex. People came and went. Tracing the child's paternity was impossible, even if the group had been interested in that sort of thing. "There was a birth, I know that," Tex Watson wrote to me from prison. "Hell, might've been mine. But we were all pretty gone, you know?"

Of the mother, the accounts mention only how young she was. No name, no explanation of how she came to the ranch. One calls her "dew-faced." In his account my father admits to having sex with her on several occasions. He says, "She was a good kid."

After police raided Spahn's on August sixteenth, California Child Protective Services placed the baby with foster parents, Al and Vaye Orlando of Orlando's Furniture Warehouse in Thousand Oaks. Vaye constantly fussed over the baby, worried at her calmness, what she called "a blankness in her face." During the child's first five years, Vaye had her examined for autism seven times, never trusting the results. She even hired a special nanny to play games with the child, encourage her cognitive development. Al thought this a waste of money.

Now the baby is a grown woman, forty. She is slender but not slight, and moves like liquid does. She has dark hair and the small brown eyes of a deer mouse. Not the eyes of those teenage girls my father met at Pali, the ones he invited to Spahn's and introduced to Charlie, the ones, later, with crosses cut into their foreheads, arms linked, singing down hallways, smiling into the camera in archived footage. I've looked. These are my father's brown eyes. Mine.

TEN YEARS AGO, LAKE STREET—THE last surviving vanity landmark of poor Myron Lake, site of Reno's original iconic arch (you know it, *Biggest Little City in the World*)—was lined with slums: dumpy neglected mansions with fire escapes grafted to their sides, bedsheets covering the windows, most of them half-way houses. But soon people were calling Lake Street and the surrounding neighborhood Newlands Heights. Op-ed columns parleyed on the topic of redevelopment. Three Fifteen Lake was converted from the single-family mansion envisioned by Himmel Green to six one- and two-bedroom apartments in 2001, one of the last to go. By then, Newlands Heights (named, of course, for Francis G. Newlands, Nevada senator, prudent annexer of Hawaii, irrigator of the American West, and great civilizer of savages) was lined with post–Comstock Lode Colonials and Victorians, their lavish parlors and sunrooms partitioned into open studio apart-ments and condos with hardwood floors. They've even torn down the original arch—it attracted vagrants and teenagers, they said. I was assured, back when things like this meant anything to me, that the city was erecting a replica, in neon, across Virginia Street, closer to the big casinos.

These days, they say Newlands Heights is worth quite a bit, and for all my bitching about gentrification, I don't mind this. A person feels just as guilty living among the poor as she does living among the rich, but at least you can be angry at the rich. I can afford to live at 315 Lake only because the landlords, Ben and Gloria (nice people, Burners turned bourgeois, role models to us all), hired my boyfriend—ex-boyfriend—J to do the cabinetwork on the building. J ended up, as he does with so many of his business associates, smoking a bunch of pot with Ben. J considers marijuana the universal ambassador of goodwill, and himself its humble steward. Gloria was pregnant and Ben was desperate, pouring money into a building with no tenants. One afternoon, J and Ben sat on a pallet of bathroom tiles passing a joint between them, and J persuaded Ben to give me a deal on the only unit they'd finished, a studio on the first floor, number two. It was probably the last nice thing I let him do before he left.

I lived through nine months of construction noise and paint smells, the rest of the building a hollow skeleton. Once, I heard someone working in the unit right above me and went up there to see who it was. I was thinking if it was Ben I'd give him my rent check, see if he had any weed I could buy off him, or that he'd just give me. But it was Gloria, standing in a room painted a crisp robin's-egg blue, splotches of the paint on her hands and overalls, speckles in her blond hair. Clear plastic drop cloths billowed in the breeze from the open windows. She rested her hands on her globe of a belly and turned to me. I saw then that the room wasn't entirely painted.

In front of her was a patch of wall the size of a playing card, dingy beige.

"I found it when we scraped the wallpaper," she said, her eyes teared up with sadness or paint fumes or both. She had a paint-

brush in her right hand. "I've been avoiding this spot for a week."
I bent to examine the patch of bare wall and saw there, scrawled in
charcoal or heavy carpenter's pencil,

H loves Leo, 1909.

"How can I do this?" said Gloria. And she said it again as she
slopped a stripe of blue over the writing.

This was just before my mom died. Before Razor Blade Baby
moved in. I didn't know what to say. Now I know better. I see
Gloria in the yard, and I'd like to give her an answer. She's had her
baby and puts a playpen under the willow tree and sings over to
the girl while she gardens. She named her Marigold. I'd like to say:
You do it because you have to. We all do.

And here we are.

The day my mom checked out, Razor Blade Baby moved in.
Upstairs. Number four. Right above me. We are neighbors at 315
Lake Street, Newlands Heights, Reno, Nevada. That first day I
heard the floorboards above my bed creak, then the hall stairs.
When I opened the door, Razor Blade Baby invited me to see a
three-dollar matinee at the old Hilton Theatre. Though I like their
popcorn (stale and fluorescent yellow, salty enough to erode a gully
in the roof of your mouth) and their hot dogs (all beef), I said what
I would say every Sunday: No. No, thank you. I closed the door,
and she sat on the stairs as she would every Sunday. She stayed
there all day.

My father, Paul Watkins, met Charles Manson at a house
party in San Francisco eleven months before Razor Blade Baby was
born. He and Charlie wrote songs together and camped around
the bay until December, when they set out for L.A., bored with the
city, sick of the rain. Paul was eighteen and handsome. Or so my
mother would tell me later.

At Spahn's, Paul moved his things into the old jail set: a sleeping bag, candles, his guitar and flute. He looked younger than his age, young enough to enroll himself in Pacific Palisades High School, though he'd already graduated the previous spring, a year early. He would become fond of pointing this out in interviews. (To Maureen Reagan on *Larry King Live*, August 23, 1987: "We were bright kids, Maureen. Not delinquents. I was the class president." Larry was out sick.) Paul went to Pali, home of the Dolphins, for two months to meet girls and bring them back to the ranch. He was good at it.

Years later, well after he was finally swallowed up by Hodgkin's disease, my mother, after one of her attempts to join him, wherever he was, called my father "Charlie's number one procurer of young girls." I couldn't tell whether she was ashamed or proud of him.

She also said, lying on her bed at University Medical Center, bandages on her wrists where she'd taken a steak knife to them, "When you go, all that matters is who's there with you. Believe me. I've been close enough enough times to know."

About once a year someone tracks me down. Occasionally it's one of Charlie's fans wanting to stand next to Paul Watkins's daughter, to rub up against all that's left, to put a picture up on his red-text-on-black-background website. Far more often, though, it's someone with a script. Producers, usually legit ones—I Google them: *True Lies*, *The Deer Hunter*. They offer to drive down from Lake Tahoe, take me out to dinner. They never want my permission to make their movie or input on who should play me (Winona Ryder); they just want to know how am I.

"How *are* you?" they say.

"I'm a receptionist," I say.

"Good," they say, long and slow, nodding as though my being a receptionist has given them everything they came for.

The day after Razor Blade Baby moved in, I rode my bike across the Truckee River to work. Razor Blade Baby followed, wearing a blazer, trailing behind me on a violet beach cruiser with a wicker basket, her long hair flapping behind her as though tugged by a hundred tiny kites. She followed me up the courthouse steps and sat in the lobby in front of my desk. She stayed there until lunch, when we sat on a bench beside the river, me eating a burrito from the cart, her dipping celery sticks into a Tupperware dish of tuna salad made with plain yogurt instead of mayonnaise. After lunch I went back to work, she back to the lobby. At five we rode home.

Some days she brings a roll of quarters and plugs the parking meters in front of the building. Others she crosses the street and browses the souvenir shops. I watch her from my office window, through the shop's glass front, running her fingers along the car-ousels of T-shirts. When the sun is very hot she simply sits on the courthouse's marble steps, drinking a cherry Slurpee, her palm pressed to the warm rock.

Some weekends I go out, and Razor Blade Baby comes along. One night, about three months after she moved in, I went to a dinner party to celebrate a friend's new condo, built high up in the hollowed-out bones of the renovated Flamingo. A row of one-legged bird silhouettes was still left on the building's façade.

It was a fine party, good food. I wore a poufy emerald green cocktail dress with pink flats, a pink ribbon in my hair. My friends, trying their very best for normalcy, sometimes pointed across the room and asked, "Claire, sweetheart, did you bring your auntie? You look just like her."

"Oh, no," I would say, swallowing the last bit of prosciutto or salmon dip or whatever it was. "That's Razor Blade Baby. She goes everywhere with me."

That night Razor Blade Baby and I left the party and started our walk back to 315 Lake. It had been raining heavily up in the Sierras for two days straight, and the Truckee was raging—the highest I'd ever seen it. The water was milky and opaque, and in it tumbled massive logs that had probably lain on the river's bed unmoved for years. Across the bridge two concrete stumps with rebar worming out the tops stood on either side of the street like sentinels, all that was left of the original arch. We stood there for a long while, Razor Blade Baby and I, sort of hypnotized with the high water thrashing by, not sure whether it was safe to cross or what we'd do when we reached the other side. I imagined taking very small steps down the wet, slippery bank and wading into the current, my pockets weighed down with silver.

At home I got stoned and thought—as I often do after tracing my fingers over the frosted glass of my cabinets, my butcher-block countertops, sanded and varnished by his hands, all that's left of him, in my life anyway—of calling J. But I was no more capable of giving him what he needed than I was the day he left.

I didn't call. Instead I smoked myself deeper into oblivion and watched my hot breath billow at the ceiling, Razor Blade Baby no doubt on the other side, and fell asleep.

I BELIEVE I FELL IN love with one of them, these producers. He e-mailed me, said his name was Andrew, that he wanted to have dinner and talk about a film he wanted to make about my father, about how he was Charlie's number two in charge (true), how he came to live in an abandoned shack in the desert (true), how he got sober and testified against Charlie, then fell off the wagon again, blacked out, and woke up in a van, on fire (mostly true). I agreed to let him buy me dinner, as it is almost always my principle to do.

I met Andrew at Louis' Basque Corner on Fourth Street. Razor Blade Baby came along. I take all the movie guys to Louis', or I used to before Andrew. Now I take them to Miguel's off Mount Rose, also very tasty.

"What's good here?" he said. He had an easy, loose smile.

"Picon Punch," I said. "If you come here and don't order the Picon Punch, you didn't really come here." This was my bit. My Picon Punch bit.

Picon Punch is the deep brown of leather oil. Only the Basques know what's in it, but we all have a theory—rum, licorice root, and gin; top-shelf rye with club soda and three drops of vanilla extract; well vodka; gin and a splash of apple juice; Seagram's, scotch, and a ground-up Ricola cough drop—all theories equally plausible, none of them the truth. One Picon Punch will make you buy another. Two is too many. That night we had three each.

For dinner we ordered the sweetbreads and two Winnemucca coffees and ate at the bar playing video poker, Deuces Wild. Razor Blade Baby played Ms. Pac-Man in the back.

We talked quietly, closely. Every once in a while Razor Blade Baby floated over and stood at my elbow. I did my best to shoo her away. I gave her another roll of quarters and found myself leaning into Andrew. He smelled of strong stinging cinnamon, like a smoker who tried hard to hide it.

A casino can make an average man lovely. The lights are dim, the ceiling low and mirrored. The machines light his face from below in a soft sweet blue. As they turn to reveal themselves on the screen, the electric playing cards reflect in his eyes as quick glints of light. The dense curtain of cigarette smoke filters the place fuzzy, as if what the two of you do there isn't actually happening. As if it were already in the past. As if your life wasn't a life but an old nostalgic movie. *Duel in the Sun*, perhaps. You don't want to know what a casino can do to a man already lovely.

It wasn't long before we were turned facing each other, and my right leg, dangling off my stool, found its way between his legs, nestled into his groin. We finished off the sweetbreads with our hands, sopping the small sinewy pieces of young lamb glands in onion sauce.

He asked about my father. I wanted to tell him what I told you, but that's nothing that can't be found in a book, a diary, a newspaper, a coroner's report. And there is still so much I'll never know, no matter how much history I weigh upon myself. I can tell you the

shape of the stain left by H. T. P. Comstock's brain matter on the
wooden walls of his cabin, but not whether he tasted the sour of the
curse in his mouth just before he pulled the trigger. I can tell you
the backward slant of Himmel Green's left-handed cursive, but not
whether Leo loved him back. I can tell you of the silver gleam of
Helen Spahn's tumors, but not whether she felt them growing inside her. I can tell you of the view from George's front porch, of the
wide yellow valley below, but not what he saw after he went blind.
I can tell you the things my father said to lure the Manson girls
back to Spahn's Ranch, but I can't say whether he believed them.
I can tell you the length and width and number of the cuts on my
mother's wrists, and the colors her skin turned as they healed, but
I couldn't say whether she would do it again, or when. Everything I
can say about what it means to lose, what it means to do without,
the inadequate weight of the past, you already know.

But the whiskey in our coffees was doing its job. I was feeling
loose. So I told him what I could. I told him of the heavy earth
scent after a desert rain, three or four times a year. That it smelled
like the breathing of every thankful desert plant, every plot of soil,
every unfound scrap of silver. That it had a way of softening you,
of making you vulnerable. That it could redeem.

After dinner we watched Razor Blade Baby until she killed
off her last life. Andrew walked us out to our bikes and helped us
unchain them. He kissed me then, or rather we kissed each other,
right in front of Razor Blade Baby. It was an inevitable kiss. A kiss
like I had caught the hem of my skirt on the seat of my bike while
trying to mount it, and toppled. A kiss like we had fallen into each
other, which I suppose we had.

Afterward, Razor Blade Baby and I rode home to 315 Lake,
headlights lighting us from behind. When I closed my front door,
my cell phone rang.

"Come outside." It was Andrew, his voice breathy, sweetly
slurred.

"What?"

My doorbell buzzed. I pulled the curtain of my living room window aside, saw him swaying slightly on the porch, glowing phone pressed to his ear.

"Or come and live with me," he said.

"You're drunk," I said.

"So are you. Let me in. We'll move to L.A., down by the ocean. You can ride your bike up and down the coast. Or forget L.A., we can live here, in the mountains. In the desert. Whatever this is. That thing you said about the rain. You and me, Claire. Just let me in."

And I wanted to let him in. It wasn't that I didn't want to. I was swaying now and reached for the wall to steady myself, trying to stop the swirl of Picon in my head, my chest. Tried not to think of the words written there under the paint. *When you go, all that matters is who's there with you. Believe me.* I rested my head against the front door and wanted badly to open it. But the story was too much, wherever I began: the borrowed revolver on the floor of a cabin near Bozeman, Montana. The sweet sizzle of Himmel Green's skin as it melted into Leopold's. Helen Spahn's withering uprooted tendrils. Bottles's dry bleached bones. My parents' own toxic and silver-gilded love. Razor Blade Baby, the simple fact of her.

"Good night, Andy," I said. "Please don't call me again."

When I hung up, I heard the sound I had already come to know: a quick creak in the floorboards above me. Razor Blade Baby's body shifting. The unpressing of her ear from the floor.

WHEN RAZOR BLADE BABY CAME to my door the next morning—this morning—I did not say, No. No, thank you. We rode our bicycles to the old Hilton Theatre, down Lake Street. Her hair flapped behind her as though lifted by George Spahn's Pennsylvanian swarm.

I bought a hot dog before the matinee from the concession stand. I covered it with mustard, onions, kraut, jalapeños. Razor Blade Baby nervously fingered a Ziploc bag of peeled carrot sticks hidden in her purse.

Here in the theater I know I ought to try, ought to carry that weight, ought to paint over the past. But I can only do my best. I hold my hot dog near her face. "Want a bite, Razor Blade Baby?"

"Claire," she says. "I could be your sister."

And though we have known this since she moved in—well before—this is the first time either of us has said it aloud. And I admit now, it sounds softer than it felt. There is something thankful in the saying.

I nod. "Half sister."

The lights in the theater dim. Technicolor figures—ghosts, cowboys, Gregory Peck—move across the screen. In *Duel in the Sun* Pearl Chavez asks, "Oh, Vashti, why are you so slow?"

"I don't rightly know, Miss Pearl, except I always have so much to remember."

GEORGE SAUNDERS

"If you feel that there's a comic riff that's based on cruelty, if you say *No, but I'm compassionate, I won't do that*, you've lamed yourself in a certain way. So the way I think of it is it's not compassion but just: Have you spent sufficient time with the character to not be missing anything that he might have to offer? If you say: *Jim was an asshole.* All right, that's not great. Well, let's be more specific. When was Jim an asshole? *On Wednesday, Jim was an asshole.* Where? *On Wednesday, Jim was an asshole at the coffee shop.* How? *Jim was an asshole when he was rude to the barista.* How? *He insulted her because she was slow.* Why did he do that? *She reminded him of his dead wife.* Boom! Suddenly, he's not an asshole. He's a sweetheart. But you didn't get there by saying, *Let's be kind to Jim.*"

"My whole trajectory in writing has been to learn that I'm better off when I don't know anything about what's going to happen. I don't want to have any real hopes for the story except that it won't be dull."

Onstage interview at The Story Prize event
March 5, 2014

Tenth of December

from *Tenth of December*

The pale boy with unfortunate Prince Valiant bangs and cublike mannerisms hulked to the mudroom closet and requisitioned Dad's white coat. Then requisitioned the boots he'd spray-painted white. Painting the pellet gun white had been a no. That was a gift from Aunt Chloe. Every time she came over he had to haul it out so she could make a big stink about the wood grain.

Today's assignation: walk to pond, ascertain beaver dam. Likely he would be detained. By that species that lived amongst the old rock wall. They were small but, upon emerging, assumed certain proportions. And gave chase. This was just their methodology. His aplomb threw them loops. He knew that. And reveled in it. He would turn, level the pellet gun, intone: Are you aware of the usage of this human implement?

Blam!

They were Netherworlders. Or Nethers. They had a strange bond with him. Sometimes for whole days he would just nurse their wounds. Occasionally, for a joke, he would shoot one in the butt as it fled. Who henceforth would limp for the rest of its days. Which could be as long as an additional nine million years.

Safe inside the rock wall, the shot one would go, Guys, look at my butt.

As a group, all would look at Gzeemon's butt, exchanging sullen glances of: Gzeemon shall indeed be limping for the next nine million years, poor bloke.

Because yes: Nethers tended to talk like that guy in *Mary Poppins.*

Which naturally raised some mysteries as to their ultimate origin here on Earth.

Detaining him was problematic for the Nethers. He was wily. Plus could not fit through their rock-wall opening. When they tied him up and went inside to brew their special miniaturizing potion—*Wham!*—he would snap their antiquated rope with a move from his self-invented martial arts system, Toi Foi, a.k.a., Deadly Forearms. And place at their doorway an implacable rock of suffocation, trapping them inside.

Later, imagining them in their death throes, taking pity on them, he would come back, move the rock.

Blimey, one of them might say from withal. Thanks, guv'nor. You are indeed a worthy adversary.

Sometimes there would be torture. They would make him lie on his back looking up at the racing clouds while they tortured him in ways he could actually take. They tended to leave his teeth alone. Which was lucky. He didn't even like to get a cleaning. They were dunderheads in that manner. They never messed with his peen and never messed with his fingernails. He'd just abide there, infuriating them with his snow angels. Sometimes, believing it their coup de grace, not realizing he'd heard this since time in memorial from certain in-school cretins, they'd go, Wow, we didn't even know Robin could be a boy's name. And chortle their Nether laughs.

Today he had a feeling that the Nethers might kidnap Suzanne Bledsoe, the new girl in homeroom. She was from Montreal. He just loved the way she talked. So, apparently, did the Nethers, who planned to use her to repopulate their depleted numbers and bake various things they did not know how to bake.

All suited up now, NASA. Turning awkwardly to go out the door.

Affirmative. We have your coordinates. Be careful out there, Robin.

Whoa, cold, dang.

Duck thermometer read ten. And that was without windchill.

That made it fun. That made it real. A green Nissan was parked where Poole dead-ended into the soccer field. Hopefully the owner was not some perv he would have to outwit.

Or a Nether in the human guise.

Bright, bright, blue and cold. Crunch went the snow as he crossed the soccer field. Why did cold such as this give a running guy a headache? Likely it was due to Prominent Windspeed Velocity.

The path into the woods was as wide as one human. It seemed the Nether had indeed kidnapped Suzanne Bledsoe. Damn him! And his ilk. Judging by the single set of tracks, the Nether appeared to be carrying her. Foul cad. He'd better not be touching Suzanne inappropriately while carrying her. If so, Suzanne would no doubt be resisting with untamable fury.

This was concerning, this was very concerning. When he caught up to them, he would say: Look, Suzanne, I know you don't know my name, having misaddressed me as Roger that time you asked me to scoot over, but nevertheless I must confess I feel there is something to us. Do you feel the same?

Suzanne had the most amazing brown eyes. They were wet now, with fear and sudden reality.

Stop talking to her, mate, the Nether said.

I won't, he said. And Suzanne? Even if you don't feel there is something to us, rest assured I will still slay this fellow and return you home. Where do you live again? Over in El Cirro? By the water tower? Those are some nice houses back there.

Yes, Suzanne said. We also have a pool. You should come over this summer. It's cool if you swim with your shirt on. And also, yes to there being something to us. You are by far the most insightful boy in our class. Even when I take into consideration the boys I knew in Montreal, I am just like: No one can compare.

Well, that's nice to hear, he said. Thank you for saying that. I know I'm not the thinnest.

The thing about girls? Suzanne said. Is we are more content-driven.

Will you two stop already? the Nether said. Because now is the time for your death. Deaths.

Well, now is certainly the time for somebody's death, Robin said.

The twerpy thing was, you never really got to save anyone. Last summer there'd been a dying raccoon out here. He'd thought of lugging it home so Mom could call the vet. But up close it was too scary. Raccoons being actually bigger than they appear in cartoons. And this one looked like a potential biter. So he ran home to get it some water at least. Upon his return, he saw where the raccoon had done some apparent last-minute thrashing. That was sad. He didn't do well with sad. There had perchance been some pre-weeping, by him, in the woods.

That just means you have a big heart, Suzanne said.

Well, I don't know, he said modestly.

Here was the old truck tire. Where the high-school kids partied. Inside the tire, frosted with snow, were three beer cans and a wadded-up blanket.

You probably like to party, the Nether had cracked to Suzanne moments earlier as they passed this very spot.

No, I don't, Suzanne said. I like to play. And I like to hug.

Hoo boy, the Nether said. Sounds like Dullsville.

Somewhere there is a man who likes to play and hug, Suzanne said.

He came out of the woods now to the prettiest vista he knew. The pond was a pure frozen white. It struck him as somewhat Switzerlandish. Someday he would know for sure. When the Swiss threw him a parade or whatnot.

Here the Nether's tracks departed from the path, as if he had contemplatively taken a moment to gaze at the pond. Perhaps this Nether was not all bad. Perhaps he was having a debilitating conscience-attack vis-à-vis the valiantly struggling Suzanne atop his back. At least he seemed to somewhat love nature.

Then the tracks returned to the path, wound around the pond, and headed up Lexow Hill.

What was this strange object? A coat? On the bench? The bench the Nethers used for their human sacrifices?

No accumulated snow on coat. Inside of coat still slightly warm.

Ergo: the recently discarded coat of the Nether.

This was some strange juju. This was an intriguing conundrum, if he had ever encountered one. Which he had. Once, he'd found a bra on the handlebars of a bike. Once, he'd found an entire untouched steak dinner on a plate behind Fresno's. And hadn't eaten it. Though it had looked pretty good.

Something was afoot.

Then he beheld, halfway up Lexow Hill, a man.

Coatless bald-headed man. Super-skinny. In what looked like pajamas. Climbing plodfully, with tortoise patience, bare white arms sticking out of his p.j. shirt like two bare white branches sticking out of a p.j. shirt. Or grave.

What kind of person leaves his coat behind on a day like this? The mental kind, that was who. This guy looked sort of mental. Like an Auschwitz dude or sad confused grandpa.

Dad had once said, Trust your mind, Rob. If it smells like shit but has writing across it that says Happy Birthday and a candle stuck down in it, what is it?

Is there icing on it? he'd said.

Dad had done that thing of squinting his eyes when an answer was not quite there yet.

What was his mind telling him now?

Something was wrong here. A person needed a coat. Even if the person was a grown-up. The pond was frozen. The duck thermometer said ten. If the person was mental, all the more reason to

come to his aid, as had not Jesus said, Blessed are those who help
those who cannot help themselves but are too mental, doddering,
or have a disability?

He snagged the coat off the bench.

It was a rescue. A real rescue, at last, sort of.

TEN MINUTES EARLIER, DON EBER had paused at the pond to
catch his breath.

He was so tired. What a thing. Holy moley. When he used to
walk Sasquatch out here they'd do six times around the pond, jog
up the hill, tag the boulder on top, sprint back down.

Better get moving, said one of two guys who'd been in discussion in his head all morning.

That is, if you're still set on the boulder idea, the other said.

Which still strikes us as kind of fancy-pants.

Seemed like one guy was Dad and the other Kip Flemish.

Stupid cheaters. They'd switched spouses, abandoned the
switched spouses, fled together to California. Had they been gay?
Or just swingers? Gay swingers? The Dad and Kip in his head had
acknowledged their sins and the three of them had struck a deal:
he would forgive them for being possible gay swingers and leaving
him to do Soap Box Derby alone, with just Mom, and they would
consent to giving him some solid manly advice.

He wants it to be nice.

This was Dad now. It seemed Dad was somewhat on his side.

Nice? Kip said. *That is not the word I would use.*

A cardinal zinged across the day.

It was amazing. Amazing, really. He was young. He was fifty-
three. Now he'd never deliver his major national speech on compassion. What about going down the Mississippi in a canoe? What
about living in an A-frame near a shady creek with the two hippie
girls he'd met in 1968 in that souvenir shop in the Ozarks, when

Allen, his stepfather, wearing those crazy aviators, had bought him a bag of fossil rocks? One of the hippie girls had said that he, Eber, would be a fox when he grew up, and would he please be sure to call her at that time? Then the hippie girls had put their tawny heads together and giggled at his prospective foxiness. And that had never—

That had somehow never—

Sister Val had said, Why not shoot for being the next JFK? So he had run for class president. Allen had bought him a Styrofoam straw boater. They'd sat together, decorating the hatband with Magic Markers. WIN WITH EBER! On the back: GROOVY! Allen had helped him record a tape. Of a little speech. Allen had taken that tape somewhere and come back with thirty copies, "to pass around."

"Your message is good," Allen had said. "And you are incredibly well spoken. You can do this thing."

And he'd done it. He'd won. Allen had thrown him a victory party. A pizza party. All the kids had come.

Oh, Allen.

Kindest man ever. Had taken him swimming. Had taken him to découpage. Had combed out his hair so patiently that time he came home with lice. Never a harsh, etc., etc.

Not so once the suffering begat. Began. God damn it. More and more his words. Askew. More and more his words were not what he would hoped.

Hope.

Once the suffering began, Allen had raged. Said things no one should say. To Mom, to Eber, to the guy delivering water. Went from a shy man, always placing a reassuring hand on your back, to a diminished pale figure in a bed, shouting CUNT!

Except with some weird New England accent so it came out KANT!

The first time Allen had shouted KANT! there followed a funny moment during which he and Mom looked at each other to see which of them was being called KANT. But then Allen amended, for clarity: KANTS!

So it was clear he meant both of them. What a relief.

They'd cracked up.

Jeez, how long had he been standing here? Daylight was waiting.

Wasting.

I honestly didn't know what to do. But he made it so simple.

Took it all on himself.

So what else is new?

Exactly.

This was Jodi and Tommy now.

Hi, kids.

Big day today.

I mean, sure, it would have been nice to have a chance to say a proper good-bye.

But at what cost?

Exactly. And see—he knew that.

He was a father. That's what a father does.

Eases the burdens of those he loves.

Saves the ones he loves from painful last images that might endure for a lifetime.

Soon Allen had become THAT. And no one was going to fault anybody for avoiding THAT. Sometimes he and Mom would huddle in the kitchen. Rather than risk incurring the wrath of THAT. Even THAT understood the deal. You'd trot in a glass of water, set it down, say, very politely, Anything else, Allen? And you'd see THAT thinking, All these years I was so good to you people and now I am merely THAT? Sometimes the gentle Allen would be inside there too, indicating, with his eyes, Look, go away, please go away, I am trying so hard not to call you KANT!

Rail-thin, ribs sticking out.

Catheter taped to dick.

Waft of shit smell.

You are not Allen and Allen is not you.

So Molly had said.

As for Dr. Spivey, he couldn't say. Wouldn't say. Was busy drawing a daisy on a Post-it. Then finally said, Well, honestly? As these things grow, they can tend to do weird things. But it doesn't necessarily have to be terrible. Had one guy? Just always craved him a Sprite.

And Eber had thought, Did you, dear doctor/savior/lifeline, just say *craved him a Sprite*?

That's how they got you. You thought, Maybe I'll just crave me a Sprite. Next thing you knew, you were THAT, shouting KANT!, shitting your bed, swatting at the people who were scrambling to clean you.

No, sir.

No sirree bob.

Wednesday he'd fallen out of the med bed again. There on the floor in the dark it had come to him: I could spare them.

Spare us? Or spare you?

Get thee behind me.

Get thee behind me, sweetie.

A breeze sent down a sequence of linear snow puffs from somewhere above. Beautiful. Why were we made just so, to find so many things that happened every day pretty?

He took off his coat.

Good Christ.

Took off his hat and gloves, stuffed the hat and gloves in a sleeve of the coat, left the coat on the bench.

This way they'd know. They'd find the car, walk up the path, find the coat.

It was a miracle. That he'd gotten this far. Well, he'd always been strong. Once, he'd run a half-marathon with a broken foot. After his vasectomy he'd cleaned the garage, no problem.

He'd waited in the med bed for Molly to go off to the pharmacy. That was the toughest part. Just calling out a normal good-bye.

His mind veered toward her now, and he jerked it back with a prayer: Let me pull this off. Lord, let me not fuck it up. Let me bring no dishonor. Leg me do it cling.

Let. Let me do it cling.

Clean.

Cleanly.

ESTIMATED TIME OF OVERTAKING THE Nether, handing him his coat? Approximately nine minutes. Six minutes to follow the path around the pond, an additional three minutes to fly up the hillside like a delivering wraith or mercy angel, bearing the simple gift of a coat.

That is just an estimate, NASA. I pretty much made that up.

We know that, Robin. We know very well by now how irreverent you work.

Like that time you cut a fart on the moon.

Or the time you tricked Mel into saying, "Mr. President, what a delightful surprise it was to find an asteroid circling Uranus."

That estimate was particularly iffy. This Nether being surprisingly brisk. Robin himself was not the fastest wicket in the stick. He had a certain girth. Which Dad prognosticated would soon triumphantly congeal into linebackerish solidity. He hoped so. For now he just had the slight man boobs.

Robin, hurry, Suzanne said. I feel so sorry for that poor old guy.

He's a fool, Robin said, because Suzanne was young, and did not yet understand that when a man was a fool he made hardships for the other men, who were less foolish than he.

He doesn't have much time, Suzanne said, bordering on the hysterical.

There, there, he said, comforting her.

I'm just so frightened, she said.

And yet he is fortunate to have one such as I to hump his coat up that big-ass hill, which, due to its steepness, is not exactly my cup of tea, Robin said.

I guess that's the definition of "hero," Suzanne said.

I guess so, he said.

I don't mean to continue being insolent, she said. But he seems to be pulling away.

What would you suggest? he said.

With all due respect, she said, and because I know you consider us as equals but different, with me covering the brainy angle and special inventions and whatnot?

Yes, yes, go ahead, he said.

Well, just working through the math in terms of simple geometry—

He saw where she was going with this. And she was quite right. No wonder he loved her. He must cut across the pond, thereby decreasing the ambient angle, ergo trimming valuable seconds off his catch-up time.

Wait, Suzanne said. Is that dangerous?

It is not, he said. I have done it numerous times.

Please be careful, Suzanne implored.

Well, once, he said.

You have such aplomb, Suzanne demurred.

Actually never, he said softly, not wishing to alarm her.

Your bravery is irascible, Suzanne said.

He started across the pond.

It was actually pretty cool walking on water. In summer, canoes floated here. If Mom could see him, she'd have a conniption. Mom treated him like a piece of glass. Due to his alleged infant surgeries. She went on full alert if he so much as used a stapler.

But Mom was a good egg. A reliable counselor and steady hand of guidance. She had a munificent splay of long silver hair and a raspy voice, though she didn't smoke and was even a vegan. She'd never been a biker chick, although some of the in-school cretins claimed she resembled one.

He was actually quite fond of Mom.

He was now approximately three-quarters, or that would be sixty percent, across.

Between him and the shore lay a grayish patch. Here in summer a stream ran in. Looked a tad iffy. At the edge of the grayish patch he gave the ice a bonk with the butt of his gun. Solid as anything.

Here he went. Ice rolled a bit underfoot. Probably it was shallow here. Anyways he hoped so. Yikes.

How's it going? Suzanne said, trepidly.

Could be better, he said.

Maybe you should turn back, Suzanne said.

But wasn't this feeling of fear the exact feeling all heroes had to confront early in life? Wasn't overcoming this feeling of fear what truly distinguished the brave?

There could be no turning back.

Or could there? Maybe there could. Actually there should.

The ice gave way and the boy fell through.

NAUSEA HAD NOT BEEN MENTIONED in *The Humbling Steppe*.

A blissful feeling overtook me as I drifted off to sleep at the base of the crevasse. No fear, no discomfort, only a vague sadness at the thought of all that remained undone. This is death? I thought. It is but nothing.

Author, whose name I cannot remember, I would like a word with you.

A-hole.

The shivering was insane. Like a tremor. His head was shaking on his neck. He paused to puke a bit in the snow, white-yellow against the white-blue.

This was scary. This was scary now.

Every step was a victory. He had to remember that. With every step he was fleeing father and father. Farther from father. Stepfarther. What a victory he was wresting. From the jaws of the feet.

He felt a need at the back of his throat to say it right.

From the jaws of defeat. From the jaws of defeat.

Oh, Allen.

Even when you were THAT you were still Allen to me.

Please know that.

Falling, Dad said.

For some definite time he waited to see where he would land and how much it would hurt. Then there was a tree in his gut. He found himself wrapped fetally around some tree.

Fucksake.

Ouch, ouch. This was too much. He hadn't cried after the surgeries or during the chemo, but he felt like crying now. It wasn't fair. It happened to everyone supposedly but now it was happening specifically to him. He'd kept waiting for some special dispensation. But no. Something/someone bigger than him kept refusing. You were told the big something/someone loved you especially but in the end you saw it was otherwise. The big something/someone was neutral. Unconcerned. When it innocently moved, it crushed people.

Years ago at *The Illuminated Body* he and Molly had seen this brain slice. Marring the brain slice had been a nickel-sized brown spot. That brown spot was all it had taken to kill the guy. Guy must have had his hopes and dreams, closet full of pants, and so on, some treasured childhood memories: a mob of koi in the willow shade at Gage Park, say, Gram searching in her Wrigley's-smelling purse for a tissue—like that. If not for that brown spot, the guy might have been one of the people walking by on the way to lunch in the atrium. But no. He was defunct now, off rotting somewhere, no brain in his head.

Looking down at the brain slice Eber had felt a sense of superiority. Poor guy. It was pretty unlucky, what had happened to him.

He and Molly had fled to the atrium, had hot scones, watched a squirrel mess with a plastic cup.

Wrapped fetally around the tree Eber traced the scar on his head. Tried to sit. No dice. Tried to use the tree to sit up. His hand wouldn't close. Reaching around the tree with both hands, joining his hands at the wrists, he pulled himself up, leaned back against the tree.

How was that?

Fine.

Good, actually.

Maybe this was it. Maybe this was as far as he got. He'd had it in mind to sit cross-legged against the boulder at the top of the hill, but really what difference did it make?

All he had to do now was stay put. Stay put by force-thinking the same thoughts he'd used to propel himself out of the med bed and into the car and across the soccer field and through the woods: MollyTommyJodi huddling in the kitchen filled with pity/loathing, MollyTommyJodi recoiling at something cruel he'd said, Tommy hefting his thin torso up in his arms so that MollyJodi could get under there with a wash—

Then it would be done. He would have preempted all future debasement. All his fears about the coming months would be mute.

Moot.

This was it. Was it? Not yet. Soon, though. An hour? Forty minutes? Was he doing this? Really? He was. Was he? Would he be able to make it back to the car even if he changed his mind? He thought not. Here he was. He was here. This incredible opportunity to end things with dignity was right in his hands.

All he had to do was stay put.

I will fight no more forever.

Concentrate on the beauty of the pond, the beauty of the

woods, the beauty you are returning to, the beauty that is everywhere as far as you can—

Oh, for shitsake.

Oh, for crying out loud.

Some kid was on the pond.

Chubby kid in white. With a gun. Carrying Eber's coat.

You little fart, put that coat down, get your ass home, mind
your own—

Damn. Damn it.

Kid tapped the ice with the butt of his gun.

You wouldn't want some kid finding you. That could scar a
kid. Although kids found freaky things all the time. Once he'd
found a naked photo of Dad and Mrs. Flemish. That had been
freaky. Of course, not as freaky as a grimacing cross-legged—

Kid was swimming.

Swimming was not allowed. That was clearly posted. NO
SWIMMING.

Kid was a bad swimmer. Real thrashfest down there. Kid was
creating with his thrashing a rapidly expanding black pool. With
each thrash the kid incrementally expanded the boundary of the
black—

He was on his way down before he knew he'd started. *Kid in
the pond, kid in the pond*, ran repetitively through his head as he
minced. Progress was tree to tree. Standing there panting, you got
to know a tree well. This one had three knots: eye, eye, nose. This
started out as one tree and became two.

Suddenly he was not purely the dying guy who woke nights in
the med bed thinking, Make this not true make this not true, but
again, partly, the guy who used to put bananas in the freezer, then
crack them on the counter and pour chocolate over the broken
chunks, the guy who'd once stood outside a classroom window in
a rainstorm to see how Jodi was faring with that little red-headed
shit who wouldn't give her a chance at the book table, the guy who

used to hand-paint birdfeeders in college and sell them on weekends in Boulder, wearing a jester hat and doing a little juggling
routine he'd—

He started to fall again, caught himself, froze in a hunched-
over position, hurtled forward, fell flat on his face, chucked his
chin on a root.

You had to laugh.

You almost had to laugh.

He got up. Got doggedly up. His right hand presented as a
bloody glove. Tough nuts, too bad. Once, in football, a tooth had
come out. Later in the half, Eddie Blandik had found it. He'd
taken it from Eddie, flung it away. That had also been him.

Here was the switchbank. It wasn't far now. Switchback.

What to do? When he got there? Get kid out of pond. Get
kid moving. Force-walk kid through woods, across soccer field, to
one of the houses on Poole. If nobody home, pile kid into Nissan,
crank up heater, drive to—Our Lady of Sorrows? UrgentCare?
Fastest route to UrgentCare?

Fifty yards to the trailhead.

Twenty yards to the trailhead.

Thank you, God, for my strength.

IN THE POND HE WAS all animal-thought, no words, no self,
blind panic. He resolved to really try. He grabbed for the edge.
The edge broke away. Down he went. He hit mud and pushed up.
He grabbed for the edge. The edge broke away. Down he went. It
seemed like it should be easy, getting out. But he just couldn't do
it. It was like at the carnival. It should be easy to knock three saw-
dust dogs off a ledge. And it was easy. It just wasn't easy with the
amount of balls they gave you.

He wanted the shore. He knew that was the right place for
him. But the pond kept saying no.

Then it said maybe.

The ice edge broke again, but, breaking it, he pulled himself infinitesimally toward shore, so that, when he went down, his feet found mud sooner. The bank was sloped. Suddenly there was hope. He went nuts. He went total spaz. Then he was out, water streaming off him, a piece of ice like a tiny pane of glass in the cuff of his coat.

Trapezoidal, he thought.

In his mind, the pond was not finite, circular, and behind him but infinite and all around.

He felt he'd better lie still or whatever had just tried to kill him would try again. What had tried to kill him was not just in the pond but out here, too, in every natural thing, and there was no him, no Suzanne, no Mom, no nothing, just the sound of some kid crying like a terrified baby.

EBER JOG-HOBBLED OUT OF THE woods and found: no kid. Just black water. And a green coat. His coat. His former coat, out there on the ice. The water was calming already.

Oh, shit.

Your fault.

Kid was only out there because of—

Down on the beach near an overturned boat was some ignoramus. Lying facedown. On the job. Lying down on the job. Must have been lying there even as that poor kid—

Wait, rewind.

It was the kid. Oh, thank Christ. Facedown like a corpse in a Brady photo. Legs still in the pond. Like he'd lost steam crawling out. Kid was soaked through, the white coat gone gray with wet.

Eber dragged the kid out. It took four distinct pulls. He didn't have the strength to flip him over, but, turning the head, at least got the mouth out of the snow.

Kid was in trouble.

Soaking wet, ten degrees.

Doom.

Eber went down on one knee and told the kid in a grave fatherly way that he had to get up, had to get moving or he could lose his legs, he could die.

The kid looked at Eber, blinked, stayed where he was.

He grabbed the kid by the coat, rolled him over, roughly sat him up. The kid's shivers made his shivers look like nothing. Kid seemed to be holding a jackhammer. He had to get the kid warmed up. How to do it? Hug him, lie on top of him? That would be like Popsicle-on-Popsicle.

Eber remembered his coat, out on the ice, at the edge of the black water.

Ugh.

Find a branch. No branches anywhere. Where the heck was a good fallen branch when you—

All right, all right, he'd do it without a branch.

He walked fifty feet downshore, stepped onto the pond, walked a wide loop on the solid stuff, turned to shore, started toward the black water. His knees were shaking. Why? He was afraid he might fall in. Ha. Dope. Poser. The coat was fifteen feet away. His legs were in revolt. His legs were revolting.

Doctor, my legs are revolting.

You're telling me.

He tiny-stepped up. The coat was ten feet away. He went down on his knees, knee-walked slightly up. Went down on his belly. Stretched out an arm.

Slid forward on his belly.

Bit more.

Bit more.

Then had a tiny corner by two fingers. He hauled it in, slid himself back via something like a reverse breaststroke, got to his knees, stood, retreated a few steps, and was once again fifteen feet away and safe. Then it was like the old days, getting Tommy or Jodi ready for bed when they were zonked. You said, "Arm," the kid lifted an arm. You said, "Other arm," the kid lifted the other arm. With the coat off, Eber could see that the boy's shirt was turning to ice. Eber peeled the shirt off. Poor little guy. A person was just some meat on a frame. Little guy wouldn't last long in this cold. Eber took off his pajama shirt, put it on the kid, slid the kid's arm into the arm of the coat. In the arm was Eber's hat and gloves. He put the hat and gloves on the kid, zipped the coat up.

The kid's pants were frozen solid. His boots were ice sculptures of boots.

You had to do things right. Eber sat on the boat, took off his boots and socks, peeled off his pajama pants, made the kid sit on the boat, knelt before the kid, got the kid's boots off. He loosened the pants up with little punches and soon had one leg partly out. He was stripping off a kid in ten-degree weather. Maybe this was exactly the wrong thing. Maybe he'd kill the kid. He didn't know. He just didn't know. Desperately, he gave the pants a few more punches. Then the kid was stepping out.

Eber put the pajama pants on him, then the socks, then the boots.

The kid was standing there in Eber's clothes, swaying, eyes closed.

We're going to walk now, okay? Eber said.

Nothing.

Eber gave the kid an encouraging pop in the shoulders. Like a football thing.

We're going to walk you home, he said. Do you live near here?

Nothing.

He gave a harder pop.

The kid gaped at him, baffled.

Pop.

Kid started walking.

Pop-pop.

Like fleeing.

Eber drove the kid out ahead of him. Like cowboy and cow. At first, fear of the popping seemed to be motivating the kid, but then good old panic kicked in and he started running. Soon Eber couldn't keep up.

Kid was at the bench. Kid was at the trailhead.

Good boy, get home.

Kid disappeared into the woods.

Eber came back to himself.

Oh, boy. Oh, wow.

He had never known cold. Had never known tired.

He was standing in the snow in his underwear near an over-turned boat.

He hobbled to the boat and sat in the snow.

ROBIN RAN.

Past the bench and the trailhead and into the woods on the old familiar path.

What the heck? What the heck had just happened? He'd fallen into the pond? His jeans had frozen solid? Had ceased being blue jeans. Were white jeans. He looked down to see if his jeans were still white jeans.

He had on pajama pants that, tucked into some tremendoid boots, looked like clown pants.

Had he been crying just now?

I think crying is healthy, Suzanne said. It means you're in touch with your feelings.

Ugh: That was done, that was stupid, talking in your head to some girl who in real life called you Roger.

Dang.

So tired.

Here was a stump.

He sat. It felt good to rest. He wasn't going to lose his legs. They didn't even hurt. He couldn't even feel them. He wasn't going to die. Dying was not something he had in mind at this early an age. To rest more efficiently, he lay down. The sky was blue. The pines swayed. Not all at the same rate. He raised one gloved hand and watched it tremor.

He might close his eyes for a bit. Sometimes in life one felt a feeling of wanting to quit. Then everyone would see. Everyone would see that teasing wasn't nice. Sometimes with all the teasing his days were subtenable. Sometimes he felt he couldn't take even one more lunchtime of meekly eating on that rolled-up wrestling mat in the cafeteria corner near the snapped parallel bars. He did not have to sit there. But preferred to. If he sat anywhere else, there was the chance of a comment or two. Upon which he would then have the rest of the day to reflect. Sometimes comments were made on the clutter of his home. Thanks to Bryce, who had once come over. Sometimes comments were made on: his manner of speaking. Sometimes comments were made on the style faux pas of Mom. Who was, it must be said, a real eighties gal.

Mom.

He did not like it when they teased about Mom. Mom had no idea of his lowly school status. Mom seeing him more as the paragon or golden-boy type.

Once, he'd done a secret rendezvous of recording Mom's phone calls, just for the reconnaissance aspect. Mostly they were dull, mundane, not about him at all.

Except for this one with her friend Liz.

I never dreamed I could love someone so much, Mom had said. I just worry I might not be able to live up to him, you know? He's so *good*, so *grateful*. That kid deserves—that kid deserves it all. Better school, which we cannot afford, some trips, like abroad, but that is also, uh, out of our price range. I just don't want to *fail* him, you know? That's all I want from my life, you know? Liz? To feel, at the end, like I did right by that magnificent little dude.

At that point it seemed like Liz had maybe started vacuuming.

Magnificent little dude.

He should probably get going.

Magnificent Little Dude was like his Indian name.

He got to his feet and, gathering his massive amount of clothes up like some sort of encumbering royal train, started toward home.

Here was the truck tire, here the place where the trail briefly widened, here the place where the trees crossed overhead like reaching for one another. Weave ceiling, Mom called it.

Here was the soccer field. Across the field, his house sat like a big sweet animal. It was amazing. He'd made it. He'd fallen into the pond and lived to tell the tale. He had somewhat cried, yes, but had then simply laughed off this moment of mortal weakness and made his way home, look of wry bemusement on his face, having, it must be acknowledged, benefited from the much appreciated assistance of a certain aged—

With a shock he remembered the old guy. What the heck? An image flashed of the old guy standing bereft and blue-skinned in his tighty-whities like a P.O.W. abandoned at the barbed wire due to no room on the truck. Or a sad traumatized stork bidding farewell to its young.

He'd bolted. He'd bolted on the old guy. Hadn't even given him a thought.

Blimey.

What a chickenshitish thing to do.

He had to go back. Right now. Help the old guy hobble out. But he was so tired. He wasn't sure he could do it. Probably the old guy was fine. Probably he had some sort of old-guy plan.

But he'd bolted. He couldn't live with that. His mind was telling him that the only way to undo the bolting was to go back now, save the day. His body was saying something else: It's too far, you're just a kid, get Mom, Mom will know what to do.

He stood paralyzed at the edge of the soccer field like a scarecrow in huge flowing clothes.

EBER SAT SLUMPED AGAINST THE boat.

What a change in the weather. People were going around with parasols and so forth in the open part of the park. There was a merry-go-round and a band and a gazebo. People were frying food on the backs of certain merry-go-round horses. And yet, on others, kids were riding. How did they know? Which horses were hot? For now there was still snow, but snow couldn't last long in this bomb.

Balm.

If you close your eyes, that's the end. You know that, right?

Hilarious.

Allen.

His exact voice. After all these years.

Where was he? The duck pond. So many times he'd come out here with the kids. He should go now. Good-bye, duck pond. Although hang on. He couldn't seem to stand. Plus you couldn't leave a couple of little kids behind. Not this close to water. They were four and six. For God's sake. What had he been thinking? Leaving those two little dears by the pond. They were good kids, they'd wait, but wouldn't they get bored? And swim? Without life jackets? No, no, no. It made him sick. He had to stay. Poor kids. Poor abandoned—

Wait, rewind.

His kids were excellent swimmers.

His kids had never come close to being abandoned.

His kids were grown.

Tom was thirty. Tall drink of water. Tried so hard to know things. But even when he thought he knew a thing (fighting kites, breeding rabbits), Tom would soon be shown for what he was: the dearest, most agreeable young fellow ever, who knew no more about fighting kites/breeding rabbits than the average person could pick up from ten minutes on the Internet. Not that Tom wasn't smart. Tom was smart. Tom was a damn quick study. O Tom, Tommy, Tommikins! The heart in that kid! He just worked and worked. For the love of his dad. Oh, kid, you had it, you have it, Tom, Tommy, even now I am thinking of you, you are very much on my mind.

And Jodi, Jodi was out there in Santa Fe. She'd said she'd take off work and fly home. As needed. But there was no need. He didn't like to impose. The kids had their own lives. Jodi-Jode. Little freckle-face. Pregnant now. Not married. Not even dating. Stupid Lars. What kind of man deserted a beautiful girl like that? A total dear. Just starting to make some progress in her job. You couldn't take that kind of time off when you'd only just started—

Reconstructing the kids in this way was having the effect of making them real to him again. Which—you didn't want to get that ball roiling. Jodi was having a baby. Rolling. He could have lasted long enough to see the baby. Hold the baby. It was sad, yes. That was a sacrifice he'd had to make. He'd explained it in the note. Hadn't he? No. Hadn't left a note. Couldn't. There'd been some reason he couldn't. Hadn't there? He was pretty sure there'd been some—

Insurance. It couldn't seem like he'd done it on purpose.

Little panic.

Little panic here.

He was offing himself. Offing himself, he'd involved a kid. Who was wandering the woods hypothermic. Offing himself two weeks before Christmas. Molly's favorite holiday. Molly had a valve thing, a panic thing, this business might—

This was not—this was not him. This was not something he would have done. Not something he would ever do. Except he— he'd done it. He was doing it. It was in progress. If he didn't get moving, it would—it would be accomplished. It would be done.

This very day you will be with me in the kingdom of—

He had to fight.

But couldn't seem to keep his eyes open.

He tried to send some last thoughts to Molly. Sweetie, forgive me. Biggest fuckup ever. Forget this part. Forget I ended thisly. You know me. You know I didn't mean this.

He was at his house. He wasn't at his house. He knew that. But could see every detail. Here was the empty med bed, the studio portrait of HimMollyTommyJodi posed around that fake rodeo fence. Here was the little bedside table. His meds in the pillbox. The bell he rang to call Molly. What a thing. What a cruel thing. Suddenly he saw clearly how cruel it was. And self-ish. Oh, God. Who was he? The front door swung open. Molly called his name. He'd hide in the sunroom. Jump out, surprise her. Somehow they'd remodeled. Their sunroom was now the sunroom of Mrs. Kendall, his childhood piano teacher. That would be fun for the kids, to take piano lessons in the same room where he'd—

Hello? said Mrs. Kendall.

What she meant was: Don't die yet. There are many of us who wish to judge you harshly in the sunroom.

Hello, hello! she shouted.

Coming around the pond was a silver-haired woman.

All he had to do was call out.

He called out.

To keep him alive she started piling on him various things from life, things smelling of a home—coats, sweaters, a rain of flowers, a hat, socks, sneakers—and with amazing strength had him on his feet and was maneuvering him into a maze of trees, a

wonderland of trees, trees hung with ice. He was piled high with
clothes. He was like the bed at a party on which they pile the coats.
She had all the answers: where to step, when to rest. She was strong
as a bull. He was on her hip now like a baby; she had both arms
around his waist, lifting him over a root.

They walked for hours, seemed like. She sang. Cajoled. She
hissed at him, reminding him, with pokes in the forehead (right
in his forehead), that her freaking *kid* was at *home*, near *frozen*, so
they had to *book it*.

Good God, there was so much to do. If he made it. He'd make
it. This gal wouldn't let him not make it. He'd have to try to get
Molly to see—see why he'd done it. *I was scared, I was scared, Mol.*
Maybe Molly would agree not to tell Tommy and Jodi. He didn't
like the thought of them knowing he'd been scared. Didn't like the
thought of them knowing what a fool he'd been. Oh, to hell with
that! Tell everyone! He'd done it! He'd been driven to do it and
he'd done it and that was it. That was him. That was part of who
he was. No more lies, no more silence, it was going to be a new and
different life, if only he—

They were crossing the soccer field.

Here was the Nissan.

His first thought was: Get in, drive it home.

Oh, no, you don't, she said with that smoky laugh and guided
him into a house. A house on the park. He'd seen it a million
times. And now was in it. It smelled of man sweat and spaghetti
sauce and old books. Like a library where sweaty men went to
cook spaghetti. She sat him in front of a woodstove, brought him
a brown blanket that smelled of medicine. Didn't talk but in di-
rectives: Drink this, let me take that, wrap up, what's your name,
what's your number?

What a thing! To go from dying in your underwear in the
snow to this! Warmth, colors, antlers on the walls, an old-time
crank phone like you saw in silent movies. It was something. Every

second was something. He hadn't died in his shorts by a pond in
the snow. The kid wasn't dead. He'd killed no one. Ha! Somehow
he'd got it all back. Everything was good now, everything was—

The woman reached down, touched his scar.

Oh, wow, ouch, she said. You didn't do that out there, did you?

At this he remembered that the brown spot was as much in his
head as ever.

Oh, Lord, there was still all that to go through.

Did he still want it? Did he still want to live?

Yes, yes, oh, God, yes, please.

Because, okay, the thing was—he saw it now, was starting to
see it—if some guy, at the end, fell apart, and said or did bad
things, or had to be helped, helped to quite a considerable extent?
So what? What of it? Why should he not do or say weird things
or look strange or disgusting? Why should the shit not run down
his legs? Why should those he loved not lift and bend and feed
and wipe him, when he would gladly do the same for them? He'd
been afraid to be lessened by the lifting and bending and feeding and wiping, and was still afraid of that, and yet, at the same
time, now saw that there could still be many—many drops of
goodness, is how it came to him—many drops of happy—of good
fellowship—ahead, and those drops of fellowship were not—had
never been—his to withheld.

Withhold.

The kid came out of the kitchen, lost in Eber's big coat, pajama
pants pooling around his feet with the boots now off. He took
Eber's bloody hand gently. Said he was sorry. Sorry for being such
a dope in the woods. Sorry for running off. He'd just been out of
it. Kind of scared and all.

Listen, Eber said hoarsely. You did amazing. You did perfect.
I'm here. Who did that?

There. That was something you could do. The kid maybe felt
better now? He'd given the kid that? That was a reason. To stay

around. Wasn't it? Can't console anyone if not around? Can't do squat if gone?

When Allen was close to the end, Eber had done a presentation at school on the manatee. Got an A from Sister Eustace. Who could be quite tough. She was missing two fingers on her right hand from a lawn-mower incident and sometimes used that hand to scare a kid silent.

He hadn't thought of this in years.

She'd put that hand on his shoulder not to scare him but as a form of praise. *That was just terrific. Everyone should take their work as seriously as Donald here. Donald, I hope you'll go home and share this with your parents.* He'd gone home and shared it with Mom. Who'd suggested he share it with Allen. Who, on that day, had been more Allen than THAT. And Allen—

Ha, wow, Allen. There was a man.

Tears sprang into his eyes as he sat by the woodstove.

Allen had—Allen had said it was great. Asked a few questions. About the manatee. What did they eat again? Did he think they could effectively communicate with one another? What a trial that must have been! In his condition. Forty minutes on the manatee? Including a poem Eber had composed? A sonnet? On the manatee?

He'd felt so happy to have Allen back.

I'll be like him, he thought. I'll try to be like him.

The voice in his head was shaky, hollow, unconvinced.

Then: sirens.

Somehow: Molly.

He heard her in the entryway. Mol, Molly, oh boy. When they were first married they used to fight. Say the most insane things. Afterward, sometimes there would be tears.

Tears in bed? And then they would—Molly pressing her hot wet face against his hot wet face. They were sorry, they were saying with their bodies, they were accepting each other back, and that feeling, that feeling of being accepted back again and again, of someone's affection for you expanding to encompass whatever new flawed thing had just manifested in you, that was the deepest, dearest thing he'd ever—

She came in flustered and apologetic, a touch of anger in her face. He'd embarrassed her. He saw that. He'd embarrassed her by doing something that showed she hadn't sufficiently noticed him needing her. She'd been too busy nursing him to notice how scared he was. She was angry at him for pulling this stunt and ashamed of herself for feeling angry at him in his hour of need, and was trying to put the shame and anger behind her now so she could do what might be needed.

All of this was in her face. He knew her so well.

Also concern.

Overriding everything else in that lovely face was concern.

She came to him now, stumbling a bit on a swell in the floor of this stranger's house.

ELIZABETH McCRACKEN

"I honestly don't know how conscious anything I do is. It all seems like a blunder, and, when it comes out right, I'm delighted."

"I can't say that I have any religious belief, but to the extent to which I believe there is redemption in the world of sadness, it is through black humor. In the worst moments of my life, there is always a joke to be made, and that's a deep comfort to me. It's not putting off feelings; it's part of sad things."

Onstage interview at The Story Prize event
March 4, 2015

Something Amazing

from *Thunderstruck & Other Stories*

Just west of Boston, just north of the turnpike, the ghost of Missy Goodby sleeps curled up against the cyclone fence at the dead end of Winter Terrace, dressed in a pair of ectoplasmic dungarees. That thumping noise is Missy bopping a plastic Halloween pumpkin on one knee; that flash of light in the corner of a dark porch is the moon off the glasses she wore to correct her lazy eye. Late at night when you walk your dog and feel suddenly cold, and then unsure of yourself, and then loathed by the world, that's Missy Goodby, too, hissing as she had when she was alive and six years old, *I hate you, you stink, you smell, you* baby.

The neighborhood kids remember Missy. She bit when she was angry and pinched no matter what. They don't feel sorry for her ghost self. They remember the funeral they were forced to attend after she died, how her mother threw herself on the coffin, wailing, how they thought she was kidding and so laughed out loud and got shushed. The way the neighborhood kids tell the story, the coffin was lowered into the ground and Missy Goodby's grieving mother leapt down and then had to be yanked from the hole like a weed. Everyone always believes the better story eventually. Really, Joyce Goodby just thumped the coffin at the graveside service. Spanked it: two little spanks, nothing serious. She knew that pleading would never budge her daughter, not because she was dead but because she was stubborn. All her life, the more you pleaded with Missy, the more likely she was to do something to terrify you. Joyce Goodby spanked the coffin and walked away and listened for footsteps behind her. She walked all the way home, where she took off her shoes, black pumps with worn stones of gray along the toes. "Done with *you*," she told them.

•

THE SOUL IS LIQUID, AND slow to evaporate. The body's a bucket and liable to slosh. Grieving, haunted, heartbroken, obsessed: your friends will tell you to *cheer up*. What they really mean is *dry up*. But it isn't a matter of will. Only time and light will do the job.

Who wants to, anyhow?

Best keep in the dark and nurse the damp. Cover the mirrors, keep the radio switched off. Avoid the newspaper, the television, the whole outdoors, anywhere little girls congregate, though the world is manufacturing them hand over fist, though there are now, it seems, more little girls living in the world than any other variety of human being. Or middle-aged men whose pants don't fit, or infant boys, or young women with wide, sympathetic, fretful foreheads. Whatever you have lost there are more of, just not yours. Sneeze. Itch. Gasp for breath. Seal the windows. Replace the sheets, then the mattresses. Pry the mercury from your teeth. Buy appliances to scrub the air.

Even so, the smell of the detergent from the sheets will fall into your nose. The chili your nice son cooks will visit you in the bedroom. The sweat from his clothes when he runs home from high school, the fog of his big yawping shoes, the awful smell, of batteries loaded into a remote control, car exhaust, the plastic bristles on your toothbrush, the salt-air smell of baking soda once you give up toothpaste. Make your house as safe and airtight as possible. Filter the air, boil the water: the rashes stay, the wheezing gets worse.

What you are allergic to can walk through walls.

THE NEIGHBORHOOD KIDS DON'T REMEMBER what Joyce Goodby looked like back when she regularly drove down Winter Terrace; they've forgotten her curly black hair, her star-and-moon earrings, her velvet leggings. It's been five years. Now that she's locked away, they know everything about her. She no longer cuts or colors her mercury hair but instead twists it like a towel and pins it to her head. The paper face mask she wears over her nose and mouth makes her eyes look big. Her clothes are unbleached cotton and hemp; an invalid could eat them. She and her son, Gerry, used to look alike, a pair of freckled hearty people. Not anymore. Her freckles have starved from lack of light. Her eyebrows are thick, her eyelashes thin. She seems made of soap and steel wool.

Something's wrong in the neighborhood, she tells her son, it gave Missy lymphoma and now it's made her sick.

Of course she's a witch. The older kids tell younger kids, and kids who live on the street tell the kids around the corner. The Winter Terrace Witch, they call her, as though she's a seventeenth-century legend. She eats children. She kills them. She killed her own daughter a million years ago. Some gangly kid not even from the street tells Santos and Johnny Mackers about the witch and the ghost. The Mackerses have just moved to Winter Terrace. Santos is nine years old, with curly hair and a strange accent, the result of nearly a decade of postnasal drip. Johnny is as tough a five-year-old as ever was, a preschool monster Santos has created on the sly. Santos steals their father's Kools and lights them for Johnny. He has taught Johnny all the swears he knows, taught him how to punch, all in hopes that their mother will love Johnny a little less and him a little more. It's not working. Already they're famous on the street, where no one has ever seen Johnny Mackers's feet touch the ground. He rides his Big Wheel everywhere: up and down the street and into the attached garage. He rides it directly into the cyclone fence.

"You're a crazy motherfucker," Santos says. "A crazy motherfucker." He doesn't like the word himself but Johnny won't learn it otherwise.

"That's Ghostland, by the fence," the gangly kid says, from the other side. "That's where all the ghosts get caught, that's why they call it a dead end."

"Nosir," says Santos.

"Yessir," says the kid. "Dead girl ghost. Plus there's a witch." He spits to be tough but he hasn't practiced enough: he just drools, then walks away, embarrassed.

Johnny Mackers is swarthy and black-haired and Italian-looking, like his mother; Santos has his Irish father's looks. He likes to shut Johnny into things. Already he's investigated the locks of their new house. The attic, the basement, the mirror-fronted closet in their parents' room—every lock sounds different: key, slide bolt, knob, hook-and-eye, dead bolt. He's glad to learn of a ghost to threaten Johnny with. "The dead girl wants to kiss you. Here she comes. Pucker up." But the dead girl isn't interested, and Johnny Mackers knows it. The neighborhood kids are lying when they say they see her. The dead girl doesn't watch as Santos stuffs Johnny into the front hall closet. The dead girl doesn't see the fingers at the bottom of the door, or the foot that stomps on them. She doesn't see Mrs. Mackers open up the door an hour later, saying, "What are you doing in there, for Pete's sake? The way you hide, it drives me nuts. Why don't you go ride your bike. Go on, now." The dead girl doesn't sleep outside, ever. Why would she? She is with her mother, who—as she cleans the kitchen (her eyesight so vigilant she can see individual motes of dust, a single bacterium scuttling along the countertop)—can hear the mortar-and-pestle sound of a plastic wheel grinding along the grit of the gutter, a noise that should surely mean more than a grimy black-haired boy getting from one end of the street to another.

A DIFFERENT CHILD MIGHT HAVE turned into a different kind of ghost, visible only to little children, a finder of lost balls, a demander of candy. She could have visited Johnny Mackers late at night, when he plotted how he would kill his brother Santos. She could have haunted Santos himself. She could have accomplished things.

Instead, she likes to snuffle close to her mother's skin.

The best spot is Joyce's skin in the hollow just below her cheekbones and just above her jaw: you have to get close, you have to get nearly under Joyce's nose to settle in. Sometimes Missy gets in the way and cuts off her mother's breath. She doesn't mean to. The biting, pinching child bites and pinches, along her mother's arms, her pale stomach.

"Look," Joyce says to her son, and displays her forearms, which are captioned with strange anaglyphic sentences, spelled out in hives.

Gerry Goodby was twelve when his little sister died. Now he's a seventeen-year-old six-foot-tall lacrosse player. He has watched his mother turn from a human woman into some immaculate vegetable substance, wan, thin, lamplit. *What will you do*, his father says. He means about college. For the past five years, Gerry and his father have had the same alternating conversation. *I want to live with you*, Gerry will say, and his father will answer, *You know that's impossible, you know your mother needs you*. Or his father will say, *This is crazy, she's crazy, come live with me*, and Gerry will answer, *You know that's impossible*.

He was the one who closed up Missy's room. A year after she died, his mother wheezing, weeping, molting on the sofa. She gave him the directions. *Don't touch a thing. Just seal it up.* He nailed over the doorway with barrier cloth, then painted over that with latex paint. His mother felt better for nearly a month.

Sometimes he stops in the hallway and touches the slumped wall where Missy's door used to be. He feels like a projection on a screen, waiting for the rest of the movie to be filled in. *This is intolerable*, he thinks. He's always thought of *intolerable* as a grown-up word, like *mortgage*.

Missy the allergen, Missy the poison. She's everywhere in the house, no matter how their mother scrubs and sweeps and burns and purges. She's in the bricks. She's in the new bedding, in the nontoxic cleaning fluid. She leeches and fumes and wishes—insofar as a ghost can, in the way that water wishes, and has a will, sometimes thwarted and sometimes not—that the house were not shut up so tight. She rises to the ceiling daily and collects there, drips down, tries again. Outside there's a world of blank skin, waiting for her to scribble all over it.

"I would die without you," Joyce Goodby tells her son one morning. He knows it's true, just as he knows he's the only one who would care. Sometimes he thinks it wouldn't be such a bad bargain, his mother's death for his own freedom. Anyone would understand. Anyhow, it's time to leave for school. She won't die during the school day; at least, she hasn't so far.

Across the street Santos shuts Johnny Mackers in a steamer trunk in the attic instead of walking him to kindergarten. Then Santos, liberated, guilty, decides to skip school himself. He walks to the corner and gets on the bus that says, across its forehead, DOWNTOWN VIA PIKE. He has just enough to pay his fare. The bus is crammed with people. A man in a gray windbreaker stands up. "Hey," he says. "Kiddo, sit here."

Santos sits.

THE WORLD GOES ON. THE world will. At any moment you can look from your window and see your neighbors. The fat couple who live next door will bicker and then bear-hug each other. The teenage boys will play basketball with their shirts off. The elderly lady next door waits for the visiting nurse; her bloodhound snoozes in the sun like a starlet, one paw across his snout. You want to drape that old, good, big dog's sun-warmed fawn-colored ears on your fists. You want to reassure the elderly lady, tease the fat couple, watch—just watch—those shirtless, heedless boys. *You have to get out*, your family says, *it's time. It's time to join the world again.* But you never left the world. You're filled with tenderness, with worry for every living being, but you can't do anything—not for your across-the-street neighbors, or for the people on the next street, or around the corner, or driving on the turnpike two blocks away, or in the city, or the whole country, the whole world, west and east and north and south. You are so unlucky you don't want to brush up against anyone who isn't.

You will not join a group. You will not read a book. You're not interested in anyone else's story, not when your own story takes up all your time. When the calamity happened, your friends said, *It's so sad. It's the worst kind of luck*, and you could tell they believed it. What's changed? You are as sad and unlucky as you were when it happened. It's still so, so sad. It's still the worst kind of luck.

The dead live on in the homeliest of ways. They're listed in the phone book. They get mail. Their wigs rest on Styrofoam heads at the back of closets. Their beds are made. Their shoes are everywhere.

THE PAINT ACROSS THE DOOR is still tacky. It's dumb to even be here. Joyce swears she can smell the fiberboard headboard of the bed through the barrier cloth, the scratch-and-sniff stickers on the desk, the old lip gloss, the bubble bath in containers shaped like animals arranged on the dresser top, the unchanged mattress, the dust. The dress from Bloomingdale's that had been hers and then Missy's, in striped fabric like a railroad engineer's hat. The Mexican jumping beans bought at a joke shop before the diagnosis, four dark little beans in a plastic box with a clear top and blue bottom that clasped shut like an old-fashioned change purse. You warmed them in your hands, and they woke up and twitched and flipped: the worms who lived inside dozed in the cold but threw themselves against the walls when the temperature rose.

"Worms?" Missy had asked. Her nose was lacy with freckles, pink around the rim. "How do we feed them?"

"We don't," said Joyce.

"Then they'll starve to death!"

Quickly Joyce made up a story: the worm wasn't a worm, it was a soul. It was fine where it was, it was eternal, and if the bean stopped moving that only meant the soul had moved on to find another home. *Back to Mexico?* asked Missy, and Joyce said, *Sure, why not.* (Who knows? Maybe that's why the worms woke up when they got warm—they thought, *At last we re back home in Oaxaca.*) Back then, reincarnation was a comforting fable. In fairy tales, people were always born again as beasts, frogs, migrating swans.

Now Joyce feels the world shake and thinks, *Mexican jumping bean.* She can't decide whether the house is the bean and she's the worm, or the bean's her body and the worm her soul.

Neither: someone has wrenched open the wooden storm door of the sun porch and let it slam behind him. Then the doorbell rings.

JOHNNY MACKERS HAS ESCAPED. HE'S kicked his way out of the trunk, the one his great-grandmother emigrated from Ireland with, still lined with the napkins and tablecloths she thought she'd need for a new life. She once told Johnny a story about a monkey that belonged to a rich family she worked for, and though he knows that monkey died in the rich family's house, he was sure the trunk smelled of monkey, as well as the inventory of every story his great-grandmother ever told him: whiskey, lamp oil, house fires, a scalded baby's arm treated with butter, horse sweat, lemon

drops, the underside of wooden dentures. The trunk turned out
to be made of cardboard held together with moldy oak and cheap
tin. He kicked one end to pieces and crawled out. The wreckage
scared him. It was as though he'd kicked his great-grandmother
apart before she'd had a chance to get on the boat and sail to
Boston and meet her future husband at an amusement park and
have children.

He rings the doorbell once, twice. Last year in their old neighborhood he helped Santos sell mints for the Y; you were supposed
to ring, count to ten slowly, and ring only once more. He counts to
ten but quickly and over and over. To keep himself from ringing
too many times, he runs a finger over the engraved sign by the bell.
He doesn't know what a solicitor is or that he's one. The air of the
sun porch is stale. He gulps at it. The front door opens.

"Lady," he says, "do you wanna buy a rock?"

The rocks in Johnny Mackers's hand have been lightly rubbed
with crayon. He found them a week ago at Revere Beach with his
father: at the beach they were washed by the water and looked
valuable and ancient. Dry, they turned gray and merely old. The
woman who has answered the door is the witch, of course, the
dead girl's mother. He's come to her first of all the neighbors
because she may be able to grant wishes, and Johnny has one.
When it's the right time, he'll ask: he wishes his brother dead.
She's the cleanest person he's ever seen and yet not entirely white.
Everything about her is blurred, like dirt beneath the surface of a
hockey rink.

He would do anything for her. He knows that right away, too.
You have to, to get your wish granted.

He has cobwebs in his hair but she doesn't smell them. She
doesn't smell the cigarette smoke or the fibers off the wall-to-
wall carpet or the must that clings to him from the trunk, the
usual immigrant disappointments, the rusty cut on his ankle
that needs medical attention. What she smells is little-kid sweat

touched with sweet bland tomato sauce. Ketchup, canned spaghetti, maybe.

"Come in," she says. "I'll find my purse."

Once he's inside she doesn't know what to do. She sits him
at the kitchen table and offers him a plate of pebbly brown cookies. He eats one. He would rather something chocolate and store-
bought, but his mother likes cookies like this, studded with sesame
seeds, and he knows that eating them is a good deed. She hooks a
cobweb out of his hair with one finger. He picks up another cookie
and rubs the side of his cheek with the back of one wrist.

"You need a bath," she says.

"OK," he answers.

Now, Joyce. You can't just bathe someone else's child. You
can't invite a strange boy into your house and bring him upstairs
and say, "Chop chop. Off with your clothes. Into your bath."

The bathroom is yellow and pink. Johnny Mackers under-
stands his new obedience as a kind of sanitary bewitching. He is
never naked in front of his mother like this: his mother likes to
pinch. "Just a little!" she'll say, and she'll pinch him on his knee
and stomach and everywhere. Santos is right, their mother loves
Johnny best. His hatred of kisses and hugs has turned her into a
pinching tickler, a sneak thief. "Just a little little!" she'll say, when
she sees any pinchable part of him.

"Bubbles?" Joyce asks, and he nods. But there's no bubble
bath. Instead she pours the entire bottle of shampoo into the tub.

So it's true, what the neighborhood kids say. She does kidnap
children.

He's not circumcised. He looks like an Italian sculpture from
a dream, a polychrome putto from the corner of a church. The tub
is rotten, pink, with a sliding glass door that looks composed of
a million thumbprints. Soon the bubbles rise up like shrugging,
foamy shoulders, cleft where the water from the faucet pours in.

The almond soap is as cracked as an old tooth. The boy steps

over the tub edge. "Careful," Joyce says, as he puts his hand on the
shower door runners. When Missy was born, Joyce was relieved:
she loved her husband and son but there was, she thought, something different about a girl. Maybe it was scientific, those as-yet-
unused girl organs speaking to their authorial organs, transmitting
information as though by radio. A strange little boy is easier to love
than a strange little girl. The water slicking down his dirty hair
reveals the angle and size of his ears. She soaps them and thinks
of Missy in the tub, the fine long hair knotted at the nape, the big
ears, the crescent shape where they attached to her head. The arch
at the base of her skull.

"Your ears are very small," she says.

"I know," he answers.

She soaps the shoulder blades that slide beneath the boy's dark
skin and is amazed to see that he's basically intact, well-fed, maybe
even well-loved.

(Of course he is. Even now his mother is calling his name on
the next block. Soon she'll phone the police.)

"What's your name?" Joyce asks.

He says, "I don't know."

"You don't know your name?"

He shrugs. He looks at his foam-filled hands. Then he says,
"Johnny."

"What's your last name?"

"Lion," he says. He drops his face in the bubbly bath water,
plunges his head down, and blubs.

When he comes up she says, smiling, "Your clothes are filthy.
You're going to need clean ones. Where were you?"

"Trunk."

"Of a *car*?"

"Trunk like a suitcase," he answers. He pounds the sliding
glass shower door, bored with questioning.

It's after school. Mrs. Mackers, the owlish pincher, is back

on Winter Terrace, asking the neighborhood kids if they've seen
Johnny, the little boy, the little boy on the trike. She doesn't know
where Santos is, either, but Santos is old enough to take care of
himself (though she's wrong in thinking this—Santos even now is
in terrible trouble, Santos, miles away, is calling for her). The last
teenage boy she asks is so freckled she feels sorry for him, a pause
in her panic.

No, Gerry Goodby hasn't seen a little kid.

He's looking up at Missy's window; he always looks at it
when he comes home, shouldering his lacrosse stick like a rifle.
He didn't remember to pull down the blinds all the way before
closing the room up and it always bothers him. You can see the
edge of the dresser that overlaps the window frame, a darkened
rainbow sticker, and just the snout-end of an enormous rocking horse named Blaze who used to say six different sentences
when you pulled a cord in his neck. Blaze had been Gerry's horse
first. It seemed unfair he had to disappear like that. Someday,
Gerry knows, they'll have to sell the house, and the new owners
will find the tomb of a six-year-old girl pharaoh. It's as though
they've walled in Missy instead of burying her in the cemetery,
as though (as in a ghost story) he will someday see her face looking back out at him, mouthing, *Why?* Gerry, in his head, always
answers, *It's not your fault, you didn't know how dangerous you
were.*

But this time he sees something appearing, then disappearing,
then appearing again: the rocking horse showing its profile, one
dark carved eye over and over.

Not only that: the front door is open.

THE BARRIER CLOTH HAS BEEN slit from top to bottom. Beyond it is the old door with the brassy doorknob still bright from
all its years in the dark. Beyond the door is Missy's room.

"Hello," says his mother. She's sitting on the bed, smoothing a pair of light yellow overalls on her lap. There's a whole outfit set out next to her: the Lollipop-brand underpants Missy had once written a song about, a navy turtleneck, an undershirt with a tiny rosebud at the sternum. The dust is everywhere in the room. It's a strange sort of dust, soot and old house, nothing human. Even so, compared to the rest of the house, this room is Oz. The comforter is pink gingham. The walls are pink with darker pink trim. Dolls of all nations lie along one wall, as though rubble from an earthquake has just been lifted from them. The 50-50 bedclothes are abrasive just to look at. He inhales. Nothing of Missy's fruit-flavored scent is left.

But his mother doesn't seem to notice. She has—he's heard this expression but never seen it—roses in her cheeks. "Look," she says, and points.

A boy. He's fallen through the chimney or he's a forgotten toy of Missy's come to life. What else can explain him here, brown and naked next to the rocking horse he's just dismounted, a gray towel turbaned around his head. He's pulling two-handed at the cord that works Blaze's voice box, but Blaze has had a stroke and can't speak, he just groans apologetically before the boy interrupts him with another tug. Through the half-drawn shades the police lights color Winter Terrace: blue, less blue, blue again.

Outside, the neighborhood kids sit on the sidewalk, their feet in the gutter, daring the cops to tell them to move along. The little smoking kid, the one who likes to swear, is missing. The kids are working on their story. *When did you last see him?* a policeman asks, but the fact is the woman, who is not crying yet, will get her boy back. That is, she'll get one of her boys back: the one she hasn't missed yet is missing for good, forever, and by tomorrow morning he will be his mother's favorite, and by tomorrow afternoon the police will have questioned everyone on the street, and the neighborhood kids will pretend that they remember Santos, though they can't even make sense of his name. He will pass into legend, too.

Inside Missy Goodby's room, Gerry obeys his mother: he looks at the little boy. He wonders how to sneak him back home. He wonders how to keep him forever.

ADAM JOHNSON

"I just love stories. And when you're writing a novel, all these sexy stories walk by, and they say: *Cheat. Leave your novel. I'm going to be awesome.* I said no to them all."

"There's something in a novel that's a political act. The characters want one thing, the plot wants another, the setting, the situation. But in a story, you can be a pure dictator. You can make every facet contribute to a total effect."

"The second it transmits its emotional cargo, the story just screeches to a halt, the way a car screeches. It transfers its energy into you, and you are thrown forward, and you believe the story in that state. I really like doing that to people, if I can."

Onstage interview at The Story Prize event
March 2, 2016

Nirvana

from *Fortune Smiles*

It's late, and I can't sleep. I raise a window for some spring Palo Alto air, but it doesn't help. In bed, eyes open, I hear whispers, which makes me think of the president, because we often talk in whispers. I know the whispering sound is really just my wife, Charlotte, who listens to Nirvana on her headphones all night and tends to sleep-mumble the lyrics. Charlotte has her own bed, a mechanical one.

My sleep problem is this: when I close my eyes, I keep visualizing my wife killing herself. More like the ways she might *try* to kill herself, since she's paralyzed from the shoulders down. The paralysis is quite temporary, though good luck trying to convince Charlotte of that. She slept on her side today, to fight the bedsores, and there was something about the way she stared at the safety rail at the edge of the mattress. The bed is voice-activated, so if she could somehow get her head between the bars of the safety rail, "incline" is all she'd have to say. As the bed powered up, she'd be choked in seconds. And then there's the way she stares at the looping cable that descends from the Hoyer Lift, which swings her in and out of bed.

But my wife doesn't need an exotic exit strategy, not when she's exacted a promise from me to help her do it when the time comes.

I rise and go to her, but she's not listening to Nirvana yet—she tends to save it for when she needs it most, after midnight, when her nerves really start to crackle.

"I thought I heard a noise," I tell her. "Kind of a whisper."

Short, choppy hair frames her drawn face, skin faint as refrigerator light.

"I heard it, too," she says.

In the silver dish by her voice remote is a half-smoked joint. I light it for her and hold it to her lips.

"How's the weather in there?" I ask.

"Windy," she says through the smoke.

Windy is better than hail or lightning or, God forbid, flooding, which is the sensation she felt when her lungs were just starting to work again. But there are different kinds of wind.

I ask, "Windy like a whistle through window screens, or windy like the rattle of storm shutters?"

"A strong breeze, hissy and buffeting, like a microphone in the wind."

She smokes again. Charlotte hates being stoned, but she says it quiets the inside of her. She has Guillain-Barré syndrome, a condition in which her immune system attacks the insulation around her nerves so that when the brain sends signals to the body, the electrical impulses ground out before they can be received. A billion nerves inside her send signals that go everywhere, nowhere. This is the ninth month, a month that is at the edge of the medical literature. It's a place where the doctors no longer feel qualified to tell us whether Charlotte's nerves will begin to regenerate or she will be stuck like this forever.

She exhales, coughing. Her right arm twitches, which means her brain has attempted to tell her arm to rise and cover the mouth. She tokes again, and through the smoke she says, "I'm worried."

"What about?"

"You."

"You're worried about me?"

"I want you to stop talking to the president. It's time to accept reality."

I try to be lighthearted. "But he's the one who talks to me."

"Then stop listening. He's gone. When your time comes, you're supposed to fall silent."

Reluctantly, I nod. But she doesn't understand. Stuck in this bed, having sworn off TV, she's probably the only person in America who didn't see the assassination. If she'd beheld the look in the president's eyes when his life was taken, she'd understand why I talk to him late at night. If she could leave this room and feel the nation trying to grieve, she'd know why I reanimated the commander in chief and brought him back to life.

"Concerning my conversations with the president," I say, "I just want to point out that you spend a third of your life listening to Nirvana, whose songs are by a guy who blew his brains out."

Charlotte tilts her head and looks at me like I'm a stranger. "Kurt Cobain took the pain of his life and made it into something that mattered. What did the president leave behind? Uncertainties, emptiness, a thousand rocks to overturn."

She talks like that when she's high. I tap out the joint and lift her headphones.

"Ready for your Nirvana?" I ask.

She looks toward the window. "That sound, I hear it again," she says.

At the window, I peer out into the darkness. It's a normal Palo Alto night—the hiss of sprinklers, blue recycling bins, a raccoon digging in the community garden. Then I notice it, right before my eyes, a small black drone, hovering. Its tiny servos swivel to regard me. Real quick, I snatch the drone out of the air and pull it inside. I close the window and curtains, then study the thing: its shell is made of black foil stretched over tiny struts, like the bones of a bat's wing. Behind a propeller of clear cellophane, a tiny infrared engine throbs with warmth.

"Now will you listen to me?" Charlotte asks. "Now will you stop this president business?"

"It's too late for that," I tell her, and release the drone. As if blind, it bumbles around the room. Is it autonomous? Has someone been operating it, someone watching our house? I lift it from its column of air and flip off its power switch.

Charlotte looks toward her voice remote. "Play music," she tells it.

Closing her eyes, she waits for me to place the headphones on her ears, where she will hear Kurt Cobain come to life once more.

I WAKE LATER IN THE night. The drone has somehow turned itself on and is hovering above my body, mapping me with a beam of soft red light. I toss a sweater over it, dropping it to the floor. After making sure Charlotte is asleep, I pull out my iProjector. I turn it on, and the president appears in three dimensions, his torso life-size in an amber glow.

He greets me with a smile. "It's good to be back in Palo Alto," he says.

My algorithm has accessed the iProjector's GPS chip and searched the president's database for location references. This one came from a commencement address he gave at Stanford back when he was a senator.

"Mr. President," I say. "I'm sorry to bother you again, but I have more questions."

He looks into the distance, contemplative. "Shoot," he says.

I move into his line of sight but can't get him to look me in the eye. That's one of the design problems I ran across.

"Did I make a mistake in creating you, in releasing you into the world?" I ask. "My wife says that you're keeping people from mourning, that *this you* keeps us from accepting the fact that the *real you* is gone."

The president rubs the stubble on his chin. He looks down and away.

"You can't put the genie back in the bottle," he says.

Which is eerie, because that's a line he spoke on *60 Minutes*, a moment when he expressed regret for legalizing drones for civilian use.

"Do you know that I'm the one who made you?" I ask.

"We are all born free," he says. "And no person may traffic in another."

"But you weren't born," I tell him. "I wrote an algorithm based on the Linux operating kernel. You're an open-source search engine married to a dialog bot and a video compiler. The program scrubs the Web and archives a person's images and videos and data—everything you say, you've said before."

For the first time, the president falls silent.

I ask, "Do you know that you're gone . . . that you've died?"

The president doesn't hesitate. "The end of life is another kind of freedom," he says.

The assassination flashes in my eyes. I've seen the video so many times—the motorcade slowly crawls along while the president, on foot, parades past the barricaded crowds. Someone in the throng catches the president's eye. The president turns, lifts a hand in greeting. Then a bullet strikes him in the abdomen. The impact bends him forward, his eyes lift to confront the shooter. A look of recognition settles into the president's gaze—of a particular person, of some kind of truth, of something he has foreseen? He takes the second shot in the face. You can see the switch go off—his limbs give and he's down. They put him on a machine for a few days, but the end had already come.

I glance at Charlotte, asleep. "Mr. President," I whisper, "did you and the first lady ever talk about the future, about worst-case scenarios?"

I wonder if the first lady was the one to turn off the machine.

The president smiles. "The first lady and I have a wonderful relationship. We share everything."

"But were there instructions? Did you two make a plan?"

His voice lowers, becomes sonorous. "Are you asking about bonds of matrimony?"

"I suppose so," I say.

"In this regard," he says, "our only duty is to be of service in any way we can."

My mind ponders the ways in which I might have to be of service to Charlotte.

The president then looks into the distance, as if a flag is waving there.

"I'm the president of the United States," he says, "and I approved this message."

That's when I know our conversation is over. When I reach to turn off the iProjector, the president looks me squarely in the eye, a coincidence of perspective, I guess. We regard each other, his eyes deep and melancholy, and my finger hesitates at the switch.

"Seek your inner resolve," he tells me.

CAN YOU TELL A STORY that doesn't begin, it's just suddenly happening? The woman you love gets the flu. Her fingers tingle, her legs go rubbery. Soon she can't grip a coffee cup. What finally gets her to the hospital is the need to pee. She's dying to pee, but the paralysis has begun: the bladder can no longer hear the brain. After an ER doc inserts a Foley catheter, you learn new words— *axon, areflexia, ascending peripheral polyneuropathy.*

Charlotte says she's filled with "noise." Inside her is a "storm."

The doctor has a big needle. He tells Charlotte to get on the gurney. Charlotte is scared to get on the gurney. She's scared she won't ever get up again. "Please, honey," you say. "Get on the gurney." Soon you behold the glycerin glow of your wife's spinal fluid. And she's right. She doesn't get up again.

Next comes plasmapheresis, then high-dose immunoglobulin therapy.

The doctors mention, casually, the word *ventilator.*

Charlotte's mother arrives. She brings her cello. She's an expert on the siege of Leningrad. She has written a book on the topic.

When Charlotte's coma is induced, her mother fills the neuro ward with the saddest sounds ever conceived. For days, there is nothing but the swish of vent baffles, the trill of vital monitors, and Shosta-kovich, Shostakovich, Shostakovich.

Two months of physical therapy in Santa Clara. Here are dunk tanks, sonar stimulators, exoskeletal treadmills. Charlotte becomes the person in the room who makes the victims of other afflictions feel better about their fate. She does not make progress, she's not a "soldier" or a "champ" or a "trouper."

Charlotte convinces herself that I will leave her for one of the nurses in the rehab ward. She screams at me to get a vasectomy so this nurse and I will suffer a barren future. To soothe her, I read aloud Joseph Heller's memoir about contracting Guillain-Barré syndrome. The book was supposed to make us feel better. Instead, it chronicles how great Heller's friends are, how high Heller's spir-its are, how Heller leaves his wife to marry the beautiful nurse who tends to him. And for Charlotte, the book's ending is particularly painful: Joseph Heller gets better.

We tumble into a well of despair that's narrow and deep, a place that seals us off. Everything is in the well with us—careers, goals, travel, children—so close that we can drown them to save ourselves.

Finally, discharge. Yet home is unexpectedly surreal. Amid familiar surroundings, the impossibility of normal life is ampli-fied. But the cat is happy, so happy to have Charlotte home that it spends an entire night curled on Charlotte's throat, on her tracheal incision. Goodbye, cat! While I'm in the garage, Charlotte watches a spider slowly descend from the ceiling on a single thread. She tries to blow it away. She blows and blows, but the spider disap-pears into her hair.

Still to be described are tests, tantrums and treatments. To come are the discoveries of Kurt Cobain and marijuana. Of these times, there is only one moment I must relate. It was a normal night. I was beside Charlotte in the mechanical bed, holding up her magazine.

She said, "You don't know how bad I want to get out of this bed."

Her voice was quiet, uninflected. She'd said similar things a thousand times.

"I'd do anything to escape," she said.

I flipped the page and laughed at a picture whose caption read, "Stars are just like us!"

"But I could never do that to you," she said.

"Do what?" I asked.

"Nothing."

"What are you talking about, what's going through your head?"

I turned to look at her. She was inches away.

"Except for how it would hurt you," she said, "I would get away."

"Get away where?"

"From here."

Neither of us had spoken of the promise since the night it was exacted. I'd tried to pretend the promise didn't exist, but it existed.

"Face it, you're stuck with me," I said, forcing a smile. "We're destined, we're fated to be together. And soon you'll be better, things will be normal again."

"My entire life is this pillow."

"That's not true. You've got your friends and family. And you've got technology. The whole world is at your fingertips."

By friends, I meant her nurses and physical therapists. By family, I meant her distant and brooding mother. It didn't matter: Charlotte was too disengaged to even point out her nonfunctional fingers and their nonfeeling tips.

She rolled her head to the side and stared at the safety rail.

"It's okay," she said. "I would never do that to you."

•

IN THE MORNING, BEFORE THE nurses arrive, I open the curtains and study the drone in the early light. Most of the stealth and propulsion parts are off the shelf, but the processors are new to me, half hidden by a Kevlar shield. To get the drone to talk, to get some forensics on who sent it my way, I'll have to get my hands on the hash reader from work.

When Charlotte wakes, I prop her head and massage her legs. It's our morning routine.

"Let's generate those Schwann cells," I tell her toes. "It's time for Charlotte's body to start producing some myelin membranes."

"Look who's Mr. Brightside," she says. "You must have been talking to the president. Isn't that why you talk to him, to get all inspired? To see the silver lining?"

I rub her Achilles tendon. Last week Charlotte failed a big test, the DTRE, which measures deep tendon response and signals the *beginning* of recovery. "Don't worry," the doctor told us. "I know of another patient who also took nine months to respond, and he managed a full recovery." I asked if we could contact this patient, to know what he went through, to help us see what's ahead. The doctor informed us this patient was attended to in France, in the year 1918.

After the doctor left, I went into the garage and started making the president. A psychologist would probably say the reason I created him had to do with the promise I made Charlotte and the fact that the president also had a relationship with the person who took his life. But it's simpler than that: I just needed to save somebody, and with the president, it didn't matter that it was too late.

I tap Charlotte's patella, but there's no response. "Any pain?"

"So what did the president say?"

"Which president?"

"The dead one," she says.

I articulate the plantar fascia. "How about this?"

"Feels like a spray of cool diamonds," she says. "Come on, I know you talked to him."

It's going to be one of her bad days, I can tell.

"Let me guess," Charlotte says. "The president told you to move to the South Pacific to take up painting. That's uplifting, isn't it?"

I don't say anything.

"You'd take me with you, right? I could be your assistant. I'd hold your palette in my teeth. If you need a model, I specialize in reclining nudes."

"If you must know," I tell her, "the president told me to locate my inner resolve."

"*Inner resolve*," she says. "I could use some help tracking down mine."

"You have more resolve than anyone I know."

"Jesus, you're sunny. Don't you know what's going on? Don't you see that I'm about to spend the rest of my life like this?"

"Pace yourself, darling. The day's only a couple minutes old."

"I know," she says. "I'm supposed to have reached a stage of enlightened acceptance or something. You think I like it that the only person I have to get mad at is you? I know it's not right—you're the one thing I love in this world."

"You love Kurt Cobain."

"He's dead."

We hear Hector, the morning nurse, pull up outside—he drives an old car with a combustion engine.

"I have to grab something from work," I tell her. "But I'll be back."

"Promise me something," she says.

"No."

"Come on. If you do, I'll release you from the other promise."

I shake my head. She doesn't mean it—she'll never release me.

She says, "Just agree to talk straight with me. You don't have to be fake and optimistic. It doesn't help."

"I am optimistic."

"You shouldn't be," she says. "Pretending, that's what killed Kurt Cobain."

I think it was the shotgun he pointed at his head, but I don't say that.

I know only one line from Nirvana. I karaoke it to Charlotte:

"With the lights on," I sing, "she's less dangerous."

She rolls her eyes. "You got it wrong," she says. But she smiles.

I try to encourage this. "What, I don't get points for trying?"

"You don't hear that?" Charlotte asks.

"Hear what?"

"That's the sound of me clapping."

"I give up," I say, and make for the door.

"Bed, incline," Charlotte tells her remote. Her torso slowly rises. It's time to start her day.

I TAKE THE 101 FREEWAY south toward Mountain View, where I write code at a company called Reputation Curator. Basically, the company threatens Yelpers and Facebookers to retract negative comments about dodgy lawyers and incompetent dentists. The work is labor-intensive, so I was hired to write a program that would sweep the Web to construct client profiles. Creating the president was only a step away.

In the vehicle next to me is a woman with her iProjector on the passenger seat; she's having an animated discussion with the president as she drives. At the next overpass, I see an older man in a tan jacket, looking down at the traffic. Standing next to him is the president. They're not speaking, just standing together, silently watching the cars go by.

A black car, driverless, begins pacing me in the next lane. When I speed up, it speeds up. Through its smoked windows, I can see it has no cargo—there's nothing inside but a battery array big enough to ensure no car could outrun it. Even though I like driving, even though it relaxes me, I shift to automatic and dart into the Google lane, where I let go of the wheel and sign on to the Web for the first time since I released the president a week ago. I log in and discover that fourteen million people have down-loaded the president. I also have seven hundred new messages. The first is from the dude who started Facebook, and it is not spam—he wants to buy me a burrito and talk about the future. I skip to the latest message, which is from Charlotte: "I don't mean to be mean. I lost my feeling, remember? I'll get it back. I'm try-ing, really, I am."

I see the president again, on the lawn of a Korean church. The minister has placed an iProjector on a chair, and the president ap-pears to be engaging a Bible that's been propped before him on a stand. I understand that he is a ghost who will haunt us until our nation comes to grips with what has happened: that he is gone, that he has been stolen from us, that it is irreversible. And I'm not an idiot. I know what's really being stolen from me, slowly and irrevocably, before my eyes. I know that late at night I should be going to Charlotte instead of the president.

But when I'm with Charlotte, there's a membrane my mind places between us to protect me from the tremor in her voice, from the pulse in her desiccated wrists. It's when I'm away that it comes crashing in—how scared she is, how cruel life must seem to her. Driving now, I think about how she has started turning toward the wall even before the last song on the Nirvana album is over, that soon even headphones and marijuana will cease to work. My off-ramp up ahead is blurry, and I realize there are tears in my eyes. I drive right past my exit. I just let the Google lane carry me away.

•

WHEN I ARRIVE HOME, MY boss, Sanjay, is waiting for me. I'd messaged him to have an intern deliver the hash reader, but here is the man himself, item in hand. Theoretically, hash readers are impossible. Theoretically, you shouldn't be able to crack full-field, hundred-key encryption. But some guy in India did it, some guy Sanjay knows. Sanjay is sensitive about being from India, and he thinks it's a cliché that a guy with his name runs a start-up in Palo Alto. So he goes by SJ and dresses all D-School. He's got a Stanford MBA, but he basically just stole the business model of a company called Reputation Defender. You can't blame the guy—he's one of those types with the hopes and dreams of an entire village riding on him.

SJ follows me into the garage, where I dock the drone and use some slave code to parse its drive. He hands me the hash reader, hand-soldered in Bangalore from an old motherboard. We marvel at it, the most sophisticated piece of cryptography on earth, here in our unworthy hands. But if you want to "curate" the reputations of Silicon Valley, you better be ready to crack some passwords.

He's quiet while I initialize the drone and run a diagnostic.

"Long time no see," he finally says.

"I needed some time," I tell him.

"Understood," SJ says. "We've missed you, is all I'm saying. You bring the president back to life, send fifteen million people to our website and then we don't see you for a week."

The drone knows something is suspicious—it powers off. I force a reboot.

"Got yourself a drone there?" SJ asks.

"It's a rescue," I say. "I'm adopting it."

SJ nods. "Thought you should know the Secret Service came by."

"Looking for me?" I ask. "Doesn't sound so secret."

"They must have been impressed with your president. I know I was."

SJ has long lashes and big, manga brown eyes. He hits me with them now.

"I've gotta tell you," he says, "the president is a work of art, a seamlessly integrated data interface. I'm in real admiration. This is a game changer. You know what I envision?"

I notice his flashy glasses. "Are those Android?" I ask.

"Yeah."

"Can I have them?"

He hands them over, and I search the frames for their IP address.

SJ gestures large. "I envision your algorithm running on Reputation Curator. Average people could bring their personalities to life, to speak for themselves, to customize and personalize how they're seen by the world. Your program is like Google, Wikipedia and Facebook all in one. Everyone on the planet with a reputation would pay to have you animate them, to make them articulate, vigilant . . . eternal."

"You can have it," I tell SJ. "The algorithm's core is open-source—I used a freeware protocol."

SJ flashes a brittle smile. "We've actually looked into that," he says, "and, well, it seems like you coded it with seven-layer encryption."

"Yeah, I guess I did, didn't I? You're the one with the hash reader. Just crack it."

"I don't want it to be like that," SJ says. "Let's be partners. Your concept is brilliant—an algorithm that scrubs the Web and compiles the results into a personal animation. The president is the proof, but it's also given away the idea. If we move now, we can protect it, it will be ours. In a few weeks, though, everyone will have their own."

I don't point out the irony of SJ wanting to protect a business model.

"Is the president just an animation to you?" I ask. "Have you spoken with him? Have you listened to what he has to say?"

"I'm offering stock," SJ says. "Wheelbarrows of it."

The drone offers up its firewall like a seductress her throat. I deploy the hash reader, whose processor hums and flashes red. We sit on folding chairs while it works.

"I need your opinion," I tell him.

"Right on," he says, and removes a bag of weed. He starts rolling a joint, then passes me the rest. He's been hooking me up the last couple months, no questions.

"What do you think of Kurt Cobain?" I ask.

"Kurt Cobain," he repeats as he works the paper between his fingers. "The man was pure," he says, and licks the edge. "Too pure for this world. Have you heard Patti Smith's cover of 'Smells Like Teen Spirit'? Unassailable, man."

He lights the joint and passes it my way, but I wave it off. He sits there, staring out the open mouth of my garage into the Kirkland plumage of Palo Alto. Apple, Oracle, PayPal and Hewlett-Packard were all started in garages within a mile of here. About once a month, SJ gets homesick and cooks litti chokha for everyone at work. He plays Sharda Sinha songs and gets this look in his eyes like he's back in Bihar, land of peepal trees and roller birds. He has the look now. He says, "You know, my family downloaded the president. They have no idea what I do out here, as if I could make them understand that I help bad sushi chefs ward off Twitter trolls. But the American president, that they understand."

The mayor, barefoot, jogs past us. Moments later, a billboard drives by.

"Hey, can you make the president speak Hindi?" SJ asks. "If

you could get the American president to say 'I could go for a Pepsi' in Hindi, I'd make you the richest man on earth."

The hash reader's light turns green. Just like that, the drone is mine. I disconnect the leads and begin to sync the Android glasses. The drone uses its moment of freedom to rise and study SJ.

SJ returns the drone's intense scrutiny.

"Who do you think sent it after you?" he asks. "Mozilla? Craigslist?"

"We'll know in a moment."

"Silent. Black. Radar deflecting," SJ says. "I bet this is Microsoft's dark magic."

The new OS suddenly initiates, the drone responds, and using retinal commands, I send it on a lap around the garage. "Lo and behold," I say. "Turns out our little friend speaks Google."

"Wow," SJ says. "Don't be evil, huh?"

When the drone returns, it targets SJ in the temple with a green laser.

"What the fuck," SJ says.

"Don't worry," I tell him. "It's just taking your pulse and temperature."

"What for?"

"Probably trying to read your emotions," I say. "I bet it's a leftover subroutine."

"You sure you're in charge of that thing?"

I roll my eyes and the drone does a backflip.

"My emotion is simple," SJ tells me. "It's time to come back to work."

"I will," I tell him. "I've just got some things to deal with."

SJ looks at me. "It's okay if you don't want to talk about your wife. But you don't have to be so alone about things. Everyone at work, we're all worried about you."

•

INSIDE, CHARLOTTE IS SUSPENDED IN a sling from the Hoyer Lift, which has been rolled to the window so she can see outside. She's wearing old yoga tights, which are slack on her, and she smells of the cedar oil her massage therapist rubs her with. I go to her and open the window.

"You read my mind," she says, and breathes the fresh air.

I put the glasses on her, and it takes her eyes a minute of flashing around before the drone lifts from my hands. A grand smile crosses her face as she puts it through its paces—hovering, rotating, swiveling the camera's servos. And then the drone is off. I watch it cross the lawn, veer around the compost piles, and head for the community garden. It floats down the rows, and though I don't have the view Charlotte does in her glasses, I can see the drone inspecting the blossoms of summer squash, the fat bottoms of Roma tomatoes. It rises along the bean trellises and tracks watermelons by their umbilical stems. When she makes it to her plot, she gasps.

"My roses," she says. "They're still there. Someone's been taking care of them."

"I wouldn't let your roses die," I tell her.

She has the drone inspect every bloom. Carefully, she maneuvers it through the bright petals, brushing against the blossoms, then shuttles it home again. When it's hovering before us, Charlotte leans slightly forward and sniffs the drone. "I never thought I'd smell my roses again," she says, her face flushed with hope and amazement. The tears begin streaming.

I remove her glasses, and we leave the drone hovering there.

She regards me. "I want to have a baby," she says.

"A baby?"

"It's been nine months. I could have had one already. I could've been doing something useful this whole time."

"But your illness," I say. "We don't know what's ahead."

She closes her eyes like she's hugging something, like she's holding some dear truth.

"With a baby, I'd have something to show for all this. I'd have a reason. At the least, I'd have something to leave behind."

"You can't talk like that," I tell her. "We've talked about you not talking like this."

But she won't listen to me, she won't open her eyes.

All she says is "And I want to start tonight."

LATER, I CARRY THE IPROJECTOR out back to the gardening shed. Here, in the gold of afternoon light, the president rises and comes to life. He adjusts his collar and cuffs, runs his thumb down a black lapel as if he exists only in the moment before a camera will broadcast him live to the world.

"Mr. President," I say. "I'm sorry to bother you again."

"Nonsense," he tells me. "I serve at the pleasure of the people."

"Do you remember me?" I ask. "Do you remember the problems I've been talking to you about?"

"Perennial is the nature of the problems that plague man. Particular is the voice with which they call to each of us."

"My problem today is of a personal nature."

"Then I place this conversation under the seal."

"I haven't made love to my wife in a long time."

He holds up a hand to halt me. He smiles in a knowing, fatherly way.

"Times of doubt," he tells me, "are inherent in the compact of civil union."

"My question is about children. Would you have still brought yours into the world, knowing that only one of you might be around to raise them?"

"Single parenting places too much of a strain on today's families," he says. "That's why I'm introducing legislation that will reduce the burden on our hardworking parents."

"What about your children? Do you miss them?"

"My mind goes to them constantly. Being away is the great sacrifice of the office."

In the shed, suspended dust makes his specter glitter and swirl. It makes him look like he is cutting out, like he will leave at any moment. I feel some urgency.

"When it's all finally over," I ask, "where is it that we go?"

"I'm no preacher," the president says, "but I believe we go where we are called."

"Where were you called to? Where is it that you are?"

"Don't we all try to locate ourselves among the pillars of uncommon knowledge?"

"You don't know where you are, do you?" I ask the president.

"I'm sure my opponent would like you to believe that."

"It's okay," I say, more to myself. "I didn't expect you to know."

"I know exactly where I am," the president says. Then, in a voice that sounds pieced from many scraps, he adds, "I'm currently positioned at three seven point four four north by one two two point one four west."

I think he's done. I wait for him to say "Good night and God bless America." Instead, he reaches out to touch my chest. "I have heard that you have made much personal sacrifice," he says. "And I'm told that your sense of duty is strong."

I don't think I agree, but I say, "Yes, sir."

His glowing hand clasps my shoulder, and it doesn't matter that I can't feel it.

"Then this medal that I affix to your uniform is much more than a piece of silver. It is a symbol of how much you have given, not just in armed struggle and not just in service to your nation. It marks you forever as one who can be counted upon, as one who in times of need will lift up and carry those who have fallen." Proudly, he stares into the empty space above my shoulder. He says, "Now return home to your wife, soldier, and start a new chapter of life."

•

WHEN DARKNESS FALLS, I GO to Charlotte. The night nurse has placed her in a negligee. Charlotte lowers the bed as I approach. The electric motor is the only sound in the room.

"I'm ovulating," she announces. "I can feel it."

"You can feel it?"

"I don't need to *feel* it," she says. "I just know."

She's strangely calm.

"Are you ready?" she asks.

"Sure."

I steady myself on the safety rail that separates us.

She asks, "Do you want some oral sex first?"

I shake my head.

"Come join me, then," she says.

I start to climb on the bed—she stops me.

"Hey, sunshine," she says. "Take off your clothes."

I can't remember the last time she called me that.

"Oh yeah," I say, and unbutton my shirt, unzip my jeans. When I drop my underwear, I feel weirdly, I don't know, naked. I swing a leg up, then kind of lie on her.

A look of contentment crosses her face. "This is how it's supposed to be," she says. "It's been a long time since I've been able to look into your eyes."

Her body is narrow but warm. I don't know where to put my hands.

"Do you want to pull down my panties?"

I sit up and begin to work them off. I see the scar from the femoral stent. When I heft her legs, there are the bedsores we've been fighting.

"Remember our trip to Mexico," she asks, "when we made love on top of that pyramid? It was like we were in the past and the future at the same time. I kind of feel that now."

"You're not high, are you?"

"What? Like I'd have to be stoned to recall the first time we talked about having a baby?"

When I have her panties off and her legs hooked, I pause. It takes all my focus to get an erection, and then I can't believe I have one. Here is my wife, paralyzed, invalid, insensate, and though everything's the opposite of erotic, I am poised above her, completely hard.

"I'm wet, aren't I?" Charlotte asks. "I've been thinking about this all day."

I do remember the pyramid. The stone was cold, the staircase steep. The past to me was a week of Charlotte in Mayan dresses, cooing at every baby she came across. Having sex under jungle stars, I tried to imagine the future: a faceless *someone* conceived on a sacrificial altar. I finished early and tried to shake it off. I focused only on all those steps we had to make it down in the dark.

"I think I feel something," she says. "You're inside me, right? Because I'm pretty sure I can feel it."

Here I enter my wife and begin our lovemaking. I try to focus on the notion that if this works, Charlotte will be safe, that for nine months she'd let no harm come to her, and maybe she's right, maybe the baby will stimulate something and recovery will begin.

Charlotte smiles. It's brittle, but it's a smile. "How's this for finding the silver lining—I won't have to feel the pain of childbirth."

This makes me wonder if a paralyzed woman *can* push out a baby, or does she get the scalpel, and if so, is there anesthesia, and all at once my body is at the edge of not cooperating.

"Hey, are you here?" she asks. "I'm trying to get you to smile."

"I just need to focus for a minute," I tell her.

"I can tell you're not really into this," she says. "I can tell you're still hung up on the idea that I'm going to do something drastic to myself, right? Just because I talk about crazy stuff sometimes doesn't mean I'm going to do anything."

"Then why'd you make me promise to help you do it?"

The promise came early, in the beginning, just before the ventilator. She had a vomiting reflex that lasted for hours. Imagine endless dry heaves while you're paralyzed. The doctors finally gave her narcotics. Drugged, dead-limbed and vomiting, that's when it struck her that her body was no longer hers. I was holding her hair, keeping it out of the basin. She was panting between heaves.

She said, "Promise me that when I tell you to make it stop, you'll make it stop."

"Make what stop?" I asked.

She retched, long and cord-rattling. I knew what she meant.

"It won't come to that," I said.

She tried to say something but retched again.

"I promise," I said.

Now, in her mechanical bed, her negligee straps slipping off her shoulders, Charlotte says, "It's hard for you to understand, I know. But the idea that there's a way out, it's what allows me to keep going. I'd never take it. You believe me, don't you?"

"I hate that promise, I hate that you made me make it."

"I'd never do it, and I'd never make you help."

"Then release me," I tell her.

"I'm sorry," she says.

I decide to just shut it all out and keep going. I'm losing my erection, and my mind wonders what will happen if I go soft—do I have it in me to fake it?—but I shut it out and keep going and going, pounding on Charlotte until I can barely feel anything. Her breasts loll alone under me. From the bedside table, the drone turns itself on and rises, hovering. It flashes my forehead with its green laser, as if what I'm feeling is that easy to determine, as if my emotion has a name. Is it spying on me, feeling sympathy or executing old code? I wonder if the drone's OS reverted to a previous version or if Google reacquired it or if it's in some kind of autonomous mode. Or it could be that someone hacked the Android glasses, or maybe . . . That's when I look down and see Charlotte is crying.

I stop.

"No, don't," she says. "Keep going."

She's not crying hard, but they are fat, lamenting tears.

"We can try again tomorrow," I tell her.

"No, I'm okay," she says. "Just keep going and do something for me, would you?"

"All right."

"Put the headphones on me."

"You mean, while we're doing it?"

"Music on," she says. From the headphones on her bedside table, Nirvana starts to hum.

"I know I'm doing it all wrong," I say. "It's been a long time, and . . ."

"It's not you," she says. "I just need my music. Just put them on me."

"Why do you need Nirvana? What is it to you?"

She closes her eyes and shakes her head.

"What is it with this Kurt Cobain?" I say. "What's your deal with him?"

I grab her wrists and pin them down, but she can't feel it.

"Why do you have to have this music? What's wrong with you?" I demand. "Just tell me what it is that's wrong with you."

THE DRONE FOLLOWS ME TO the garage, where it wanders the walls, looking for a way out. I turn on a computer and download one of these Nirvana albums. I play the whole thing, just sitting there in the dark. The guy, this Kurt Cobain, sings about being stupid and dumb and unwanted. In one song, he says that Jesus doesn't want him for a sunbeam. In another song, he says he wants milk and laxatives along with cherry-flavored antacids. He has a song called "All Apologies," but he never actually apologizes. He doesn't even say what he did wrong.

The drone, having found no escape, comes to me and hovers silently. I must look pretty pathetic, because the drone takes my temperature.

I lift the remote for the garage door opener. "Is this what you want?" I ask. "If I let you go, are you going to come back?"

The drone silently hums, impassive atop its column of warm air.

I press the button. The drone waits until the garage door is all the way up. Then it snaps a photograph of me and zooms off into the Palo Alto night.

I stand and breathe the air, which is cool and smells of flowers. There's enough moonlight to cast leaf patterns on the driveway. Down the street, I spot the glowing eyes of our cat. I call his name, but he doesn't come. I gave him to a friend a couple blocks away, and for a few weeks the cat returned at night to visit me. Not anymore. This feeling of being in proximity to something that's lost to you, it seems like my whole life right now. It's a feeling Charlotte would understand if she'd just talk to the president. But he's not the one she needs to speak to, I suddenly understand. I return to my computer bench and fire up a bank of screens. I stare into their blue glow and get to work. It takes me hours, most of the night, before I'm done.

It's almost dawn when I go to Charlotte. The room is dark, and I can only see her outline. "Bed incline," I say, and she starts to rise. She wakes and stares at me but says nothing. Her face has that lack of expression that comes only after it's been through every emotion.

I set the iProjector in her lap. She hates the thing but says nothing. She only tilts her head a little, like she's sad for me. Then I turn it on.

Kurt Cobain appears before her, clad in a bathrobe and composed of soft blue light.

Charlotte inhales. "Oh my God," she murmurs.

She looks at me. "Is it him?"

I nod.

She marvels at him. "What do I say?" she asks. "Can he talk?"

I don't answer.

Kurt Cobain's hair is in his face. Shifting her gaze, Charlotte tries to look into his eyes. While the president couldn't quite find your eyes, Kurt is purposefully avoiding them.

"I can't believe how young you are," Charlotte tells him. "You're just a boy."

Kurt mumbles, "I'm old."

"Are you really here?" she asks.

"Here we are now," he sings. "Entertain us."

His voice is rough and hard-lived. It's some kind of proof of life to Charlotte.

Charlotte looks at me, filled with wonder. "I thought he was gone," she says. "I can't believe he's really here."

Kurt shrugs. "I only appreciate things when they're gone," he says.

Charlotte looks stricken. "I recognize that line," she says to me. "That's a line from his suicide note. How does he know that? Has he already written it, does he know what he's going to do?"

"I don't know," I tell her. This isn't my conversation to have. I back away toward the door, and just as I'm leaving, I hear her start to talk to him.

"Don't do what you're thinking about doing," she pleads with him. "You don't know how special you are, you don't know how much you matter to me," she says, carefully, like she's talking to a child. "Please don't take yourself from me. You can't do that to me."

She leans toward Kurt Cobain like she wants to throw her arms around him and hold him, like she's forgotten that her arms don't work and there's no him to embrace.

RICK BASS

"Sometimes, you can know a thing, as a writer, too well, and you lose the necessity of imagination. You're just hitting your marks. You're saying: *Okay, this happened this way. This happened this way.* You see it in a lot of writing students. Ron Carlson says: *Don't confuse the facts with the truth.* The more imagination you can bring in and the specificity of the senses is what attaches a reader to a story."

"I try to go in not knowing. That way, you and the reader go in as partners in equity, encountering each change in the landscape of the story with equal discovery. And that's a really powerful shared experience between the reader and the writer. It develops a certain bond."

"I live in the woods and have a lot of whack ideas. One I have is that the elegant, orthodox, traditional, mainstream, classic, beginning-middle-and-end, lens-shaped, six-to-eighteen-page vessel of the short story has evolved with us as a species. It's a way that we have to process information, mostly emotional information. And we've grown very comfortable with that lozenge, that thirty-minute telling (or thirty-minute showing). If that's the case, then the ending will write itself. You have the narrow beginning and then you swell out into the middle of the lens—where obstacles and conflicts come in—and then, when you get toward the terminus of that lens, the end is when the end happens. You don't have any control over it. You run out of space, and all of this emotion and conflict and narrative comes to the point where it can't go any further, and that's the end."

"If you get into the senses and let the story go, you're going to make discoveries as a writer that transcend your skills as a writer. That's why we do it. It's addictive."

Onstage interview at The Story Prize event
March 2, 2016

How She Remembers It

from *For a Little While*

They left Missoula with a good bit of sun still left—what would be dusk any other time of year. The light was at their backs, and the rivers, rather than charging straight down out of the mountains, now meandered through broader valleys, which were suspended in that summer light, a sun that seemed to show no inclination of moving. Lilly's father had only begun to lose his memory, seemed more distracted than forgetful then. He had been a drinker, too, once upon a time, though Lilly did not know that then; it had been long ago, before she was even born. A hard drinker, one who had gone all the way to rock bottom—good years wasted, her mother would later tell her—but he was better now. Though some of his memories—the already reduced or compromised roster of them, due to his years of drinking—were now leaving. Sometimes what left was the smallest thing, from the day or a week before, other times more distant memories, but nothing serious yet.

The pastures were soft and lush, the grass made emerald by May's alternations of thunderstorms and sunlight, and the farmers had not yet begun their first cutting of hay. The rivers had cleared up and were running blue, scouring the year's silt from the bottoms, cleaning every stone. From time to time she and her father would see a bald eagle sitting in a cottonwood snag overlooking the river. There were more deer in the fields than cattle—occasionally they'd see a few black Angus, like smudges of new charcoal amid the rainwashed green, but mostly just deer, some of them swollen-bellied with fawns that would be born any day, while others were round with lactation, their fawns already having been dropped, but not yet visible, in those tall grasses. The velvet antlers of the bucks glowed when they passed through shafts and slants of that slowly flattening light. Lilly was twelve, and her father was only fifty-two.

They rode with the windows down. The air was still warm but not superheated now, and in the brief curves of canyons they could detect a cooling that felt exquisite on their bare arms, with so much sun elsewhere, all around. It was only another four hours to the Paradise Valley, south of Livingston, where her father had friends, though he said if she wanted to stop and get a room or camp before that, they could. Lilly said she didn't care, and she didn't. It was enough to just be driving with the windows down, with her father, looking around and thinking about things.

Now the tinge of valley light was shifting, the gold and green becoming infused with purple and blue, and the touch of the air on their arms was more delicious yet. Mayflies were hatching out along the river, drifting columns of them rising dense as fog or smoke and bouncing off their arms like little needles. Farther on, the larger stone flies began to emerge and were soon thudding off the windshield and smearing it with a bright pastel of green and yellow and orange, which the windshield wipers turned to slurry before wiping the glass clear again.

Nearing Deer Lodge at the beginning of true dusk, just before ten, they saw the colorful lights of a tiny carnival, one of the portable setups that's able to fit all of its equipment onto a single long flatbed tractor-trailer, with the various parts for five or six ancient rides so cloaked with grease and blackened with oil, and the hydraulic hoses so leaky and patched together with pipe clamps, that no self-respecting parent would let a child ride; and yet in the summer, when a carnival suddenly appeared on a once-vacant lot in the middle of such a small town, and knowing that in only a few days the carnival will be gone, what self-respecting parent could say no?

Passing through Deer Lodge, the highway was slightly elevated above the town, so that from their vantage they were looking slightly down on the carnival. Viewed through the canopy of summer green cottonwoods, the lights of the fair—and, in particular, the lights of the Ferris wheel, which seemed to rise up into, and then somehow rotate through, the foliage—gave the impression of slow-budding continuous fireworks going off, at their peak barely rising above the canopy. It looked like a secret, private festivity. They exited as though it had been their planned destination all along.

The carnival was so tiny that once they were on the downtown streets of Deer Lodge they couldn't even find it at first. The streets were wide and dusty, and they could smell the waxy buds of the cottonwoods, which were just opening. Both sides of the street were lined with the white fluff of cottonwood seeds, piled like drifts of snow. Up ahead, they could hear the grinding machinery of the fair, the squeak and rattle of ancient gears, though there was no loudspeaker music, so the atmosphere was not so much one of frivolity as instead a more dutiful, even morose, labor.

Still, it was a fair, and when they rounded the last corner they could see the lights again: a weak yellow 40-watt glow coming from the popcorn stand, as well as a few lights still burning on various whirligig rides. A portable yellow iron fence surrounded the vacant lot on which the carnival had set up shop.

The Ferris wheel, along with the other rides, had stopped since they turned off the highway, and there were no other children around, despite darkness only just now descending. They parked beneath one of the big cottonwoods and got out. The sweet-scentedness of the buds and new leaves was almost overwhelming, and a strong dry wind was blowing from the west, sending cotton-wood fluff sailing past them. There was no one at the well-worn turnstile, so they walked right through. They wandered around, looking at the rickety equipment, marveling at the decrepitude of the infrastructure—rides that had been manufactured in the 1940s and '50s, with puddles of oil already staining the dust of the gravel lot and scraps and flanges of steel welded into patches atop the oil-darkened machinery, so fatigued now by time and the friction of innumerable revolutions that it seemed the wind itself might be sufficient to snap some of the rides off at the base.

The carnival laborers, nearly as oil-stained as the machinery, were smoking their cigarettes and beginning to disassemble the rides. The tractor-trailer on which it would all be folded and stacked and strapped down was already being revved up, rumbling and smoking—in no better shape than the rides—and as Lilly and her father went from one ride to the next, asking if any might still be open, might be cranked back up one last time, the men who were busy with wrenches and sockets shook their heads and spoke to them in Spanish, not unkindly but in a way that let them know the momentum of their world was different from the leisurely pace of Lilly and her father's. In a perfect summer evening in the country, she and her father would have ridden in the Ferris wheel up above the canopy of the green cottonwoods, high enough to look out at the last rim of purple and orange sunlight going down behind the Pintler Mountains, their crests still snowcapped; but in the real world they were just able to buy a cotton-candy cone before walking back out to their truck and continuing on their journey.

And it was enough, was more than enough, to have the pink cotton candy, and to be driving on, and to simply imagine, rather than really remember, what it would have been like, riding the Ferris wheel around and around, with the whole carnival to themselves. It's been so long now that in Lilly's mind she almost remembers it that way—they were only a few minutes removed from having it happen like that—and yet in a way she can't explain or know, it was almost better to not; better to miss, now and again, than to get everything you want, all the time, every time.

They stopped for gas at a Cenex convenience store. Her father still wouldn't shop at an Exxon, for what they had done at Prince William Sound—not the spill so much as the cover-up—and while he went inside to get a cup of coffee, having decided they would drive on through the night, all the way to the Paradise Valley, Lilly looked out her window at the woman in the car parked next to them.

She was sitting behind the wheel of an old red Cadillac, the paint so faded it was more of a salmon color, and the fender wells rusted out from decades of plowing through salty winter slush. It was a soft top, with a once-crisp white vinyl roof crackled and stained a sickly greenish yellow by years of parking outdoors and under trees.

Lilly noticed that the Caddy's tires were not only balding but mismatched in size and style. Though the woman had not asked Lilly's counsel, Lilly found herself recalling one of her father's many strongly held opinions—always invest in the best tires possible—and she found herself wanting to tell the lady to replace them. The car was an eyesore, but the tires themselves, fraying steel wires sprung from the thin rubber, were an actual affront, and a hazard, her father would have said.

The woman was perhaps in her early fifties, though possibly simply hard used and much younger—or, just as possible, much older and simply preserved, pickled somehow, by toxins. She had brittle orange hair, a sleeveless red T-shirt—what Lilly's father called a wifebeater—and a weight lifter's shoulders, though with pale, flabby arms. She wasn't so much fat, Lilly recalls now—not really fat at all—as loose; as if once she had been hard but no longer and never again, and she was just sitting in her car smoking a cigarette, smoking it down to a nub. She labored at it a short while longer, then flicked it out the window in Lilly's direction without even looking, or noticing that Lilly was looking, and then turned away from Lilly to murmur some endearment to her traveling companion, a nasty rat-colored Chihuahua.

The woman lifted a pink ice cream cone—which must have been her reason for stopping—and held it up for the little dog to eat. He scampered into her lap and began licking at it, fastidiously at first, but then really gnawing at it, wolfing it down, and she continued to hold it for him, fascinated and charmed by his appetite, as the ice cream—bubblegum? strawberry?—began to froth around his muzzle. She was still murmuring her adoration to him, enchanted by what she clearly perceived to be his singular skill, when Lilly's father came back out and got in the car.

He barely glanced at the woman, and as they backed out and then pulled away, the Chihuahua was still attacking the ice cream cone, both sticky paws up on the woman's chest now, laboring to get down into the cone, and still the woman beheld the little dog as if he were an amazement; and for all Lilly knew, when he had finished that cone, she was going to go in and get him another one. She appeared to have completely lost track of time and easily could have remained there all night, slumping a little lower in her seat, settling, seemingly intent upon going nowhere. It was terrifying in a fascinating way, and as they continued on through the night— satisfied for having simply gotten off the road briefly and having at least seen the fair, if not actually ridden any of the rides—Lilly ate her cotton candy leisurely, slumping down in her seat and pretending, for a moment, with a delicious thrill, that she was the woman in the Cadillac: that her life would or might end up there—lonely and lost, and needing to feed a nasty little dog ice cream to have even that friendship.

As they drove, the stars blinked brightly above them—her father had cleaned the windshield again—and Lilly pulled little stray tendrils of her cotton candy and released them out the window, into the wind, where she imagined birds up from South America finding them and, not knowing they were edible, weaving them into their nests.

She thought up stories about the woman with the dog: She had just gotten out of jail after serving twenty years and didn't have a friend in the world, or her husband had just that day been sent to prison for life, or maybe her whole family. Or maybe she had found

out that her little dog was going to have to be put down—maybe
he had a tumor the size of a grapefruit, or at least a ping-pong
ball, hidden in his stomach. Maybe the woman had been a great
beauty once, in another life, another town, another state, thirty or
more years ago—back when her car had been new—and maybe,
at times, she still believed herself to be. Maybe . . .

"What are you thinking?" her father asked.

"Nothing," she said.

They rode, putting safe distance between themselves and the
woman with the dog, with music playing from a cassette mix Lilly's
father had made. Lilly tries to remember, now, but can't recall every song—Emmylou Harris and Neil Young, she knows—though
if she were to hear one of the other songs it would come back to
her in an instant.

Driving on, peering forward into the night, and thinking
about Yellowstone.

WHEN SHE WOKE UP, THEY had crossed over the Divide. It was
the middle of the night and they were in the Paradise Valley. They
were driving slowly down a rain-slicked winding road, and hail
was bouncing off their roof and windshield like marbles. Her first
image, and the reason she had awakened, was of her father slowing
to a stop, with the hail coming down so hard he couldn't see far
enough ahead to continue. The roar on the roof was so loud that
even by shouting they could not hear each other.

They sat there for a few minutes with the engine running, the
hail streaming all around them, and then the storm began to ease
off, loosening back into drumming rain, and the road ahead reap-
peared, steaming and hissing in their headlights, paved with hail
three inches deep.

They proceeded, the mist clearing in tatters like smoke from
a battlefield, and with the road untraveled before them. They

crossed the Yellowstone River, which was still running muddy and was frothy already with the quick runoff from the storm. Green boughs of cottonwoods drifted past crazily, bobbing and pitching, so that Lilly knew the storm must have originated farther upstream, earlier in the evening—the high snowy mountains attracting lightning as soon as the evening began to cool—and as they cracked their windows in order to clear the fog from the windshield, the summery scent of hail-crushed mint from along the riverbanks was intense, as was that of the shredded cottonwood leaves and black riverside earth, loam-ripped by the rushing waters.

The grass was tall on either side of the narrow road, taller than the roof of their car. Bright white fences lined both sides, and more cottonwoods grew close along the road, forming a canopy above. The road was covered with a mix of hail and leaves, some of the leaves with their bright green sides up and others with the pale silvery undersides showing.

Several times her father had to stop and get out and clear the road of limbs downed by the storm. He dragged them to the side as if pulling a canoe, his breath leaping in clouds, his tracks crisp and precise in the fresh hail.

For a while it rained lightly, with a south wind sending the fallen green leaves skittering across the top of the hail. They turned up a gravel side road and drove past a series of old red barns. Her father seemed surprised to see them, stopped and looked for a minute, then gestured toward one and said he and Lilly's mother had slept in it once when they first visited this part of the state, but there had been an owl living in there, and it had kept them awake most of the night.

Farther on, the road came to its end at a trailhead, where there was barely room in the tall summer grass for the car to turn around; and when they did—the neatness and solitude of their tracks revealing them to be the only travelers out in such a storm, and in such a world—the effect was profound: as if all of the mountains, and all of the valley through which they had driven, were theirs and theirs alone. As though they were not exploring lands that had already been traversed many times over but instead territories not yet dreamed of or discovered.

The rain had picked up and was drumming and blowing past them now in curtains and sheets, and Lilly stayed in the car while her father set up the tent in the steaming blaze cast by their headlights. The rain appeared to be drifting in a curtain only along the foothills because she could see now in the valley below them a few faint and scattered lights, farmhouses and ranches spaced far apart but with their infrequent lights defining the shape of the valley and the course of the river. When her father finished putting the tent up, he unrolled their sleeping bags, and Lilly raced from the car to the tent, crawled into her bag, as warm and dry as she could remember feeling, and slept without dreams or recollections of the day.

THE VALLEY WAS GILDED WITH light when they awoke in the morning. The air was cool and scrubbed clean from the storm, and the hail had already melted. Other than the downed limbs and branches and leaves, there was no evidence the hail had been there in the first place. The sound sleepers in the valley would awaken and look out and think they had slept through a thunderstorm, and would know nothing of the winter scene they had missed completely.

There was a rainbow over the valley and steam rising from the river far below. Lilly turned and looked behind them and was stunned to see the Beartooths right at their feet. She could feel the cold emanating from their glaciers, as when one opens a freezer or refrigerator door. It made her laugh out loud to see such immense and jagged mountains rising right before them and for her to have been standing there with her back to them, unknowing, as she stared out at the green valley.

She and her father were at the front gate of the mountains, next to the trailhead leading up into the crags and ice fields. Lilly kept looking back out at the valley, then turning and looking up at the Beartooths. How could any traveler decide? She chose both, and stared out at the Paradise Valley for a while, and then at the Beartooths, as her father stowed the sleeping bags and shook the water from the tent fly before spreading it in the back windshield of the car to dry in the morning sun as they drove.

They got in the car and traveled down the winding road, away from the mountains and down into the lush summer valley, puddles splashing beneath them.

They drove down to a diner with some little guest cabins along one of the side creeks that fed into the fast and broad Yellowstone River. A series of tiny log cottages, painted dark brown, lined the edges of the rushing, noisy creek—Lilly's father and mother had stayed there a few nights when they were young, exploring and wandering around.

A garish 1950s-style faux-neon sign above the diner—hugely oversize and illuminated by bright rows of painted lightbulbs— was welded to an immense steel post to hold its weight: the kind of sign one might see outside a lounge advertising itself as the Thunderbird or the Wagon Wheel, but would generally not expect to encounter back in a quiet grove of trees far off the beaten track in southern Montana. *Pine Creek Lodge.*

It pleased her father to see that the sign was still there, by the rushing creek, and he got out and took a picture of it to show her mother, though he said that to appreciate it fully one needed to see it at night.

A cardboard sign hung on the door said that the restaurant was closed for the day. As they left, they saw that the other side of the marquee, visible only to northbound traffic, advertised an upcoming outdoor concert the very next night—Martha Scanlan and the Revelators—and it was strange to see how quiet and isolated the hidden little grove was in contrast to the garish ambition of the sign. Lilly felt bad for Martha Scanlan, whoever she was, and her Revelators. No one would ever find this place, and no one would ever see the spectacular illumination of her name in the colorful lights. Perhaps a few cows from the pasture across the road, and the horses on the other side of the creek. At least Martha would maybe get to eat breakfast in the diner. Lilly found herself loving the name Martha, loving the musician herself.

Lilly could imagine the cigarette smoke, and the dusty display case of Certs breath mints by the ancient cash register. She imagined Martha Scanlan tuning her guitar, beginning to prepare already, days ahead of time, for this bad idea of a concert. A barbecue was advertised to go along with it. Perhaps Martha was in one of the Dakotas at this very moment, hurrying on toward Pine Creek Lodge in an old Volkswagen bus, imagining a throng awaiting her, and a buzzing building, rather than this quiet, secret little grove of seven cabins. Perhaps the same storm that had washed over Lilly and her father the night before was now lashing Martha, out on the prairie somewhere, out in the Badlands.

THEY STOPPED INSTEAD AT A KOA along the river, where an elderly couple was just opening their store, still a few minutes before seven. Lilly and her father saw them walking over together, holding hands, to unlock the building. There were pink and yellow rosebushes blooming by the log-cabin storefront—back home, the roses would not bloom for another week or two—and the storm had torn loose numerous petals, which were cast onto the damp pavement like alms. The bushes had surely been planted and tended by the old lady or perhaps both her and the old man, but they appeared not to notice the spoilage, or, if they noticed, not to mind.

Their breath rose in clouds as they spoke quietly to each other, and perhaps they simply thought the storm's residue was pretty.

There were no other residents up and about. Perhaps a dozen or more behemoths—Winnebangos, her father called them—rested back among the old cottonwoods, their silver sides as shiny as salmon, but not even a generator was stirring. Lilly imagined it must have been a pretty rough night for all the old folks, no more able to sleep through the storm than had they been in a giant popcorn popper. After the storm had passed through, they must have wandered outside to inspect the damage, hoping for the best: that if the hail had caused any blemishes to their beloved, shiny homes, the damage would not be visible to the larger world, but would be confined to the roofs, unseen by anyone or anything but the birds passing overhead.

Lilly and her father gave the old couple a minute or two to get the lights turned on and the cash register opened up, and then they went inside and bought a breakfast bar each, some dry and unsatisfactory crumbly little thing. Her father got a coffee and added cream to it, which surprised her—she'd never seen him do that before—while she got an orange juice, and then they were on the road again, driving early, through the greenest part of the summer.

They were just riding, she and her father. She didn't know then that something was wrong with him, and that he wasn't going to get better—though she did know that there was something wonderfully right with her, something gloriously good. She didn't know then, though she suspects now, that he had a clue what was up. That he must have.

They had not traveled five miles before they saw the faded red Cadillac broken down on the side of the road, its hood elevated like the maw of a shark. Despite the chill of the morning, smoke and steam boiled out from the engine's interior. It was not the simple white steam of a boiling radiator, but instead a writhing column of black smoke from burning oil. One of her father's many great gifts to Lilly was to make sure she understood how engines worked, and, looking at the car, Lilly saw the smoke of an expensive repair bill, or maybe no repair bill at all.

The woman with the dog was sitting on the side of the road next to the car. The dog, clutched in her arms like a teddy bear, appeared to be concerned by the situation, occasionally writhing and struggling, but the woman herself was the picture of reflective calm, save for the half-empty bottle of vodka sitting in the gravel beside her. She seemed resigned, so accustomed to this type of situation that her relaxed demeanor could almost be viewed, Lilly supposed, as a form of confidence.

Lilly's father hesitated—Lilly thought she detected a quick burst of annoyance, and she understood: there was now a complication to their perfect day, this unwelcome challenge or summons to Good Samaritanhood—but she was surprised by the flare of something almost like anger in him.

He looked straight ahead then and drove on past the woman, not so much deliberating—she and her father both knew he was going to stop and turn around and go back—as allowing himself, she thinks now, the brief luxury of believing he could keep going. Of believing he was free to keep on going.

The woman watched him pass but made no gesture, no outreach or call for help other than to make a sour face briefly as she confirmed once again that she understood how the world was—that there was no mercy in it for her, and that people could not be expected to do the right things and could in fact be counted upon to do the wrong things—but then she quickly settled back into her I-don't-give-a-fuck serenity, just sitting there and watching the western skies and holding tightly to the dog.

She was surprised, Lilly could tell, when her father pulled over and, checking for traffic, made a wide loop of a turnaround and headed back. The woman was already drunk and a little unsteady as she labored to rise from her cross-legged position, still gripping

the dog, and whether her inebriation was the result of new efforts
in that direction already begun that morning or left over from the
previous night, Lilly had no way of knowing.

Where had she spent the night during the storm, Lilly wondered, and what had she thought of it? Had she even noticed?

Lilly stayed in the car but with her window rolled down while
her father got out and walked over to assess the woman's smoking
car. Even over the scent of the burning oil, she could smell the
woman now—old sweat and salt and above all else stale alcohol—
and Lilly heard her ask her father in a raspy growl if he would like
a sip, holding the bottle up to him as if it were a particularly fine
vintage.

"I was going to Yellowstone," the woman said, staggering a bit.
The dog in her arms like a sailor in a crow's nest was ready to leap
free should she topple, but with the practiced familiarity also of a
veteran who had weathered many such tempests. "I wanted to go
see the buffalo," she said. She made a small flapping motion with
one hand. "*Wooves*, and all that shit." Danger. Excitement. Now she
looked at the dying car, her pride and freedom, her other self. Her
better self. "I don't reckon you can fix it," she said to Lilly's father.

THERE WAS A PAY PHONE back at the KOA. The woman and her
dog got in the back seat. Lilly turned and smiled at both of them,
hoping not to betray her revulsion at the stench.

The day was warming and not in their favor. Her father drove
fast, and he and Lilly each experimented with the windows. It was
hard to tell which was more unbearable: to have them rolled down
and the foul aromas swirling around their heads, or rolled up, with
the noxious odors heavy and still. They finally settled on a combi-
nation that left each window cracked several inches.

Their passenger was becoming more talkative, even in that
short distance, telling them about—surprise—an unhappy rela-

tionship, a disappointing man, and now Lilly's father was pressing
the accelerator so hard that the woman, none too steady to begin with, was pinned against the back seat, though still she kept
talking, an occasional curse spilling from her lips followed by a
surprised look in Lilly's direction—how did this child get here?—
and an overwrought apology.

They skidded into the gravel parking lot of the KOA—a plume
of white dust announcing their arrival—and the old couple, who
were out watering their roses, looked up with mild curiosity,
prepared for some level of disapproval. Lilly's father got out and
opened the door for the woman, who was having difficulty with
the task.

Lilly heard her father offer the woman twenty-five cents for the
phone, but the woman declined, insisting with great protest that
she had more than enough money for a phone call.

"Do you need anything else?" Lilly's father asked. "Are you
sure you'll be all right?"

The woman held the Chihuahua under one arm like a purse
and the vodka bottle in her other hand. Unobserved by the woman,
the icy breath of the Beartooths mingled with the rising lovely
warmth of the day. The sound of the Yellowstone River, full runoff,
in the distance.

"I'll be fine," she slurred. "Right as rain."

Hostility now rushed into her, and she all but snarled at Lilly's
father, with a scornful glance in Lilly's direction, and said, "Y'all
go on with your little vacation, don't you worry about me at all.
I'll be just hunky-dory." The last two words took stupendous effort
to pronounce, and she turned and weaved her way toward the pay
phone, stopping now and again as if to ascertain whether it was
retreating from her and seeming surprised that she had not already
reached it.

The old man and woman turned their hoses off and came
walking over to see what the problem was.

"She's in a bad relationship," Lilly's father said—the truth, certainly, though also the closest Lilly would ever hear him come to telling a lie. He opened his billfold and handed the old man six twenty-dollar bills—enough for four nights' lodging in one of the cabins, and some modest amount of groceries, assuming she didn't spend it all on booze. Lilly was surprised—flabbergasted—for they were not in the least bit rich, and it was a huge outlay for them.

"I don't know her," Lilly's father said to the old man and woman, and nothing more. They saw that the woman was not making a phone call—who really would she call and what was there to say?—but was instead just resting, leaning against the inside of the Plexiglas shell framing the phone, seemingly satisfied, momentarily, for having achieved some destination; and Lilly and her father left before she emerged from her reverie, fearing she might hail them, might seek to lay claim with some nebulous moral obligation, or fearing, perhaps, that they might simply have to witness more humiliation, more desperation.

Lilly for one didn't feel at all bad about leaving her behind. The woman could stay and hear Martha Scanlan, could go to the barbecue. She might not get to see Yellowstone but she would be close; one never knew, it might work out somehow. And Lilly remained astounded by her father's generosity.

THEY STARTED BACK IN THE direction they had already traveled. They didn't say anything about what had happened, and it amazes Lilly now to consider that her father had the restraint and discipline not to try to put too fine a point on what they had seen. She knew—and knows—it would have been well within his rights to look over at Lilly and say, *Don't drink, ever.*

They drove with the windows down, the clean valley winds scouring the green fields and washing through the car, blasting away the scent of their previous occupant. They drove past the

woman's car, which was still smoldering, and then, not much farther on, her father got excited and pulled off the road.

At first Lilly had no idea why, thinking—fearing—he had
spied another stranded motorist, another pilgrim. But instead
he grabbed the binoculars from the back seat and pointed out a
yellow-headed blackbird in a clump of cattails not far from the
road—a sunken little wetland in which a few dairy cattle stood
and beside which old metal barrels and an abandoned tractor
rusted back down into squalor, while just upslope, a dingy mobile
home perched crookedly on an irregular stacking of cinder blocks,
the trailer tilting toward the black-water pond below.

Two white PVC pipes jutted from the earthen bank above the
pond—overflow, no doubt, for various effluents—but it was the
shocking beauty of the bird, its boisterous, exuberant singing, incredible yellow head thrown back and trilling to the blue sky, having survived the storm, that fixed their attention.

"Would you look at that," her father kept exclaiming, handing
her the binoculars so she could see the bird's beauty close up, and
then, moments later, asking for them back, wanting to see it again,
then growing more excited and passing them back to her, while the
bird sang on and on.

A grizzled middle-aged man, probably no older than her father but much worse for the wear, came out onto the porch, un-
nerved by their scrutiny, and Lilly began to imagine all the days
that might have been that led him to this place—this downward
slide, this rendezvous with failure.

What would it be like to be him, Lilly wondered—the man
in the stained T-shirt, staggering onto the porch and blinking at
the bright sunlight? Only her own victory of being loved deeply
allowed her the luxury of such indulgent imaginings.

They waved to the man—he did not wave back—and drove
on. They began to see other travelers streaming toward Yellowstone: a landscape all the travelers had surely heard described as

mythical, beautiful, otherworldly. She could sense her father's excitement as well as mild confusion. He told her they were going into an old and vast caldera that long ago had been a fountain of gurgling, uncontrollable fire but had since cooled to stone, and where—across the many millions of years—every kind of beauty had crept in, reborn and flourishing.

He told her he couldn't wait for her to see it. That it was a fantastic land of geysers and bears, ocher cliffs and cascading waterfalls, burbling mud pots and hot springs: a fantastic land, he said, something she would remember always.

There was only one main road leading into Yellowstone, but her father seemed tentative, kept looking at side roads as if lost, as though unsure whether memories attached to those branching little roads or not. He was wondering, she thinks now, if there were important or interesting stories at the end of some of those side roads, and that he had been trying—bluffing—to remember them, there on the main road.

The blackbird had been good. She leaned her head out the open window and breathed in deeply.

There was no way for him to tell her then in words the truth that he must have been discovering each day: that to be increasingly isolate is better than being numb, if it comes down to a choice. That even forgetting might be all right, eventually, after a long enough time, if the first-burning is hot enough.

She remembers stopping at the stone archway outside the park so they could take a picture, her father setting the camera up on the hood, pressing the timer, then running quickly to join her. Huffing, when he got there, having sprinted into the wind, as if into the past. His arm tight around her. How vast our brains must be, she thinks now, to remember even such tiny and essentially useless and fleeting things. How dare anyone sleep through even a moment of it?

ELIZABETH STROUT

"The people in this book were very real for me. They have to be for me to continue to write them. Otherwise, if they're not, then they just get tossed on the floor—literally. But these people were very, very real to me. I didn't write the stories in order because I don't write anything in order. I don't even write a story from beginning to end."

"If I could take whatever was most pressing in my own chest and just put that emotion—completely transpose it but use that emotion in a scene—the scene would probably last or have a better chance of lasting than if I was just trying to write the beginning of a story. That's when I learned to write in scenes that would, hopefully, have a heartbeat to them."

Onstage interview at The Story Prize event
February 28, 2018

The Sign

Tommy Guptill had once owned a dairy farm, which he'd inherited from his father, and which was about two miles from the town of Amgash, Illinois. This was many years ago now, but at night Tommy still sometimes woke with the fear he had felt the night his dairy farm burned to the ground. The house had burned to the ground as well; the wind had sent sparks onto the house, which was not far from the barns. It had been his fault—he always thought it was his fault—because he had not checked that night on the milking machines to make sure they had been turned off properly, and this is where the fire started. Once it started, it ripped with a fury over the whole place. They lost everything, except for the brass frame to the living room mirror, which he came upon in the rubble the next day, and he left it where it was. A collection was taken up: For a number of weeks his kids went to school in the clothes of their classmates, until he could gather himself and the little money he had; he sold the land to the neighboring farmer, but it did not bring much money in. Then he and his wife, a short pretty woman named Shirley, bought new clothes, and he bought a house as well, Shirley keeping her spirits up admirably as all this was going on. They'd had to buy a house in Amgash, which was a run-down town, and his kids went to school there instead of in Carlisle, where they had been able to go to school before, his farm being just on the line dividing the two towns. Tommy took a job as the janitor in the Amgash school system; the steadiness of the job appealed to him, and he could never go to work on someone else's farm, he did not have the stomach for that. He was thirty-five years old at the time.

The kids were grown now, with kids of their own who were

also grown, and he and Shirley still lived in their small house; she had planted flowers around it, which was unusual in that town. Tommy had worried a good deal about his children at the time of the fire; they had gone from having their home be a place that class trips came to—-each year in spring the fifth-grade class from Carlisle would make a day of it, eating their lunches out beside the barns on the wooden tables there, then tromping through the barns watching the men milking the cows, the white foamy stuff going up and over them in the clear plastic pipes—to having to see their father as the man who pushed the broom over the "magic dust" that got tossed over the throw-up of some kid who had been sick in the hallways, Tommy wearing his gray pants and a white shirt that had *Tommy* stitched on it in red.

Well. They had all lived through it.

THIS MORNING TOMMY DROVE SLOWLY to the town of Carlisle for errands; it was a sunny Saturday in May, and his wife's eighty-second birthday was just a few days away. All around him were open fields, the corn newly planted, and the soybeans too. A number of fields were still brown, as they'd been plowed under for their planting, but mostly there was the high blue sky, with a few white clouds scattered near the horizon. He drove past the sign on the road that led down to the Barton home; it still said SEWING AND ALTERATIONS, even though the woman, Lydia Barton, who did the sewing and alterations had died many years ago. The Barton family had been outcasts, even in a town like Amgash, their extreme poverty and strangeness making this so. The oldest child, a man named Pete, lived alone there now, the middle child was two towns away, and the youngest, Lucy Barton, had fled many years ago, and had ended up living in New York City. Tommy had spent time thinking of Lucy. All those years she had lingered after school, alone in a classroom, from fourth grade right up to her senior year in high school; it had taken her a few years to even look him in the eye.

But now Tommy was driving past the area where his farm had been—these days it was all fields, not a sign of the farm was left—and he thought, as he often thought, about his life back then. It had been a good life, but he did not regret the things that had happened. It was not Tommy's nature to regret things, and on the night of the fire—in the midst of his galloping fear—he understood that all that mattered in this world were his wife and his children, and he thought that people lived their whole lives not knowing this as sharply and constantly as he did. Privately, he thought of the fire as a sign from God to keep this gift tightly to him. Privately, because he did not want to be thought of as a man who made up excuses for a tragedy; and he did not want anyone—not even his dearly beloved wife—to think he would do this. But he had felt that night, while his wife kept the children over by the road—he had rushed them from the house when he saw that the barn was on fire—as he watched the enormous flames flying into the nighttime sky, then heard the terrible screaming sounds of the cows as they died, he had felt many things, but it was just as the roof of his house crashed in, fell into the house itself, right into their bedrooms and the living room below with all the photos of the children and his parents, as he saw this happen he had felt—undeniably—what he could only think was the presence of God, and he understood why angels had always been portrayed as having wings, because there had been a sensation of that—of a rushing sound, or not even a sound, and then it was as though God, who had no face, but was God, pressed up against him and conveyed to him without words—so briefly, so fleetingly—some message that Tommy understood to be: *It's all right, Tommy.* And then Tommy had understood that it was all right. It was beyond his understanding, but it was all right. And it had been. He often thought that his children had become more compassionate as a result of having to go to school with kids who were poor, and not from homes like the one they had first known. He had felt the presence of God since, at times, as though a golden color was very near to him, but he never again felt visited by God as he had felt that night, and he knew too well what people would make of it, and this is why he would keep it to himself until his dying day— the sign from God.

Still, on a spring morning as this one was, the smell of the soil brought back to him the smells of the cows, the moisture of their nostrils, the warmth of their bellies, and his barns—he had had two barns—and he let his mind roll over pieces of scenes that came to him. Perhaps because he had just passed the Barton place he thought of the man, Ken Barton, who had been the father of those poor, sad children, and who had worked on and off for Tommy, and then he thought—as he more often did—of Lucy, who had left for college and then ended up in New York City. She had become a writer.

Lucy Barton.

Driving, Tommy shook his head slightly. Tommy knew many things as a result of being the janitor in that school more than thirty years; he knew of girls' pregnancies and drunken mothers and cheating spouses, for he overheard these things talked about by the students in their small huddles by the bathrooms, or near the cafeteria; in many ways he was invisible, he understood that. But Lucy Barton had troubled him the most. She and her sister, Vicky, and her brother, Pete, had been viciously scorned by the other kids, and by some of the teachers too. Yet because Lucy stayed after school so often for so many years he felt—though she seldom spoke—that he knew her the best. One time when she was in the fourth grade, it was his first year working there, he had opened the door to a classroom and found her lying on three chairs pushed together, over near the radiators, her coat as a blanket, fast asleep. He had stared at her, watching her chest move slightly up and down, seen the dark circles beneath her eyes, her eyelashes spread like tiny twinkling stars, for her eyelids had been moist as though she had been weeping before she slept, and then he backed out slowly, quietly as he could; it had felt almost unseemly to come upon her like that.

But one time—he remembered this now—she must have been in junior high school, and he'd walked into the classroom and she was drawing on the blackboard with chalk. She stopped as soon as he stepped inside the room. "You go ahead," he said. On the board was a drawing of a vine with many small leaves. Lucy moved away from the blackboard, then she suddenly spoke to him. "I broke the chalk," she said. Tommy told her that was fine. "I did it on purpose," she said, and there was a tiny glint of a smile before she looked away. "On purpose?" he asked, and she nodded, again with the tiny smile. So he went and picked up a piece of chalk, a full stick of it, and he snapped it in half and winked at her. In his memory she had *almost* giggled. "You drew that?" he asked, pointing to the vine with the small leaves. And she shrugged then and turned away. But usually, she was just sitting at a desk and reading, or doing her homework, he could see that she was doing that.

He pulled up to a stop sign now, and said the words aloud to himself quietly, "Lucy, Lucy, Lucy B. Where did you go to, how did you flee?"

He knew how. In the spring of her senior year, he had seen her in the hallway after school, and she had said to him, so suddenly open-faced, her eyes big, "Mr. Guptill, I'm going to college!" And he had said, "Oh, Lucy. That's wonderful." She had thrown her arms around him; she would not let go, and so he hugged her back. He always remembered that hug, because she had been so thin; he could feel her bones and her small breasts, and because he wondered later how much—how little—that girl had ever been hugged.

Tommy pulled away from the stop sign and drove into the

town; right there beyond was a parking space. Tommy pulled in to it, got out of his car, and squinted in the sunshine. "Tommy Guptill," shouted a man, and, turning, Tommy saw Griff Johnson walking toward him with his characteristic limp, for Griff had one leg that was shorter than the other, and even his built-up shoe could not keep him from limping. Griff had an arm out, ready to shake hands. "Griffith," said Tommy, and they pumped their arms for a long time, while cars drove slowly past them down Main Street. Griff was the insurance man here in town, and he had been awfully good to Tommy; learning that Tommy had not insured his farm for its worth, Griff had said, "I met you too late," which was true. But Griff, with his warm face, and big belly now, continued to be good to Tommy. In fact, Tommy did not know anyone—he thought—who was not good to him. As a breeze moved around them, they spoke of their children and grandchildren; Griff had a grandson who was on drugs, which Tommy thought was very sad, and he just listened and nodded, glancing up at the trees that lined Main Street, their leaves so young and bright green, and then he listened about another grandson who was in medical school now, and Tommy said, "Hey, that's just great, good for him," and they clapped hands on each other's shoulders and moved on.

In the dress shop, with its bell that announced his entrance, was Marilyn Macauley, trying on a dress. "Tommy, what brings you in here?" Marilyn was thinking of getting the dress for her granddaughter's baptism a few Sundays from now, she said, and she tugged on the side of it; it was beige with swirling red roses; she was without her shoes, standing in just her stockings. She said that it was an extravagance to buy a new dress for such a thing, but that she felt like it. Tommy—who had known Marilyn for years, first when she was in high school as a student in Amgash—saw her embarrassment, and he said he didn't think it was an extravagance at all. Then he said, "When you have a chance, Marilyn, can you help me find something for my wife?" He saw her become efficient then, and she said yes, she certainly would, and she went into the changing room and came back out in her regular clothes, a black skirt and a blue sweater, with her flat black shoes on, and right away she took Tommy over to the scarves. "Here," she said, pulling out a red scarf that had a design with gold threads running through it. Tommy held it, but picked up a flowery scarf with his other hand. "Maybe this," he said. And Marilyn said, "Yes, that looks like Shirley," and then Tommy understood that Marilyn liked the red scarf herself but would never allow herself to buy it. Marilyn, that first year Tommy worked as a janitor, had been a lovely girl, saying "Hi, Mr. Guptill!" whenever she saw him, and now she had become an older woman, nervous, thin, her face pinched. Tommy thought what other people thought, it was because her husband had been in Vietnam and had never afterward been the same; Tommy would see Charlie Macauley around town, and he always looked so far away, the poor man, and poor Marilyn too. So Tommy held the red scarf with the gold threads for a minute as though considering it, then said, "I think you're right, this one looks more like Shirley," and took the flowery one to the register. He thanked Marilyn for her help.

"I think she'll love it," Marilyn said, and Tommy said he was sure she would.

Back on the sidewalk, Tommy walked up to the bookstore. He thought there might be a gardening book his wife would like; once he was inside he walked about, then saw—right there in the middle of the store—a display of a new Lucy Barton book. He picked it up—it had on its cover a city building—then he looked at the back flap, where her picture was. He thought he wouldn't recognize her if he met her now, it was only because he knew it was her that he could see the remnants of her, in her smile, still a shy smile. He was reminded once again of the afternoon she said she had broken the chalk on purpose, her funny little smile that day. She was an older woman now, and the photo showed her hair pulled back, and the more he looked at it, the more he could see the girl she had been. Tommy moved out of the way of a mother with two small children, she moved past him with the kids and said, "'Scuse me, sorry," and he said, "Oh sure," and then he wondered—as he sometimes did—what Lucy's life had been like, so far away in the City of New York.

He put the book back on the display and went to find the salesclerk to ask about a book on gardening. "I might have just the thing, we *just* got this in," and the girl—who was not a girl, really, except they all seemed like girls to Tommy these days—brought him a book with hyacinths on the cover, and he said, "Oh, that's perfect." The girl asked if he wanted it wrapped, and he said, Yes, that would be great, and he watched while she spread the silver paper around it, with her fingernails that were painted blue, and with her tongue sticking slightly out, between her teeth, as she concentrated; she put the Scotch tape on, then gave him a big smile when it was done. "That's perfect," he repeated, and she said, "You have a nice day now," and he told her the same. He left the store and walked across the street in the bright sunshine; he would tell Shirley about Lucy's book; she had loved Lucy because he had. Then he started the car and pulled out of the parking space, started back down the road toward home.

The Johnson boy came to Tommy's mind, how he couldn't get off drugs, and then Tommy thought of Marilyn Macauley and her husband, Charlie, and then his mind went to his older brother, who had died a few years back, and he thought how his brother—who had been in World War II, who had been at the camps when they were being emptied—he thought how his brother had returned from the war a different man; his marriage ended, his children disliked him. Not long before his brother died, he told Tommy about what he had seen in the camps, and how he and the others had the job of taking the townspeople through them. They had somehow taken a group of women from the town through the camps to show them what had been right there, and Tommy's brother said that although some of the women wept, some of them put their chins up, and looked angry, as if they refused to be made to feel bad. This image had always stayed with Tommy, and he wondered why it came to him now. He unrolled the window all the way down. It seemed the older he grew—and he had grown old—the more he understood that he could not understand this confusing contest between good and evil, and that maybe people were not meant to understand things here on earth.

But as he approached the sign that declared SEWING AND AL-TERATIONS, he slowed his car and turned down the long road that led to the Barton house. Tommy had made a practice of checking in on Pete Barton, who of course was not a kid now but an older man, ever since Ken—Pete's father—had died. Pete had stayed living in the house alone, and Tommy had not seen him for a couple of months.

Down the long road he drove, it was isolated out here, a thing he and Shirley had discussed over the years, isolation not being a good thing for the kids. There were cornfields on one side and soybean fields on the other. The single tree—huge—that had been in the middle of the cornfields had been struck by lightning a few years back, and it lay now on its side, the long branches bare and broken and poking up toward the sky.

The truck was there next to the small house, which had not been painted in so many years it looked washed out, the shingles pale, some missing. The blinds were drawn, as they always were, and Tommy got out of his car and went and knocked on the door. Standing in the sunshine, he thought again of Lucy Barton, how she had been a skinny child, painfully so, and her hair was long and blond, and almost never did she look him in the eye. Once, when she was still so young, he had walked into a classroom after school and found her sitting there reading, and she had jumped—he saw her really jump with fear—when the door opened. He had said to her quickly, "No, no, you're fine." But it was that day, seeing the way she jumped, seeing the *terror* that crossed her face, when he guessed that she must have been beaten at home. She would have to have been, in order to be so scared at the opening of a door. After he realized this, he took more notice of her, and there were days he saw what seemed to be a bruise, yellow or bluish, on her neck or her arms. He told his wife about it, and Shirley said, "What should we do, Tommy?" And he thought about it, and she thought about it, and they decided they would do nothing. But the day they discussed this was the day Tommy told his wife what he had seen Ken Barton, Lucy's father, do, years before when Tommy had his dairy farm and Ken worked on the machinery at times. Tommy had walked out behind one of the barns and seen Ken Barton with his pants down by his ankles, pulling on himself, swearing—what a thing to have come upon! Tommy said, "None of that out here, Ken," and the man turned around and got into his truck and drove off, and he did not return to work for a week.

"Tommy, why didn't you tell me this?" Shirley's blue eyes looked up at him with horror.

And Tommy said it seemed too awful to repeat.

"Tommy, we need to do something," his wife said that day. And they talked about it more, and decided once again there was nothing they could do.

THE BLIND MOVED SLIGHTLY, AND then the door opened, and Pete Barton stood there. "Hello, Tommy," he said. Pete stepped outside into the sunshine, closing the door behind him, and stood next to Tommy, and Tommy understood that Pete didn't want him inside the house; already a rank odor came to Tommy, maybe coming off Pete himself.

"Just driving by, and I thought I'd see how you were doing." Tommy said this casually.

"Thanks, I'm okay. Thank you." In the bright sun Pete's face looked pale, and his hair was almost all gray now, but it was a pale gray, and it seemed to match the pale shingles of the house he stood in front of.

"You're working over at the Darr place?" Tommy asked.

Pete said he was, though that job was almost done, but he had another lined up in Hanston.

"Good." Tommy squinted toward the horizon, all soybean fields in front of him, the bright green of them showing in the brown soil. Right on the horizon was the barn of the Pederson place.

They spoke of different machines then, and also of the wind turbines that had been put up recently between Carlisle and Hanston. "We've just got to get used to them, I guess," said Tommy. And Pete said he guessed Tommy was right about that. The one tree that stood next to the driveway had its little leaves out, and the branches dipped for a moment in the wind.

Pete leaned against Tommy's car, his arms folded across his chest. He was a tall man, but his chest seemed almost concave, he was that thin. "Were you in the war, Tommy?"

Tommy was surprised at the question. "No," he said. "No, I was too young, just missed it. My older brother was, though." Up and down quickly, once, went the branches of the tree, as though it had felt a breeze that Tommy had not.

"Where was he?"

Tommy hesitated. Then he said, "He was assigned to the camps, at the end of the war, he was in the corps that went to the camps in Buchenwald." Tommy looked up at the sky, reached into his pocket, pulled out his sunglasses and slipped them onto his face. "He was changed after that. I can't say how, but he was changed." He walked over and leaned against his car, next to Pete.

After a moment, Pete Barton turned toward Tommy. In a voice without belligerence, even with a touch of apology to it, he said, "Look, Tommy. I'd like it if you didn't keep coming over here." Pete's lips were pale and cracked, and he wet them with his tongue, looking at the ground. For a moment Tommy was not sure he heard right, but as he started to say "I only—" Pete looked at him fleetingly and said, "You do it to torture me, and I think enough time has gone by now."

Tommy pushed himself away from the car and stood straight, looking through his sunglasses at Pete. "Torture you?" Tommy asked. "Pete, I'm not here to torture you."

A sudden small gust of wind blew up the road then, and the dirt they stood on swirled a tiny bit. Tommy took his sunglasses off so that Pete could see his eyes; he looked at him with great concern.

"Forget I said that, I'm sorry." Pete's head ducked down.

"I just like to check on you every so often," Tommy said. "You know, neighbor to neighbor. You live here all alone. Seems to me a neighbor should check in once in a while."

Pete looked at Tommy with a wry smile and said, "Well, you're the only man who ever does that. Or woman." Pete laughed; it was an uncomfortable sound.

They stood, the two of them, Tommy's arms unfolded now; he slipped his hands into his pockets, and Pete slipped his hands into his pockets as well. Pete kicked at a stone, then turned to look out over the field. "The Pedersons should take that tree away, I don't know why they don't. It was one thing to plow around it when it was standing up straight, but now, sheesh."

"They're going to, I heard them talking." Tommy did not quite know what to do, and this was an odd feeling for him.

Still looking toward the toppled tree, Pete said, "My father was in the war. He got all screwed up." Now Pete turned and looked at Tommy, his eyes squinting in the sunshine. "When he was dying he told me about it. It was terrible what happened to him, and then—then he shot these two German guys, he knew they weren't soldiers, they were almost kids, but he told me he felt every day of his life that he should have killed himself in return."

Tommy listened to this, looking at the boy—the man—without his sunglasses, which he held in his hand in his pocket. "I'm sorry," he said. "I didn't know your father was in the war."

"My father—" And here Pete unmistakably had tears in his eyes. "My father was a *decent* man, Tommy."

Tommy nodded slowly.

"He did things because he couldn't control himself. And so he—" Pete turned away. In a moment he turned partway back to Tommy and said, "And so he went in and turned on those milking machines that night, and then the place burned down, and I never, ever forgot it, Tommy, it was like I *knew* he had done it. And I know you know that too."

Tommy felt his scalp break out into goosebumps. It continued, he felt the bumps crawling across his head. The sun seemed very bright, and yet it seemed it shone in a cone around only him. In a moment he said, "Son"—the word came out involuntarily—"you mustn't think that."

"Look," Pete said, and his face had some color to it now. "He knew the milking machines could cause trouble—he'd talked about it. He'd said it wasn't a very sophisticated system and they could get overheated in a hurry."

Tommy said, "He was right about that."

"He was mad at you. He was always mad at someone, but he was mad at you. I don't know what happened, but he was working at your place, and then he stopped. I think he went back eventually, but he never liked you after whatever happened had happened."

Tommy put his sunglasses back on. He said with deliberateness, "I found him playing with himself, Pete, pulling on himself, behind the barns, and I said that was something he couldn't do there."

"Oh, man." Pete wiped at his nose. "Oh, man." He looked

up at the sky. Then he looked at Tommy quickly and said, "Well, he didn't like you. And the night before the fire, he went out— sometimes he would just do that, go out, he wasn't a drinker, but sometimes he'd just leave the house and go out, and that night he went out and he got back around midnight, I remember because my sister couldn't sleep, she was too cold, and my mother—" Here Pete stopped, as though to catch his breath. "Well, my mother was up with her, and I remember she said, Lucy, go to sleep, it's midnight! And my father came home. And the next morning when I was at school— Well, we all heard about the fire. And I just knew."

Tommy steadied himself against the car. He said nothing.

"And you knew too," Pete finally said. "And that's why you stop by here, to torture me."

For many moments, the two men stood there. The breeze had picked up and Tommy felt it ripple the sleeves of his shirt. Then Pete turned to go back inside the house; the door opened with a squeak. "Pete," Tommy called. "Pete, listen to me. I don't come here to torture you. And I still don't know—even with what you just told me—that it's true."

Pete turned back; after a moment he closed the door behind him and walked back to Tommy. His eyes were moist, either from the wind that was whipping up or from tears, Tommy didn't know. Pete spoke almost tiredly. "I'm just telling you, Tommy. He wasn't supposed to go and do those things in the war that he had to do. People aren't *supposed* to murder people. And he did, and he did awful things, and awful things happened to him, and he couldn't live *inside* himself, Tommy. That's what I'm trying to say. Other men could do it, but he couldn't, it ruined him, and—"

"What about your mother?" Tommy asked suddenly.

Pete's face changed; a blankness of expression came to it. "What about her?" he asked.

"How did she take all this?"

Pete seemed defeated by this question. He shook his head

slowly. "I don't know," he said. "I don't know what my mother was like."

"I never really knew her myself," Tommy said. "Just saw her out and about once in a while." But it came to him now: He had never seen the woman smile.

Pete was gazing at the ground. He shrugged and said, "I don't know about my mother."

Tommy's mind, which had been spinning, rearranged itself; he felt himself again. "Now listen, Pete. I'm glad you told me about your father being in the war. I heard what you said. You said he was a decent man, and I believe you."

"But he *was*!" Pete almost wailed this, looking at Tommy with his pale eyes. "Whenever he did something, he felt terrible about it later, and after your fire he was so—so *agitated*, Tommy, for weeks and weeks he was worse than ever."

"It's okay, Pete."

"But it's *not*."

"But it is." Tommy said this firmly. He walked over to the man and put his hand on Pete's arm for a moment. Then he added, "And I don't think he did it, anyway. I think I forgot to turn the machines off that night, and your father was mad at me, and he probably felt bad about what happened. He never told you he did it, am I right? When he was dying, and told you about killing those men in the war, he never confessed to burning my barns down. Did he?"

Pete shook his head.

"Then I suggest you let it go, Pete. You've had enough to contend with."

Pete ran a hand over his hair, a piece of it stood up briefly. With some confusion he said, "Contend with?"

"I saw how you were treated by the town, Pete. And your sisters, too. I saw that when I was a janitor." Tommy felt slightly winded.

Pete gave a small shrug. He still seemed vaguely confused. "Okay," he said. "Okay, then."

They stood a few more moments in the breeze and then Tommy said he was going to get going. "Hold on," said Pete. "Let me drive down the road with you. It's time I got rid of that sign of my mother's. I've been meaning to do that, and I'll do it now. Hold on," he said again. Tommy waited by the car while Pete went inside the house, and very soon Pete came back out, holding a sledgehammer. Tommy got in the driver's seat, and Pete got in on the passenger's side, and together they drove down the road; the rank odor Tommy had smelled before was stronger now with the man next to him. As he drove, Tommy suddenly remembered how one time he had put a quarter near the desk where Lucy would sit when she was in junior high school. She always went to Mr. Haley's room; the man taught Social Studies for a year, then went into the service, but he must have been kind to Lucy because that was the room, even when it later became the science room, that Lucy preferred to be in. And so one day Tommy left a quarter near the desk he knew she sat at. The school had just gotten a vending machine and there were ice cream sandwiches you could buy for a quarter, so he left the quarter there where Lucy could see it. That night, after she had gone home, Tommy went into the room and the quarter was still there, exactly where he had left it.

He almost asked Pete, then, about Lucy, if they were in touch, but he had already pulled up next to the sign that said SEWING AND ALTERATIONS and so he just said, "Here you go, Pete. You be well." And Pete thanked him and got out of the car.

After a few moments, Tommy glanced in his rearview mirror, and what he saw was Pete Barton hitting the sign with the sledgehammer. Something about the way he hit it—the force—made Tommy watch carefully as he drove down the road. He saw the boy—the man—hit the sign again and again with what seemed to be increasing force, and as Tommy's car dipped down just slightly,

losing sight for a moment, he thought: Wait. And when his car
came back up he looked again in the rearview mirror and he saw
again this boy-man hitting that sign with rage, with a ferocity that
astonished Tommy, it was astonishing, the rage with which that
man was hitting that sign. It seemed indecent to Tommy that he
was witnessing it, for it felt as private in its anguish as what the
boy's father had been doing out behind Tommy's barns that day.
And then as Tommy drove he realized: Oh, it was the mother. It
was the mother. She must have been the really dangerous one.

He slowed the car, then turned it around. As he drove back, he
saw that Pete had stopped smashing the sign, and was now kicking
at the pieces with a tired dejection. Pete looked up, surprise showing on his face, as Tommy approached. Tommy leaned to unroll
the passenger's window and said, "Pete, get in." The man hesitated,
sweat on his face now. "Get in," Tommy said again.

Pete got back into the car and Tommy drove down the road,
back to the Barton home. He turned the car engine off. "Pete, I
want you to listen to me very, very carefully."

A look of fear passed over Pete's face, and Tommy put his hand
briefly on the man's knee. It was the look of terror that had passed
over Lucy's face when he surprised her in the classroom. "I want to
tell you something I had never in my life planned on telling anyone. But on the night of the fire—" And Tommy told him then,
in detail, how he had felt God come to him, and how God had let
Tommy know it was all okay. When he was done, Pete, who had
listened intently, sometimes looking down, sometimes looking at
Tommy, now looked at Tommy with wonder on his face.

"So you believe that?" Pete asked.

"I don't believe it," Tommy said. "I know it."

"And you never even told your wife?"

"I never did, no."

"But why not?"

"I guess there are some things in life we don't tell others."

Pete looked down at his hands, and Tommy looked at the man's hands as well. He was surprised by them, they were strong-fingered, large; they were a grown man's hands.

"So you're saying my father was doing God's work." Pete shook his head slowly.

"No, I'm telling you what happened to me that night."

"I know. I hear what you're telling me." Pete gazed through the windshield. "I just don't know what to make of it."

Tommy looked at the truck that sat next to the house; its fender glinted in the sunlight. The truck was old and gray-brown. It almost matched the color of the house. It seemed to Tommy that he sat there for many minutes looking at that truck and how it matched the house.

"Tell me how Lucy is," said Tommy then, moving his feet, hearing them scrape over the grit on the floor of the car. "I saw she's got a new book."

"She's good," said Pete, and his face lit up. "She's good, and it's a good book, she sent me an early copy. I'm really proud of her."

Tommy said, "You know, she wouldn't even take a quarter I left her once," and he told Pete about leaving the quarter and finding it later.

"No, Lucy wouldn't have taken a penny that wasn't hers," Pete said. He added, "My sister Vicky, well, she's another story. I bet she would have taken the quarter and then asked for more." He glanced at Tommy. "Yeah. She'd have taken it."

"Well, I guess there's always that struggle between what to do and what not to do," Tommy said, attempting to be jocular.

Pete said, "What?" And Tommy repeated it.

"That's interesting," said Pete, and Tommy was struck with a sense of being with a child, not a grown man, and he looked again at Pete's hands.

The car engine made a few clicking sounds as they sat in silence. "You asked about my mother," Pete said after a few moments.

"Nobody has ever asked me about my mother. But the truth is, I don't know if my mother loved us or not. I don't know about her in some big way." He looked at Tommy, and Tommy nodded. "But my father loved us," Pete said. "I know he did. He was troubled, oh, man, was he troubled. But he loved us."

Tommy nodded his head again.

"Tell me more about what you just said," Pete asked.

"About what? What was I just saying?"

"The—struggle, did you say that? Between doing what we should and what we shouldn't do."

"Oh." Tommy looked through the windshield at the house sitting so silently and so worn out there in the sunshine, its blinds drawn like tired eyelids. "Well, here's an example on a large scale." And then Tommy told Pete about what his brother had seen in the war, the women who had walked through the camps, how some had wept and others had looked furious and would not be made to feel bad. "And so there's a struggle, or a contest, I guess you could say, all the time, it seems to me. And remorse, well, to be able to show remorse—to be able to be sorry about what we've done that's hurt other people—that keeps us human." Tommy put his hand on the steering wheel. "That's what I think," he said.

"My father showed remorse. He's what you're talking about, in one person. The contest."

"I suppose you're right."

The sun had grown so high in the sky it could not be seen from the car.

"I never have talks like this," said Pete, and Tommy was struck once again by how young this boy-man seemed. Tommy experienced a tiny physical pain deep in his chest that seemed directly connected to Pete.

"I'm an old man," said Tommy. "I think if we're going to have talks like this one I should stop by more often. How about I see you two Saturdays from now?"

Tommy was surprised to see Pete's hands become fists that he banged down on his knees. "No," Pete said. "No. You don't have to. No."

"I want to," said Tommy, and he thought—then he knew—as he said this that it was not true. But did that matter? It didn't matter.

"I don't need someone coming to see me out of obligation." Pete said this quietly.

The pain deep in Tommy's chest increased. "I don't blame you for that," he said. They sat together in the car, which was now warm, and the smell, to Tommy, was palpable.

In a moment Pete spoke again, "Well, I guess I thought you were coming here to torture me, and I was wrong about that. So I guess maybe I'd be wrong to think you were just obliging me."

"I think you'd be wrong," said Tommy. But he was aware, again, that this was not true. The truth was that he did not really want to visit this poor boy-man seated next to him ever again.

They sat in silence for a few moments more; then Pete turned to Tommy, gave him a nod. "All right, I'll see you then," said Pete, getting out of the car. "Thanks, Tommy," he said, and Tommy said, "Thank *you*."

DRIVING HOME, TOMMY WAS AWARE of a sensation like that of a tire becoming flat, as though he had been filled—all his life—with some sustaining air, and it was gone now; he felt, increasingly as he drove, a sense of fear. He could not understand it. But he had told what he had vowed to himself never to tell—that God had come to him the night of the fire. Why had he told? Because he wanted to give something to that poor boy who had been smashing the sign of his mother so ferociously. Why did it matter that he had told the boy? Tommy wasn't sure. But Tommy felt he had pulled the plug on himself, that by telling the thing he would never tell he had diminished himself past forgiveness. It really frightened him. *So you believe that?*, Pete Barton had said.

He felt no longer himself.

He said, quietly, "God, what have I done?" And he meant that he was really asking God. And then he said, "Where are you, God?" But the car remained the same, warm, still slightly smelling from the presence of Pete Barton, just rumbling over the road.

He drove more quickly than he usually did. Going past him were the fields of soybeans and corn and the brown fields as well, and he saw them only barely.

At home, Shirley was sitting on the front steps; her glasses twinkled in the sunlight, and she waved to him as he drove up the small driveway. "Shirley," he called as he got out of the car. "Shirley." She pulled herself up from the steps by holding on to the railing, and came to him with worry on her face. "Shirley," he said, "I have to tell you about something."

At the small kitchen table, in their small kitchen, they sat. A tall water glass held peony buds, and Shirley pushed it to the side. Tommy told her then what had just happened that morning at the Barton home, and she kept shaking her head, pushing her glasses up her nose with the back of her hand. "Oh, Tommy," she said. "Oh, that poor boy."

"But here's the thing, Shirley. It's more than that. There's something else I need to tell you."

And so Tommy looked at his wife—her blue eyes behind her glasses, a faded blue these days, but with the tiny shiny parts from her cataract surgery—and he told her then, with the same detail he had told Pete Barton, how he had felt God come to him the night of the fire. "But now I think I must have imagined it," Tommy said. "It couldn't have happened, I made it up." He opened both his hands upward, shook his head.

His wife watched him for a moment; he saw her watching him, saw her eyes get a little bit bigger then begin to break into a tenderness around their corners. She leaned forward, took his hand, and said, "But, Tommy. Why couldn't it have happened? Why couldn't it have been just what you thought it was that night?"

And then Tommy understood: that what he had kept from her their whole lives was, in fact, easily acceptable to her, and what he would keep from her now—his doubt (his sudden belief that God had never come to him)—was a new secret replacing the first. He took his hand from hers. "You might be right," he said. A paltry thing he added, but it was true: He said, "I love you, Shirley." And then he looked at the ceiling; he could not look at her for a moment or two.

ACKNOWLEDGMENTS

I'd like to thank The Chisholm Foundation, Julie and Jay Lindsey, Alice Elliott Dark, and Pat Strachan. Without the support of any one of whom, this book would not have come about.

ABOUT THE AUTHORS

RICK BASS is the author of *For a Little While*, which won The Story Prize for books published in 2016. He has published fourteen works of fiction—including *The Lives of Rocks*, which was a 2006 finalist for The Story Prize—and sixteen nonfiction books. He grew up in Houston, worked as a petroleum geologist in Jackson, Mississippi, and lives in the remote Yaak Valley of Montana, where he works to protect his adopted home from roads and logging. He has received several O. Henry Awards, numerous Pushcart Prizes, awards from the Texas Institute of Letters, and fellowships from the National Endowment for the Arts and the Guggenheim Foundation, among other honors, along with having several stories included in *The Best American Short Stories*.

EDWIDGE DANTICAT is the author of *The Dew Breaker*, which won The Story Prize for books published in 2004. Her other works include *Breath, Eyes, Memory* (an Oprah Book Club selection), *Krik? Krak!* (a National Book Award finalist), *The Farming of Bones*, *Create Dangerously*, and *Claire of the Sea Light*. She is also the editor of *The Butterfly's Way: Voices from the Haitian Dyaspora in the United States*, *Best American Essays 2011*, *Haiti Noir*, and *Haiti Noir 2*. Her memoir, *Brother, I'm Dying*, was a 2007 finalist for the National Book Award and a 2008 winner of the National Book Critics Circle Award for autobiography. She is a 2009 MacArthur fellow.

ANTHONY DOERR is the author of *Memory Wall*, which won The Story Prize for books published in 2010, the story collection *The

Shell Collector, the memoir *Four Seasons in Rome*, and the novels *About Grace* and *All the Light We Cannot See*, which was awarded the 2015 Pulitzer Prize for fiction and the 2015 Andrew Carnegie Medal for Excellence in Fiction. His work has been translated into over forty languages and has won the Barnes & Noble Discover Prize, the Rome Prize, the New York Public Library's Young Lions Award, a Guggenheim Fellowship, an NEA Fellowship, an Alex Award from the American Library Association, the National Magazine Award for Fiction, four Pushcart Prizes, two Pacific Northwest Book Awards, four Ohioana Book Awards, and the *Sunday Times* EFG Short Story Award. He lives in Boise, Idaho, with his wife and two sons.

MARY GORDON is the author of *The Stories of Mary Gordon*, which won The Story Prize for books published in 2006, and eight novels, including *There Your Heart Lies*, *Final Payments*, *Pearl*, and *The Love of My Youth*; six works of nonfiction, including the memoirs *The Shadow Man* and *Circling My Mother*; and two other collections of short fiction. Her honors include a Lila Wallace–Reader's Digest Writers' Award, a Guggenheim Fellowship, and an Academy Award for Literature from the American Academy of Arts and Letters. She teaches at Barnard College and lives in New York City.

ADAM JOHNSON is the author of the story collection *Fortune Smiles*, which won The Story Prize for books published in 2015 and the National Book Award for Fiction, as well as *The Orphan Master's Son*, which won the Pulitzer Prize in fiction, the Dayton Literary Peace Prize, and the California Book Award, and was a finalist for the National Book Critics Circle Award. Johnson's other awards include a Guggenheim Fellowship, a Whiting Writers' Award, a National Endowment for the Arts Fellowship, and a Stegner Fellowship. He is also the author of *Emporium*, a story collection, and the novel *Parasites Like Us*. Johnson teaches creative writing at Stanford University and lives in San Francisco with his wife and children.

ELIZABETH McCRACKEN is the author of *Thunderstruck & Other Stories*, which won The Story Prize for books published in 2014, as well as *Bowlaway*, *An Exact Replica of a Figment of My Imagination*, *The Giant's House*, *Here's Your Hat What's Your Hurry*, and *Niagara Falls All Over Again*. A former public librarian, she is now a faculty member at the University of Texas, Austin, and has received grants and awards from numerous organizations, including the American Academy of Arts and Letters, the Guggenheim Foundation, the Radcliffe Institute for Advanced Study, and the American Academy in Berlin.

STEVEN MILLHAUSER is the author of *We Others*, which won The Story Prize for books published in 2011, and numerous other works of fiction, including the novels *Edwin Mullhouse* and *Martin Dressler*, which was awarded the Pulitzer Prize in 1997, and the story collections *Voices in the Night*, *Dangerous Laughter*, *The Knife Thrower*, *The Barnum Museum*, and *In the Penny Arcade*. His work has been translated into fifteen languages. He is Professor Emeritus at Skidmore College.

DANIYAL MUEENUDDIN is the author of *In Other Rooms, Other Wonders*, which won The Story Prize for books published in 2009. He was brought up in Lahore, Pakistan, and Elroy, Wisconsin. A graduate of Dartmouth College and Yale Law School, his stories have appeared in *The New Yorker*, *Granta*, *Zoetrope*, *The Best American Short Stories 2008* (selected by Salman Rushdie), and *PEN/O. Henry Prize Stories 2010*. For a number of years he practiced law in New York. He lives on a farm in Pakistan's southern Punjab.

PATRICK O'KEEFFE is the author *The Hill Road*, which won The Story Prize for books published in 2005, and the novel *The Visitors*. Born in Ireland's County Limerick, O'Keeffe later moved to the United States, where he eventually earned an undergraduate degree from the University of Kentucky and a master's in creative writing from the University of Michigan. He is a Whiting Writers' Award recipient and teaches in the graduate creative writing program at Ohio University.

GEORGE SAUNDERS is the author of *Tenth of December*, which won The Story Prize for books published in 2013, was a finalist for the National Book Award, and won the inaugural Folio Prize (for the best work of fiction in English). He is also the author of the novel *Lincoln in the Bardo*, which won the Man Booker Prize. His other story collections are *In Persuasion Nation*, *Pastoralia*, and *CivilWarLand in Bad Decline*. He has received MacArthur and Guggenheim Fellowships and the PEN/Malamud Prize for excellence in the short story. He teaches in the Creative Writing Program at Syracuse University.

JIM SHEPARD is the author of *Like You'd Understand, Anyway*, which won The Story Prize for books published in 2007. He has also published seven novels, including *The Book of Aron*, which won the PEN/New England Award for fiction, and several other story collections, including *The World to Come*, *You Think That's Bad*, and *Love and Hydrogen*. He has won the Rea Award for the Short Story, and six of his stories have been chosen for the *Best American Short Stories*, two for the *PEN/O. Henry Prize Stories*, and two for a Pushcart Prize. He teaches at Williams College.

ELIZABETH STROUT is the author of *Anything Is Possible*, which won The Story Prize for books published in 2017, and of the Pulitzer Prize–winning *Olive Kitteridge*, as well as the novels *My Name*

Is Lucy Barton, *The Burgess Boys*, *Abide with Me*, and *Amy and Isabelle*, which won *The Los Angeles Times* Art Seidenbaum Award for First Fiction and the *Chicago Tribune* Heartland Prize. *Anything Is Possible* was also named one of the best books of the year by *The New York Times Book Review*, *USA Today*, and *The Washington Post*, among other publications.

CLAIRE VAYE WATKINS is the author of the novel *Gold Fame Citrus* and the story collection *Battleborn*, which won The Story Prize for books published in 2012, the Dylan Thomas Prize, New York Public Library's Young Lions Fiction Award, the Rosenthal Family Foundation Award from the American Academy of Arts and Letters, and a Silver Pen Award from the Nevada Writers Hall of Fame. She was born in Bishop, California, in 1984 and raised in the Mojave Desert, in Tecopa, California, and across the state line in Pahrump, Nevada. A graduate of the University of Nevada Reno, she earned her MFA from Ohio State University. She was named one of the National Book Foundation's "5 Under 35" authors. A Guggenheim Fellow, she has been a professor at Bucknell University, Princeton, and the University of Michigan. She is also the co-director, with Derek Palacio, of the Mojave School, a free creative writing workshop for teenagers in rural Nevada.

TOBIAS WOLFF is the author of *Our Story Begins*, which won The Story Prize for books published in 2008, and three other short story collections (*In the Garden of the North American Martyrs*, *Back in the World*, and *The Night in Question*), a novella (*The Barracks Thief*), a novel (*Old School*), and two memoirs (*This Boy's Life* and *In Pharaoh's Army*). His honors include the PEN/Malamud Award and the Rea Award—both for excellence in the short story—the *Los Angeles Times* Book Prize, and the PEN/Faulkner Award. He lives in Northern California.

ABOUT THE STORY PRIZE

The Story Prize is an annual book award for short story collections established in 2004 by its founder, Julie Lindsey, and director, Larry Dark, with the backing of The Chisholm Foundation. Eligible books are written by living authors and published in the United States during a calendar year. Every January, The Story Prize announces three books as finalists and names one Spotlight Award winner. Three independent judges choose The Story Prize winner, who receives the $20,000 top prize, while the other two finalists each receive $5,000. The winner is announced after an evening of readings by and interviews with the three finalists, an event hosted by and co-sponsored with the New School Creative Writing Program.

WINNERS, FINALISTS, AND JUDGES OF THE STORY PRIZE

(2004–2018)

2007

Winner: *Like You'd Understand, Anyway* by Jim Shepard
            (Alfred A. Knopf)
Finalists: *Sunstroke & Other Stories* by Tessa Hadley (Picador)
            Bloodletting & Miraculous Cures by Vincent Lam
            (Weinstein Books)
Judges: Author David Gates, librarian Patricia Groh, and
            author/editor Meghan O'Rourke

2008

Winner: *Our Story Begins* by Tobias Wolff (Alfred A. Knopf)
Finalists: *Unaccustomed Earth* by Jhumpa Lahiri (Alfred A.
            Knopf)
            Demons in the Spring by Joe Meno (Akashic Books)
Judges: Editor Daniel Menaker, bookseller Rick Simonson, and
            author/editor Hannah Tinti

2009

Winner: *In Other Rooms, Other Wonders* by Daniyal Mueenuddin
            (W. W. Norton)
Finalists: *Drift* by Victoria Patterson (Mariner)
            Everything Ravaged, Everything Burned by Wells Tower
            (Farrar, Straus and Giroux)
Judges: Author A. M. Homes, librarian Bill Kelly, and
            journalist Carolyn Kellogg

2010

Winner: *Memory Wall* by Anthony Doerr (Scribner)
Finalists: *Gold Boy, Emerald Girl* by Yiyun Li (Random House)
            Death Is Not an Option by Suzanne Rivecca (Little,
            Brown)
Judges: Bookseller Marie Du Vaure, editor John Freeman, and
            author Jayne Anne Phillips

2011

Winner: *We Others* by Steven Millhauser (Alfred A. Knopf)
Finalists: *The Angel Esmeralda* by Don DeLillo (Scribner)
            Binocular Vision by Edith Pearlman (Lookout
                Books)
Judges: Author Sherman Alexie, translator Breon Mitchell, and
            reading series curator Louise Steinman

2012

Winner: *Battleborn* by Claire Vaye Watkins (Riverhead
                Books)
Finalists: *Stay Awake* by Dan Chaon (Ballantine Books)
            This Is How You Lose Her by Junot Díaz (Riverhead
                Books)
Judges: Author/critic Jane Ciabattari, bookseller Sarah McNally,
            and author Yiyun Li

2013

Winner: *Tenth of December* by George Saunders (Random
                House)
Finalists: *Archangel* by Andrea Barrett (W. W. Norton)
            Bobcat by Rebecca Lee (Algonquin Books)
Judges: Librarian Stephen Enniss, author Antonya Nelson, and
            editor Rob Spillman

2014

Winner: *Thunderstruck* by Elizabeth McCracken (Dial Press)
Finalists: *The Other Language* by Francesca Marciano (Pantheon
                Books)
            Bark by Lorrie Moore (Alfred A. Knopf)
Judges: Bookseller Arsen Kashkashian, literary center director
            Noreen Tomassi, and author Laura van den Berg

2015

Winner: *Fortune Smiles* by Adam Johnson (Random House)

Finalists: *There's Something I Want You to Do* by Charles Baxter
            (Pantheon)

            Thirteen Ways of Looking by Colum McCann (Random
            House)

Judges: Author Anthony Doerr, librarian Rita Meade, and critic
         Kathryn Schulz

2016

Winner: *For a Little While* by Rick Bass (Little, Brown)

Finalists: *Goodnight, Beautiful Women* by Anna Noyes (Grove
            Press)

            They Were Like Family to Me by Helen Maryles
            Shankman (Scribner)

Judges: Former literary awards director Harold Augenbraum,
         author Sarah Shun-lien Bynum, and bookseller Daniel
         Goldin

2017

Winner: *Anything Is Possible* by Elizabeth Strout (Random House)

Finalists: *The King Is Always Above the People* by Daniel Alarcón
            (Riverhead Books)

            Homesick for Another World by Ottessa Moshfegh
            (Penguin Press)

Judges: Author Susan Minot, critic Walton Muyumba, and
         librarian Stephanie Sendaula

LIST OF PERMISSIONS